MY NAM
JACOB R

by
Ben Trebilcook

DISCLAIMER

This is a work of fiction. Names, characters, businesses, places, events and incidents are either the products of the author's imagination or used in a fictitious manner. Any resemblance to actual persons, living or dead, or actual events is purely coincidental.

DEDICATION

To the hundreds of students I have worked with over the years
whose traumatic and brave stories often go unheard.
Thank you

ACKNOWLEDGEMENTS

First book, so a lot of thanks to be passed out. To Dad, the last action hero, for always being the inspiration; a real life John McClane, who told me thrilling adventure stories of his own. To my Mum for laughing and raising me brilliantly. My brother, Steven, for being proud of me. To my dad's former colleague and friend, Andy Day, for the expert forensic science help. To Ann Davies, an educational dream, true creative and for simply being the best boss. To Tom Cruise for a launch-pad. Cheers to my fellow writer pals and peers Jake Adelstein, Rex Picket, Sarah Pinborough, Doug Richardson, Ed Neumeier, Polly Courtney, Jaq Burns, Jeff Norton, John Fusco, Steven E. deSouza, Matt Hamby, Louis Leterrier, Amy Goldberg, Zachary Leeman, Grant Fieldgrove and Sean Hood for the encouraging flag waving. My good mate, designer Ant Gardner, for the cover, my super editor, Stephanie Dagg - and to my Jen for the love, motivation and continued belief in me.

CONTENTS

I. SINATRA UMBUNDO

"I will fockin' rape you, blud!" The deep voice of a teenage male echoed down the alley way, becoming one with the wind and night. Veins pulsated between the knuckles of brown fists, clenched tightly by the hips of low-slung jeans, which exposed boxer-short-covered buttocks. In one hand, a Versace belt, complete with a mean-looking metal buckle. "Get back here, man!" the shout continued. "If I find you, I will rape you, man. I will rape you. You understand?"

Rape was not solely for the purpose of committing a violent act of sexual intercourse, but was also used as a weapon. It had become the weapon of choice amongst gangs. Police couldn't arrest you for possession of a penis. They could with a knife.

Further down the alley, in the cover of night, a heart pumped super-fast; a chest inflated and deflated like it belonged to a scared animal. The eyes stared blankly and remembered a not-too-distant past.

A dark blue Ford F-150 truck churned up the rust-coloured dusty road of Cuando Cubango, in the south-eastern province of deepest Angola.

Sinatra thought the dust looked like orange smoke as it floated up around the truck's wheels.

The chrome glistened in the smouldering heat. A sticker of the red and black flag of Angola was pasted upon the rear of the truck. Sinatra believed the red represented the blood that had been spilt by the thousands of Angolans in their many conflicts. The black depicted the continent of Africa, while in the middle of the flag was a golden cog wheel, crossed with a machete. The cog signified the workers of industry and the machete was for the peasantry. There was a lone gold star fixed above the two symbols. Sinatra convinced himself the cog embodied the never-ending cycle of violence and the machete merely one of the weapons of choice.

A dirty, cream tarpaulin flapped in the wind as the truck sped along the road. The material opened out to reveal a ten-year-old Angolan boy, who tightly grasped onto it. Whether he shielded himself from the dust and stones or was simply hiding was anyone's guess, though from the traumatized, trance-like expression upon his face, that guess would probably favour the latter. An old Arsenal Football Club shirt, half tucked into his bloodstained, pale blue jeans. Bare ankles above his oversized Nike trainers. His eyes were wide and his lower lip quivered, moistened by the drool which escaped his mouth. They revealed a frightened, fearful boy. In his recent past, the boy had been fishing near the Luvuei River, in the Province of Moxico. A place he shouldn't have been fishing at all as an army offensive was in full swing.

The offensive, "Kissonde", was known also as "Bissonde". It meant ants: giant, violent ants that attacked chickens, dogs, springbok, zebra with devastating results. Sinatra knew they were all the same to the kissonde. They were all prey, the enemy.

Operation "Violent Ant" took place; a horrendous fire-fight between Angolan government troops with a handful of South African mercenaries and Jonas Judas Savimbi, the sixty-seven-year-old Angolan rebel leader.

Bullets tore up the ground and pierced and punctured everything in sight, creating one hell of a thunderous noise.

The boy cupped his ears as he crouched on the wet earth. He tried his hardest to close his eyes as tight as he could. He seemed to be completely invisible as soldiers passed him by, gripping their weapons with clenched hands.

They pulled the triggers of their guns and caused utter destruction with every tiny squeeze of their fingers. The sound was similar to a pneumatic drill as they peppered everything in sight.

The boy turned his scrunched-up, fearful face this way and that as he saw Jonas Savimbi's bodyguards riddled with bullets all around him.

Men, who resembled Israeli Special Forces, took notice of the boy. One hardened his face as he locked eyes with him, giving him a disappointed look. He pushed him down further, lower into the reeds and out of sight. The Israeli suddenly jolted, as he received a bullet to his right arm. It spun him round and down to the boy's level. The soldier held his finger up to the boy's face as he quickly knelt beside him and screwed in a suppressor that muffled the sound of gunfire. He let loose a spray of silent bullets which drilled into half a dozen men.

The cheap, green fabric that made up the rebels' uniforms was shredded by bullets, which pierced their flesh and ripped them apart. The green cotton clothing and grassland turned red with blood; blood of all shades of red.

Sinatra knew that blood came in these many different shades and it all depended on its type and whether it was oxygenated, deoxygenated or even cancerous. This would vary from person to person. Like a pre-school kid squeezing a paint bottle, a bright red spurt of blood jetted out of a rebel's neck as an artery, his jugular, was speared by a nine millimetre round.

His brown flesh flapped open like an inside out jean pocket. A shade of scarlet suddenly spread across the chest of another rebel as a bullet entered one of his lungs. A deeper maroon appeared, along with a brownish-black from a shot-up kidney.

Bullets zigzagged around Sinatra. He lowered himself and pressed one hand to steady himself upon the wet, blood-drenched soil. He stared at his hand, moistened by the gritty, grainy mess upon it. Then he looked up; dazed. Widening his eyes further he saw the rebel leader shot in the throat.

Blood spurted from his neck like a water sprinkler. The back and sides of Savimbi's head suddenly forced outwards as he was shot twice by government bullets. His lifeless body dropped to the ground, shot several more times, including in the arms and legs, which folded on him like lengthy tubes of jelly. His body tumbled to the ground like a felled mighty oak.

Sinatra heard Jonas Savimbi was buried under a tree near to where he died. Many told him that Operation Kissonde was a success.

Many told him it wasn't.

The boy in the truck remembered the horrific event. Was it the one he was currently escaping from in his mind or the fact that his village had recently been attacked by rogue rebels with no code or loyalty to anyone but themselves? The boy had a scarred mind. Sinatra wondered if it could be repaired, especially having just witnessed barbaric rebels tearing open the bellies of pregnant women with machetes and hunting knives, whilst betting on whether they were carrying a son or a daughter. The boy had seen deranged, murderous men chopping off the hands and heads of fathers, including his own. He had been forced to smoke crack cocaine and even been injected with heroin. The boy had gripped tightly and fired an AK47 Assault Rifle and had killed men he respected.

The boy was Sinatra Umbundo and he was leaving in the back of the Ford F-150 truck.

2. HISTORICAL GREENWICH / HYSTERICAL GANGS

Michael Thompson, a thirty-three-year-old white man from south-east London. A spectacle-wearing, loveable geek, though by no means an IT geek or even a bookworm, train-spotting geek. He was a geek with charm. A ladies' man geek, but not in any shape or form a player. He couldn't have played the field if he tried. Not with women and certainly not in sport. He was a patient, kind-hearted, creative man, who knew random facts. He hoped one day they'd be used to full effect; more often than not on his hardworking girlfriend, Rebecca, with whom he lived.

Michael had just driven out of Luxor Street and shortly after entering the main road, he joined the many other motorists in the all too familiar traffic jam that occurred around that time every weekday morning. Sitting in his beaten-up silver, X-registration Volkswagen Golf at the traffic lights in Cold Harbour Lane, which met Denmark Hill, Michael changed out of gear and shifted into neutral. As he raised the handbrake and sighed, he stared at the red lights and the red bus that blocked the road from two sides of traffic. Seeing red had never been so uncannily apt before. He was flustered and disliked traffic intensely, but hated being late more so. He just didn't like to let people down. Michael was a never-say-no kind of guy.

Michael drove his Volkswagen into the almost deserted Greenwich Park and headed up the hill. It was a terrific view, with the luscious green grass and trees either side of the road. The morning sunshine beamed through the leaves on the crisp, mid-March day.

Greenwich Park, the oldest Royal Park in London. Reverted to the people from the Crown in 1427 and its two hundred acres, almost perfectly rectangular, were landscaped in the seventeenth century by André Le Nôtre.

A grey squirrel darted across the road twenty feet ahead, which made Michael smile warmly. He had a fondness for squirrels and every time he saw one, for some peculiar reason he thought of his late grandmother, with warm affection. He wondered why, convincing himself that perhaps she had been reincarnated as a squirrel. Not that she had resembled this tree-rat-vermin in any way whatsoever. She certainly did not. She had been the definition of kindness. Michael viewed squirrels as permanently smiling creatures. That made him happy.

The hill captured some of the most spectacular views of London. Canary Wharf and the two levels of parkland could be seen, along with the National Maritime Museum, the Queen's House, The Royal Observatory and Greenwich Hospital.

"This is going to be a good day," Michael said to himself as he drove the car out of the park and made his way to Charlton.

Charlton House, in Charlton, south-east London, a Jacobean mansion, was built in 1607 for Sir Adam Durham. He'd been a tutor for Prince Henry, the brother of Charles the First. The estate passed to his son, Sir Henry Newton, but during the English Civil War of 1642 to 1651 between the Parliamentarians and the Royalists, Sir Henry had to leave Charlton. In 1647 Sir William Ducie purchased it and later sold it on to Sir William Langhorne. Langhorne was a hugely wealthy East India merchant. For many years the house remained empty. Its last private owner was Sir Spencer Maryon-Wilson, a former officer in the British Army turned MP. During the First World War the house became a hospital for Army officers and was bought by the Metropolitan Borough of Greenwich in 1925. The house was used as a community centre. However, to the residents of Greenwich, the grounds and especially the postcode had become home to one of the most dangerous gangs in London.

The gang gathered from flats upon the Cherry Orchard Estate, from where they gained their name: Cherry. The Cherry Boys were predominantly West African males, hailing from Sierra Leone, Liberia, Angola and Democratic Republic of the Congo. Many had been boy soldiers in their own native country. Their ages ranged dramatically from a startling eight years old to a pathetic twenty-eight.

The Cherry Boys' colour was red and with slight variations. To join The Cherry Boys, their initiation process couldn't have been simpler, yet no less barbaric. Would-be members were bundled into the back of a van, where they encountered several older male members who kicked, punched, slapped, jabbed, elbowed, head-butted and kneed the young wannabe into a state of utter distress, in order to create an uncontrollable rage deep within. It caused the youth to react. How they reacted differed every time. They cried and broke, cut and bled, became defenceless or defensive in ways unimaginably raw that only The Incredible Hulk, a caveman, a passionate parent fighting for their child or a woman fending off an attacking bastard rapist could ever know about. Once they had experienced their pummelling inside the van, then they had gained themselves gang member status. They ended up leaving that van a Cherry Boy. The gang needed new members; new blood to recruit and control.

There was a hierarchy within street gang culture. The older, more experienced members were known as Olders. They were usually in their later teen years. Then there were your Youngers. They averaged around fourteen years. Below the Youngers were Tinies and, although rare, there were Tiny Tinies. Ironically, one didn't have to be too old to be an Older. It was all in what you did to gain notoriety or some form of respect among your peers. Burgled a house. Robbed a shop. Dealt drugs. Used drugs. Stole a car. Hired a Bugatti. Robbed someone's phone. Carried a knife. Threatened someone using a knife. Beat a rival gang member to a pulp. Put someone in a comatose state. Bottled someone. Had a number of girlfriends. Pimped your girlfriends out to fellow gang members. Raped someone. Stabbed someone. Carried a gun. Shot a gun. Shot someone. Killed someone. Killed again. Killed some more.

Everywhere in the world had an area in its cities and outskirts and suburbs considered to be dodgy. Who would have ever thought a quaint looking place like Charlton Village, in the Royal Borough of Greenwich, had an unpleasant, often no-go zone for even the Metropolitan Police at night? This, of course, wasn't night. Eight-thirty in the morning. Gang members tended not to be early risers.

Michael drove past the Cherry Orchard Estate and indicated right. He passed Charlton House as a young black boy, eating fried chicken from a greasy box, crossed the street.

The youth was the Angolan, Sinatra Umbundo, and he looked highly Westernised in his jeans, Nikes and hooded top, completed with an intense scowl. His jeans slung low. His belt tightened around his thighs and caused him to walk not just slowly, but practically waddle. Sinatra glanced up and locked eyes with Michael. He kissed his teeth as he watched the vehicle pass him by.

"Fockin look at me, man," Sinatra said to himself, with a mouthful of oily chicken.

The lollipop lady at the end of the street stopped an approaching car to the right, which enabled a group of primary school children and their mothers to cross the street.

Michael had the opportunity to continue without slowing. He turned left and made his journey towards Woolwich.

Woolwich was home to the Royal Arsenal, historical Woolwich Dockyard, the Royal Horse Artillery and the Royal Military Academy. Even Arsenal Football Club originally hailed from here in 1886, before moving to the Arsenal Stadium in Highbury in 1913. Woolwich was still very much an army base, however it wasn't at all Royal. It was also home to The Woolwich Boys.

The Woolwich Boys, an extremely dangerous, physically and emotionally fearless and reckless gang, was made up of youths from Somalia, Eritrea and Ethiopia. They weren't just a gang, they were an outfit, an organised crime unit. Their gang colour: blue. More often than not, members would wear tops and t-shirts with the Warner Bros insignia, because the symbol was simply WB. Into their guns, drugs and knives as much as the next gang, however this group of people would even rob the shoes from someone's feet in broad daylight. The Woolwich Boys lived on the Woolwich Common Estate.

Michael had just passed Nightingale Vale, one of The Woolwich Boys' surrounding streets. His car headed towards Plumstead Common.

In 960AD King Edgar gave away four plough lands to St Augustine's Abbey near Canterbury in Kent, which was collectively known as Plumstede. It wasn't long before the lands were taken away from the monastery, by an Earl called Godwin, who gave the area to one of his sons.

William the Conqueror, after the 1066 Battle of Hastings, gave an area known as Plumfted to his half-brother Odo. Odo was also known as the Earl of Kent, John Baynard.

Another John Baynard was the son of a man who worked upon a farm. During the eighteen hundreds, Baynard became a drunk. His wife eventually gave him no alternative than to attend local services at a Methodist chapel run by a Wesleyan sect. Baynard became a regular attendee and soon became a preacher himself. However, in Plumstead, the Wesleyan people were also known as the Peculiar People.

Michael believed not much had changed in hundreds of years. He neared Abbey Wood, which was also covered by the area of Greenwich.

In the year 1178 foundations were laid at the site of the Abbey of St Mary and St Thomas the Martyr at Lesnes. Lesnes Abbey was in Abbey Wood. The site and the surrounding area was home to T-Block, aka Blok Gang, a notorious group of males made up of young Nigerian-born youths, whose criminal activity included drugs, firearms and knife-related incidents. They lived in nearby Thamesmead. Their colour was green and their main rivals were The Cherry Boys.

One day, boxes of green bandanas were deposited outside the homes of young black youths. This was their instant recruitment drive and it worked, whether through fear or a thirst for excitement.

Michael turned into the car park of a former primary school which, although it housed school pupils on a daily basis, they were not your average students.

The building was in the middle of a triangle. At one point of the triangle was the Blok Gang. At another were The Woolwich Boys and at the third point, The Cherry Boys. All housed in Greenwich. The London Borough of Greenwich, where Michael worked.

Michael's job was a mixed bag. His title was Seclusion Manager, but he often worked as a Media Tutor, showing films to and then discussing them with a variety of pupils who would not normally choose to see them. His main role within the school was that of a Learning Mentor: a qualified counsellor to children aged between eleven and sixteen.

The students were predominantly permanently-excluded children from mainstream school. There were also EAL (English as a second language) students. Asylum seekers. Refugees. Looked After Children (LAC/fostered). Abused and on the Child Protection Register. Those who had moved into the UK from other EU countries or elsewhere in the world, or even elsewhere in the UK, and required a new school. They lived in homes in Plumstead, Eltham, Charlton, Greenwich, Kidbrooke, Woolwich, Abbeywood and Thamesmead.

They were residents of the Royal London Borough of Greenwich.

3. A KIDIFIED UNITED NATIONS

Michael, with five folded copies of the free Metro newspaper under his arm, swiped his entrance card into the reader, which enabled him to open the front door to the school and step inside the cold, dimly-lit, brown-painted concrete stairwell. His beige canvas workbag over one shoulder as he ascended the stairs, passing a piece of paper tacked to the wall that read "ONLY 78 STEPS TO GO!" Also on the paper was a yellow smiley face. Michael smiled and in lengthy strides he climbed the stairs two at a time, gaining momentum, picking up pace and breathing heavily, in and out, in and out. He ate healthily enough, but he wasn't particularly fit. Michael drove everywhere. He disliked sport and the only exercise he got was probably the stairs he climbed each day.

Along the walls, up the stairwell, were beautiful pieces of artwork. Acrylic paintings of the O2 in Greenwich, formerly known as The Millennium Dome. Line drawings featuring Canary Wharf and watercolours of the Thames Barrier. All pupils' artwork mounted and tacked to the wall.

Michael reached a set of wooden double doors and opened one half. He paused to look at a felt pen picture of a gasmask, peeling from the wall. He pushed his thumb on the corner, which was coming away, and re-attached it. He eyed the picture, frowning at its dark, gloomy portrayal of the army equipment, before going beyond the doors.

Within a brightly fluorescent-lit corridor, Michael entered a staffroom, where a half-sized filing cabinet rested in one corner. Upon it was a list of various names. Michael retrieved a pen from the top of the cabinet and wrote in the time of 8:45am beside his name. He looked at the clock mounted on the wall nearby and saw it was actually nearing 9:00am.

He sighed and entered another room. Michael unlocked a full-sized filing cabinet and opened the second drawer down. He placed his beige canvas bag inside, then closed and locked the cabinet. He removed his grey fleck, Dandy-style overcoat and placed it on the chair in the incredibly small box-room, more like an oversized cupboard, with a desk, an office chair and two soft chairs. A host of junk in an assortment of boxes. Varied laminated pictures lined the wall consisting of a butterfly knife, a .38 revolver, an Uzi and some drug paraphernalia. On another wall was a drawing of a Bow Street Runner. Michael adored history and storytelling. If a student gazed around the room, they would fix their eyes on something to spark a question and encourage conversation. The place was like room-bait. British Board of Film Classification symbols - U, PG, 12, 12A, 15 and 18 certificates - and the abbreviation BBFC also laminated. Everything was laminated in fact. Michael remembered the day he first met Rebecca and gave her a laminated picture of a bunch of flowers. On another wall, various gang names, their colours, races, places and crimes. Michael knew his stuff and his room was a comfortable place to be in.

The large kitchen housed four classroom desks. They were pushed together to make one larger table, with ten blue plastic chairs set around it.

Michael placed his copies of Metro down. He looked up and smiled.

Paul Jones was a sixty-year-old white Liverpudlian man. He was a gentleman no end and brought cheer and experience wherever he stepped. Every year, near the Christmas holidays, he invited the core members of the team to his house for a meal. He always said that it was a 'thank you' to Helen, their boss, for choosing him to join such a happy, trusting, enjoyable work environment. Paul was a maths teacher and had been made redundant from a previous school as well as having retired twice. He was onto a winner and he knew it, but he was worth every penny. He was an outdoors type, often teaching the students games and taking them for walks. "I'm a mountain man and I like mountain women," he would joke. He wore dark blue corduroy trousers with a blue shirt under a mint green sweater. His hair was practically white and his kind face beamed a smile.

"I was wondering where the paperboy had got to. Cheers, sir," Paul said to Michael, as he sat down to read the front page of the paper. He often called his work colleagues "miss" or "sir". It saved remembering names. It saved getting names wrong. He even called the pupils "sir" or "miss". It was much simpler.

"Tea, vicar?" Michael patted Paul on the shoulder and stepped to a sink. He plucked a mug from a cupboard.

"Please, matron," replied Paul.

Michael started to prepare several cups of tea. The hot water came from a fitted urn upon the wall, so there was no hanging around for a kettle to be boiled.

"Eh, I might get an iPhone, you know. Whadya reckon, Mikey?" Paul called out.

"I was thinking of upgrading, Paul. Could do with someone actually giving me one," Michael said.

"I bet you could!" Paul joked. "Wor hey! I could do with someone giving me one. Especially someone like that new Countdown lass!" Paul continued. He buried his head and innuendos into the newspaper.

Michael smiled and poured some milk into the tea. He stirred it and stepped over to Paul, placing the mug beside his paper.

"They'll soon be in," Michael said, returning to the urn.

"Oh, dammit. Really? I thought I come 'ere to just hang out with you and drink tea all day," joked a smiley Paul once more.

Helen Martin was an attractive fifty-five year old woman. She was a Deputy Head, white and originally from Liverpool too. On that day, she wore black leggings and a colourful purple dress, with maroon velvet boots. She had been Michael's boss, Line Manager and first point of call since she interviewed him and took him on as part of her team five years prior. Kind, well-travelled, firm but fair, adventurous with education, outgoing and fun, she would back you up and support you no end. She first met Michael after he applied and successfully gained an interview for a Learning Mentor position at another provision of the Pupil Referral Unit.

Michael had turned up for his interview in dirty blue jeans, a t-shirt and scuffed trainers as well as having a rather sweaty appearance. He apologised for his attire as he had just been playing football with some Special Needs Children in a nearby park. It was his job at the time, not a peculiar hobby.

Helen liked him instantly and was impressed with his potential and so he got the job, although the Head Teacher wasn't convinced at all.

A few years passed and Deputy Head Helen was asked to take on the many responsibilities of a secondary site. Helen's first loyal team mate to join her on the new and exciting mission into the unknown was none other than Michael.

Helen, like Paul, lit up the room as she entered.

"Morning Mike. Hi Paul," she said, as Michael handed her a cup of tea. "Thanks, Michael. Boy, 'ave we got some starting today. They're ready to come up," she continued.

Paul shrugged and tilted his cup of tea. "Nature of the beast. Always ready. You know that, Helen."

Michael sipped his own cup of tea and sighed.

Helen looked at him and walked over. "How was your journey in today? OK?" she asked.

"Surprisingly yes. You're just whacked out before you even start. The journey's a killer," Michael replied.

"Three new EAL starting today. One Romanian, one Somali boy and a Russian girl, with two more I think starting tomorrow. Both Afghani. It's tipping the balance," replied Helen, regretfully.

"Are we meant to be taking in this many kids from overseas?" asked Paul.

Helen sighed. "Not really. Year nine should go straight to school."

"And what about the ones who look twenty-nine?" chirped Michael, smirking.

Paul cackled a laugh. He turned around on his chair to look at him. He winked and raised his thumb.

Helen raised her eyebrows. She tilted her head at him. This was her 'I know what you're saying' look. "Well, I'm on the case, so don't think I'm not doing anything about moving them on. I am. We'll just have to..."

"Cope?" Paul completed her fading sentence.

Helen nodded as she clutched her warm cup.

Patricia Banerjee was a plain-looking forty-six-year-old mixed raced Bengali woman. Not unattractive, just slightly below average. Although married, she retained her maiden name of Banerjee. She was a woman with a fuller figure and fairly tall to go with it. Patricia, on this day, wore a brown trouser suit and a cream blouse. Her designer glasses partly obscured her pained face. Her crow's feet ran deep. They were like cracks upon a dried-up riverbed caused by - perhaps - a lot of laughter and certainly a great deal of pain. Twice married, it was not too long ago that her second husband, David, had committed suicide.

He had been a store manager of a multi-chain supermarket, somewhere in another borough. He didn't leave a suicide note. He had met Michael's parents on several occasions. David would greet them at the doors of the supermarket when they did their weekly shop. He was well liked by his colleagues and members of the community. All that was known to Michael and some of his colleagues, as well as his parents, was that David was extremely unhappy and no longer wanted to work at the store.

David had driven his car and parked up near Waterloo from where he walked to Gabriel's Wharf along the South Bank. He had pulled a length of rope from a supermarket carrier bag and securely tied it to the rail. In one swift motion, he suddenly placed the other end of the rope, tied like a traditional hangman's noose, over his head and clambered over the rail. David took in the view for just a couple of seconds and simply stepped off the pier. His neck snapped instantly and his body dangled above the still waters. He remained there, unnoticed, for twenty minutes, dead.

A colleague informed Michael the next day. She looked extremely upset when Michael set foot into the corridor. She wrapped her arms around him and blurted out, tearfully, that Patricia's husband had committed suicide.

Michael held his colleague tight and wondered what could have possibly happened, as well as about what kind of day it would be for him and the rest of the team. He contacted his father and told him the sad news.

His father said that he had shaken hands with David the day before he took his life. As kind and caring as they always were, Michael's parents offered support to a stranger, who in this case was Patricia. They helped her with the many forms, interviews and what to expect from the police and coroner, not to mention managing to overturn the decision to rule a straight suicide verdict to a death by misadventure verdict.

Patricia was thus enabled to receive a significant payout. It entitled her to David's pension and a weekly sum for a child of hers until she reached a certain age.

Michael's parents and Helen invested a great deal of time and effort into Patricia's well-being and general mental health, despite not actually being friends with her. They would invite her round for an Indian take-out and even on an occasional day trip somewhere in the country.

Helen would visit Patricia at her home and never fail to call her each Sunday morning. Patricia had been helped a great deal professionally and emotionally by many, enabling her to be in the position she was today.

In her grasp was a red clipboard. Patricia looked at Michael with a smile.

He handed her a cup of tea.

"Ooh, thank you. How was your journey? Bad?"

Michael nodded as he sipped his newly-made cup of ginger and lemon tea. He looked past Patricia to see there were three Afghan boys, in jeans and hooded tops, sitting themselves down against a far wall. They were older than their so-called official documented age of fourteen. They were probably nearing twenty.

Some, in the past, had certainly been in their mid-twenties.

Michael smiled and stuck his thumb up to them. The boys nodded and held up their hands to wave.

He gestured a drinking motion. "Tea?" he called out.

The Afghan boys shook their heads.

"Well, that was easy," Michael said to Patricia.

"What a night of TV last night. I was in telly heaven," she said to Michael.

"Don't tell me," he replied, "Master Chef and-"

"ER double bill. Box-set, of course. Also caught up on Dancing on Ice," completed Patricia, smiling. Her conversations usually revolved around ER or Master Chef. It depended, of course, on the season. Sometimes she would throw in the odd question about 24 with Kiefer Sutherland.

Two more children entered the room. They, too, sat at the table.

A fifteen-year-old Nigerian girl in a heavy Puffa jacket. Next, a tall Eastern European girl around seventeen in black, with dark, heavy make-up around her eyes and dark lipstick. More than a little Gothic. She was a vamp, with a beehive hairstyle. She sat down next to the Nigerian girl and exposed a bright, sparkling red thong. Her name was Olga and she looked and sounded a lot older than her age too. Her English was outstanding. She was more of a mature student, however one couldn't say she was out of place here. She fitted in well. Another fellow misfit.

Michael raised his left eyebrow and exchanged a look with Patricia. "A little too much pant-showing today," he said, looking in the direction of the Eastern European girl.

Patricia gulped her tea. "Mm, saw her knickers showing this morning. Did have a word, obviously didn't do much good."

"Olga, would you like a cup of tea?" Michael asked her.

She turned and knocked her silvery purse to the floor. As she smiled with slight embarrassment, she bent down to pick it up, showing yet more of her underwear.

"Whoa! Olga! Say no to crack!" bellowed Paul. He shielded his eyes with the back of his hand and beamed a smile as he looked to his adult audience for a reaction.

Patricia and Michael smiled and Helen smirked, shaking her head.

Olga grinned and looked up, holding her purse, eyeing each member of staff curiously.

"What? What have I done?" she laughed, bemused and then frowned, with her face still smiling. "I don't understand."

The Nigerian girl, known as Juliet, whispered into Olga's ear.

Olga widened her eyes with shock. "No! Am I doing it now?" Olga quickly pulled her jeans up and, even quicker, pulled her jumper down, subsequently showing off her cleavage.

Patricia sighed and closed her eyes briefly. She re-opened and smiled. "Olga, it's best if you just leave your clothes alone and perhaps turn up tomorrow in something more suitable."

"You don't like my clothes? They're fashionable. They're not dirty," replied Olga, somewhat hurt by Patricia's words.

"No, I know they're not unclean and yes, you are fashionable, but maybe a little too fashionable for school," said Patricia, quickly.

"Tea please, Michael," said Olga.

Michael tended to the tea request as a tall, skinny Somali boy of around sixteen entered the room. His head was lowered and his feet shuffled as he walked. He had an unhappy demeanour. Guled Omar-Ali had been in the United Kingdom for three months. Found wandering around Terminal 5 of Heathrow Airport with his name in black felt pen written on a piece of cardboard and tied with string around his neck.

Also attached to the string was a clear plastic bag containing a passport-sized photograph of himself, his airline ticket stub and seventy US dollars. They were crumpled, torn and some had bloodstains on them. He'd been wearing men's shoes, four sizes too big for him, dark blue socks, Hawaiian style swimming shorts and a large, blue, pin-striped shirt, completed by a pink tie. Obviously an incredibly unusual sight, but whoever had dressed him had tried their utmost to make him the smartest kid on the planet and make his tailor the proudest person, too. With no idea of his true age, the Home Office dentist assessed him to be sixteen and a half. That type of assessment, at the time, was deemed ninety-eight percent accurate.

Michael and his fellow work colleagues questioned this method all the time.

Guled's birthday was on the first of the first, a common date in that line of work when it came to dealing with children from overseas. Whenever a refugee, asylum seeker or anyone entered the United Kingdom without the correct paperwork, documentation or passport that stated their age, it was often the case that the person in question would be given a birth-date of January the first.

Today was Guled Omar-Ali's first day in Michael's care.

Michael stepped to where Guled sat and crouched down to his level. He placed a friendly hand upon Guled's shoulder and smiled at him. "Good morning, I'm Michael. Michael," he said, pointing at himself.

Guled nodded and extended his hand.

Michael shook his hand.

"Would you like a drink?" Michael asked.

Guled frowned at him.

"Tea? Would you like a cup of tea?" repeated Michael.

"Thank you. Thank you," said Guled. He formed a pained smile.

Michael stood and patted Guled on the back. He walked back to his tea-making area and passed Patricia.

"Did he talk?" she asked.

"Just a thank you. Who does he live with?" Michael asked.

"Semi-independent living," replied Patricia.

"What? Pats, that's nuts. He's been in the UK for what, three months? Why isn't he in care?" Michael was shocked and concerned.

"In care for a month. His age was reassessed. He went into a hostel and then given semi-independent living accommodation."

Patricia reeled off information like The Terminator, churning out facts when asked to. She would spew out any details on demand about a pupil, or a document, a diary date, a term date, an address and even a shoe size. She had OCD with organization.

Helen made sure she kept her well in line, as she often became extremely objective and far too by-the-book, especially when she believed the book to be her own. She, like the rest of the team, was cherished. To the team, she was reliable and trustworthy, or so they all thought.

Patricia used to be a Learning Support Assistant, once known as General Assistant. Patricia the GA used to be bullied by an old fashioned female teacher. She belittled her. Gave her the worst jobs in the classroom; sharpening pencils accompanied by constant put-downs. Making her feel like a child, instead of utilising her skills to assist a pupil's learning. Patricia was given an opportunity, by Helen, to rise through the admin ranks. First, by taking the role of an administration job, dealing with registers, pupils' files, parents and stock ordering. It fuelled the jealousy fire of the stuck-in-her-ways teacher as she was always placing stock orders left, right and centre. Patricia, in charge of the budgeting and signing the final ordering document, was slowly getting her own back.

A new role within the school became somewhat hard to define as it was completely made up on the spot: Parent-Pupil Support Coordinator. It was a glorified admin role and, in the future, would be known as Pastoral Manager. She was the first point of call when it came to a student being referred to the workplace and there were a number of ways that a pupil could be referred.

A referral form or a telephone call would come in, faxed or posted from the Head Office in deepest, darkest Woolwich. A referral could also be made at the Fair Access Panel. Previously known as the Pupil Placement Panel, the three Ps in a row became difficult for some people. They would buzz the intercom and say "I have come to sit at the PPP." It was like listening to Colin Firth in The King's Speech. The stuttering sound of the PPP quickly changed.

Head Teachers of Greenwich Borough secondary schools sat in a boardroom with other leading professionals, together with NHS school nurses and psychologists from Child and Adolescent Mental Health Services (CAMHS, pronounced CAMS). For a couple of hours they would toss around files of various children, most permanently excluded, as well those newly arrived into the country. Some were on the Attendance Advisory list, having been out of school for a considerable length of time. Sometimes there would be a great deal of pupil information but, more often than not, there would hardly be any at all. Just a name and an address.

Patricia amended the documents so it made sense to others. She interviewed foster carers and parents; spoke to social workers on a regular basis. She dealt with Attendance Advisory Workers, Youth Offending Team Workers, court officials, interpreters, siblings of pupils, School Governors and Head Teachers. If the workplace were a brand, Patricia would want to be the logo. That said, Patricia needed to be kept in line and Helen did it brilliantly.

Helen guided her into the team's way of thinking. She would halt her interviewing too many new-referred students, as the team had to take their time in getting to know certain children first. If Patricia had her way, she would fill the place up constantly like a conveyor belt and forget to move children on to the next phase.

Fill, fill, and fill. It was Patricia's mentality. She was a real box ticker.

Anna was a blonde, petite twelve year old with a stern expression. She stood in the doorway, staring into the kitchen.

Paul stepped over to Patricia and Michael.

"Who's that? She new?" he whispered to Patricia.

"Oh, that's Anna. She's Russian," Patricia ticked Anna's name in the register.

"She's not rushing, she's standing still," chuckled Paul. He looked at Michael, who smiled and stepped up to where the girl was standing.

"Hello. Would you like to sit down?" he asked her.

She nodded her head and sat on the nearest blue plastic chair. Well postured, hands interlinked, feet crossed and tucked under the chair, Anna stared straight ahead.

Michael squatted beside her. "I'm Michael."

"Anna. My name is Anna. Not Ann or Annie. Anna."

"Would you like a drink of anything, Anna?" he asked.

"Anything of what?" Anna said curiously, with a frown.

"Tea, or hot chocolate perhaps?"

"Tea. I want tea," she said, abruptly.

"Please. Tea, please," corrected Michael, with a smile.

"Yes." Anna nodded her head and turned away to look elsewhere. She retrieved a copy of the Metro newspaper and flicked through the pages rapidly, as if on a page-seeking mission, honing in like a guided missile until she locked onto her target: the Sudoku page.

Michael raised an eyebrow and straightened. He made his way back to the tea-making area.

"She's as coldski as ice-ski," he joked, in a stereotypical Eastern European accent to Paul, who responded in a similar fashion, smiling.

"Niet, I see she will be good fun here."

Patricia shook her head. "Entertaining for you, you mean Mr Jones."

Michael gave Anna her cup of tea.

"It has sugar, yes?" she asked.

"No sugar. We don't have any today."

Anna shrugged like it didn't matter either way.

Michael headed to the wall where the trio of boys were sitting.

They were more like men and straightened when Michael approached. They had set themselves apart from the other pupils. One by one each extended their hand to Michael, with a smile.

19

"Good morning," said one, shaking Michael's hand.

"See you yesterday," said another, causing Michael to frown.

"Good morning," he said. "You say 'good morning'."

The Afghan nodded his head. More like a Royal Variety Performance, with Michael moving along the line.

He shook hands with the variety acts. In fact, it was exactly that. He was Royalty to them.

They adored his presence and the positive vibe he gave off. They were an unusual, performing trio, forever surprising and interesting for Michael's monarch-like status.

He shook the third boy's hand.

Abdul Rah-Maan was supposed to be a fourteen. He looked, like his fellow Afghani students, nearly twice that age. Handsome, with a friendly smile, yet his eyes spoke of pain that viewed a continually frustrating journey. Born in Pakistan, he'd lived his whole life in Herat and Kabul.

Herat province was taken over by the Taliban in 1995 and prior to that, the Mujahedeen and the Soviets battled each other no end throughout the nineteen eighties. Armed forces of the United States and the Coalition, assisted by the Afghan Northern Alliance in 2001, removed the Taliban from the province.

There were around fifty-seven different tribes and ethnic groups in Afghanistan. The population included Pashtun, Baloch, Aimak, Turkoman, Tajik, Hazara, Pashtoon and Uzbek. With all the groups naturally came many different languages, the most common being Dari and Pashto. They were the official languages of the country and came originally from Iran. Other languages included Farsi and Hazaragi, spoken by the Hazara people. Lesser languages included Pashai, Balochi, Brahui, Nuristani, Pamiri languages and Hindko.

Ninety-nine per cent of Afghans were Muslim. Shia and Sunni.

Abdul Rah-Maan was a Muslim and spoke seven different languages. He was in foster care and being looked after by a Pakistani family in Royal Greenwich. Abdul was found by Kent police officers at a set of traffic lights, by the roundabout at the Swanley and M25 junction. He was an extremely polite and respectful young man.

The Home Office assessed his age and officially classed him as fourteen. His school file revealed Abdul's mother was killed by the Taliban and the whereabouts of his siblings and journalist father were unknown to him.

Michael smiled at Abdul. "Good morning, Abdul."

"Good morning, Teacher," replied Abdul.

"Michael. You can call me Michael."

Abdul smiled politely, but masked his awkwardness.

"No, Teacher. I say Teacher. In Afghanistan, I say Teacher because it is, um, what is the word for respectful?" asked Abdul.

"No, you're right. Respectful is right," said Michael.

"Understand. So, it is difficult? Yes, difficult for me to say your name."

"But that is my name. Michael is my name. Abdul is your name."

"Example please, Teacher," Abdul asked.

"In England, when somebody gives you permission..."

"Permish?"

"Permission. It means you are allowed to do something."

"Understand. Please. Continue."

"When somebody says you are allowed to call them by their name, you should."

"Because it is respectful in England?" questioned Abdul.

"Yes. It is respectful everywhere."

"Not in Afghanistan. It is very different. I find it difficult, but I will try," said Abdul.

"Your English is excellent," replied Michael, impressed by the new student.

Abdul smiled, bashfully. "I speak seven languages, Teacher Michael," he said.

Michael straightened. He patted Abdul on the shoulder.

Abdul's smile was wiped immediately to practically a wary and sudden scowl, which caused Michael to turn to where Abdul aimed his glare.

A tall, gangly Kurdish teenager stood awkwardly in the doorway. He wore light blue jeans and brilliant white Reebok trainers with a neatly-pressed dark blue shirt. His name was Shaheen and he, too, looked older than his given fourteen years.

Michael turned to Patricia, who had already spotted Shaheen and made her way to him. Michael met her halfway.

"Who's this?" he asked quietly, stepping up to him with a smile.

Patricia gestured to Shaheen and then Michael.

"This is Shaheen," she said.

"Good morning, Shaheen. I'm Michael."

Michael extended his hand towards him.

He looked at the friendly hand and gripped it.

"Shaheen." He felt uncomfortable.

"You're early, Shaheen. Three days early," Patricia chuckled.

"Early? No, I start today." Shaheen scowled and looked around the room. He fixed on the Afghans several feet away.

"Well, you can start today, Shaheen," Patricia said.

"Tomorrow Home Office." His eyes were glassy and he looked concerned. He pointed a finger at the group of Afghans nearby. "Who they?" he asked. "Afghani?"

"Yes, they're from Afghanistan," answered Patricia.

"No problem. No problem," Shaheen said. He held his palms upwards and stepped back into the corridor.

Michael turned to Patricia when Helen approached.

"What's the matter?" Helen said.

"It's uncertain yet, but he seems troubled by our Afghans," said Michael.

"How was he in the interview, Pats?" asked Helen.

"A bit unsettled. He wants to start school as soon as possible. Likes money and said he doesn't want to be near any Afghans."

"Well, that's going to be difficult," Michael remarked as he closely monitored Shaheen pacing the corridor several feet away.

"It can't be done. He has to accept everyone. We don't take demands here. Have we got all of his files, Patricia?" Helen asked, also watching Shaheen.

"Well, as much of a file as it can be. Details of his foster carers and what I quickly jotted down through the interpreter in the interview."

"I'll have a read later, but can you brief us now before he comes back in?" requested Helen.

"Arrived at Dover in the back of a lorry. He travelled alone from Iran and escaped trouble. Says he's angry. Doesn't like the US and British governments; said his father was some kind of freedom fighter. I wrote it down. I've got it here. There are a few to choose from." Patricia flicked over a couple of pages on her red clipboard and read from it. "The Kongra-Gel. Kurdistan Freedom and Democracy Congress. KADEK. Kurdistan Workers' Party. The PKK. Partiya Karkeran. Kurdistan Workers' Party People's Defence Force." She turned the page back over and noticed Michael and Helen both looking like they had a thousand thoughts running through their minds.

Michael raised his eyebrows and gritted his teeth.

"Look at him. He looks older than my twenty-four-year-old son. What do you think, Mike?" asked Helen.

He exhaled a deep breath, considering. He looked at Patricia and Helen. "Said he doesn't like the US and British governments. Maybe he got on the wrong lorry?"

"Why is he angry?" added Helen.

"I don't know," shrugged Patricia.

"I don't want any upset. We're out of our depth," Helen sighed.

"Why have we got so many at the moment?" Michael asked.

"Admissions had a new member of staff. Didn't fully understand the process," Helen replied.

"He's coming back," Michael said, watching.

"Okay. We'll see how it goes. He may just be nervous. What's his problem with Afghanis?" Helen asked Patricia.

Patricia shrugged again, not knowing what to say as Shaheen walked back in with a nervous smile.

Patricia, Helen and Michael - tight as tight can be. Although not always sociable outside of work, in the workplace the three of them were an open book. Nothing was really withheld when it came to the politics of the Education Service. Their personal lives often exposed and discussed.

All three were trustworthy and loyal, assets to any workforce, and should probably have been renamed 'The Three Musketeers'. Wherever one went, the other two weren't too far behind, working and creating something that would benefit the young people and their own team.

It wasn't long, however, before the dreaded Cardinal Richelieu entered the room.

Catherine Riverdale was sixty years old. She was a short, white woman, with a slight hunch and a protruding chin. She resembled an archetypal school mistress of the 1950s or even, at times, a slave driver in charge of a Victorian workhouse. Riverdale was the temporary manager of a newly formed Assessment Centre. She psychologically mind-whipped fellow staff members, let alone the young, impressionable and extremely vulnerable children she was there to educate. If there was ever a spanner in the works, Riverdale was surely that very spanner.

It wasn't such a bad thing. After all, she only had one month of her temporary contract left. Her job, manager of the Assessment Centre, was definitely in a limbo state. She left colleagues stressed; mentally and emotionally exhausted on a daily basis. Her random statements, social attitude and general approach to life itself were simply peculiar. She did, however, always put the children first, despite her methods being unusual, to say the least.

Riverdale would, for instance, suddenly enter another teacher's classroom, or if Michael was in the midst of counselling a student, she would stare and point at them. She waggled her forefinger and removed them from class to the bemusement of the staff member. Riverdale took a handful of children outside to grow vegetables, rake up some grass or pull up weeds. She stood on the edge, watching each one like a prison warden. She'd return the pupils back to their classroom, grubby as hell, and expect them to settle back into their lesson, even though they would have missed the vitals.

Michael often found Catherine Riverdale sobbing at her desk or in the corner of a classroom.

One day she explained to him that her partner of fifteen years was addicted to cannabis and it concerned her that she, also, smoked too much weed. It naturally surprised Michael to learn this, but it quickly lessened when she told him she hadn't been getting a lot of sex either. At first she reminded Michael of a troll, but then he settled on the fact that she was more of a dead-ringer of Fenella the Kettle Witch from 1970s children's animation Chorlton and the Wheelies.

"Good morning everybody," said Catherine Riverdale. She nodded and smiled with her crooked teeth at some of the children sitting in the room. She waddled, in a witch-like manner, nodding to Michael, hearing him sighing. "Morning. How are you today, on this lovely, crisp morning?"

Michael caught sight of the other staff.

Paul raised his eyebrows and also his cup of tea. He smiled and lowered his head.

"I'm good, thank you, Catherine," replied Michael. He pressed his back against the edge of the work-surface. Trapped.

Riverdale moved her head rapidly up and down, like one of those annoying nodding dogs positioned on the parcel shelves of a number of cars. Pointless. Utterly and completely. Likened only slightly to those fortune cats found in Chinese restaurants. However, at least those nodding, paw-waving cats actually had a positive purpose. To bring good luck, health and fortune.

Michael couldn't help but frown and stare at her as she nodded her head.

Riverdale jutted her chin out and looked back at him, as if he was a biological study sample. "I've never understood answers like that, Michael."

"Answers like what, Catherine?"

"Answering with the word 'good' when somebody asks how another person is. Surely 'very well, thank you' or a simple 'fine' would be just as well. I'll set that as homework for you, Michael. Ha. Get your mother to respond to my notes in your daily planner," she nodded, grinning and revealing her brown, decaying teeth, cackling an uncertain giggle. If only she was joking. At least it would be an excuse for an attempt at humour, but it wasn't a joke. She was serious. Her sole mission was to control and to gain status. Riverdale had always made it known that she left a high-profile trophy school and took a considerable significant drop in her salary in order to work here. Questionable. With everything in life there have been always three sides to every story: yours, theirs and the truth, as Michael's father always used to say.

Michael hid his face with his cup of tea, raising his eyebrows as he sipped his drink.

"Who's that then?" Riverdale said, pointing a spindly finger towards the Afghan quarter of the room.

Shaheen scowled, catching sight of her looking at him. He pointed at his own chest.

"No problem here. I have no problem. Are you making problem at me?" Shaheen called out. He suddenly kicked out from his chair and marched out the room.

Everyone was affected by this, most notably the Afghan trio, who were tight against the back wall.

Michael saw Abdul looking at him.

Abdul managed a smile but appeared highly concerned.

"Oh, what did I say? Something I said? Think somebody might have missed his breakfast this morning or at least woken up on the wrong side of the bed," mocked Riverdale, turning to look at Michael. "Cup of tea then, Michael."

Michael knew full well she meant for him to make her one.

She could never have brought herself to say 'please' or 'thank you', nor did she ever once make anyone a drink at all. Since her arrival at the centre ten months ago, Michael had always been treated as the lowest of the low in terms of staff hierarchy. It didn't fuss anyone else.

From Helen to Paul, Patricia and Michael, and despite their different levels of pay, they were a team. Each knew their job and there had never once been an issue of a power struggle. However, with Catherine Riverdale, there was.

Michael turned and took a step ahead, to pass her.

"Sure, go for it, Catherine. The urn's on."

He made his way past Helen, who quickly exited the room after him, leaving without Catherine noticing her due to her tea-making duty.

In the corridor outside the kitchen, Michael stood with Helen Martin. Together they watched Shaheen pace up and down, heavy footed and flustered, clenching his fists.

He caught sight of Michael and stopped to lean his back against a wall, lifting one leg to press the sole of his shoe upon the cold wall tiles.

Helen looked at Michael, whose mind raced. "What do you think, Mike? Shall we leave him?"

"Not really a good sign for a first day," he replied.

"No. It's not, is it? This one's going to be trouble. Don't you reckon?"

"I'm unsure what to think, really," Michael said.

Shaheen tightened one of his fists and thumped it against the wall behind him.

"I'll ask what's wrong, shall I?"

"Would you rather deal with him or deal with Catherine Riverdale for another month?" Helen asked, smiling.

"I'd rather deal with a dozen of these situations than one more day of...."

Michael stopped to see Shaheen suddenly launching himself towards a set of wooden double doors. He kicked them violently open, causing one to crack back on itself and shudder one of the glass panels. He then disappeared down a short series of concrete steps, rounding a corner.

"Do you think he's gone?" Helen asked.

There wasn't a need for Michael to reply as a series of repetitions of "No, fuck you," were heard from a lower level.

Michael and Helen entered a reception area where the front door of the building was sited. The door had just slammed to a close.

Michael stepped down to the door and opened it to look out over to the street beyond. Helen joined him and together they saw Shaheen on the pavement, striding up the road.

Michael stopped and turned to see another boy nearing Shaheen.

He was a white boy. A stereotypical kind for this area. A chav, who wore the usual uniform of such a teenage male: dark blue tracksuit bottoms made of the thinnest, cheapest material, a pair of white Reebok classics, also known as 'the Pub Shoe', a dirty, fake England football shirt and, of course, the hair, shorn with zigzag shapes and lines at the back and side. He was Lee Mace, a fourteen year old who had recently been excluded from his school for persistent disruptive behaviour during class, continuous abuse towards staff, bullying pupils, selling illegal drugs on and around the school grounds, damage to school property, pushing a teacher down the stairs, punching a different teacher in the face, and lastly revealing a knife to yet another teacher and implying he would "use it" on him.

The teacher whom Lee had punched in the face just happened to be the Head Teacher and the teacher he'd pushed down the stairs, minutes before, was the Head's wife.

She was four months pregnant. Fortunately, neither teacher-wife nor the baby inside her were injured, but the violent act did, as it should, warrant a permanent exclusion for Lee from that particular school.

Lee's single-parent, alcoholic, former-heroin-addict mother tried and failed in her quest to make a successful case for appeal. With a file literally eight inches thick, that consisted purely of negative reports on her son, the outcome was pretty much a dead cert. Lee's twenty-nine-year-old mother, however, left the appeal hearing content by rendering the Board of Governors speechless after calling them all "a bunch of smelly-breath, fucking dick-bag teachers."

Lee picked up a broken house brick from the roadside gutter. Michael widened his eyes and raced down the steps to the front gate of the school. Helen froze for a moment and watched closely from the front steps, which overlooked the street.

The view was blocked every so often by tree branches, swaying in the breeze, beside the fence. Beyond the fence, Michael saw Shaheen.

A few feet ahead of him was Lee, complete with the angriest and most aggressive expression one could ever imagine. Not the look a fourteen year old should ever express, but Lee wasn't the usual run-of-the-mill, happy-go-lucky teenager. He was a violent, 'act first and don't care to think later' type. Lee advanced, brick in hand, with the most intense scowl and a never-blink, mad-eye stare. It could burn a hole into someone's soul.

"I'll smash this on your 'ed, man," Lee called out.

Michael held the palms of his hands upwards to face Lee, who simply stared beyond him at Shaheen. "Lee? Lee, can you hear me?" Michael asked, calmly. "Lee, look at me. Lee. Put the brick down and look at me." Michael's voice was firm and calm. He looked into Lee's eyes, trying to break his stare. "Lee, give me the brick," Michael extended his hand towards the house brick.

"I'm gonna fucking kill the prick. What's he staring at? WHAT ARE YOU FUCKING STARING AT!" shouted Lee, who pushed forward into Michael.

Michael glanced around behind him and saw Shaheen nearing, with a similar wide-eyed stare, but his eyes were more glassy and close to tears.

Paul stepped out onto the pavement just as Shaheen set foot to launch himself into a hop, skip and a jump toward Lee. Paul wrapped his arm around Shaheen's arms and chest.

"Hold on, hold on. It's okay, Shaheen, mate," Paul said calmly.

Shaheen panted heavily. He breathed in a deep, growling manner, as if he was going in for a kill.

Lee suddenly lunged forth. He pushed up against Michael, who, without physically touching him, was actually restraining him.

Michael stopped him from going forward, simply by using his body as a shield. Shaheen zipped past Paul and grabbed the house brick right out of Lee's grasp and gripped it tight.

Lee was surprised and shocked by the sudden weapon take-over and his body language changed. He hid behind Michael, lowered his shoulders and lost the scowl. However, he retained his foul mouth. "Come on, fucking Afghan prick. Hit me. Knock me out, ya prick."

Michael sidestepped every split second to block Lee's view of Shaheen. It was as if Michael was invisible to him. His body had become an ever-sliding wall: back and forth, this way and that. It was a difficult task to predict what tactics would work on a particular student.

Lee spat a mouthful of gob, but missed his intended target completely and hit Michael on the shoulder.

The act, fortunately, caused Lee to break his maddening stare for a moment and fix upon the mucus spittle that was bubbled upon Michael's clothes. His eyes met with Michael's.

"It's okay. Let's go inside," said Michael.

"He's a fucking terrorist, Mike."

"You call me terrorist? I not terrorist!" shouted Shaheen.

"Sshh. Choose different language, Lee. Don't be abusive and lower yourself. You've done well this week. I don't want to make a bad phone call home."

"Don't call my dad! Please don't call my dad," Lee said, flustered.

Michael glanced round to see Paul tending to Shaheen in a similar manner.

Shaheen gripped the brick tight. He stared wildly and brought the brick down on his own head. "Is this what terrorist do? You think I terrorist now?" He pressed the corner of the brick against the skin of his forehead and dragged it across one side to the other, leaving a trail of grit and blood.

Paul tightened his mouth and gently took the brick from Shaheen's grasp. He saw blood trickle down his forehead and the side of his nose.

Michael looked past Lee, who glanced around and then looked back to Michael.

"Who you looking at?" Lee asked.

Michael responded quickly. "I thought I saw that friend of yours."

"Who?"

"I can't remember his name. Who were you with yesterday?" Michael asked, as Lee scrunched his face up, thinking, confused.

"I dunno. What, yesterday night or at school?" Lee turned around and started to walk down the street, with Michael alongside him, leading him away from Shaheen.

Michael stuck his thumb out and raised it behind his back for Paul to see.

"Did he go in the other gate, sir?" asked Lee.

"I think so. I'm sure it was your friend."

"The playground entrance, sir? Maybe we can have a kick-about or somefin' or table tennis? Yes mate. Table tennis!" said Lee, as they neared another gate that led into a playground.

Of course, Michael had made it all up. He hadn't seen anyone at all, but the bizarre distraction tactic appeared to have worked and together they disappeared from sight.

Paul and Shaheen stood further up the street. Shaheen was still flustered and was pacing up and down. Paul watched him closely.

"He call me terrorist, sir. Fuck you Shaheen. Always fuck you.

Everyday. I tired, sir. I no done wrong. Why he say this fuck you, Afghani. I'm not Afghani. I don't like Afghani. He don't like Afghani. We should be friends. I don't understand. He make problem with me. In my country, he would have..." Shaheen mimed a cutting of his throat with his fingers.

"Well, we don't do that here. Not in England. It's all right. He's just very angry."

"Yes, sir. He's angry. Why he angry with me?"

"He's angry with everyone. It's okay," said Paul.

"Angry with everybody? Angry with you, sir?"

"Even me. Yes," chuckled Paul, smiling as the sides of Shaheen's mouth started to curl into a half smile, feeling the comfort of Paul's gentle patting on his shoulder.

"Is everything okay with you? Are you feeling angry today?"

"Yes, but no problem, sir. No problem. I make no problem for you, sir. It is all right, sir," said Shaheen.

"We need to know if you're all right, Shaheen. Your head is bleeding and you walked out at breakfast."

"I have no breakfast, sir. I am fine, sir. No problem," Shaheen said as Paul tightened his face, sympathetically.

"We need to know."

"Peoples. They stare at me. They talk about me."

"What people?" Paul asked.

"Teachers. They look at me. They are police. I'm sure of it. I tell you, sir. I know."

"There are no police here. Just teachers. We're all here to help."

"I make no problem, sir. I want my own house. I live on my own, sir. You help me do this."

"Shaheen, you live with your foster family," Paul stated.

"Yes, foster family no good, sir. I want to live on my own. In my own house. Semi-independent living, sir. In hostel. I can do. I have Iranian friends. They tell me I can."

"Well, if they tell you that you can, then it is best if you ask them how. Come on, let's go inside. Sort that head out, so to speak." Paul stepped to one side and gestured for Shaheen to enter.

He frowned at Paul.

"I go home, sir. I have headache."

"I'm not surprised! We'll call the family and tell them. Come on."

Paul and Shaheen walked up the steps and met Helen. Shaheen passed her as he entered the building. Paul made a face at her.

"What's he say, Paul?"

"He wants to live on his own. Semi-independent living."

"Knows his stuff, then," Helen replied, as she sidestepped to let Paul enter. "He can go home. I'm not having him here acting like that. Too unpredictable. If he wants to live on his own, we'll feed that back to the social worker. He's nearing sixteen. We can't have that violent, unprovoked behaviour," she said, closing the door.

"There's always bigger and tougher," chuckled Paul.

"Yeah, and we'll be getting one tomorrow," replied Helen.

"That's life," shrugged Paul.

"That's apt," Helen quipped. "Our new lad is called Sinatra."

"Ain't that a kick in the head!" sang Paul.

4. SONG BIRD

Rebecca Samson was a pretty twenty-five year old. Her rosy red cheeks were extra prominent upon her pale, creamy skin. She crossed into a calm and fairly quiet Beak Street in the crisp afternoon sunshine. The wind blew against her fresh, young, kind face and into her large blue eyes, causing them to glaze over and release tears from each of them. Rebecca wiped the rolling tears with the back of her left hand and headed into the much busier Carnaby Street. Held tight in her right hand was a bunch of beautifully cheerful sunflowers, with each petal dancing gently in the breeze. The edges of the paper wrapped around them flapped back and forth. The wind picked up and Rebecca's cream woollen cardigan blew against her slight frame and tiny waist, covered by a white shirt. Her pale legs took her quicker in the cream skirt and her tan high-heeled shoes hurried her towards Regent Street. Rebecca's honey brown, shoulder length hair was in a ponytail. It darted this way and that behind her shirt collar.

She took herself into Fouberts Place and slowed her pace as she became shielded from the wind within the narrow side street. Then across Kingly Street. The traffic on Regent Street was in clear view, along with the dozens upon dozens of diverse groups of people, who spanned the pavements of the popular tourist destination.

The Jaeger Store on the corner of the street caught Rebecca's attention as a poppy print silk dress hanging in the window signaled her.

She stared at it, with an 'I want one of those' smiles.

In the reception area of an advertising agency off Regent Street, Rebecca stood, clutching her flowers. She turned to see a young, suited woman in her thirties striding towards her, with a confused expression upon her face.

"Rebecca! So good to see you instead of only talking on the phone all the time! Unfortunate about today," the ad company exec woman said.

"Oh, I'm so, so sorry about the girl we placed with you. I've got you some flowers," said Rebecca, apologetically.

"Bex, don't. It's ok. Really, you shouldn't have. It's just how things work out - or people." She took the flowers from Rebecca, breathing in their scent.

"I was told she had a sudden mental breakdown in front of you and walked out," Rebecca said.

"Well, to say the very least she did go a little psycho and it was at the start of the day."

"But then we replaced her with somebody who simply didn't turn up. I'm sorry," apologised Rebecca.

"Ssh, nonsense. It's perfectly fine and what was said over the phone to you was probably exaggerated to the max, so please don't feel bad at all," said the exec. She sniffed in the flowery scent again and then sneezed. "Oh dear. Had it coming."

"Bless you," Rebecca replied.

The exec smiled.

Rebecca worked in Media Recruitment and despised it. There was a time when she once enjoyed the work, but it was probably more to do with the team than the actual role itself. It didn't help that she helped complete strangers get a much better occupation than her own.

The company had five other women, which included her boss. She was a complete 'mad as a hatter' cokehead, who desperately fought against aging and the fact that the eighties were long gone. Estranged from her husband, due to an affair with an advertising executive, and balanced it with a relationship with Botox.

Rebecca endured daily, erratic rants from her unstable, paranoid boss. It caused her to come home exhausted and often in floods of tears, but always to the comfort of her boyfriend. She had met him on an internet dating site. Rebecca wasn't really all that fussed about signing up, but did so for her friend, whom she'd worked with at another recruitment agency, prior to the one with the cokehead boss.

Her friend was on the hunt for a new man. With that particular dating website you needed a close friend to write about you in order to be propelled forth to the thousands who scanned through your significant details. The said close friend was also required to join.

Rebecca was game for a laugh and signed up alongside her colleague, who wrote about her too. In an odd twist of fate, after several dates, Rebecca found true love. It was incredibly unexpected and caused slight bitterness, along with a touch of jealousy, for those who had intended to land a decent date for them. Rebecca had been in the relationship for four years and was just as starry-eyed with the man she fell for as the day she met him. You would have thought that friends, especially good friends, would be happy and joyous for another's happiness and success at finding love and, more to the point, true love.

Within the Jaeger Store, Rebecca stood at the counter, ready to pay, as a sales assistant folded the poppy print dress, placing it into a bag. Another assistant scanned the barcode. Both were young girls, early twenties, and were in mid conversation.

Rebecca twiddled her debit card between her fingers and watched them, tuning into their chat.

"I did ask him, cos I was worried. Well, not so much worried, but wondering why we hadn't. I mean, everybody has one, don't they?" replied the sales girl packing the dress into a bag.

"I dunno, do they? Does everybody have one though? I don't think I do," responded the other girl.

Rebecca formed a look of total curiosity, transfixed by the girls and their conversation. What on earth were they discussing?

"Well, you have to be with someone. I mean, when you were with Blake, did you have a favourite song then? You were with each other for a few years. What was your song?" asked the sales girl.

The girl at the cash register took Rebecca's card and slotted it into the chip and pin machine.

"Enter your pin please. I dunno if we actually did have a song. I always thought it was just people at weddings," said the girl.

Rebecca entered her four-digit pin number and looked up, with a smile. She then received a smile from both girls simultaneously.

"Well, couples getting married and dancing to their song had to have a song in the first place. They had to have a song originally, d'you know what I mean? You don't just get married and the vicar or whatever gives you a list of songs to choose from."

"That'd be cool, though," the girls giggled.

One tore the receipt off the chip and pin machine and, along with the debit card, handed it to Rebecca, accompanied with another automated, robotic, yet pleasant smile. Her teeth were brilliant white. Like the doors of a fridge. Obviously over-bleached.

Rebecca tilted her head as she fixed her gaze on the girl's teeth.

As well as the ultra-whiteness, they were perfectly straight and not one glimpse of an irregular gum line. The modelesque mouth reminded Rebecca of the time when she and her boyfriend were due to visit Los Angeles. It would be her first time, though for him, it would have been his third. Rebecca was informed that everyone in LA had amazing teeth that sparkled and glistened. She was also told that everyone roller-bladed here, there and everywhere, wearing bikinis and exposed their flat, sculpted stomachs. That gave her the frustrating urge, along with her teeth, to do something about it. With that, Rebecca ordered some teeth whitening kits over the internet for her and her boyfriend, who already had a plastic mould of his own teeth, and set about gaining herself a fresher look. Whitening her teeth would involve Rebecca having to dip a short plastic strip into a cup of boiling water and then cool it before inserting it into her mouth, biting down, first with her top set, then secondly with her lower set of teeth. Fortunately for Rebecca, there was a couple of short plastic strips available to her as the first and second were boiled so much they twisted into a melted lump. She still tried to bite into it, making an impression not too dissimilar to when you bite into the rim of a polystyrene cup. As well as what became a waste of time with the teeth whitening exercise, came exactly that: exercise, in the vein of an ab-roller. Consisting of a rubber-coated metal frame and an extremely thin piece of foam, intended for the user to lie on, Rebecca attempted to flatten her stomach.

"It doesn't help rolling on the floor in front of Master Chef," Rebecca stated.

"Nor drinking red wine," replied her boyfriend, who spoke through a plastic gumshield filled with a whitening bleach gel and was unscrewing the cap off a bottle of Rioja.

Rebecca winced as she pulled herself up from the floor and smiled a loving smile at her boyfriend. The boyfriend she utterly adored.

"Thank you. Have a good day," replied the sales girl who then placed the item in the bag.

"Thank you. Bye," replied Rebecca, turning with her new gift to herself. She then made out of the store.

Outside, in Fouberts Place, leading back to Carnaby and Beak Street, Rebecca retrieved her Samsung mobile phone and pressed a few digits. She then placed the phone to her ear.

"Hi Mikey, just quickly. Do we have a song?"

Michael was in the school kitchen filling up the dishwasher with tea-stained cups, whilst holding his iPhone to one ear.

He frowned. "A song? What, on the top of my head, like... is this a new office game?" he replied to Rebecca.

"No, I was just thinking on whether we had a song. You know, a shared song? Is there one that reminds us of one another?" Rebecca asked, as she walked down Carnaby Street.

Michael was, of course, Rebecca's boyfriend. He was the man she had met on the dating website nearly four years prior. He, like Rebecca, had signed up to the dating website for a friend. He was on his way out to the pub when a particular friend telephoned him and asked if he'd log in to the site, as well as register, write a short and wonderful blurb about him, saying how talented a musician he was, mention he was in a rock band and women should date him because of it.

"But I'm off out," Michael told his friend.

He felt guilty not long after reading his friend's description of him, stating how kind and generous he was and how he worked with vulnerable and disaffected children as well as having a loving family. It was such a good blurb that Michael, to his astonishment, never felt the urge to contact any women himself as they got in touch with him. "Mate, this is brilliant! I've had eight beautiful women message me. How many have you had?"

"None, ya bastard," replied Michael's down-in-the-dumps friend.

Michael, in the school kitchen, pondered Rebecca's question. "I'd like to say it was Duran Duran's 'A View to a Kill' and we had just watched it at the cinema, but I didn't know you then and as you were born in the year it was released, it'd be a bit weird for a ten-year-old me taking a newborn-baby you to a Bond film on a date," Michael said, curling his lip as he wiped his hand on a tea towel, freeing himself from a cup that dripped the remnants of tea or coffee or hot chocolate on his fingers.

"Yes, that would be a little weird. I don't even think I've seen a James Bond film at the cinema. I've only ever seen one in my entire life, but anyway, listen, was there a particular song playing when we first met, or when we did anything, or even when we've been away?" Rebecca dodged the thousands of people milling about in Carnaby Street.

Michael scrunched his face up, thinking, as he crouched down to a cupboard and retrieved a dishwasher tablet from a box. With one hand and his teeth, he tore the tiny wrapper off the tablet, spitting out a piece that had come off in his mouth.

"Ugh. Pptthh," he sounded out.

"What are you doing? Are you eating?" Rebecca asked him, as she crossed into the darker, narrower, less busy Beak Street.

"No, I'm just filling up the dishwasher. I had to open one of the tablets with my teeth."

"Why don't you use your hands?"

"Because I can only use one hand. I have the phone in one hand."

"Did you put the dishwasher tablet in your mouth?"

"Not intentionally, well... I guess... but not to deliberately feast upon it. Anyway, a song. I suppose it wasn't exactly playing, but do you remember when you first telephoned me before our first date?" Michael asked.

"You were at the school and it was lunch time."

"Yeah, well, in the background was a noise and you asked me what it was."

"It was Paul from your work singing or doing some guitar noise or something. I remember that because it nearly put me off from meeting up with you," Rebecca commented, as she entered Upper James Street and went into Soho's Golden Square.

"You nearly didn't go out with me because somebody at my work was singing in the background?" Michael was a little concerned.

"Well, not - I don't know. Maybe. You also called me 'buddy' and 'mate', which was another negative point, and more so when you said them together.

"I called you 'buddy mate'?"

"Yes, don't you remember?" Rebecca asked.

"I may have blanked it from my memory."

"I wish I could blank it from mine. So what was Paul singing in the background?"

"He was singing 'Born to be Wild' by Steppenwolf," Michael said, quite proudly.

Rebecca stopped on the street outside the Absolute Radio building. She frowned. "Is that one of those rock anthems?"

"It's definitely an anthem of some sort. It's like when Huey helicopters swooped over the paddy fields during the Vietnam War. Speakers were fitted inside them and blasted out the song. The guitar kicked in; Dahh dum dahh dum der dum dum, dahh dum dahh dum der dum dum." Michael was excited, as he tried to mimic the classic 'Born to be Wild' guitar rift.

"I don't really understand, and your guitar voice doesn't work too well over the phone. Maybe you could form a band with that bloke from Britain's Got Talent," Rebecca said.

"What, the one who did a saxophone voice, but really just sounded like an annoying, squealing cartoon baby?"

"That's the one," said Rebecca.

"Hmm, could be good. Think I'll look him up. So yeah, that's what you heard in the background when you first spoke to me."

"So, what you're saying is that our song, whether we like it or not, is some Liverpudlian maths teacher who hummed a seventies rock anthem in the background when we first heard one another's voice? That's our song? The song that will forever remind us of one another?" Rebecca raised her eyebrows and walked into Shaftesbury Avenue.

"A song that defines our relationship. It's a classic. When played, it will fill our hearts with so much love, words will be non-existent. The only way to communicate and express ourselves to one another would be to perform the most passionate kiss ever," Michael said with a smile. He slotted the tablet into the drawer, closed the dishwasher door and pressed the start button.

"Oh. I hadn't expected that. So our song, if anybody asks, is 'Born to be Wild' by Wolf Man?" Rebecca accepted the disappointing fact.

"Steppenwolf. It's Steppenwolf. 'Born to be Wild'," Michael corrected.

"Right. OK. I've got another call. I'll see you later. I have a candidate to interview at half six, so hope to be back home by half seven or eight. Have we got potatoes?"

"I've got stuff already. I may pop to my folks for a bit, then. See you later on. Love you."

"Love you too. Byeeee."

5. BRIEF

The staffroom had worn, square, black sponge chairs. The walls were off-white, with cracks zigzagging across them. The upper half was a completely different colour: a mouldy green, pea soup shade with sections of plaster missing. Twenty-year-old John Lewis coffee tables placed next to each other were in the middle of the room, with a kitchen area in one corner.

Michael slouched against the back wall, next to Helen. A cup of tea in his grasp. He had spent the past two hours constructing a file which didn't previously exist as it consisted of the school experience of a former pupil: a boy from Nepal.

The boy had only ever received schooling from a goat herder, information that the IT course at the college he was applying for wouldn't particularly find useful or helpful.

Helen placed her cup of tea upon the table in front of her.

Paul sat himself on a chair opposite. He wore a cheap pair of off-the-shelf glasses and started to read a newspaper clipping. Patricia plumped herself near Helen, with a green card file on her lap.

Catherine Riverdale waddled into the room. She eyed everybody. Her chin jutted out and she nodded at Helen. Riverdale formed a most peculiar smile, yet it was delivered with a slight touch of suspiciousness.

"There's a cup of tea here, Catherine," Michael informed her.

She turned her back and eyed up the work-surface. She scanned the top like a forest creature crossed with The Terminator and a hob-goblin. A bizarre mix, though an extremely uncanny and accurate description. "Hmm? Oh, I'm getting coffee, thanks. Thanks anyway, Michael." Catherine fumbled inside a cupboard and rattled a jar of Nescafé coffee. "Oh actually, I think I will have a cup of tea. Why not? Live dangerously. Break a habit, as they say."

She turned around and eyeballed the seating arrangements. The only free seat was opposite Patricia. Catherine shuffled herself right next to her.

Patricia couldn't stand her. It showed in her face and body language. She became instantly uncomfortable and crossed her left leg over her right, with her left arm across her lap, upon her card files. Patricia exchanged a quick look with Michael, who raised an eyebrow.

Catherine caught his look. "What's on the agenda then?" She fixed her gaze on Patricia's lengthy finger on the top of her file.

Patricia managed a smile. It was more of a one-hundred-mile-an-hour mouth twitch.

The telephone rang and Michael rose to walk to the work-surface, where the telephone was.

"Hello?" he said, in a deep, peculiarly mysterious sounding voice. "Yep, we're all here. Just a mo."

Michael turned to see the team looking at him. He gritted his teeth at Helen. "That woman is on the phone."

Helen clambered up off her seat and made toward Michael, who handed her the telephone receiver.

"Can you put it through to my office? Okay, thank you." Helen replaced the receiver and an immediate ringing sounded from another room nearby. "I've got to get this. She's been trying to call me all day. She probably wanted me to be at the other site for the rest of the week. Start without me." Helen winced as she passed Michael.

"Are you okay?" he asked.

"Just my knee again. Bite your tongue and let me know how it goes," she whispered, as she left the room.

It was only four minutes into the staff meeting and Catherine had formed the reddest, angriest expression upon her face. Her jaw was jutting forth so much Michael was becoming transfixed by it.

"I don't really feel it's necessary for you to be here at these meetings, Patricia. It's like you're a spy for senior management. No. I dislike it. I should be the only one making telephone calls to the parents and children and foster parents and social workers," Catherine said, abruptly.

Michael instantly defended Patricia. "I can understand what you're saying, Catherine. You are the Manager and do need to know, however, to be fair to Pat, she is the first face the children and parents see and the first voice they hear, and, oddly enough, Patricia has liaison in her title."

"Oh, so we're throwing titles out now are we? Well, as your Line Manager, Michael..."

"But you're not my Line Manager, Catherine. You're the Manager of this Department, not my Line Manager," Michael blurted.

That infuriated Catherine further. Her face reddened and it spread down her neck as she bellowed out, "I AM YOUR LINE MANAGER!"

Everybody jolted.

Patricia edged away. Any further and she would be part of the wall.

She exchanged a look with Paul.

Michael raised his eyebrows and smiled, with shock. "Catherine, you're not my Line Manager. Don't worry about it. We're straying away from the initial subject."

"I am your Line Manager. Who do you think controls you?" Catherine asked.

"Nobody controls me. How do you mean, Catherine?" Michael frowned.

Riverdale searched the eyes of Patricia and Paul who each sat awkwardly, waiting anxiously for the conversation or even the day to be over. "I control you. I control you."

"No, you don't. Quit the power trip, Catherine, and let's move on."

"Who do you go to if you have a problem in work? Me. You go to me, Michael."

"Er, no, because most of the problems I have at work are you, Catherine, so I am hardly going to discuss my concerns with you and vent because you're not a neutral party. To lay down a fact, I'm managed by Helen. She's my boss. She took me on and we set it up together. Patricia then came on board, followed by Paul. You were next, and, being on a temporary eleven-month contract, you are not my Line Manager. Whoever your successor is, once the contract ends, you or someone else, they won't be my Line Manager either."

It was an arrogant move and he knew damn well Catherine could be his line manager with the click of a finger if the bosses said so. He had never warmed to her and the feeling was mutual.

Catherine stared at Michael. "I think you have an issue with authority," she said.

"Absolutely not," Michael said, calmly.

"Then maybe it's a female thing," Catherine nodded her head.

"Because I have an issue with Patricia or Helen or any other female colleague?" he said, sarcastically.

"Like our client group, I think this briefing has gone wayward," Paul chirped. He got to his feet and made for the door. He raised his hand, attempting a wave. "See you tomorrow," he said, leaving the room.

"See you, mate," Michael stood up and headed to his room.

"See you tomorrow, Mikey," Patricia called out.

"Safe journey home, Pats," Michael replied.

Catherine sipped her cup of tea and tilted her head. She gazed around the empty room.

Michael entered Patricia's office in a lower part of the school.

She smiled at him as he sat on a spare chair next to her desk, exhaling a weary sigh.

"That woman drives me nuts," he said.

"Oh Michael, she's impossible," Patricia replied. She slid some paperwork into a file.

"Are you okay?"

"Me? Yes. You kind of get used to her bluntness after-"

"-After the hundred and eleventh time?" interrupted Michael.

Patricia laughed and opened a file on her desk. "This one's interesting. Thought it'd be up your street. It's just come through, unfortunately."

"Unfortunately how, Pats?" he asked.

"Unfortunately for Catherine so that she can't ruin the whole ethos of this nurturing, child-centred environment," responded Patricia, coldly.

Michael turned and caught sight of somebody in the office doorway.

Patricia turned and instantly turned red with embarrassment, as did the uniformed man who was standing in the office.

His name was Norman Clarke and he was the 'Safer Schools' Police Officer. Norman was a typical wally of a policeman, whose main job was to look after a school. His voice was a camp monotone. Although he wasn't an unpleasant character, nor unattractive, he was somewhat of a plank and seemed to want to prove himself capable of being a super-cop.

Michael had him checked out months ago by his father, who said he already knew of him from his own days as a police officer in the City.

Norman, once a Special Policeman. A hobby bobby given the usual jobs. He guarded concrete roadblocks, looked for illegally parked vehicles. Mostly jobs that kept him in one place and never got in the way. He once worked in a bank and tried out for the police force. He couldn't get into the City of London Police Force, so tried for the British Transport Police. They, too, turned him down. The ever faithful "we will take anybody" Metropolitan Police Service eventually accepted Norman and subsequently positioned him in a school. Usually a junkyard to rid the old and useless.

As Michael's father once put it: "They don't send Sherlock Holmes in to look after a school, they send Inspector Clouseau." It was perhaps a little unfair, but would you really and honestly put your best man in to serve and protect in a place of education?

"Hiya. Am I disturbing you? I was just passing," said Norman. He always happened to be simply 'just passing' Patricia's office. His gangly frame lingered awkwardly in the doorway.

Patricia giggled like a nervous schoolgirl and slid a piece of A4 from the file to Michael.

Michael eyed it over and started to read about the Angolan Sinatra Umbundo. He sighed an exhausted breath, having read many a similar story before. However, each one tugged his heartstrings, disappointing him time and time again.

6. THE UNDERCOVER

Michael drove his car along an uneven, unmade road with potholes and weeds. His tyres churned up dust as the vehicle scrolled along with a rolling crunch. Fields either side of the road; a cornfield on the left and a neatly fenced-off section, with a couple of horses, grazing free. He passed stables, hit a stretch of tarmac and passed an enormous mansion. It was slightly obscured by trees with branches that dangled over the road. Large homes, each different in style and size.

Michael rounded a corner and drove over concrete humps in the road. Patches of tarmac outside the larger homes, dusty gravel outside others. The humps were meant to slow cars down, despite the owners of such homes being the ones who sped along the private road in their oversized jeeps and their wild and untamed children the ones hurtling out of control upon their quad bikes or scramblers.

Michael passed a slightly overweight man in his mid-forties. His face showed depression. His body hunched over and his feet shuffled along in his baggy blue tracksuit bottoms and lightweight jacket. He was white and his thinning hair danced upon his head in the breeze as he walked a black and white cross-breed dog of some sort. The man was Simon and he nodded his head to acknowledge Michael as he drove along, leaving him in a cloud of dust.

Upon the driveway of a small bungalow was a man in his mid-sixties. A kind, white face with silver hair. The man was six feet tall and that day wore a pair of army green shorts and a lighter green polo shirt. On his feet was a pair of slippers. He opened a metal gate as Michael drove his car up the drive and pulled to a stop.

Michael cut his engine and exited the car to greet the man, his father Edward Thompson, with a kiss and a hug.

"Hello Mikey. Good to see you. Leave the keys in. I'll turn the car around for you. Go in and see Mum. She's probably got a big load of fruit for you to eat."

Michael's dad took the car keys from him and clambered inside, as Michael rounded the vehicle and entered the house. Edward tutted as he retrieved a white handkerchief from his pocket and spat on it. He wiped it on the dirty, dusty and oddly sticky dashboard, freeing it from whatever it was that was on the surface. He smiled, fondly recalling a vivid memory of when his son was five years old, sitting at a kitchen table of long ago, painting a picture whilst eating a peeled pear; slippery, juicy and sticky.

"Hello, Mum? Hello?" Michael called out as he took his shoes off, entering the living room. He found his mother, kneeling upon a brown leather Chesterfield sofa.

"Oh, hello Mike. Ah. Ooh. Help. I've got pins and needles now."

"Are you okay, Mum?" Michael frowned as his mother awkwardly twisted and maneuvered herself off the sofa and hobbled over to hug her son. Her left hand grasped a yellow dusting cloth.

"Oh, sorry, son," she kissed his cheek and took a step backwards. "I'll get you something to eat."

"No, I'm OK," he responded, reluctantly.

His mother winced as she arched her back, straightening. "Aw eh. My bones," she laughed. "Sorry, I'm getting old, Mikey."

"Getting?" he teased as she grasped his shoulder and passed him, laughing again and leaving the room.

His mother, Violet, a sixty-three-year-old woman of Irish descent, looked at her youngest son lovingly. Being so patient, trusted and affectionate, she adored him the most and he was forever her child, no matter how old he was.

Upon the three-seater Chesterfield, Michael sipped his gigantic cup of hot chocolate. The white china cup was huge and bowl-like. Upon a plate, on the wooden coffee table and wrapped up in two sheets of kitchen paper, were two pains au chocolat - chocolate croissants to Michael and many others.

Edward sat upon the two-seater sofa nearby. "I spoke to Simon, the detective, outside a minute ago. He was walking three of his dogs."

"How many dogs does he have?" asked Michael.

"Five," answered his father. "He's really interested in your work and the types of children you have there. He said he'd be back in half an hour if you'd like to knock on his door and talk to him."

"What does he want to know?" Michael unwrapped the croissants and took a bite of one.

His father removed his gold-rimmed spectacles and looked at his son. "He's interested in gang members. He said the amount of gangs and teenagers killing each other is really worrying him. He's just been assigned a new team and I told him about the types of children at your school. It's worth talking to him. You'll get money for it."

"Money for what?" Michael asked, frowning.

"For any information you give him," his father, Edward, replied.

"Like what?"

"You could start paying off your bills with the amount of information you have on those pupils."

"What, I'd be an informant?" Michael formed a slight smirk.

His father smiled at his son.

"Like a super-grass?"

"Well, best if you speak with him first and see what he has to say," his father replied.

He always wanted to help his son out whenever he could, especially when it regarded some extra money, and if the deed caught a few criminals along the way, then that was surely a plus in his book. And his book was certainly a unique one.

Michael nodded and chomped another bite of his croissant as his mother re-entered the room. She perched on the wooden coffee table. "How's Rebecca and her job? Are they still being horrible to her?" she asked Michael.

"Mmm. Yeah. Utterly," he said, with his mouth full. "The Botox-faced boss makes her cry every other day. Bec calls me at work crying her eyes out. Get this: the other day, everyone in the office was given special beauty treatment, manicures and facials except for Bec. How mean is that?"

"Oh that's awful!" said his mother.

"I know. She's treated like a schoolgirl."

"Why? I don't understand. What does she do to deserve such harsh treatment?"

"Nothing. That's the thing. She does more than she's required to do and she's treated and paid the worst. Last week she was flavour of the month, with Botox woman emailing her across the room to say she's received good words regarding Becca and how professional she is, but this week, it's the complete reverse."

"Sounds like the woman is bi-polar or something," chipped in his father. "Poor girl."

"She ought to get out of there," said his mother.

"If she can," said Edward.

"She's been looking and applying for anything and everything. She will," Michael responded, positively.

His parents loved Rebecca as if she were their own daughter. His mother was especially pleased for Michael to have such a wonderful girlfriend, as she cared for him so lovingly and cooked amazingly.

Violet even dreamt of Rebecca's cooking, that was how much she liked her food. Both Violet and Edward were equally relaxed and happy that Michael was happy and had finally found somebody who put as much effort and energy and love into a relationship as he did.

"Has Bec read The Secret?" she asked.

"Ha! I've read various bits of it to her and have written some of her wants and goals in the Gratitude book you bought me."

"Does anyone know of it at her work?"

"Mm, yeah, but they think it's something you simply do; a quick fix to things as opposed to a practice or way of life and constant thought," Michael said, food in his mouth once again.

"How do you mean?" his mother asked, curiously.

"Like, 'Oh, we should do The Secret on that client' someone will say in her office. As if it was a magic spell or something. Grr. I can't stand them. They're all a bunch of Ab-Fab wannabe, Botox-filled, bloated-faced fakes. There's no loyalty in that place at all." Michael was passionate about his girlfriend, Rebecca. It frustrated him that she was unhappy in her workplace.

Rebecca was somewhat envious of Michael and the varied days he had at his job and the closeness of his staff team.

He thought about the types of students he had. His mind raced with a thousand and one thoughts. Becca disliked her job so much and if she suddenly left and handed her notice in, how would they pay their rent and other bills? Would being a police informant be of any benefit to him? To them? Could it be easy to simply tell on the teenagers at his work to the police? What would they want to know? What did he know about them anyway?

Simon was a slightly overweight white man in his mid-forties. His greying blond hair was thin and wavy and his appearance implied a man depressed and deep in thought. This was the man Michael had seen as he drove by. He walked bow-legged up the driveway to Michael's parents' home as Michael exited the house. Only the metal gate separated the two of them.

"I was just on my way to you," Michael smiled, extending his hand to shake Simon's over the gate.

The mournful-looking Simon formed an awkward half-smile. He was unsure how to initiate the conversation, looking around the driveway and everywhere else but Michael's face.

"I spoke to your Dad earlier and he said you have a lot of contact with gang members. I've got a... a special unit. A new team under my control. It's quite a secretive division. It's just a very difficult and hard task to achieve anything with any positive outcome," he rambled.

"With regards to...?" asked Michael, curiously.

"The gangs of south-east London," answered Simon, looking him in the eye for the first time.

Simon was a Detective Chief Inspector. Worn out and exhausted before his actual age commanded it to be so. Stressed out because of his job and the amount of pet dogs he and his wife had. His wife was rarely sighted, let alone seen walking the pets at all.

"There are so many guns in Thamesmead. So many automatic weapons. It's alarming. The shootings are kept out of the press, but we can't keep them out forever."

"So, what would you like from me?" Michael asked.

"I don't know until I hear what you can tell me about the types of kids you have," Simon stated.

Michael nodded his head, thinking seriously. He raised his eyebrows and looked at Simon.

"It's daily. Pretty much. T-Blok, Cherry Boys, Woolwich Boys, the stereotypical chavy racist attackers from Bexleyheath."

"The RA. We've got them all watched," Simon said.

Michael rested one arm upon the gate and assumed a more solemn expression.

"I've dealt with children who have been charged for rape, attempted murder, sexual assaults, ABH and GBH. One boy, the other week, came in with stab wounds all over his head."

"Interesting. So, would you be willing to meet some colleagues of mine in the week at all?" Simon asked.

"Sure," said Michael, positively.

"You'll be paid for any information you tell them that can be used in evidence against somebody you identify, but it has to be signed over. It's not like it was in your dad's days, where it was meeting somebody in a pub and they handed over an envelope full of cash. It has to be all recorded now. It's all quite official," Simon stated again.

Michael nodded his head. He understood.

At their top-floor conversion flat within a terrace town house in Luxor Street, Michael and Rebecca slouched on the L-shaped sofa, watching Jamie Oliver on their oversized Sony television. They sipped glasses of an Australian Pinot Noir. Always red. They loved their wine. The colours, the aromas and, of course, the taste.

Michael would dip his nose into the glass and breathe in the scent, as if he was about to duck underwater.

"Raspberry, vanilla, no licorice; maybe even cola."

Rebecca often scrunched up her nose and curled her lip. "Cola? Just smells like wine."

Michael told her he gained his wine knowledge when, in his youth, he'd worked in the beers, wines and spirits department at a local supermarket.

Rebecca believed he'd gained what he knew about wine by simply watching the movie Sideways and winging it, like everybody else.

Michael dabbed a sheet of kitchen towel against Rebecca's cheek, wiping a tear away.

"I just don't know what I have to do in order to please her anymore," she sniffed.

"She's a nutcase, Becca. You're so professional and she's not worth a single tear of yours, so don't cry, baby. I bet tomorrow will be completely different for you and she'll be singing your praises again," Michael reassured her.

"I doubt that. I'm sorry you have to see me crying when you come home and hear how crap my job is all the time. How was your day, Mikey?" she asked, as she placed her glass of wine on the black Ikea coffee table and snuggled into his arms.

"It was a little weird. The usual at work. A complete psycho kicking off. This Iranian man-boy."

"Did you see your mum and dad?"

"Yeah. You know they have a neighbour, next door but one, who's a detective?"

"No, but carry on," replied Rebecca, hurrying him up.

"Well, there's this detective couple next door but one from Mum and Dad and they got talking to him the other day and told him I dealt with a bunch of gang kids."

"And he knows the gang kids you teach?"

"Not really. Well, maybe, I don't know. Perhaps. But he wants me to meet up with his undercover guys and discuss stuff. They've set up this new undercover police gang unit near where I work and are out of their depth. They underestimated the amount of kids with knives and guns in the area where the school is and, well, it's worth meeting up with them."

"When?" Rebecca asked.

"I don't know. Could be tomorrow. Sometime this week anyway."

"Is there any money in it for you?"

"Yeah, but I don't know how much. It all depends on what information I give them, I suppose. I'll find out more when I meet up with them," Michael replied.

"I'd like a Jamie Oliver book for my birthday," Rebecca randomly stated, as she reverted to watching the television.

"Which one? He has so many," Michael asked.

"Not the American one or the garden one. Something traditional."

"Does he have a traditional cook book?"

"He must do." She finished her wine and settled the glass down, lightly prodding the stem with her fingertips, pushing it away from the edge. She yawned, covering her mouth with the back of her hand.

"That was a mega yawn," Michael observed.

Rebecca grasped his face gently, kissed his nose, and released it again.

"And that was a warm, yawn hand on my face," he continued.

She grinned a beautiful smile.

"Oh, no," he said.

"What?" asked Rebecca, as she looked at his suddenly disappointed expression.

He quickly pulled up her top to expose her stomach, nestled his face into her belly button and blew a big, squidgy sounding raspberry, lasting four or five seconds. He covered her stomach up and exhaled.

"It's a condition. It comes and goes. It could have been worse," he said.

"Yeah, it could have been your belly. All fluffy and hairy," she yawned again, arching her neck slightly.

"Right, Monkey Pants. Shall we do bedtime?" Michael asked.

"Mm, I'm tired. Been a stressy day," she replied. "Race you to the bathroom."

Rebecca rolled off the sofa and conducted a trot-like walk to the bathroom.

Michael smiled, collected the TV remote control and zapped it onto Sky News.

The Sony television was an oversized beast of technology. Black and silver and as sturdy as an ox. A motionless, frozen, black and silver metal and plastic, electrical ox. Carrying that beast up to their flat was backbreaking hell. Michael's mind recounted that very day whenever he looked at that TV. He smiled. The memory exhausted him.

Rebecca had stood at the top of the carpeted stairs, looking on in a combined state of amazed horror and concern at a hunched Michael, with his claw-like hands practically becoming one with the side of the television set. His blue eyes had bulged at the weight, clearly evident upon his reddening, sweaty face. Michael remembered the shady Rastafarian man who'd assisted him from the car to the hallway, but gave up far too quickly. He was clearly deceived by the Rasta's bulky frame and glistening Reebok tracksuit and spotlessly clean Reebok Classics trainers. Obviously unqualified in the carrying of ridiculously heavy television sets. Michael set about, frantically out of breath, knocking on his new neighbours' doors. The only one to answer was none other than Gay Gary, an even slighter-framed and whiter-skinned man than Michael.

Gay Gary lived a floor below Rebecca and Michael and was extremely pleased to meet and assist his new neighbours, at least until he cast his eyes upon the mass of television blocking the communal hallway door.

Together Gay Gary and Michael had heaved the electronic bulk up four flights of carpeted stairs, through their front door, to their flat and up another set of stairs into their loft conversion, positioning it in the corner of the living area, where it had remained for a further four years.

A TV news report featured Iranian President Mahmoud Ahmadinejad. There was a discussion on the terrorist groups that Iran supported, including Hezbollah and Lebanese Shiite militants, as well as Palestinian Islamic Jihad and Hamas.

An expert spoke on the various organisations and revealed some minor facts that stimulated Michael momentarily. He revealed the following: Hezbollah is Arabic and means "Party of God". Primarily based in Lebanon, they are a paramilitary Shi'a Islamist organisation. Some stated supporters of the late Lebanese Shiite resistance leader Sheikh Ragheb Harb to be the founders of Hezbollah. Ragheb Harb was killed by the Israelis on February 16th 1984.

Michael yawned and stood up from the sofa. He turned off the television and closed his Mac Book down. On his way to the fridge freezer, he opened the door and fumbled inside the lower drawer to retrieve an orange plastic Sainsbury's carrier bag, placing it upon the side. Michael filled the kettle and switched off the light, making his way into the bathroom where he stared at his reflection. He tweezed out an in-growing hair from his neck, just below his jaw line. The metal point of the tweezers scrolled over his delicate skin gently, but drew blood. His thumb smeared the blood down his neck. Michael continued to lightly scrape the tip of his instrument over and over until he caught his prize; hooking the black hair from under his skin. It dangled like a piece of cotton thread. Michael pinched his thumb and forefinger and pulled the hair tight, slowly dragging it from within its blood-filled comfort zone of a home. Michael inspected the hair held in the metallic clasp of the tweezers. He was somewhat proud as he eyed it, like a fisherman and their grand catch of the day. Beauty! He looked into the mirror at his messy, bloodstained face. A reddish brown streak of faint dried blood was smeared from his jaw and down one side of his neck.

7. WHAT ON EARTH HAPPENED TO NASIF FARAH?

Nasif Farah was of the Hazara people of Afghanistan. He made up the trio of Afghani students sitting, as they regularly did, against the far wall of the kitchen at Michael's workplace. His shoulders were rounded and his face thin, humbled and pained. His eyes told tales of trauma and a lifetime of serving others. Nasif sat by the water cooler and handed his fellow Afghan students - Abdul Rah-Maan and the streetwise and very tall Rabee - a plastic cup of cold water each.

They took it and sipped the water. Like a servant, Nasif sat. He stood up when Michael entered the room and cast his eyes upon the only three students in the room.

Michael smiled and greeted each Afghani as he did without fail every morning. Nasif always held Michael's hands with both of his own and in his extremely poor, not even broken, English, he managed a "Goo-man." Whether this was "good man" or "good morning" remained uncertain to Michael, however, to him, it was a pleasantry nonetheless. He looked into Nasif's sad eyes that so wanted to be filled with hope.

Nasif had been a student here for over a year. He was too vulnerable to be simply transferred to a mainstream school. He wouldn't have coped with their curriculum. He looked like a withered old man. Wrinkled and beaten by the weather, and goodness knows what else. The team had deliberately kept him for as long as they could. To protect him. To give him life skills. To give him love. His first word to Michael had been simply "America?" As if it were a question.

Michael told him that he was safe, though "America" was uttered continuously until Michael led Nasif to a map and pointed to the United Kingdom and said, "England. This is England." Nasif frowned and hugged Michael, wrapping his thin, scarecrow-like arms around Michael's own slight frame.

Helmand Province in Afghanistan was where Nasif grew up. Due to his fellow Afghani students not fully understanding the Dari language Nasif spoke, it was unclear through the various translations whether Nasif was born mentally retarded or had been psychologically scarred in the war-torn country he had fled from.

Michael wondered about this and then his mind raced onto whether him even thinking the term "mentally retarded" was politically correct or not, as the PC Brigade were forever changing once suitably accepted phrases. Mentally challenged / developmentally challenged / Mentally Handicapped / Learning Disability, or even Cognitively Impaired. That's a good one too. To put it in the simplest of terms, Nasif Farah was a very slow thinker, but was incredibly reliable in the physical sense. Nasif had been an assistant to a cigarette seller on the streets of Helmand and also Kabul; a looked-down-upon Hazara who had suffered torment at every step of his life, in every town and country.

During an art session, Michael noticed Nasif was drawing eggs with feet and expressionless faces dotted around what looked like a hilly landscape. The task was for students to do their own version of Mondrian's Broadway Boogie Woogie. A colourful account of Manhattan on a grid, so titled because of Mondrian's love of the Boogie Woogie dance.

Nasif had never touched a pencil before coming to England, let alone attended an art class or even school, so allowing him free run in class was acceptable and interesting for both staff and student.

"Maybe he's drawing children," suggested Helen.

"Ah, yes. Maybe," replied Michael, as they both stood near Nasif, who was pressing his pencil down hard upon the white cartridge paper. "Actually, there's a test, the Goodenough test. I think it's the Goodenough 'draw a man test' or something," Michael said, impressing and intriguing Helen. "I'm pretty sure it assesses a person's intelligence levels when they're asked to draw a man just by using a pencil and piece of paper. You get points on how accurately the man is drawn."

Helen nodded her head, thinking. "So we can assess Nasif's levels using this method, d'you think?"

"Maybe. I suppose," shrugged Michael.

He was correct. In fact, the method was created by Florence Laura Goodenough in 1926. Florence was an American pioneer in child psychology, and wrote the acclaimed books Measurement of Intelligence by Drawings and, in 1933, Handbook of Child Psychology. The method, previously known as the 'Goodenough Draw-A-Man Test' is today called the 'Goodenough-Harris Draw-A-Person Test.'

"You get points for various elements such as arms, legs, head, fingers, eyes, that kind of thing, and those points equal a person's mental age I believe," Michael said, as he and Helen lowered their eyes to Nasif's first ever drawing.

"We should call it 'Egg Men on a Hill'," smirked Michael.

Helen chuckled.

Nasif looked up at them as together they raised their thumbs in approval. Nasif scowled and shook his head. "Bad. Very bad," he said, impressing both Helen and Michael with this addition of two words to his English vocabulary.

"No, it's good. Good work, Nasif," Michael noted, gently patting him upon the back.

Helen raised her eyebrows and stepped to the door.

"I'm going to look up the Goodenough test thing. Good work on that, Mike," she nodded.

The Goodenough Test didn't do justice to Nasif in the study and accuracy of his mental age. Helen and Michael were wrong in thinking Nasif might possibly have had the mental age of a four or five year old just because he was drawing people resembling eggs with legs, or eggs on sticks, scattered around yellow and brown hills with small, red rocks. In fact, his drawing was an accurate depiction of the Afghan terrain where he once lived.

The egg people were real people. The egg shapes were their bodies, which had either two legs, one leg or no legs, along with two arms, one arm or no arms, as well as each having no head. Why didn't they have a head? It was because the red rocks on the yellow brown hills and on the ground were the heads. It was the aftermath of an air-strike by foreign forces, raining their bombs down upon Nasif's hometown, killing, maiming and blowing apart literally all of his friends and family. The scattered arms and legs, severed heads and the walking, hopping dying and dead surrounded Nasif as he returned to his home from selling cigarettes that day. His village, his home, had been obliterated.

Was Nasif Farah mentally challenged, developmentally challenged, learning impaired or simply disabled before the air-strike? Or had the slaughter of innocent farmers, women and children caused this trauma to the harmless, blameless and once pure mind of Nasif Farah? Maybe something else contributed to the Nasif Farah who Michael saw before him. For Nasif, it was a year long journey from Afghanistan through Iran, Syria, Egypt, Libya, Algeria, Morocco, Spain and France in order to reach England. How many lorries Nasif Farah had travelled inside before he arrived in the French town of Calais was uncertain. Even he couldn't recall exactly how many. What was certain and clearly evident to Michael was that Nasif Farah showed every sign that he had been abused. Physically, mentally and sexually.

Nasif Farah was scarred.

The squeal of a metal door howled like a distressed animal in the indigo night sky. The door was large and caught the moonlight in its sheer metal, shiny side.

A number of feet lined up and trod upon the dusty, stony ground before stepping up onto a horizontal metal plate. Some feet seemed to levitate into darkness.

The feet, some bare, some in running shoes, some in sandals, were all male and tanned in colour. Dirty and dusty with cuts and sores. The feet were Afghani feet. At the ankles were traditional Afghani clothing. The shalwar kameez, the dress tunic worn by men and women. Pyjama-like trousers. Wide and baggy. Some wore jogging pants and t-shirts.

The men climbed up into an awaiting truck. Some were yanked upwards, disappearing into a black hole. A portal to another time and hopefully a safer time.

The thin, wiry Nasif Farah in his pale coloured shalwar kameez and black leather sandals, was pulled up with a jerking motion by a larger, heftier Afghani man, dressed in similar garb.

The grip on Nasif's hand was tight and strong.

His look into Nasif's eyes was equally tight and equally strong.

Nasif smiled and looked behind him. A second-long glimpse of his homeland, Afghanistan. He took it all in.

The beautiful jagged mountains.

The bright and full moon.

The chilled night air.

Gone in an instant.

The door to the truck slammed shut leaving nothing but pitch black and shuffling feet and then the vehicle's engine started up.

The flame of a cheap plastic, disposable cigarette lighter flared up and flickered in the darkness. The tiny light captured several gasps and faces huddled in corners and along the sides.

With his knees held tight to his chest and eyes wide like a frightened dog on Fireworks Night, Nasif Farah looked at the big Afghani man holding the lighter.

He beckoned him over with the quick wag of his forefinger, threateningly.

Nasif's eyes glazed over.

The flame danced as it reflected in his pupils.

Other men, each in their late teens and early twenties, formed fearful faces.

"Hazara," said the big man to the Hazara Nasif Farah.

The Hazara were reviled by other races in the country. Blamed for apparent suicide bombing attacks on Coalition Forces and Afghan people, they were easy targets in a game of propaganda.

The Taliban took control of the city of Mazar-i-Sharif. It had been a massacre of thousands of Hazara people. Mullah Manan Niazi was the new Taliban governor and vowed to kill every Hazara.

"Hazaras are kuffar. They are not Muslim. They are Shia. They are Infidels," said Mullah Manan Niazi in a speech he made in one of the many mosques he visited.

Hazara were for female rights. They even had an equal number of female students in the country, engendering further hatred in the Taliban.

Afghan President, Hamid Karzai, was bringing Taliban members into his government, rapidly changing laws, leading them down the path towards getting rid of human rights, making it even more difficult for the Hazara people to live at all, let alone live a normal life.

A tracksuit-wearing Nasif Farah, inside that truck full of Afghan and also Iranian men, was en route to Calais, the town that had acquired the nickname of 'the Jungle'. He had travelled thousands of miles and was thinner than ever.

His expression was trance-like as several flames from cigarette lighters jerked this way and that.

The big Afghan man pulled up a pair of dirty white underpants over his hairy backside and buckled a belt to a pair of blue jeans.

The other men inside tried their hardest not to look at him.

A tear rolled down Nasif's cheek.

There were close to a thousand people inside the camp, based on the outskirts of Calais. It was all due to the closure of the Red Cross Reception Centre in nearby Sangatte.

Authorities in France and the UK had hoped that the removal of the centre would decrease the number of migrants determined to cross into England. They couldn't have been more wrong.

It was Nicolas Sarkozy, the then Interior Minister, who closed the camp.

A single tap on the roadside gave the mainly Afghan men drinking water. Rows of blue and grey tarpaulin sheets flapped in the wind. Dirty bodies infected the air. Their clothes were stained by goodness knows what and the stench of desperation was ever-present. Makeshift toilets had been constructed out of wood and plastic. Five or six men shared tent-like structures, assembled from cardboard and corrugated iron sheets and tarpaulin. Blue light from the plastic sheeting above shone down on Nasif Farah as he knelt on a piece of carpet, with several other men, praying to a God who would hopefully listen to them. It cost each of them hundreds and more often thousands of dollars just to get to this stage of their journey to the UK. How on Earth could the recently-orphaned son of a peasant farmer from Afghanistan have paid his way through all those countries in order to reach the goal of safety in the United Kingdom? Nasif Farah had been there for six months.

An Eastern European truck left the port of Dover and rumbled towards the A2 road of southern England. An ancient Celtic route that the Romans developed further still, with Anglo-Saxons calling it Wæcelinga Stræt. It was renamed into modern English as Watling Street and simply meant "a paved road". Britons used this as the main route between Canterbury and St Albans.

The Romans paved the track, using it as their gateway from London to Dover.

The Polish driver of the truck frowned when he heard a loud thumping noise from within the trailer. He slowed his vehicle down, pulled it over to the hard shoulder and clambered out of his cab, rounding to the rear.

The metal strip security seal had been bent and twisted. It was broken, and the additional metal cable which should have hooked into a fixed U-shaped loop had been cut.

The driver tightened his face, disappointed and disheartened. He reached up and opened the rear doors, like it had happened to him before; like it happened to him often.

A casually-dressed North African man leapt out the back, followed by several Iranian men, each nodding their head to the driver.

The driver retrieved a cigarette from a pack of L&Ms and placed it between his lips. He delved into his jean pocket and pulled a Zippo lighter, looking up to see Nasif Farah awkwardly making his way out of the truck.

Nasif extended his hand, smiling painfully at the driver.

"America?" Nasif managed to say.

The driver nodded his head, patted Nasif on the shoulder twice, gently moving him aside as he closed the door and made his way to the cab.

Cars raced past Nasif on the major road as he walked along the roadside. His shoulders hunched. His oversized trainers clobbered upon the ground, wet from the driven rain. His long, plain black t-shirt stuck to his disheveled body like cling-film. His baggy tracksuit bottoms became heavier with each step. He was having to hold them up as he walked. He stopped and looked upwards.

The rain spat in his face and dripped down his chin. The raindrops glistened white on his cheeks and on the tip of his nose and slowly turned into blue sparkles. They caught the swirling light of a police traffic vehicle parked behind him.

Nasif Farah's age was assessed by the Home Office as being fourteen. Like many of the overseas' students, he was given the birth-date of the first of the first. January 1st. It stood out like a sore thumb every single time it appeared on a referral form or register. Nasif Farah was in foster care. A strict, hardworking Muslim Pakistani family. He was continuously bullied by his Afghani peers who were the more streetwise and Pashto-speaking kids from

Kabul. He was simply a slave and servant to their daily needs, whether it was inside or outside of their UK education.

Michael and Nasif looked at one another in the classroom as he held up his artwork.

"Picture," Nasif smiled.

"Good picture," Michael replied, returning the smile and holding up his thumb, to which Nasif beamed more, held up his own thumb and giggled.

Rabee, his fellow Afghani student, slapped Nasif round the head and laughed.

Nasif giggled again.

"Nasif do picture," mocked Rabee.

"Yes, picture. Picture good. Good picture," Nasif said, choosing a brown pencil from the tray, holding it like a knife.

As much as Michael and the staff tried to put a stop to Nasif's peers barking orders at him, they could not watch their every move outside. It was simply a cultural thing. It was tribal and it saddened Michael and his colleagues just to look at the weak Nasif Farah.

Nasif giggled again and looked at Michael. "Good picture. Good picture," he said with a smile.

8. AUSTRALIAN WINE
AND NEIGHBOURS

Michael sat on a table next to his colleague Paul in his classroom. Despite mathematics not being his strong point, he had supported the lesson; however, it had become more of a 'if you think it's the right answer, put it down' type of support. That type of response meant Michael had no idea if it was the correct answer or not. A reassuring pat on the back and a "Keep going, you're doing well" statement often accompanied Michael's maths support technique.

In front of Michael and Paul sat a row of six laptops on four classroom tables. Sitting at the computers were the three Afghan students: Rabee, Abdul Rah-Maan and Nasif Farah. Also there was the Iranian boy, Shaheen, the Somali boy, Guled Omar-Ali and the Angolan, Sinatra Umbundo.

Sinatra had been there for a few weeks and so had the harsh scowl on his face. Michael and Paul watched each of them curiously as the kids tapped away and engaged themselves in their free time. Each had headphones on that allowed just the faintest tinny sound to escape into the otherwise quiet classroom.

Shaheen was watching YouTube. It was an Iranian woman belly dancing.

Next was Nasif Farah, who looked blankly at the Google homepage, glancing every so often at his fellow Afghani, Abdul Rah-Maan, who was also on YouTube, as was the third Afghani, Rabee, who was sitting next to Abdul.

Michael frowned and looked at Paul, gesturing him to look at Nasif.

"Does Nasif want to just stare at Google?"

"Maybe he's plugged himself into it and we don't know. Perhaps he's controlling it that way," chuckled Paul, as Michael shuffled off the table and squatted beside Nasif.

He lowered his headphones and turned to Michael. "Michael Jackson?" questioned Nasif.

"Michael Jackson! Michael Jackson!" shouted out Rabee, with a smirk, staring straight ahead at his screen, depicting some scantily clad Indian dancer on a hilltop. Rabee reclined on his seat.

Paul gently pushed the back of Rabee's chair with his foot, putting him upright. Rabee turned his head to give Paul a large grin and then returned to his viewing.

Michael entered the YouTube URL into the browser and typed "Michael Jackson Thriller" into the YouTube search box. He clicked on the first link which enabled Nasif to watch the full Thriller video on full screen.

"That's thirteen minutes out the way."

He glanced over to Sinatra Umbundo who was viewing some poor quality video of the Peckham Grime rapper known as Giggs. Giggs sometimes went by the name Hollowman. His real name was Nathan and he was an ex-offender, imprisoned for gun charges in 2003 and affiliated with various Peckham gangs. For some reason, his very distinctive, cheaply-produced music videos were extremely popular amongst the various students Michael encountered daily. More often than not, however, the majority of the students discreetly disclosed to him that they didn't like Giggs' music at all, nor rap in general, but just wanted to fit in with everybody.

Next to Sinatra was Guled, who watched a gang video. He slyly glanced round and clicked onto the Miniclip games website, pausing a motorcycle dirt bike game and returning to the mobile-phone-filmed gang music video.

Michael sat himself back on the table.

"It's weird, isn't it? Afghani, Angolan, Iranian and Somali in one class, individually watching their own personally selected YouTube videos," he observed.

"What have we got here then? Giggs." Paul adopted a street style accent. "Giggs. It's about Giggs init?" he then chuckled to himself. "What else? Michael Jackson. Of course! Belly dancers," he glanced over Abdul's shoulder to see him looking at a Mr Bean video.

Abdul turned round to Michael and Paul, smiled and lowered his headphones. "It is Mr Bean. In Afghanistan he is known as Baba Gee. He is funny."

Abdul replaced his headphones and returned to his Baba Gee viewing.

"Baba Gee. Ha! What about him, look? Thinks we can't see him looking at gang vids," said Paul, gesturing with a nod towards the sly and suspiciously-behaving Guled.

"I saw it a minute ago. He keeps switching between that dodgy motorbike game and the Ferrier video," replied Michael.

"Clearly a gang kid."

"I know!" said Michael. "Patricia always asks about gangs when she interviews. They always tell her they're not in one, despite their weird haircuts and coloured scarfs."

"Maybe they're Morris Dancers," Paul mocked. "Which one of 'em is tagged?"

"The one with the tag on," Michael smiled.

Paul laughed and looked to see Michael discreetly pointing his forefinger down at Sinatra Umbundo's feet, tucked under his chair. A glimpse of an electronic tag fitted to one ankle was clearly visible.

Michael eyed the clock on the wall. Two o'clock. "Well, that day went quick."

Paul looked up and then to the window to see the dark skies and heavy rain beyond. He slid himself off the table and gently placed a hand upon Rabee's shoulder.

Rabee removed his headphones. "Finished?"

"Finished," Paul mocked his accent.

Rabee slid his chair out, stood and patted Abdul on the head.

Abdul looked up at him and then at the clock, twisting further to Michael, who raised his thumb.

"Can we go, teacher?" he asked, politely.

Michael nodded.

Abdul removed his headphones and gently touched Nasif on the arm.

"Nasif! Nasif! Go! Hurry yes!" called out Rabee, impatiently. He made his way to the door, turning with every step, smiling at Michael, cheekily. He opened the door and waited for Nasif to get up from his chair with Abdul and exited the class.

Nasif and Abdul shook Paul's and Michael's hands as they left.

"Cheerio," said Paul, taking hold of the door and keeping it open as Guled and Sinatra passed them.

Guled pulled up his hood, slyly glancing at Michael as he left the room.

"See you, guys," Michael called out.

Paul released the door to a close and exhaled. He seated himself on a desk.

"He's trouble that one, eh?" he said.

It was only a few minutes later when the various members of staff were each sitting on the chairs in the staffroom.

Michael sipped a Twining's fruit tea: raspberry and cranberry flavour.

Paul sat next to him, with his back against a radiator, eyeballing Michael's drink and gripping his own cup of tea.

"D'you really like that?" Paul asked.

Michael tilted his head. "Not really."

"All right, Patsy, who you got for us now?"

Patricia sighed as she opened a bulky green card file. "Well, nobody new really, just some extra information, or rather just information as we weren't sent any when he arrived. Right. Lee Mace." Patricia looked around at her fellow staff members.

Michael whistled a cuckoo sound and rolled his eyes.

"Exactly," Paul agreed, understanding Michael's whistling response.

"As you know when Lee started with us we didn't have a file. All we knew was that he came from a school in Bexley. Now, as you can see, we have a file." She patted the large bulky mass of paperwork, accompanied with a cynical smile and a raise of her eyebrows. The file was four inches thick. "An out-of-borough child who was excluded for persistent disruptive behaviour, verbally abusive to staff, assaulted one male member of staff with a chair, but refuses to accept he did so. He's a regular cannabis user and a diagnosed schizophrenic. Lee continuously raps in class, ignores instruction and when told to do something by teaching staff, he immediately becomes aggressive, very threatening and starts swearing and usually walks out."

"Then we let him walk," replied Helen, who stood up and exited due to a telephone ringing in another room off the corridor.

"It's pretty evident that we've seen all this from him already." continued Patricia. "He was living with his mother and is now living in care in Woolwich."

"He told me that he was living with his dad," Michael stated.

"I don't think so. Maybe he doesn't want people to know his mother can't handle him anymore and thus sent him into the care of the authorities."

Catherine Riverdale stroked her large, witch-like chin, nodding and weighing up something that had obviously circled in her mind for a considerable amount of time.

Michael caught sight of this. He never missed a trick and knew that whatever escaped Catherine's mouth was sure to hit a nerve.

"I quite like the boy and believe he has great potential," commented Catherine to the staff members, looking around at each of them individually, nodding like one of those plastic dogs again.

Michael's mind raced. What was the point of those nodding dogs anyway? Exactly. They were pointless. Rather like the yellow 'Child On Board' signs that had become a bizarre phenomenon of the past two decades or so. What was their main purpose? Were the three words a shorter replacement for 'Do Not Crash Into Me Please'? If so, then it should have been law for everyone in the world to have one because, surely, nobody in their right mind really and truly wanted to crash into someone on purpose. "Oh, a child is in that car, I'd best not crash into them," or "Ah, look dear, a yellow child on board notification, I think we should drive a little slower and with more caution." Shouldn't every single driver in the world do that anyway? After all, that was what you took your test for. Child on board. So what? What were they trying to say? Was a child more important than anyone else? That child could grow up to be a violent gang member... Michael's imagination continued to whirl.

Catherine's pointless nodding and comments were intended to frustrate and did exactly that. Just like those pointless nodding dogs. "I do. I think he has great potential," Catherine repeated.

"Great potential to be a schizophrenic murdering young man maybe," responded a judgmental Michael. It was like a game of 'How To Annoy The Other Person More' as Michael batted his words across like a tennis ball over the coffee table towards Catherine.

"I disagree. He's been quite a gentleman and is a brilliant rapper." Whoosh. Catherine replied, slinging her peculiar response back over the table to Michael.

"The 'Gentleman Rapper'. Sorry, Simon Cowell, but I don't see it. It's a no from me, Simon." Before his words made their full impact, he continued, looking at Paul and Patricia. "Randy Jackson, Jennifer Lopez, yes or no?"

Smash! Michael sent it hurling back at Catherine, perhaps immaturely, with the combined full force of cynical sarcasm and a total dislike for her.

Her lips quivered and mouth moved, her head tilted to one side. Speechless. A moment of silence was upon them.

Paul uncrossed his legs and sat up. "It's a no from me, Simon," he said, as he arched his back and slowly stood up. "I'm falling asleep here and I think it's time to go." He walked out of the room, raising his hand in farewell.

Patricia closed the file. "I know I'm not in the classrooms with him-"

"No, you're not in the classrooms, Patricia," snapped Catherine.

"But I did interview him and I have been on a review with him and his parents and many of his social workers, current and previous, so I think I am qualified to pass comment," Patricia answered.

"Personally and professionally, Patricia, I don't think you are qualified to pass any comment or judgment on these young people and I don't really believe you should be in on any of our meetings in future. I find it to be quite a hurdle actually."

"A hurdle?" Patricia was lost for words, and a little hurt. She stood quickly and walked out of the room, with her head lowered.

Michael and Catherine were now alone in the staffroom.

"Maybe the police could use you to disperse crowds or late night parties. You certainly know how to clear a room, Catherine." Michael stood up, taking his empty mug to the sink.

"Sit down, Michael. I'd like a chat," Catherine instructed.

She didn't know how to separate adults from children and definitely had a St Trinianesque teaching manner about her. She was a very old-fashioned lady, with a peculiar world view. She stood as Michael neared the door. "Did you not hear me? I said, sit down," Catherine repeated assertively and bordering on the downright rude.

Michael turned and frowned. "Catherine, I'm not a child."

"I'm old enough to be your mother, Michael. If I was your mother, I'd have you punished and sent to your room without any dinner."

Michael raised one eyebrow as he looked at her with gritted teeth.

"I'm really not into that, Catherine. Thanks for the offer though."

She didn't get his humour at all and just nodded again as he formed a pleasant, but very fake, smile and turned away.

"Have a good evening. See you tomorrow," he said as he exited the room and walked down the corridor.

Catherine nodded her head, despite nobody being present. She formed a frown and marched up the corridor after Michael, but it was empty and quiet. She stopped in the middle of the corridor and turned around.

In the car park, Michael approached his vehicle, slowing as he looked up to see Catherine standing by the driver's side.

Her head wobbled at him.

Michael wondered whether if it was actually a medical condition or a habit that had formed into a nervous twitch. Whatever it was, it bloody annoyed the hell out of him and he wasn't the type of person who got annoyed at anything.

Something a child whom Michael dealt with would say, "She gets my goat," summed her up quite nicely.

Catherine placed her hands on her hips like a gunslinger.

Michael rolled his tongue around inside his mouth, filling out his cheeks and gums. He slowly pulled his car keys from his back pocket as he stopped a couple of feet away from her, ready to draw.

"You're a rebel," she said to him, with a slight smirk.

"With a cause," he quipped.

Her smirk disappeared fast.

"Tomorrow I'm going to give you some mentees," she said.

"But I'm not ill."

"I don't understand your humour, Michael, and this isn't the place for laughs anyway," Catherine replied.

"Oh, I think it is, and should carry on to be, Catherine. Humour works very well in this place. It's an important ingredient of why we're so successful."

"I disagree."

"You would, Catherine. You see, these children arrive angry and leave happy or at least happier than when they walked through the door. They have the crappiest of lives. For the majority, there has never been a laugh or a smile in any of their lives from the moment they were born," Michael said, passionately.

"You don't know that," interrupted Catherine.

"Well, it's pretty evident from their files, their behaviour, their attitude and their ever-present scornful faces, so please, grant me those pretty important facts."

"As your Line Manager, I'm-"

"We've been through this, you're not my Line Manager," he cut in.

"As your Line Manager, I'm going to-"

"You're not my Line Manager, Catherine."

"I am your Line Manager!" She raised her voice.

"No, you're not."

"I am!" she practically yelled and became more and more flushed. Her neck instantly reddened.

"Catherine, I dislike this phrase, but with all due respect, you are not my Line Manager. You are not in charge of me."

"I control you!" she said, huffing, like a child having a tantrum and not getting its own way.

"No, don't be silly, you don't control me and you're not my Line Manager."

"Who controls you? Who? Who is it?" she demanded.

"Nobody controls me. My Line Manager is Helen. My role is pretty much a self-defined one," Michael said calmly.

"No. I strongly disagree. As the Centre Manager, I control you. You're under my command. You're the mentor and I send you a list of mentees," Catherine stated, almost out of breath and nodding simultaneously.

"Catherine, it's no big deal, really, but please understand: Helen is my line manager. I can have students recommended to me from you, Patricia or other teachers, or the students can choose to come to me for themselves. I can enter classrooms and observe certain pupils and I can assist the teachers."

"So you have free will to do as you please?"

"Like I said, my role is self-defined. If Helen had a problem with me and the work I do here, she'd say so. She hasn't so far in the five years that I've worked with her, so I must be doing OK in her eyes."

"Go on. Go on."

"Go on what, Catherine?"

"Go on and tell me what else you do. You breeze in and out of classrooms at will, play the occasional game of basketball and then go home."

"If that's what you think I do, then fine, but I'd suggest you look a little closer, without making it so obvious to everyone that you're trying your damnedest to inspect me."

"You just want to be their friend," she said to him.

"I'm a friendly face, but I'm by no means their friend. There's always a boundary, Catherine. I take what a child says and does very seriously and professionally and I always note it down. I'm a reliable member of the team and that's what Helen, above all else, can trust. It's about that, Catherine. Trust." Michael gripped his car key and inserted it into the lock.

She looked at the car door and sidestepped. At least she got that right.

"You're just a bit of a clown really, aren't you?" she said, giving it one last attempt at pushing a button.

"I'm not a clown and this isn't a circus." Michael opened his car door and clambered into the driving seat. He quickly inserted his key into the ignition and brought the vehicle to life. He shoved it into gear and drove out of the car park, pulling on his seatbelt.

Catherine watched the car become more distant, nodding her head.

"What a nutcase," sighed Michael.

He was first at a set of roadwork traffic lights as he slowed to a halt.

There were so many roadwork signs, dug up holes and traffic lights in Greenwich. If Greenwich was a heart and the road a major artery, then the roadworks were clogging up that artery. Huge stress was being placed on the heart. Worse still, more often than not workmen were hardly ever visible. The lights took a lifetime to change from red to green. Michael's mobile phone rang. He retrieved it and noticed an unfamiliar number. He glanced up at the traffic lights. Still red. He took the call.

"Hello?" the voice on the other end was Scottish. Soft. Maybe Edinburgh.

"Hello, is that Michael?"

"Who's calling?" replied Michael, glancing up at the red light.

"This is Detective Constable Malcolm Crowe. My boss, Simon, is a neighbour of your parents."

"Oh, right," said Michael, looking up at the red traffic light and sighing.

"I was wondering if you have time to meet today. Just on the off chance. Today would be ideal though. Is it possible that would fit into your schedule?" replied the now identified DC Malcolm Crowe.

"Erm, when and where did you have in mind?" asked Michael.

"Well, we're near Blue Water. Would that be all right for you?"

Michael knew that if the lights changed and he drove beyond them, he would now have to head back on himself and be on the opposite side to where he currently was. Back at a set of annoying traffic lights. "And you'd like to meet today?" he asked.

"Would that be OK for yer?"

"No problem."

"Good stuff. When you arrive, just give us a call."

The lights changed to amber.

"OK. See you then," Michael quickly said, tossing the phone onto the passenger seat and shoving the vehicle into first gear, turning the wheel as far as it would go to the right.

Green light.

A car from the opposite direction had obviously gone over their own red light and narrowly missed Michael as he conducted an excellent U-turn, with his front wheel nearly touching the curb on the other side.

Second gear.

He accelerated and sighed as he was on the move once again.

Third gear.

He wiped his sweaty brow with the back of his right hand.

Fourth gear.

He pressed a button and scrolled his driver's side window down.

Fifth gear.

He exhaled and drove a steady pace behind a car. His eyes fixed on something on the car in front. It was a nodding, plastic dog. Michael sneered and then his eyes diverted to something else. Dangling inside the car was none other than a yellow "Child On Board" sign.

Upon the A2, Michael drove, heading past the Crayford turn-off. He called his father, Edward, who was tidying some boxes in his garage.

"Hello Mike. Everything all right?"

"Hey Dad. I just got a call from a detective wanting to meet me in Bluewater."

"When?"

"Now. Well, I'm on my way. He said for me to call him when I arrive." Michael steadied the wheel as he drove in the middle lane.

"Would you like me to meet you there?" his father asked.

"Yes please. If you don't mind." Michael formed a relieved expression.

"Of course not! I'll see you there," his father said, comfortingly.

"I'll park near Marks and Spencer," said Michael.

"OK. I'll call you when I get there."

Bluewater was a shopping centre that opened in 1999. It was in Greenhithe, in the county of Kent, and was the rival to and, to many, a more upmarket version of Lakeside Shopping Centre in West Thurrock in Essex. Way before the days of Westfield. It had a code of conduct. A policy that had banned certain types of clothing that obscured the face. Hoodies mainly, and baseball caps. Swearing was also a no-no, as were large groups of people who had no intention to shop. This came at a time when gangs were fast on the rise and Bluewater's policies were warmly welcomed. Mostly by the middle class and not by the hood-wearing youths lacking direction or any kind of purpose other than to intimidate, steal, cause trouble, walk around aimlessly or linger and swear at the true shoppers who visited there.

The high profile shops suited the tone and the place was hailed as a design revelation. It was a place Michael knew well as he had spent many an hour there over the years. It was also just a ten minute drive away from his parents' home.

Michael drove into the covered section of the car park near Marks and Spencer. It was quiet and although there were plenty of spaces available, he parked between two vehicles and switched off his engine. His phone rang and 'Mum and Dad' flashed up on his iPhone screen. Michael sat in the dark and answered his phone.

"Hello Dad."

"Hello Mike. I can see you, so don't worry about anything."

"Thanks Dad. I'll give the bloke a call. See you soon."

Michael scrolled through his phone to the recent calls section. He called the number of Malcolm Crowe. It rang a couple of times. Michael's heart was beating fast. He felt a little nervous, even more so when the phone was answered by DC Malcolm Crowe.

"Hello." His voice was chirpy and upbeat.

"Hi, it's Michael. I've arrived."

"Hey. OK. Great stuff. We've just parked up too, so maybe if you'd like to make your way to the Marks and Spencer entrance where the flower section is, that'd be great. Would that be OK for yer?" said DC Crowe.

"I'm on the other side, so I'll see you in a few minutes," Michael replied.

"Sure. No problem. See you."

At the Marks and Spencer entrance Michael glanced around, but there was nobody to see nearby. However, in the shadows, fifty feet away, was his father in a tweed flat cap and a dark green wax jacket.

Edward followed his son at a safe enough distance not to be seen.

A handful of people were milling around the lingerie section of Marks and Spencer as Michael passed through. His eyes were everywhere and he wondered if he was being watched by the people who'd called him, but he felt comfortable that his own father was also present.

Michael's father, Edward, held a hand-basket as he followed twenty feet behind, looking at various goods on shelves. He looked up to see his Michael enter the food section.

Michael walked past the fruit and vegetable aisle and weaved around several people as he made through a checkout, heading for the entrance near the fresh flower counter.

His father slowed his pace and put his basket on the floor. He noticed Michael had exited the store. Outside the other entrance of Marks and Spencer, Michael surveyed his surroundings. He saw a bald man in his late forties lingering beside a Range Rover and smoking a cigarette. He turned to see two young men with a trolley of bagged groceries.

A woman in her late twenties, in tight jeans and a loose fitting top, caught his eye thirty feet or so away as she put shopping into her car.

Michael waited patiently and scanned the car park some more. He squinted to look further, seeing a man in a dark green baseball cap, discreetly hidden by the cover of a couple of cars. Michael's phone rang.

"Hello," answered Michael.

"Hi, I'm wearing a white t-shirt. If you just make your way to the start of the pathway in the carpark and follow me from about fifteen feet behind, that'd be great," instructed DC Malcolm Crowe, before hanging up the phone.

Michael crossed over, exaggerating a scratching of the head as he stepped onto the pathway. He noticed a man turn around and then start to walk.

He was in his early forties. On that day, he wore a dark green baseball cap, light blue jeans, Timberland boots and a white t-shirt.

Michael smirked, knowing full well that he saw him.

His father was a short distance away and saw the man in the white t-shirt near a new silver Volkswagen Passat. The rear windows were heavily tinted.

Edward looked at the registration plate. He then clocked the exits to the carpark. There was one close by, but it led back to the underground section. He watched his son retrieve his phone as his own phone rang.

"Michael, what's up?"

"They've just called me to say make for a silver Volkswagen with tinted windows," Michael said hurriedly.

"OK. Don't worry. I've got you. They'll probably flash their lights to you," his father said.

"Dad, what if they drive me away?" asked Michael, nervously.

"They may do but I doubt they'd go far. Tell them you don't have much time to spare. There's nowhere else really for them to go, so they might just park up somewhere else. Like I said, I've got you. I've always got you, Mikey, and I'll always find you. Do you understand?"

"Yes," replied Michael softly, as he neared the Volkswagen.

The headlights flared up, flashing twice as Michael approached. His father saw it, turned and headed back inside the store. Michael opened the rear passenger door and clambered inside.

Michael's father paced back the way he came, through the food section of Marks and Spencer and then past the shoes and then the cosmetics. The exit was in sight.

Inside the Volkswagen Passat, Michael sat on the backseat. The driver turned around, greeting him with a smile. He was a dark-haired, white man, around forty. Handsome, and on that day he was casually dressed in lightweight, Chino-like trousers and a dark polo t-shirt. His name was Detective Sergeant James "Jim" Cole.

He extended his hand to Michael. "All right? I'm James Cole. Detective Sergeant."

"Michael. Michael Thompson."

They shook hands.

Michael's father passed the lingerie section of Marks and Spencer, darted out of the store and into the carpark. He hot-footed it several car lengths to his silver Daewoo Matiz. He liked that car. He said it didn't have a tracker built into it, whatever that meant.

In the back of the Volkswagen Passat, Michael turned to see the front passenger door open. A man clambered inside before closing the door. It was the dark green baseball cap guy. He was DC Malcolm Crowe, the softly spoken Scottish man who'd telephoned Michael. He turned and smiled pleasantly, extending his hand towards Michael. They shook hands.

"Michael is it? I'm DC Malcolm Crowe. This is DS James Cole or Jim, as we like to call him. Well, to his face anyway. I won't say in front of him what his name is at the station as he might get annoyed." He beamed a smile, reassuring Michael. "So, how you doing?"

"Good thanks. A long day, but, well, you know," Michael replied, nervously.

"Cool. Well, what we're gonna do, Michael, is take a wee drive and park up elsewhere," replied DC Crowe.

"Where you'll what, pop me in the back of the head?" Michael said, masking his nervousness with a joke.

"Ha, yeah, double tap," replied DS Cole, as he started up the vehicle and reversed.

Michael remembered how his father always told him to reverse into a parking space and not drive straight in, even though it might be easier to do so. It made for an easy getaway.

These guys didn't do that, but Michael's father did.

Michael's father was old school. He was retired from the City of London Police Force and had represented both force and country overseas. He was also a 'retired' secret intelligence officer, who had served Queen and country. A cadet at just sixteen years of age, he was recruited into the City of London Police Force and later discovered he was part of a parallel division of the police force run by MI-5 and MI-6. He had protected Royalty, shot bad guys, tracked down terrorists, been blown up by the IRA, arrested pop stars, delivered gold to South Africa on the quiet, received commendations and awards for bravery, but above all, he had always been there for the family. Michael's father, Edward, was his absolute hero.

Edward was behind the wheel of his vehicle. He could see every exit and entrance to the car park. His car also had tinted windows. He saw the VW Passat leave Marks and Spencer's car park and enter an underground section.

"Too fast and a complete giveaway," he said to himself, sighing as he saw the Passat drive up a ramp with a slight screech of the tyres as it ascended to a higher level. He removed his flat cap and tossed it to the back seat. "To the top, no doubt," he muttered as he struggled to pull off his jacket to reveal a shirt and jumper.

He exited his car and walked briskly to a stairwell that led to the other levels of the car park. The second level saw the Volkswagen Passat drive speedily upward and head up to the third level.

Edward paced up the stairs. His breath was heavy as he reached the roof section. Discreetly hidden by many cars, he had a clear view of the entire car park and saw the Volkswagen Passat roll up the ramp and pull into a space.

"And here's Hot Fuzz once again." He exhaled a deep breath as he watched the car from a safe distance.

Inside the parked Volkswagen, DS Cole switched the engine off. Both he and DC Crowe turned around to Michael.

"All right?"

"Fine," replied Michael.

"It'll just be a quick chat really, Michael. Is it Michael? Or do you prefer Mike or what?" asked DC Crowe.

"Whichever you feel comfortable in saying," shrugged Michael.

DC Crowe smiled and glanced to DS Cole.

"Ah, you can tell you work in a school, eh Jim?"

"Yeah, very polite and making you feel at ease," DS Cole responded.

"Isn't making people feel at ease your job?" asked Michael. He felt comfortable with these guys.

"I guess it is our job, but some aspect of it is to make people feel uncomfortable. Maybe the types of people you come into contact with from day to day. I don't know. Would you like to tell us what kind of kids you deal with? We only got a brief overview from the top boss. Your parents' neighbour," said DC Crowe.

"Ah, the man who walks many dogs," commented Michael.

Crowe and Cole laughed. "Yeah, we heard he's got a lot of dogs. Cats too, apparently," replied Crowe.

"I've not seen him walk any of those," smiled Michael.

"But I can imagine him being made to do that," mocked DS Cole.

"I think the wife would make him do anything," chuckled Crowe.

"I've only ever heard her shout and swear in the garden," noted Michael, already fitting in with the cop twosome.

"Oh yeah, she's a whip cracker," replied Cole.

"She's in the job, too, isn't she?" asked Michael.

"Yeah, she is. A higher rank than he is. Isn't your old man in this line of work?" asked Crowe.

"Dad worked in the City and also for the security services," Michael confirmed.

"By security I take it you don't mean by the counter in WH Smith?" said Crowe.

Michael just responded with a smile.

Michael's father was on his mobile to his wife as he watched the Volkswagen Passat from near the stairwell.

"He's all right. I'm watching him. Do you want me to pick up a couple of French sticks from Marks while I'm here?"

Crowe brought out an A4 notebook and opened it. "OK, I'm just going to take some notes, if you don't mind. Maybe you can tell me about the place you work at and the types of children you work with. In your own time. Just for us to get an image, you know?"

"Sure. Well, erm. All types really. Anyone new to the borough of Greenwich child-wise. Be they from another school in a different borough and they require a new school. Be they excluded and need a new school. They might have moved house or they may even be from another country. Any child, aged eleven to sixteen, new to this borough comes through us and we assess them academically and socially and determine what the next step is for them. So, they may end up at the PRU, if they're excluded."

"What's 'excluded'?" asked Cole.

"It's the new term for expelled," replied Crowe.

"Right," continued Michael.

"And the PRU is what?" asked Cole.

"Pupil Referral Unit," replied Crowe.

"Right," continued Michael.

"So the ones that go to the PRU? The expelled excluded ones? What do they go there for?" inquired Crowe.

"All kinds of reasons. Persistent disruptive behaviour in their previous school or schools or centres. Violence. Drug use in schools. They might have hit a teacher, or thrown a chair at a teacher, or brought a gun or a knife into school, or something like that," Michael answered, intelligently and confidently.

"Wow. So they're all excluded in the PRU?" asked Cole.

"Not always, but pretty much. Sometimes they call it a 'Managed Move'. It's so political and some teachers say it's like chess with kids. It's like a game. Seriously. You're playing with lives. I don't have time to say much, but it's crazy. Each child is worth a certain amount of cash to a school, and more if they're... say... special. Anyway, some children may not be able to handle school life and feel more comfortable in a smaller class, so end up at the PRU," Michael told them.

"So, what, they choose to go to the Referral Unit?" asked Crowe, curiously.

"No, they won't choose. It's often chosen for them. A head of a school will speak with a head of a PRU and tell them that they'll accept a certain child if the PRU will take a different one back. Sale or return. That kind of thing."

"That's crazy!" blurted Crowe.

"What's sale or return?" asked Cole.

"It's like if a child from the unit is given a chance to return to a mainstream school again and they screw up, the school they're sent to can return them back to the PRU, no problem. Is that right?" said Crowe.

"Something like that," replied Michael.

"And what do you mean by 'special'?" asked Cole.

"In foster care or they get a free school lunch. Statemented. That kind of thing," responded Michael.

"So, tell us about the types of kid you have there," Crowe asked.

"Well, we have boys and girls. They're aged eleven to sixteen. We have the stereotypical Chavy type. Hoodie-wearing, cannabis-dealing, smoking, scowling, cheap-tracksuit-wearing insecure white kid. We have children from abroad who are new to the UK. They could be from absolutely anywhere: China, Nepal, West Africa, Afghanistan, Iran, Italy, India, Pakistan, Philippines, Nigeria, Jordan, Ethiopia, Eritrea, Somalia. To name just a few. Oh and Canada, but from my experience, they've been surprisingly OK," Michael smirked, as did Cole and Crowe.

"Any gang kids?" asked Cole.

"Lots," replied Michael, in a firm tone.

"Do you know any of the gangs in Greenwich?" asked Crowe.

"All of them," Michael said, positively. "You could have gang members from T-Block, Cherry, the Ferrier and The Woolwich Boys in one class, not to mention ones from maybe Peckham or Lewisham."

"Do they ever fight in class?" asked Cole.

"I wouldn't say never," replied Michael. "It's happened, but it's rare. They're wary of one another, sure, but we hardly ever have a fight. There's the occasional spat at the main PRU, our other site, but we haven't really had an incident at our one. No."

"OK, so what about the other countries? How does that work?" asked Crowe, as he scribbled a few notes down on the A4 pad.

"This one's a little odd, or rather, more confusing at times. The overseas students - I don't think half of them are actually children. They're far too old-looking to be children. These are men."

"You have men in the same class as the kids?" asked Cole.

"Not officially. But it's plain to see they are men. Grown men. Predominantly from Afghanistan or Iran. These guys are big, unshaven and arrive not knowing their age or date of birth, so the Foreign Office gives them a date of birth, which is usually the first of the first," Michael reeled off, confidently.

"First of the first? What do you mean by that?" asked Crowe, with a frown.

That was all new to the detectives. They were in the dark on all of this, but they were learning fast.

"If they don't know their date of birth and if we don't, then our people will guess and say something like 'Hmm, they look like they could be what? Fourteen? OK, fourteen it is.' And they'll give them the birthday of the first of January two thousand and whatever it is. You see, it stands out like crazy when the limited amount of paperwork arrives. Usually it is just one sheet of paper telling you where they live and who their foster parent is," Michael explained.

"They're all fostered?" Cole muttered.

"Pretty much. The foster parents are another story altogether," answered Michael.

"So, the kids from abroad. What are they like? Are they gang members?" asked Crowe, with his pen poised, readying himself to make yet more notes.

"Not really, but give it time. They're often troubling, let alone troubled. They could be children of Taliban members. They could have had their families killed by the Taliban. They could have had their families killed by us. They could be boy soldiers from Somalia or Angola. They could be children of revolutionaries in Iran. They could be autistic children from Nigeria whose parents are in denial that their child has anything wrong with them, medically, so have literally beaten the devil out of them or scarred them in some way that they become incredibly messed up. They could be a child of the working classes, white and incredibly strange, with a fascination for mermaids and believe everyone they come into contact with is actually a character from

Doctor Who, and when you meet each of their parents, you then realise why they are like they are," Michael informed them.

"Which is usually fucked up. Pardon my French," commented Crowe.

"Exactly," nodded Michael.

Michael's father glanced at his wrist watch and sighed as he looked at the Volkswagen Passat still parked where it had been for the past half an hour. Inside the Passat, Crowe rubbed his chin as he looked at Michael with a pondering expression.

"So, what kind of crimes are the kids involved in or have possible links to, do you think?"

"What crimes can you name in ten seconds?"

"You being serious?" asked Crowe.

"Shall I start the timer now or five seconds ago when I asked it?" Michael said.

"Fuck me. Really?" replied Crowe.

"Four seconds left," continued Michael.

"Flipping heck. Drug dealing. GBH. ABH. Burglary. Possession of a knife or firearm. Any of those?" Crowe asked, with sheer disbelief.

"All of the above, as well as sexual assault, rape, kidnapping, attempted murder, murder, attempting to derail a train and a whole lot more," completed Michael.

"Shit, well, OK, I think we have something to go on here. Are you aware of anybody or does any pupil stand out as a particular concern to you?" asked Crowe.

"Anyone at all?" reinforced Cole.

Michael stared ahead at the windscreen of the car. His mind raced with the names and faces of the children he came into contact with.

The Somali, Guled Omar-Ali.

The Iranian boy called Shaheen.

The Afghan pupils, Abdul Rah-Maan, Rabee and Nasif Farah.

The Angolan, Sinatra Umbundo.

The white, working-class boy, Lee Mace.

The Russian girl called Anna appeared in his mind.

The quiet Nigerian girl called Juliet.

The lively, fun Polish girl called Olga. That was just a handful. There were a dozen more as he thought and nodded to himself, looking at the two undercover detectives in front of him.

"Yeah, all of them," he said, holding his stare. He exhaled.

"OK, this is what we need to do," replied Crowe. "If there is anything you think of that you feel needs police attention, then give us a call. We also need to work out a safe place for you. It's in case you feel unsafe or if you're in danger; if you suspect someone is going to hurt you and we need to pick you up," continued Crowe.

"How'd you mean?" asked Michael.

"Well, say for instance you give us information on a certain pupil and they find out that you did, then that could place you in immediate danger, so we need to get you out of there fast and to a place nobody you're in contact with knows about," explained Cole.

"So, is there a place you'd prefer us to take you to?" asked Crowe.

Michael shrugged. "I... I have no idea. Maybe back home?" he suggested.

 "That's not a problem. Maybe we could take you to your parents' house or something like that? We can talk about that and arrange it at a later date maybe. So, we also need to come up with an undercover name for you. We can give you one or you can come up with your own. It's up to you," Crowe continued.

Michael's mind raced. He had suddenly found himself in an incredibly different situation. It was almost like he had signed for a Time Share apartment or something and couldn't get out of it.

The two policemen looked at him. "It may seem a bit heavy going at the moment and a lot to take in, so just relax and take your time to think about it. Weigh it all up," said Crowe, noting Michael's expression.

"So, what are you up to this evening? Watching Neighbours?" asked Cole, flippantly.

"I think that's probably finished now, Jim," chuckled Crowe.

"Maybe he'll need some wine after he finishes with us. Do you drink wine? What's your poison, as it were? French, South African or Aussie wine?"

"Australia has great wine," Michael said, with a blank expression. "Hardy's, Jacob's Creek. Both of those," Michael continued, robotically.

"Bit of an Aussie fan eh? Neighbours, Ramsey Street and Jacob's wine and all that," joked Crowe.

Michael rolled his eyes up to meet DC Malcolm Crowe's.

Michael's father, Edward, sighed and lowered his mobile phone as he watched the car. It was getting darker outside.

Inside the car, Crowe scribbled something down on his A4 pad.

"Works fine for me. Does it work for you, Jim?"

"Works fine for me, Malcolm," replied Cole, who retrieved a brown envelope filled with cash. He counted out sixty pounds and turned to Michael, who frowned as he was passed the money. "This is for you and your time. It might be more or might be less when we see you next, depending on the information and if there's an arrest of charge, that kind of thing."

"What we need now, though, is for your new signature next to this number here," Crowe explained, pointing at a scribbling scrawl of an inky £60.00 on the notepaper.

Michael took the biro offered to him and pressed the ballpoint to the paper, thinking quickly as he instantly made up a signature.

"OK then. Thank you very much. We'll await your call whenever you have any information for us. Next time we meet, we might have a few forms for you to complete. It'll just be your address and place of work. You know? That kind of thing. No biggie," said Crowe, hurriedly, knowing time was getting on.

"We'll see you soon maybe," added Cole.

Michael nodded his head, summing it all up. He raised his eyebrows and clutched the door handle.

"We'll take you back to your car if you want, mate," offered Cole.

"I might have a browse of some shops as I'm here," Michael replied.

The undercover cops nodded their heads. They understood.

Michael shook their hands.

"OK, take care," said Cole.

"Yeah, see you later, mate," chirped Crowe as Michael opened the door and clambered out of the car.

Edward watched carefully as he saw his son close the door to the VW Passat and stand back before walking past a few cars as the Volkswagen started up, reversed and drove back down the ramp, leaving his sight. Edward whistled.

Michael turned and smiled when he saw his dad walk towards him. Edward placed an arm around his shoulders, squeezing his neck gently.

"You all right? That was a long one eh?"

"Yeah, too long," Michael replied.

"Ah, were they a couple of goons?" said his father.

"They were OK. They reminded me of the two detectives from Hot Fuzz."

"Doesn't surprise me," Edward commented.

"We'll go down the stairs, shall we? Tell me all about it then. Did they give you a code name or did you choose it?"

"I chose it," Michael said.

"What's your name then?" asked his father as he and Michael descended the stairs, reaching a new level.

Michael turned to his father and said, "My name is Jacob Ramsay."

9. THE BOOKLET

Michael pulled his car up in Greenwich Park. There weren't too many vehicles there at all, but there was a healthy number of people on foot.

A few joggers.

An elderly couple.

A yummy mummy with her hands full, pushing a buggy, holding the hand of a three year old and trailing a lead with a Golden Retriever following slowly behind.

Michael took out his little Paperchase notebook and opened it, glancing briefly at one of the pages that revealed the words 'NAME: JACOB RAMSAY. ADDRESS: LUXOR ST NR DENMARK HILL'. He smiled and looked out of his car windows when his iPhone rang. He took the call and brought it to his ear. Still looking through the windows, his eyes searched.

"Hello?" he said.

"Hey, Jacob, how are you, mate? All right?" came the familiar Scottish accent that belonged to DC Malcolm Crowe. He sounded a little out of breath and was possibly outside. It was hard to tell.

Michael's eyes searched the pathways, looking for his contact.

"Hi. I'm good, you?" replied Michael.

"Yeah, not bad, mate. Listen, I'm near the bandstand. D'you wanna make your way over and then you can give us a call when you're there," Crowe instructed.

"Sure. See you in a bit," replied Michael, beeping out as he exited his car.

Upon a pathway, passing a drinking fountain, Michael headed for the bandstand. It was a good few minutes away. His eyes diverted to a young woman.

The woman was dressed in grey jeans, white Reeboks and a black jacket. She was white and walked across the grass.

Michael could see the bandstand wasn't too far away. Nobody was in sight. He pulled his phone and scrolled through his retrieved calls, pressing the name 'Jacob Ramsay'. It rang once and was answered by Crowe.

"Hello," the voice was chirpy.

"Hi, it's Jacob," replied Michael. "I'm at the bandstand." He wasn't at all, but he was close enough for him to say he was. He could still see the young woman twenty feet or so away and then he caught sight of a man, way ahead, on a bench. He was dressed in blue jeans, a white t-shirt and a brown jacket. It was Crowe.

Michael smiled. "I can see you," Michael said.

"What am I wearing?" chuckled Crowe.

"Jeans, a brown jacket and that old white t-shirt you wore when I first met you. Very different to the faded black clothes favoured by the young woman doing her best to follow me," quipped Michael.

Crowe chuckled again. "There's no woman, Jacob. It's just us. OK, if you wanna follow me, keeping about fifteen feet behind, we'll go to the car," instructed Crowe, who walked further up the path and was becoming more and more distant.

Michael didn't believe that the young woman wasn't part of the undercover police operation and continued to be conscious of her as he walked up the pathway, passing the bandstand that was upon his right hand side.

The beautiful park and greenery was all around him. It was Michael's favourite London park, probably because it was forever part of his childhood memories. He knew this park incredibly well.

After his elder brother, Jason, had passed his driving test, he used to bring Michael skateboarding here. There was a particular favourite pathway that dipped so deeply it enabled Michael the skateboarder and his roller-skating brother to gain great speed and excitement as their wheels roared and raced across the tarmac.

Earlier still, Michael's parents would take Michael and his elder brothers to a part of the park for a picnic or a bike ride and perhaps a view of the Cutty Sark ship upon which Michael would pretend to be a pirate. He recounted a different, happy memory with every step. In his more recent years, when Michael was first dating Rebecca, they would lay out a tartan blanket and sit in the shade of an oak tree as they removed several picnic foods from a cold storage bag. Chicken drumsticks, cocktail sausages, strawberries, crisps and small cheeses. The fair-haired couple, in the first stages of sharing a new love for one another, shielding themselves from the sun yet enjoying the outside fun and nature of a simple pleasurable experience. Michael passed a large, green, practically tree-free area and remembered a time where he sat with Rebecca, viewing Ferris Bueller's Day Off on a large screen with a few hundred other people in the late summer of goodness knows when.

DC Crowe walked along the narrow pathway. He neared an exit of the park, practically hidden within an ancient-looking brick wall. It was like the Secret Garden, and beyond the gate was the so-called normal, outside world. Crowe rounded the corner and disappeared from view as he left the park entirely.

Michael, as instructed, fifteen feet behind. He glanced into the glass screen of his iPhone, holding it steady and tilting it slightly to see the young woman following him close behind. He was indeed his father's son. Michael removed his jacket and slowed his pace. He stopped and diverted to a bench a couple of feet away and sat himself down.

Three or four seconds passed and the woman stepped up, looking a little surprised as she tried her hardest not to look directly at Michael as she walked on. She looked dead ahead as Michael stared at her. She continued out of the park gate, with Michael quickly getting to his feet again to walk up the path.

He glanced behind him, taking in one last view of the park before he stepped beyond the wall, out of what he imagined to be the Secret Garden. The street beyond the wall was Maze Hill and it was deserted. Michael looked left and right and couldn't see any cars he recognised. He looked ahead to Vanbrugh Park and there it was: the silver Volkswagen Passat with tinted rear windows. Michael got the sense that eyes were watching him as he saw the lights of the Passat flash once. He glanced to the right as he crossed the street and saw a figure dart out of sight.

It was the young woman.

Michael frowned as he neared the Volkswagen and grasped the door handle to the rear passenger door. Inside the VW Passat sat the familiar DS James Cole behind the wheel and DC Malcolm Crowe in the passenger seat next to him.

Michael clambered inside onto the rear seat and saw the extended hand of Cole, which he shook, followed by Crowe's.

"All right?" said Crowe as the rear door opened.

Michael swivelled to see the young woman clamber inside to sit next to him on the back seat and close the door.

"How you doing?" Michael asked her.

She released an embarrassed, awkward smile and exchanged a look with Crowe.

"This is DC Jo Blake. Jo's new to the team, so you might see her with us every so often," said Crowe.

"Did I throw you when I sat on the bench?" asked Michael.

"A little," replied DC Blake, unimpressed.

"Did you spot her then?" asked DS Cole, as he glanced up at Michael in the rear view mirror.

"She was either one of you guys or was going to mug me," sneered Michael, glancing at DC Blake who retrieved a black folder from under the seat in front.

"So you didn't think she was gonna ask you out?" quipped Crowe with a smile on his face.

"That's what I first thought of you," joked Michael, quick-wittedly.

"I'll hand over to Jo, who's just gonna ask you a few questions and whatnot," replied DC Crowe.

Michael looked at DC Jo Blake. She was attractive in a plain sort of way. A brunette and pear-shaped. She should work out a little more as she was becoming quite dumpy. Maybe the new move in her career was a healthier exercise plan that would keep her trim and fit.

Michael looked at her pale white hands. No rings on her fingers. Fingernails were short, stubby and bitten. She opened the folder containing thirty or so transparent plastic covers. She looked at Michael.

He felt like he was one of them and already believed he had 'got one over' having spotted the new DC Jo Blake in the park. He adopted a slightly superior expression that bordered on the smug side.

"These are a few CCTV pictures of youths from various boroughs. Some are from shops and street cameras and some are taken from public transport. Buses and underground, so if you would like to look through the booklet and tell us if you recognise any of them." She looked up at Crowe as if for approval.

"Great stuff," Crowe nodded. "Just browse through them, Jacob. It's a big booklet, so flag up any faces that might stand out."

Michael studied the first sheet. Underneath each photocopied colour photograph was a name, a type of crime and a date. Michael studied the first one. A CCTV image capture depicted a white youth in a cap and white tracksuit on the top deck of a bus, walking down the aisle. The crime stated 'theft/pickpocket'.

He moved on to the next picture: two black youths in a petrol garage aiming a firearm at the cashier.

The next picture was of the inside of a railway station and a collection of youths surrounding another youth lying on the floor, appearing to be protecting himself from the violent kicks of the youths.

"How's the school?" asked DS Cole as Michael turned the page to a similar set of pictures.

"Exhausting," Michael said. "Can't wait for the break really," he continued, looking down at the booklet, turning another page. "Nice looking bunch, aren't they?"

"Oh yeah, they're pretty," chuckled Crowe. "I don't think you'd find their faces on any dating websites."

"D'you have a girlfriend, Jacob?" asked Cole.

Michael looked up at him in the rear view mirror.

"Yeah, I do," replied Michael. "We met on a dating website." He smiled as he turned another page, scanning over the pictures.

"Bet you have some stories from all of that," chipped in DC Crowe.

"Yeah, a few," answered Michael. "Ah, this girl here," he said, pointing to a picture of a large-framed Somali girl. The image was clear and depicted the girl on a street corner. Underneath the photograph was her name, Nadifa Dodi, along with her crimes: 'burglary/street robbery/knife crime'.

"I know this one," Michael stated.

Crowe craned his neck round to see who the face was. "Nadifa Dodi," he said.

"That's not her name though," Michael told him.

"It's not?" Crowe asked, with Cole turning round.

"No, this picture is of Aziza Dodi. Nadifa Dodi is her sister. They're both equally as horrible as one another. Vile girls. They're pretty local actually."

"Oh, right. You don't have an address, do you?" asked Crowe.

"They're Kidbrooke girls. Always hanging out on that estate," Michael confirmed. "There's a number in her family. I remember her mother came into work once, bringing in her daughter for a meeting as she's a threatening, nasty piece of work. You should have seen her. Her mother, who's this big, hefty lump, found it extremely hard to even get up from the chair she was sitting on, let alone reach down between her feet to her handbag where she flicked through different envelopes."

"Envelopes for what?" asked Crowe.

"Each envelope was marked with a different name and address. All benefit entitlements. It was a real eye-opener. Lying, deceitful, violent and just plain horrible. Brothers and sisters. There's a bunch of them," informed Michael, in his element.

"So, the names and addresses?" uttered Crowe again.

"I can get you anything," Michael said.

"I'd like to clarify something?" chipped in Jo Blake.

"What is it, Jo?" muttered Crowe.

"I'd like to ask why you're doing this? Is it a revenge or vengeance thing? Have you been wronged by this kid?" Jo asked Michael, pen poised between her fingers.

Michael rolled his tongue around inside his mouth, filling out his cheeks and gums, thinking. "Why am I doing this? Can you honestly say that you would like these people on our streets? They're dangerous children who will soon become dangerous adults. That, to me, is dangerous times ten. This girl has about four different official ages. Does that mean she's four different people?

I don't know. The school certainly doesn't know. The government obviously doesn't know either. I first dealt with her when she was apparently thirteen. She was a massive girl then and she told me she had a twenty-year-old boyfriend and she winked at me, pressing her finger to her lips, like it was a secret. I told her that if they were in a sexual relationship then he was breaking the law. She said it couldn't be illegal if she's eighteen. A year or so later, I saw her again. She was being taught in a different department, separated from her peers. We had a young IT support guy tending to a computer in a room that she was in. This guy was twenty-one years old that day and had a birthday card, with a badge fixed to it, on a nearby desk. This girl, this woman. Her hands picked at the card and she slyly stole the badge just as I was walking into the room. I asked her to put the badge back on the desk and she moaned, saying, 'But I is twenty-one tomorrow init?' I said if she was twenty-one, then due to the health and safety of our children, she couldn't be in this building any longer. She threw the badge across the room. She told me to F off and said she had her eye on a laptop anyway and didn't need no effing badge. This is one of many and this is why I'm doing this. Revenge is Bruce Wayne running about Gotham dressed as Batman. Vengeance is Gladiator. What I'm doing is a moral justice."

10. THURSDAY NIGHT

"Well, it looked like your tip came off for us, Jacob. Aziza Dodi or Nadifa Dodi or whoever the heck she is was rounded up in her flat. She had a load of Apple Macs and laptops and iPods and a shit load of stolen goods. She's been charged," stated Crowe, in the undercover police officers' vehicle, parked in Greenwich Park. Crowe counted out seven hundred pounds in twenty-pound notes in front of Michael, who was on a back seat.

Michael's eyes were wide and he couldn't help but smile.

"We just need a Jacob Ramsay signature."

Michael walked briskly down a darkened section of a stairwell, deep within the school. His mobile phone pressed hard against one ear.

"It's Jacob. Jacob Ramsay. I've just overheard a conversation in the playground from one our new lads. He's a T-Blok member. Heard him on the phone talking about meeting up in Stockwell to get even with a gang up there. Apparently there's about twenty to thirty of them. On a bus. Heading from Blackheath."

"We arrested and charged eleven of your guys on a bus near the Oval tube station. All of them were carrying knives, baseball bats, one gun and a replica firearm. That gets you about this much, I'd say," stated Crowe as he counted out six hundred and fifty pounds, sitting next to Michael in the back of the Volkswagen undercover vehicle.

Michael locked himself within a cubicle, somewhere in the staff toilets of the school. He talked quietly into his phone.

"Hi, it's Jacob Ramsay. I've learned of a gang of girls who sit at cashpoints. ATMs. They beg to people as they withdraw cash. I was told they have a baby, but I know for certain that they don't. The baby is just a bundle of blankets. These girls are dangerous. They follow the person whose cash has just been withdrawn from the machine and literally set upon them like a pack of wolves. One girl definitely has to be watched. I have her name and address here. You ready?"

"That girl you mentioned a few months ago? The one who sits at cash machines? You know she's now up for murder?" replied Crowe, handing over some cash to Michael, sitting on the back seat of the Volkswagen, in Blackheath railway station car park.

"Murder?"

"Yeah," said Cole.

"She pushed a girl off a high-rise," added Crowe.

"Wow. No way?" blurted Michael.

"She was arrested in the act. Silly girl attempted to mug a plain clothes copper."

"Wow!" exclaimed Michael again, with surprise.

"Oh, she's a real nut job. She spat at the magistrate."

Michael walked across the school playground, heading towards a row of wooden huts. He stepped round behind one, pulling out his mobile. He scrolled to his 'Favourites' list and pressed a number. "Hi, it's Jacob Ramsay. There's this Nigerian boy at the school. He's fairly new to us. He didn't make it on that bus that day to Stockwell. He was mates with all those others, but he was too fat to run for the bus. Anyway, that doesn't make him any less dangerous because he's bad. Seriously, he's really bad. He carries this comb. He has cut the teeth of the plastic comb so it's an easier grip. Fashioned it like a knife. The end of the comb is a long, pointed length of metal. Yeah, that's right: it's an Afro comb. A spike. He carries this around in school, out of school, but that's not all. He's got access to a flat or a house. He uses it to sell drugs, weigh drugs and erm... I'm pretty sure it's a brothel. The boy is fourteen years old. The house... The house is, erm... It's either number forty-five or forty-nine and the address is... You ready? OK, it's..."

Time had passed quickly from their first meeting six months ago.

Michael had received several thousand pounds from the detectives.

"You're definitely one of our top guys," stated Crowe, in the passenger seat of the Volkswagen undercover vehicle.

"Yeah, I enjoy your company. Love to hear the school stories," chirped Cole, sitting behind the wheel as usual.

"Thanks, guys," replied Michael, sliding a wad of cash into his wallet.

"Ya might need an elastic band to secure that," Crowe laughed, gesturing to Michael's bulging wallet. "We were wondering if you're around of an evening."

"When?" asked Michael.

"Oh, I dunno," muttered Crowe.

"This Thursday or Friday, if you want," said Cole.

"Just a couple of hours in the car, driving around the streets with us and Jo," Crowe said.

"We know it's late notice, but if you can manage this Thursday, that'd be great," elaborated Cole.

"Nobody will see you. You'll be in this or a similar car. All tinted glass and all that jazz," continued Crowe.

"What would you like me to do at night?" inquired Michael, curiously and with a touch of wariness.

"Well, we'll be driving around Woolwich and Charlton and if you see anyone you know, just say so and we'll call a uniform car to go pick them up," answered Crowe.

"Pick them up for what?" Michael asked.

"I dunno. Search them. Random. Procedure," Cole said.

"So what do you say?" asked Crowe, turning round.

"Can I call you later?"

Rebecca sipped a glass of Rioja as she sat on the sofa, looking at Michael who was staring into nothingness.

"What's up?" she asked him.

"I met up with the undercovers today," he replied.

"Yeah, I know. You told me."

"They asked if I would go out one evening with them."

"What, like a drink? When?" Rebecca asked him.

"No, not a drink. A drive."

"In a police car? With flashing lights and stuff?"

"Ah, no, but kind of. It'll be in their undercover car," he explained to her.

"So, what would you be doing in it? Just driving around?" she asked him, sipping her wine, intrigued.

"I think so. They've asked if I'll point out anybody I recognise, gang-wise."

"Well, if you don't want to do it, don't. When do they want you to go out with them?"

"Thursday," Michael replied.

"That's OK because I'll be out with Steph. What will you do for food?"

"Huh? I don't know." Food wasn't on Michael's mind at all.

"Whether you're out with them or not, you'd best eat something decent," she insisted, swallowing her last mouthful of red wine and eyeing up the half empty bottle on the table.

"Of course I will," Michael said, refilling Rebecca's glass.

"Whatever you decide, just be careful, OK?" She kissed him with her red-wine-stained lips upon his, instantly putting him at ease with his thoughts.

Thursday came around all too quickly for Michael. He felt a mixture of excitement and anxiety, which wasn't at all an equal balance. Angst was tipping his see-saw of emotion within his mind as he waited on the corner of Luxor Street, off Cold Harbour Lane where he lived.

The streets were darkening. Despite it being his home turf, it wasn't really a place for someone to be just standing still on a street corner.

"Excuse me, I've been attacked. Help me."

Michael jolted, turning to see a young white woman beside him.

She was wearing what at first appeared to be a new white knee-length coat. Across the bridge of her nose was a cut. Bleeding.

Michael took a step back, looking her up and down, assessing her in 'body blocks' like The Terminator.

"Are you going to help me? I've been attacked by my boyfriend. He took all my money and I can't get home. Look at me! This isn't a scam. I'm tired and I need to get home and sort this out," she said, in a fairly well-spoken tone.

"I'll take you to the police station," Michael responded quickly.

"No. No, I've been there. They're too busy to see me," she snapped.

"What? That's crazy. Your face is bleeding. We should go to a hospital or something," Michael said.

"No. I just need to get home first. If you have twenty pounds for a taxi, I'll be most grateful," she continued.

"It's a scam, mate," came another voice into Michael's ear.

He turned to see a guy in a suit striding past him.

"It's not a bloody scam! That's my boyfriend there!" yelled the young woman, pointing at the passing man.

Michael curled his lip, turning to see the man round a corner. He eyed the woman up and down again, very quickly.

Her fingernails were stubby, dirty, with scratched hands. One earlobe looked like a forked tongue where an earring had once been and no doubt ripped out a long time before. Underneath her new coat was a filthy looking T-shirt. Her shoes were scuffed, with a hole in the side of one of them. She was obviously homeless.

"You should go to a hospital. I can walk you to the station where there'll be First Aid, but I'm not giving you any money," Michael said, with sympathy.

Her eyes were trance-like. Beaten, defeated, like misted glass. Drugged. "Oh great! Screw you! That's all anybody says!" spouted the woman, marching off into the darkness.

Michael turned and caught sight of headlamps flaring once. It was a parked car. The undercover car. Parked in Michael's road. He made his way to it, opened the door and clambered into the back.

"Who was that you were chatting to back there?" asked Cole with a smirk on his face, glancing up at Michael in the rear view mirror.

"Yeah, looked a real treat. Hope it wasn't your girlfriend," chipped Crowe, turning round with an extended, welcoming hand.

"Either that or I hope your girlfriend doesn't find out about her," mocked Cole.

Michael shook the hands of Crowe and Cole and buckled up his seatbelt.

"Seatbelt occasionally slips. You'll bust your pelvis, but at least you won't crack your face in the windscreen. How was your day, OK?" asked Crowe, as Cole pulled the car into Cold Harbour Lane.

"Exhausting." Michael peered out of the tinted window to the street as they passed the young woman in the white coat talking to another passer-by.

"More vile kids telling you to F off, eh?" Crowe gazed out of the window.

"Yeah, pretty much," said Michael, relaxing.

"So how d'you feel about this evening?" Cole asked.

"There's really nothing to worry about, Jacob. We do this thing pretty often and we really appreciate your time," explained Crowe.

"No problem." Michael's eyes glazed over with sheer nervousness, as Crowe passed the usual black folder that contained sheets of CCTV images and photographs of a mixed bunch of teen criminals, encased in clear plastic sleeves.

"Let me know if you spot anybody you recognise."

"We're on our way to pick Jo up. Shouldn't be long."

The undercover police vehicle zipped up Denmark Hill, passing King's College Hospital and The Maudsley, the psychiatric hospital. They turned into Champion Park, then Grove Lane and into Dog Kennel Hill, passing East Dulwich Rail Station, into Grove Vale and East Dulwich Road.

"Do you ever drive this way to work?" asked Crowe.

"No. Never," replied Michael, peering out of his window.

"It'll cut about fifteen to twenty minutes off your journey," Crowe continued.

Michael nodded his head, taking it in. "Where does this lead us?" he asked.

"This'll take us through Brockley." Cole slowed to stop at the lights at the Peckham Rye junction.

"More bloody flowers, Malcolm." Cole indicated to a large collection of flowers tied to a lamppost at the corner of the opposite side of the road.

"Yeah, I think it was a lorry. Sometime in the week. Poor kid," nodded Crowe.

The vehicle scrolled along Drakefell Road. There were a lot of speed-humps as they headed uphill toward Malpas Road and into Brockley.

Brockley was once a very affluent town. The rich and powerful built factories and large houses there during the early nineteenth century and, for over a hundred years afterwards, it was an incredibly wealthy part of town. However, soon after the end of World War One, the area lost its exclusivity and residents relocated elsewhere. The German V2 rocket made the town a target during World War Two. After the war and into the early nineteen fifties, the large houses of yesteryear were divided up into flats and made ideal accommodation for the arrivals of Caribbean people setting up home in the new-build council blocks and neighbouring Deptford. Once regarded as a low-rent and somewhat deprived area of London, with an increasing crime-rate, Brockley was now very much an up and coming part of town, with the large Victorian houses once again being inhabited by young professionals and well-off families.

"Well, this has certainly changed over the years, eh?" said Cole, passing down the aptly named Friendly Street.

"Used to be a right hole. Still a few gangs round here though, mate," responded Crowe, glancing round to Michael with a smile.

Stopping at the lights at Brookmill Road, the door suddenly opened, causing Michael to jolt with shock. Detective Jo Blake clambered inside next to him and smiled.

"Hi," said Jo.

Michael responded with a smile.

"How's it going, Jo?" asked Crowe, twisting round to see her.

"Good. You?"

"Same old same old. You know how it is," he said.

Jo unzipped her dark, lightweight jacket to reveal a black vest, which showed her cleavage and exposed her flat stomach, due to the vest riding upwards above her low-slung dark blue jeans. She had certainly become more toned over the past few months.

Michael's eyes wandered to fix on Jo's hip bones and the glimpse of her black lacy knickers. She was definitely sexy, slim and well-defined. Different from when he first saw her. Fitter. Perhaps she was in disguise. Perhaps she had gone through a dramatic workout regime. She arched her back and straightened her top, tucking herself in and caught Michael's gaze.

He turned away and saw Cole eyeing her up in the rear view mirror, also witnessing his stare. Michael turned to the window as Cole smirked.

"Once you get yourself sorted out, Jo, can you brief Jakey on what to expect?" uttered Crowe.

"That's brief, not debrief," Cole quipped. He shifted gears and rounded onto Blackheath Hill.

Jo snorted and shook her head. She probably experienced remarks like that often.

"From Blackheath, we'll head towards Charlton and the Cherry Orchard Estate. We'll drive around the surrounding roads for a bit and see if you can recognise anyone. Point them out and we'll call a uniformed car to check them out. We'll then head to Woolwich and do the same there," Jo said to Michael.

He tried to concentrate his eyes on hers, without diverting to her chest, however her eyes were equally as distracting. Piercing light blue pools. He conducted a quick second look at her lips.

Between each sentence, she paused briefly, biting gently upon her lower lip.

Michael blinked and looked at her forehead.

Her hair was tied back and upwards: trendy, yet slightly powerful. "How does that suit you, Michael, um, Jacob, sorry."

Cole and Crowe exchanged a look. They smirked at one another, like teenagers.

Jo shot them a look and narrowed her eyes.

Michael coughed and straightened. He nodded and became more confident.

"Yeah, sounds fine. As long as nobody sees me," he said, looking at each person in turn, leaving Jo last. His gaze lingered on her and he managed an awkward smile.

She glanced away.

Michael turned to his nearside window as Jo looked back round again at him. Her eyes practically scanned his entire body, from head to toe. She turned back to her window. She liked him. Was intrigued by him. She felt he was a completely different character from the males she worked with, both colleagues and criminals. Being around Michael, no matter how briefly, gave her a sense of normality. She imagined what it would be like to be his girlfriend. To come home to somebody who wasn't in her line of work. Someone to ask how her day was and share a bottle of wine with. Jo, however, lived alone. She ate, drank and slept alone. She let loose a deep sigh as the car drove up Blackheath Hill.

The light was fading fast. Greenwich Park was on their left and the roads were almost empty.

They headed for Vanbrugh Park and into Charlton Road, the road to Charlton Village and indeed the Cherry Orchard Estate.

"What's your feeling about all this?" asked Cole.

"I don't know," shrugged Michael. What was he supposed to feel? Nervousness? Deep concern? A sense of excitement maybe? Should a rush of adrenaline have jetted around his body, like an out-of-control locomotive? Perhaps he should have felt nothing because he hadn't thought it through enough. He hadn't weighed up the various outcomes to this particular scenario. Michael was an extremely perceptive and intuitive guy. He was cautious, quick-thinking and took in every word he heard and image he saw, analysing information like computer code and more often than not, he made the right choice every single time. However, it was guaranteed to be one of those times where Michael wasn't perceptive or intuitive. What on Earth did he think? Nothing. Nothing at all.

"Is everything all right?" asked Jo.

"Huh? Me? Yes, fine. Why d'you ask?"

"Eh up, gang alert," interrupted Cole, as the car passed a group of twelve or so black youths standing on a corner or sitting on a wall.

The youths were hooded and of West African origin. Darkly dressed with hints of red, whether it was their footwear, a bandana, a baseball cap, an armband, a trace of a t-shirt or a rag dangling out of the back pocket of their baggy pants.

The car passed them and the youths eyeballed it.

One of them even had a facemask, covering the lower half of his face. He looked like a cast member of GI Joe. Ice hockey-style, black plastic, with a skeleton feel.

Through tinted glass, on the back seat, Michael stared at each of the youths.

"It's da Feds, man," noted one youth, staring at the car.

"Yeah, boy two, boy two," responded another.

"Fuck dat shit and fuck dem pussies. What they gonna do? What? What joo want?" called out a third.

"Shit!" Cole slammed on the brakes real hard. The car suddenly screeched to an abrupt halt.

Michael jerked forward. His head and shoulders moved into the front part of the car. He stopped himself, grasping the passenger seat head-rest.

Crowe jolted and looked at Michael and smiled.

"The bloody nerve of them," frowned Cole, looking ahead through the windscreen at another hooded black youth crossing the street in front of the car, eating from a box of deep fried chicken and without a care, flinging chicken skin to the ground.

The youth bopped to the pavement and looked at the gang assembled around the wall.

"It's da Feds, blud!" called the first youth, as the chicken eater approached.

"Joo eatin ma fuckin chicken, bitch?" yelled the second youth, as chicken eater turned his head to glance at the car. It was then that his eyes locked onto Michael's eyes, staring back at him through Crowe's passenger side window.

"What the fuck!" cried the chicken eater. His jaw dropped. A piece of chicken skin stuck to his bottom lip as he stared.

Michael struggled and pushed himself backwards. His heart raced at full speed. He swallowed and breathed heavy, in and out, in and out.

Crowe turned around and smirked at him, with his grin, fast becoming a frown. "Don't worry, mate. The next one, we'll make sure we knock him down, eh?"

"Is he okay?" asked Cole, who looked up.

"Michael?" Jo said.

On the street corner, with the youths, was an equal cause for concern.

"What joo lookin' at?" replied the angriest and most vocal member of the gang. He took the box of fried chicken from the chicken eater.

"Yo. TT. Tiny Taser, what the fuck, man?"

Tiny Taser, the chicken eater, was of course a Tiny, as his gang name suggested. It meant that there was also somebody out there called Young

106

Taser and an 'Elder' gang member, who, if going by the so-called rule of thumb in gang member name-tags, was an original gang member called simply Taser. However, at that particular moment in space and time, the only person to be focused on with the Taser name was Tiny Taser, the carefree young man who crossed the main road without looking to see if it was safe, casually eating his extremely greasy and over-fried chicken. The young man who discarded chicken skin and caused an oncoming car to stop suddenly, making its passengers jerk forward.

That main passenger in question was Michael, a man who counselled and mentored vulnerable and at risk young children. A man who was paid to be an undercover informant for the Metropolitan Police Service. A man who was previously shielded by the tinted glass of the back seat of an undercover, unmarked police vehicle, but who had just been jolted forward and was seen by Tiny Taser, a gang member whose real name was Sinatra Umbundo: Michael's student.

Sinatra 'Tiny Taser" Umbundo turned his head, keeping his confused eyes locked like laser sights on Michael, as the unmarked police vehicle started to move once more.

"That was my teacher, blud," commented Sinatra.

"What the fuck you talking about?" spouted one of the crew.

"With the Feds. In the car. That was my fucking teacher, man. I swear down. I ain't lying to you. I see dat face every day, blud," Sinatra continued.

"Why is he widda cops?"

"I don't fuckin' know." Sinatra was flustered.

"Joo fink he's a pig, too?"

"Nah, blud. He's safe. You get me? Well, I thought he was. Shit. Why him? He's actually all right, you know. It probably ain't nuffin, you get me, yeah?" Sinatra said, trying to relax himself.

"Probably nuttin'! Don't fuckin' believe it, blud. You're a bitch, Taser, man. What's wiv your head? He's a Fed. You know it! Day put dem in schools, man, to fuck wijoo. Be your friend. Spy onjoo anshit. He ain't no friend, guy, I'm telling you. I swear down." The angrier youth tried and succeeded in convincing Sinatra.

Michael tilted his head, thinking. He stuck his tongue firmly inside his mouth, which filled out his cheeks and gums. He looked up to the rear view mirror at the undercover police detective driving the car, then turned to the undercover police detective in the passenger seat. He looked at the undercover police detective next to him on the back seat. They were all looking at him.

"Are you OK?" asked Detective Jo Blake. "You look a little awkward."

"I feel awkward," Michael replied.

"What's up, matey?" asked Crowe.

"One of the kids on the corner. I think he saw me," said Michael, watching Crowe glance into his wing mirror, watching the youths becoming more and more distant.

"Don't worry too much. We'll radio a car to search them. That'll take the focus off from them seeing you," chuckled Cole, as he drove on.

"No, no it won't," snapped Michael. "It'll only crank up the focus. The kid who saw me is one of the kids at the school. I see him every day."

Cole glanced at Crowe and caught Jo's eye in the mirror. He nodded at her and she turned to Michael, placing a familiar, gentle and slender hand upon his. Was that for reassurance, an unwritten rule, protocol or a game-plan?

Michael looked at her hand on his and then at her face.

Her eyes were filled with genuine empathy and concern for his wellbeing. Her hand was actually placed discreetly out of her colleagues' view.

Michael also knew this.

"It'll be OK. If you want to call it a night, just say and we'll take you home. Also remember back to when you first signed on board; if it gets too heated for you, then you call us and we'll take you to the safe place that was agreed. Well away from places you're familiar with," she held her look on him.

Cole had a satisfied expression on his face as he turned into another street.

Crowe glanced up the streets.

Michael looked at Jo's hand on his again. "Drive on. I'm OK."

"Good stuff," replied Crowe, in his soft Scottish tone. "If you feel confident enough, maybe you can head out for a walk."

"I don't think that's-" Jo blurted.

"Where'd you think? Woolwich town centre?" Cole interrupted.

"Good a place as any," smirked Crowe. "You got your radio, haven't you, Jo?" He swivelled in his seat to look at his uneasy, female colleague.

Woolwich town centre was a hole. Literally. There was building work all over the place. Outside the Docklands Light Railway entrance and opposite the Woolwich Arsenal railway station. Potholes, filled with muddy puddles, dotted the uneven road near the market accompanied by the eerie presence of unsavoury eyes, watching your every move.

Footsteps echoed down the street as Jo and Michael walked side by side. Close, like a couple.

Out of the corner of his eye, Michael looked at Jo. He coughed, clearing his throat.

"D'you come here often?" he said.

Jo double-glanced at him as she caught his smirk. She formed an awkward smile. "It is grim, isn't it?"

"Just a bit," replied Michael.

"So how long have you been working with these types of kids?" she asked.

"At this particular place, about five years," Michael said, watching his step.

"How about before this particular place?" she probed.

"That was a whole bunch of different children altogether. Autistic children, wheelchair users, Downs."

"Down where?" asked Jo.

Michael frowned, wondering, briefly, if she was humouring him or not.

She awaited his answer.

"Downs Syndrome," Michael replied.

"Oh. Right," Jo obviously wasn't humouring him at all. She took this bite-sized piece of caring information about Michael, processed it quickly in her mind and gave him a satisfying and pleasant smile in return.

Their eyes locked momentarily, just for a split second, before she turned ahead, shoving her hands inside her pockets, making her frame a little tight.

"Did you enjoy it? Working with disabled kids, I mean?" Jo had a disabled mother and thought about her in that precious moment. She had only ever seen her mother in a wheelchair. The years of being confined to it had taken their toll and when seen out shopping by school classmates, they used to think Jo's mother was actually her grandmother. Jo would go along with that as it would have been too much hassle and unnecessary stress to explain the truth to them.

"I did, yeah. It was a lot of fun for not a lot of money," said Michael.

"Not like where you are now, I suppose."

"Well, not quite. I didn't leave because of just that. There were a few factors really. I loved working with them. They were happy children. Innocent children. So many stories there. One autistic boy was obsessed with his own reflection," Michael recounted, with a fond smile.

"What, like mirrors?" asked Jo, frowning again.

"Mirrors, windows, cutlery. He'd stare into whatever it was that reflected his face or body and point at his reflection. 'Don't tread on the flowerbed or I'll take your PlayStation away,' Michael put on a different voice as he reminisced about a more recent, pleasant and enjoyable past, imitating the autistic boy he once taught.

Jo didn't really get it, but smiled nonetheless. "He sounds a little like Rain Man," she said.

"When I first met this boy, he pointed at me and said 'You look like that man.' I asked him what man he meant. 'The man from the chip shop,' he said. 'When was this?' I asked. 'In the chip shop, in 1997,' he said. I wasn't in the chip shop in 1997 to my knowledge, but you never know," Michael recounted.

"Maybe you were. He could replace forensic evidence," smiled Jo, breaking an attempt at humour and relaxing somewhat.

Michael smiled and the two looked at one another. There was a definite attraction, however it was probably more to do with the angst he secretly felt and the comfort he found being with Jo. It was warmer and more genuine than just receiving banter from the male detectives.

Jo was a pretty young woman. Her fresh, immaculate skin was pale, with rosy cheeks, like scorched pads of scarlet paint on her face, due to the cold weather that night. Her dark hair occasionally fell down her face to cover one eye which she tried to blow off with a huff of breath every so often.

"What do you think when you tell us about the violent children you're dealing with?" she asked him, curiously.

"I think very hard about whether it's the right thing to do and know that I've helped take a lot of violent children off the streets, not to mention a lot of knives and guns," Michael continued. "It might just also be the swift, hard kick they need to make them realise there's another way. Another path."

"Tough love. Do you think you'll ever report an innocent person to us?" Jo enquired.

"What, by mistake?"

"Yes."

"If I did it by mistake, then hopefully you guys would be professional enough to have checked out the innocent mistake and so it'll end up OK in the end," he said, without hesitation.

Jo was satisfied by this and the two continued to walk in the darkly lit street.

They saw a row of ATMs against a wall, and standing between each of these cash machines, as people queued to withdraw their money, were four uniformed police officers in their yellow, high visibility jackets.

"Look at that!" Michael said, surprised at the sight of these illuminated money guards.

Jo looked to where Michael gestured. "That's Woolwich for you. You don't come here a lot then," she said with a smile.

"Never. When I was young, perhaps five or six, Mum would bring me here. There was a great fruit and veg market back then and an even better toy shop for me. I'd only ever want to look at the boxes the toys were packaged in and be satisfied with that. We'd leave the shop and my mum would head back in and buy me the toy I'd been staring at. I never wanted for anything, but she said I never complained or cried or moaned, so she treated me."

"What was the toy?" Jo asked.

"Usually a He-Man figure or something like that.

"Oh, before my time I think," she remarked.

"What, you weren't around when He-Man and Fisto were having it large in the forests of Eternia?" Michael grinned.

"Er, no, I certainly was not. The only toy called Fisto I know of is probably found in a shop in Soho or something," Jo quipped.

Michael raised an eyebrow.

"Really?"

"That didn't sound the way I wanted it to," Jo was embarrassed.

"I know what you meant," Michael smirked.

"No, you didn't," Jo held back the smirking, curling corners of her mouth.

"I'm wondering what you would have said if I mentioned other He-Man figures like Spikor, Ram-Man or Faker."

"Oh shut up. Stop taking the piss. Besides, I know you're making those names up now." Jo relaxed with each word and footstep.

"I'm not! They're real. They're as real as Tung Lashor, Mantenna and Whiplash. Trust me, I had them all," Michael said, almost quite passionately, with nostalgic fondness.

"The names sound quite perverted," stated Jo.

"Perhaps now, but not when you're a child."

"So who was He-Man's nemesis? Pervertor?" Jo mocked.

"Ha. Funny. Skeletor, actually. That was until the evil Horde arrived and a new line of toys and cartoon characters besieged the toyshops. Hordak became the main villain then."

"Whore Dak? Oh honestly!" cried Jo. She shook her head.

"Not whore as in a street walker prostitute. Hor. H O R. Hordak. He was Skeletor's old master," corrected Michael.

"And I suppose the man called Mantenna had a retractable penis or something," replied Jo, smugly, still believing that Michael had made up all these characters.

"No! Mantenna fired stun beams from his extended eyes, but was also a comedic character. He'd stutter a lot, too."

Jo closed her eyes briefly, taking it all in. She gritted her teeth, tossed her hair back and turned to Michael.

"Oh my God, you're actually telling the truth."

"Of course I am!"

"About Hordak and all the others?"

"Yes."

"Shit. And I went and spouted off about Antenna Dick," Jo blurted. She was hugely embarrassed.

"As well as mentioning your Fisto toy from Ann Summers in Soho," joked Michael.

"I didn't say I got one in Ann Summers, I said a shop in Soho!" Jo defended herself, pointing her forefinger at Michael.

"You actually have one!"

"No! No! Oh my God. Shut up. Shut up," she laughed, slapping his arm.

He gently barged her.

Jo barged him back with a nudging shoulder.

He leaned in as she tried again, sending her slightly off balance.

Jo stopped and looked at him.

They both smiled.

"That's assault," she said. She exhaled her visible breath into the cold night air.

Michael sneered and held his look.

She stepped up to him, closer, just a few inches away from one another.

"Are you assaulting a police officer?" She had a serious expression, reminiscent of a 1940s femme fatale. She looked Michael up and down.

He narrowed his eyes and stared at her, taking a brief glance around his surroundings.

They were in a quiet, darkly lit side street. Nobody was around.

He scoffed again, covering his awkwardness. He puffed his own warm breath into the cold, dark of the night.

"I've got your number, mister," she said, with a devilish smirk.

Michael frowned when suddenly the familiar Nokia ring-tone sounded out from Jo's pocket.

"Saved by the bell," she said, as she retrieved the phone and brought it to her ear.

"Where are you two lovebirds at then?" came the distinct Scottish tone of DC Crowe on the other end of the mobile phone.

"We'll make our way to the station. Pick us up there," Jo said, bluntly. She beeped out and replaced the phone, looking up at Michael. "Did you hear him?" she asked.

"No, lovebird, what did he say?" Michael replied.

"Nothing. Come on. I know a shortcut." Jo led them both down another street.

Michael followed her lead and stopped in his stride, pausing to think of Rebecca. This wasn't him. He was a stand-up guy. Friendly banter, sure, but he wasn't an outright flirt. This role was starting to change him. He liked the money he was receiving as well as the wrongs he felt he was righting. He watched Jo walk ahead, glanced around his surroundings briefly and began to consider bringing it all to a halt.

Sinatra Umbundo, also known as Taser, tightened his hood as he walked briskly down a street in the still of the night. Looking worried and feeling disappointed, angry and betrayed, Sinatra crossed into another street and bowed his head. His eyes rolled upwards into their sockets, enabling him to see two shadowed figures ahead grouped by a streetlight.

Sinatra had crossed over into another postcode; strayed across an invisible boundary. Postcode wars were rife across London. The streets belonged to the hooded youths who terrorised, intimidated, robbed, beat, kicked, stabbed, shot and killed other gang members or teens who crossed into their territory without the required pass. You had to know somebody in a particular area, a certain street, or estate, in order for you to be a recognisable face and thus gain a pass to wherever it was you were going. The person you knew could have been a rival gang member who granted you permission to travel. It didn't matter if you were popping to a shop, going swimming or were attending your daily route to school; if you didn't have a pass, then you either received a beating, had your phone and Oyster Card taken, or chased until you gave in. Or worse, you got stabbed or shot.

A boy from Sinatra's previous school was excluded when a fellow pupil rummaged around inside his schoolbag and found a lethal looking kitchen knife. He told on him and the boy was subsequently expelled without hesitation. He had to attend the Youth Offending Team. It was quite a distance and several postcodes away from his home. He didn't attend a single session due to the fact he didn't have the unofficial street pass or know anybody in any of the areas he would cross over into. That, of course, didn't serve the boy well and got him into further trouble and complications with the law. He gained himself a curfew. It wasn't such a bad deal for him as it kept the boy safe on his own turf, though the eyes of the law didn't quite get the message when they ordered him to sign his name at the Youth Offending Team each week and, once again, repeated the same process as before.

Twice more that occurred, taking up around eighteen months of wasted time, resources, and not to mention taxpayers' money. It resulted with the boy being carted off to a Young Offenders Institute, where he was unfortunately severely beaten in his cell by a racist teenager.

The racist hit the boy round the head with a wooden chair leg whilst he slept. The wood splintered immediately upon making contact, cracking his skull. He then hit him around his ribs and chest. A piece of splintered wood pierced through his skin and punctured his left lung. The boy, unconscious from being struck on the head, couldn't breathe. He died in his cell.

Sinatra was determined to get himself across town and into another postcode because he had a secret.

"Yo, where d'you think you're going to, blud?" shouted a bulky, large-framed youth to Sinatra. He approached him with a peculiar swagger, with his arms open by his side, in a very threatening manner.

Sinatra straightened, eyeing the youth briefly, taking his presence in and weighing up the situation in ultra-quick time.

The youth was black, of Congolese origin. His head was freshly scarred, many times over. Baggy jeans worn low around his backside exposed his greying boxer shorts. His belt was buckled around his thighs. It was no wonder he walked awkwardly. The duck-like waddle was carefully orchestrated as to not make too sudden a move or cause enough friction to bring down his jeans. The cocky walk was almost an art form in its own right. He sucked on a lollipop and pointed it at Sinatra.

"So? Answer me. Where you going?"

"I know Taser, init. I'm his Younger," answered Sinatra.

"You're Younger Taser?"

"Yeah, man," answered Sinatra.

"Taser is like twenny-two or somefin, man. How the fuck joo know Taser, yeah?" questioned the youth.

"He's ma uncle, init," replied Sinatra, firmly.

"Taser is your uncle, yeah? Cool. Cool. So you a Cherry yoot?"

"I just live onda estate, init," explained Sinatra, looking around his surroundings. He just wanted to get going.

"So joo ain't hanging wiv dem?"

"Nah man. Fuck dat shit. I gotta bounce, man. You get me?" said Sinatra, making his move, trying to pass the youth.

"Where you headin' to, guy?"

"I gotta link, init." Sinatra's heart raced.

"You gotta link? Who is she? She hot?"

"Jus my girl, init. Es E free," reeled off Sinatra. He tried not to give away too many details.

"E3 yeah? What Blackheef? Whose da link, man? I might know her, yeah. You gonna see her now?"

"Yeah. I said dat."

"You gonna beat her? You gonna beat dat link?" asked the youth, staring at Sinatra, wide-eyed and intimidating, but held with a venomous smirk, which revealed a glistening gold tooth.

Sinatra contemplated his reply. He wondered whether he was going to "beat" his "link". To "beat" was to simply have sex with and a "link" usually referred to a girlfriend or at least a female you saw from time to time. Sinatra coughed and formed a big grin. He took a step past the youth as he laughed, taking in a brief glimpse of another glistening sight as he did so: the shiny handle of an automatic pistol, shoved down the back of the youth's jeans.

Sinatra tried his hardest to keep his focus on the youth's eyes and not reveal the fact he had just plainly seen the very weapon that could, in a matter of seconds, cause his death.

"Ah, man, a genta man don't reveal his conquests init. Dat shit is per-son-al, joo get me!" he chuckled and took one step, then two lengthy strides; three steps and by then he had found himself in the middle of the other youths.

Each youth grinned and glistened with blinging silver chains and diamond earrings.

One youth grinned wider than the others and turned. He flapped open his jacket as he did so, flashing a brown leather case inside which contained a machete.

Sinatra swallowed as he trod lightly on the paving slab, as if he was literally walking on air. Sinatra continued his fancy, springing footwork as he stepped past the youths.

"Tell your uncle that Younger Glock says what's happening, joo get me, blud?" called out the youth.

Sinatra stepped round into a corner, momentarily out of the youths' sight. His bouncy stride instantly picked up into a jog and in seconds he was sprinting down the street and into the night, well away from the youths, far from the street and their postcode. Sinatra's heart pounded fast with every racing footstep. His breath was visible in the darkness and resembled a steam locomotive. Blue lights suddenly flickered upon his sweaty face and within his dark brown eyes. He widened them and his heart sank, which slowed down his impressive momentum. He exhaled a deep breath and his body slumped, as if he was a robot and his power supply had just been cut. The plug had been pulled. He looked disheartened as he stopped and bent down. Then he straightened and took a step back to lean against a wall as the blue lights shone stronger, swirling angrily across his body and onto the bricks behind him.

Two uniformed police officers approached Sinatra.

He placed his hands upon his head.

"Done this before, son?" smirked the first officer.

"Think you're Usain Bolt, running like that? Where you going to?" asked the second officer.

"I'm... I'm going to Blackheath. To... to the village," answered Sinatra, barely able to speak.

"What's your name then, son?" asked the first officer.

"Sinatra. Sinatra Umbundo."

"Interesting," commented the first officer.

"Got a brother called Dean Martin, have you?" said the second officer, sarcastically.

"No. Sammy Davis Junior," said Sinatra, exhaling deep, controlled breaths as he looked up at the officers, both of whom had formed disappointed looks of disgust on their faces.

"Turn around and face the wall, son. That's it. Spread your feet apart. More. Bit more. All right, now press your hands against the wall. We're going to search you. Before we do, are you carrying any sharp objects, knives or needles in your pockets, or anything like that?"

"No, sir. Nothing like that. Just my phone, my money and Oyster Card," Sinatra said, as the first officer began to search him, patting and feeling his neck, T-shirt, jacket sleeves, arms, inside and out. Sinatra's belt buckle and waist were checked over, then his thighs, groin, down his legs, shins, ankles and trainers.

The second police officer sneered and held his radio, ready to speak into it, taking a couple of steps away.

The first officer took his pencil and notepad out. "Spell your name for me, son. Sinatra I can handle. Spell your last name for me and tell me your date of birth."

"R703 to Control. Require a check on an IC3 male. Name is Sinatra Umbundo." He looked at his colleague with Sinatra.

"U-M-B-U-N-D-O," said the first officer, jotting the name down. "Date of birth, son. Come on."

"First of January nineteen ninety-eight," said Sinatra.

The police officer quickly noted it down and handed the notepad to his colleague who read it and continued to speak into his radio.

"Umbundo is spelt Uniform, Mike, Bravo, Uniform, November, Delta, Oscar. Date of Birth. One, one, ninety-eight, over."

"So where are you going to, Sinatra?" asked the first officer as his colleague awaited confirmation of Sinatra's details. "You seemed like you were in a hurry,"

"I was running from a gang," Sinatra blurted.

"Gang, eh?"

"Details check out. No record. You're a clean boy, Sinatra. Go to church, do yer?" asked the second police officer, who stepped back to his colleague and Sinatra.

"Yes, sir."

"Says he was running from a gang. You can turn back round, son. Arms down now."

"Where was the gang, Sinatra?"

"I don't remember. A couple of streets away. Past the Standard." He turned round to face the police officers. He lowered his arms to his sides.

"You're not helping yourself, you're helping them, Sinatra. Try and remember a bit harder where they might be. You're not being a snake if you tell us."

"Near Mayhill Road, I think. Yeah. Near there. By Marks and Spencer," said Sinatra.

"How many would you say there were, Sinatra?" asked the first officer.

Sinatra thought hard. He just wanted to get on with his journey, so the quicker he got finished with the police, the better he would be. "Four. There were four," he said, truthfully.

"Were they like you?" asked the second officer.

"How'd you mean?" asked Sinatra. He knew full well what he meant, but took instant offence to the question.

"Were they black?" the officer clarified, sighing.

"Yes," replied Sinatra, abruptly.

"Weapons?"

"Maybe," Sinatra sighed.

The second officer tweaked his radio once more and spoke into it. "R703 to Control. Still with Sinatra Umbundo, over. Require assistance to Mayhill Road, Charlton. Gang sighting. Weapons highly probable, over."

"What kind of weapons, Sinatra?" inquired the first officer.

Sinatra shrugged. He wondered what the hell was in store for him if the information he was about to tell got him into deeper trouble. Not with the police, but with the gangs. What the hell. He just wanted to get on with his journey. It was a seven or eight minute jog for him across the heath.

"I saw what looked like the handle of a gun and I definitely saw a machete," Sinatra said, seriously.

The officers widened their eyes as they exchanged a look with one another, in total disbelief.

"You definitely saw a gun?" asked the second.

"I saw the handle of a gun," corrected Sinatra.

"The handle of a gun?"

"Yes. It was sticking out the back of the guy's jeans."

"And you saw him with a knife as well?"

"No. I saw a machete. A bit different to a knife," Sinatra said, firmly, holding his serious stare on the officers.

"And how would you know the difference between a knife and a machete, son?" asked the first police officer as his colleague once again took to his radio.

"R703 to Control. Still with Sinatra Umbundo and have updated info for officers en route to Mayhill Road, over."

Sinatra stared wild into the night, sending his gaze past the law enforcers in front of him. He remembered his nightmare experiences of a life long gone, in Angola.

A rebel, wild and savage, held aloft a shiny, gleaming machete as he stared wide-eyed at the screaming middle-aged man kneeling down before him. A heavy army boot pressed hard on his back. It forced him forward, into a log, while another rebel stretched his arms across the log.

The middle-aged man cried out, loudly. He looked across at his young son, horrified to see the despicable, unforgivable torture and death that surrounded him. The glistening blade of the machete was brought down hard onto the man's wrists.

The wrist links the hand to the arm. There are eight bones called carpel bones. Small and highly complex. The carpel bones are arranged in a set of two rows. One row is connected to the forearm, the radius and ulna. If you hold your hand in the thumbs-up position, the radius is the bone on the top of your forearm and the ulna is the bone on the bottom. The second row of carpel bones links to the palm of your hand. Between these are synovial joints, where the bones meet. They are covered with articular cartilage, which enables movement.

The machete cut the flesh like a hot knife slides through butter. It sliced the radius and ulna bones, severing the hand from the arm.

The boy saw a silent scream of indescribable pain in the middle-aged man's face. The boy saw his father, helpless, pained, with bleeding stumps. The boy,

Sinatra, looked at the blood dripping from the machete, held aloft once more by the mad-eyed rebel.

Sinatra rolled his eyes up to the officers. "I know the difference between a machete and a knife, sir. Trust me, I know the difference. I saw my father's hands being cut from his arms. Cut with a machete. A machete that should be used for farming, but instead was used for torture, pain and death. I know the difference between a knife and a machete, sir." Sinatra huffed and inflated his chest. He was angry and enraged, but fought not to express it any further.

The officers weren't entirely sure how to react to the seriousness of Sinatra's emotional tone and vivid response.

"Possible sighting of firearms. CO19 advised, over."

CO19 is the Central Operations Specialist Firearms Command. It was previously known as SO19: Specialist Operations Directorate. Renamed in 2005, it was responsible for providing a firearms-response.

"ARV required to Mayhill Road, over."

An ARV is an Armed Response Vehicle. They are crewed by Authorised Firearms Officers and they respond to 999 calls believed to involve firearms. They were first introduced in 1991.

"What if you catch them?" asked Sinatra.

"Then you may be in store for a reward."

"More guns and knives will also be removed from the streets." followed the second officer.

"I mean, will it get back that I reported it?" Sinatra was concerned for his safety.

"No. You'll be fine. There shouldn't be any call for you to be mentioned, son," the first officer assured him.

"Can I go? Now, I mean. Am I allowed to go?" he asked.

The officers exchanged a look.

The second nodded his head and both then turned to Sinatra, giving him the OK to leave.

The youth, with the gun handle poking out the back of his baggy jeans, stood on the street corner with his fellow gang members.

The machete-carrying youth zipped up his Puffa jacket as a siren sounded out. He looked at his friends with a confused expression.

"Let's bounce," he said.

"Nah, man. It ain't for us," replied the baggy youth.

The siren became louder and louder and there were flashing blue lights. The siren became sirens and the youths heard a combination of loud, blaring tones from both ends of the street. They saw a silver armed response vehicle.

The youths panicked, turning their heads this way and that. They wondered which way they should turn. Which way to flee.

The net closed in.

The machete youth decided to run first. He weaved in and out of parked cars, like a rat in a lab. He crouched low in the darkness, occasionally illuminated by headlights and the swirling blue, rotating flash of the police vehicles. He stooped behind a parked car and pressed his back against the bumper. Unzipping his jacket, he placed his hand inside, flicking a press-stud that released the small leather strap on the case. He pulled out his machete. Wide-eyed and wild, the youth gripped his weapon tight as he slid it out from within its sheath when something hard and metal made contact with his wrist. It forced him to lose grip of the glistening machete. A hard knee slammed into his back and he was brought face down to the ground, with his arms twisted behind his back. He was handcuffed. Click, click. The machete was kicked well away from him to the curb side and the youth was dragged to the middle of the street in front of a police patrol car. The bright, beaming headlamps forced the youth to close his eyes tight. He opened his eyes briefly to squint down the street and saw the silhouettes of his fellow gang members lined up against the wall, handcuffed by several police officers. He closed his eyes tight.

The youth with the baggy jeans stepped backwards against a hedgerow, edging himself into a front garden gate. He held his belt buckle with one hand so his jeans didn't fall down completely, and with his other hand, he reached behind himself to pull out his automatic pistol.

The pistol was a Glock 26 and had a standard capacity of ten rounds. It was a smaller variant of the Glock 19, but was little more than just a short version of it, as it could be adapted to have a capacity of thirty-three rounds.

That particular Glock weapon had been used in three separate gangland killings. Passed from gang member to gang member, and through postcodes across south-east London.

The Glock gunmaking business was founded by Gaston Glock, an Austrian engineer, born on 19 July, 1929. When Gaston Glock was seventy years old, in July 1999, a sixty-seven-year-old French ex-mercenary, called Jacques Pêcheur, was hired to murder him in Luxembourg. Gaston Glock was in a garage when he suffered severe head injuries caused, violently, by Pêcheur. However, Glock managed to defend himself, thus enabling police to capture his assailant. Gaston Glock survived the incident.

The youth gripped his Glock 26 tight and pulled back the slide. The weapon was ready to fire. He narrowed his eyes and searched through the blinding, distorted lights around him, fixed on a shadowy figure and stretched out his gun arm. The youth took one small step out of the garden gate and steadied himself. He had lined up his sight when an armed police officer suddenly raised, twisted and aimed his Heckler & Koch MP5 machine pistol at him.

"ARMED POLICE. DROP YOUR WEAPON! DO IT NOW!"

"Fark you, blud!" shouted the youth, who turned his gun toward the officer.

The officer squeezed the trigger.

BANG!

One 9mm bullet exited the barrel of the Heckler & Koch MP5 SFA3 semi-automatic weapon and was sent racing into the youth.

He had just experienced a gunshot injury to the chest.

The projectile, or bullet, is determined by its kinetic energy (KE) as one half of the mass (M). This is multiplied by the velocity (V) and then squared.

Kinetic energy could be greater, depending on the mass and velocity of the bullet, which naturally results in various states of tissue injury. Bullet velocity has a much greater effect on kinetic energy than mass does. Gunshots can cause tissue damage in two different ways. One is when a bullet enters the body and creates itself a direct route through the body tissue, severing it. Two is much more harmful. When the bullet makes contact with the body, piercing the skin and entering tissue, it immediately slows down. It's like diving into a swimming pool. The kinetic energy of the bullet transforms into heat. The tissues surrounding the bullet take on this heat and this can even produce steam that creates a cavity within the tissue, due to the steam rapidly causing it to expand. Cavities in the tissue can collapse and create shockwaves. This is known as a cavitation injury. Handguns have a lower velocity and cause less cavitation than do higher velocity weapons. Cavitation injuries tend to cause more damage than the bullet does itself.

That particular gunshot caused tremendous damage. What occurred was penetrating trauma.

The youth suffered a gunshot wound to the chest. The entrance wound was in the middle of his sternum. The bullet pierced the youth's lung, which collapsed. The left lung had been punctured and was rapidly deflating. The youth was suffering immediate breathing difficulty. Considerable internal bleeding occurred, as well as severe tissue damage. In under a second, the youth's legs had buckled, wobbling like jelly. The bullet, however, had yet to complete its journey. It entered the heart. The bullet was partially embedded in the anterior musculature of the right ventricle. The youth slumped in a twisted heap and the officer then advanced.

He trained his weapon constantly on the fallen youth, who was sprawled, bleeding, half in the front garden of a house.

His eyes stared upwards, like marbles. His body was completely motionless as blood escaped his nose and trickled out of his mouth.

"Target down and secure."

The baggy-jean-wearing youth was dead.

Sinatra Umbundo was far from this area, making his way across Blackheath. Ahead of him was the Princess of Wales pub.

The pub was named after Caroline of Brunswick, wife of George IV. Caroline of Brunswick-Wolfenbüttel, also known as Caroline Amelia Elizabeth and later Queen Caroline, was born on 17 May 1768 and died on 7 August 1821.

Caroline only became queen some twenty years after marrying in 1795, when the unpopular George, Prince of Wales, was crowned King of the United Kingdom and Hanover in 1820. Their marriage was troubled from the start and just two years in they were living apart, with Caroline in The Vicarage in Charlton and then Montagu House in Blackheath in 1797. Caroline, Princess of Wales, was appointed Ranger in 1806, whilst living in Montagu House on the west side of Greenwich Park from 1798 to 1812.

Sinatra passed the Clarendon Hotel that overlooked the heath. On his right was All Saints Church, built in 1857 as the new parish church for the village of Blackheath.

Sinatra's life was a rebellious, secretive one, which was full of struggle. He walked down the hill of Montpelier Row and crossed Wemyss Road into Montpelier Vale and towards Blackheath Village. He passed Café Rouge and onto Tranquil Vale, stopping on the corner of the street. His eyes searched the darkness. They stopped and fixed on something and the corners of his mouth curled into a warm, loving smile. Sinatra bounded across the zebra crossing and stopped. Standing in the shadows on the pavement, beside the red post box, he nodded his head. That was the most relaxed he had ever been.

"I've missed you," said Sinatra.

Stood before him was a pale-faced, fresh and kind-looking young man of seventeen. On that night he wore skinny jeans and an army green trench-coat.

Sinatra reached out to touch his hand. The hand of Jack.

Jack delivered the kind of smile only ever seen in boyband members. His teeth and skin were perfect and his eyes sparkled in the orange glow of the streetlights.

"How was college?" asked Sinatra.

"I didn't go. I had my hospital tests, remember?" replied Jack, in a well-spoken manner.

"Ah yeah. Sorry. Sorry, I forgot." Sinatra could have kicked himself as he failed to remember something so important.

"It's okay, Sinatra, you've got a lot on, too," said Jack, in a comforting tone.

He turned and led the two of them up the Vale, passing The Crown pub and continued up Royal Parade and Tranquil Vale. Changing course slightly onto Hare and Billet Road, Jack and Sinatra stepped into the shadows to catch their breath from the cold walk up the hill.

"I saw my teacher today," Sinatra said.

"I should hope so. You were at school," responded Jack, exhaling his warm breath into the cold night.

"No, no you don't understand. I saw him tonight. Near my Endz."

"He probably lives there. So what?"

"No, Jack, blud. Listen to me, cos you ain't. Listen yeah, I saw him with the Feds. Undercover Feds," explained Sinatra, passionately, with disappointment in his eyes.

"Don't speak like that," insisted Jack.

"Like what?"

"Like you're all gangster. I don't like it." Jack was sensitive and calm. He drew the gentler side out of Sinatra.

"Okay. Sorry. But listen, I got the feeling he was out spying with them. It's what they do. Trust me, I know. What if he is spying on me at school and telling the police about me?"

"What do you think he would tell them?" asked Jack.

"I don't know! Stuff!" yelped Sinatra, on the verge of freaking out.

Jack gently touched his arm, reassuringly. He looked into Sinatra's eyes, with absolute care and devotion. "It'll be okay. Trust me. Everything will be okay. Come on, it's getting cold."

They carried on past the Hare and Billet pub. It was an old school type of public house with a great deal of history. There was a ghostly myth that told of a shadowy figure: a Victorian woman who still haunted the roadside directly outside the pub. Sometimes referred to as 'the White Lady' or 'the Hare and Billet Ghost' or 'the Victorian Lady', the story had a woman fleeing her husband for a lover who never arrived.

She waited and waited and became more and more distressed at the realisation that her lover wasn't going to meet her. Tragically, the woman decided to take her own life and hanged herself from a nearby elm tree.

Sinatra and Jack shivered in the shadows beside the heath.

Jack placed an arm around Sinatra, who turned to him, glancing at the warm, comforting and inviting arm around his broad shoulders.

Sinatra giggled nervously and looked deep into Jack's eyes.

"Thanks for meeting me tonight. I know you're having a tough time at school and with your family, but we can support each other. You're more than a best friend to me," said Jack.

Sinatra took a deep breath and took hold of Jack's right hand, gently holding his fingertips.

"I think I love you," Sinatra said.

Jack widened his eyes. He was overwhelmed. "I - I don't know what to say. Nobody has ever said that to me before."

"Well, do you feel the same?" Sinatra asked.

"I do. I do." Jack stared into Sinatra's eyes.

Suddenly Sinatra's eyes widened as he stared past Jack across the heath. His stare turned into a squinting frown. Jack frowned too and glanced round to see what it was he was looking at.

"What is it?" wondered Jack.

"Is it a woman?" Sinatra answered.

"In fancy dress or something," Jack continued.

"She's walking towards us."

"But her feet aren't touching the ground. It looks weird. I don't like it," cried Jack.

"She's floating, man. Shit. Look at that shit," Sinatra gasped, covering his mouth. His chest inflated and deflated fast as he breathed.

"I think we should go. Please. Go. Please," trembled Jack, grabbing Sinatra's hand.

Together they paced across the heath, quickening as they set foot into a jog, then a run. They smiled, nervously, running into the darkness.

Sinatra and Jack found themselves crossing Blackheath Hill. They ventured toward Hollymount Close and Maidenstone Hill.

Jack stood in the road, by a garden gate. He turned to Sinatra and smiled at him, touching his hand.

Sinatra stepped up close to Jack.

The two young men closed their eyes and slowly leant their heads toward one another. Their lips made contact and the two of them shared a kiss beneath the moonlight that shone high above Greenwich.

"Goodnight." Jack opened his eyes.

"Night, Jack." Sinatra stepped backwards.

A fascinating and somewhat mysterious history lay between those two areas and involved another young man named Jack.

Sometime in 2002 a great deal of Blackheath suddenly collapsed, revealing a huge crater-like underworld, which obviously had to be repaired. The cause was excessive mining there in the seventeenth century. Mine workings formed lengthy, dark, twisting tunnels beneath Blackheath and Greenwich. One particular tunnel was known as 'Jack Cade's Cavern'. In 1780, a builder seized his opportunity and managed to open up one of the tunnels and some caves. He formed forty or so steps and charged members of the public the princely sum of sixpence to travel down and view them.

The builder even constructed a cottage at the entrance of the caves. It became quite a trend to visit the caves, however, that soon halted when a nineteen-year-old young woman by the name of Lucy Talbot apparently fainted. She lost consciousness within the dark, chalk, dusty tunnel created during the mining quarry days.

Lacking air, Lucy died before returning to the surface.

The cavern consisted of around four other caverns, twisting off from the main one and each joined together by separate tunnels. The main entrance of the cavern was a circular area of around thirty-five feet in diameter. It led to another, much larger area, double the size. A meandering passageway to a smaller chamber-like room revealed a well, consisting of pure water. It wasn't too long before business picked up as usual, though with a slight change of direction. The clientele changed with it. A chandelier was installed, as well as a ventilation shaft and also a bar and thus began the first of the party of parties: a nightclub for the elite was unveiled, revealing alcohol, naked dancers and a 'what happens in the cave, stays in the cave' rule to those paying members of the hoi polloi. In 1854 the cave was closed once the puritan Victorian Age was upon us.

It was in 1938 in the garden of number 77 Maidenstone Hill that the cave and tunnel was inspected once more, with the authorities determined to install an air-raid shelter. After inspecting the below ground remnants and ghostly past of the cave, they decided against the installation and resealed all openings.

Who was Jack Cade? His real name was John Aylmer, or sometimes John Mortimer. He was an Irishman from Kent and led a forty-thousand strong rebellion consisting of peasants as well as the wealthy, landowners and members of the clergy. They were protesting about laws and taxes and extortion by King Henry VI in 1450. Cade assembled his rebels on Blackheath in July of that year. It was said Jack had carried out Pagan rituals in the caves below before marching on towards London. It was in Southwark, at the White Hart Inn, where Cade made his headquarters. Jack struck his sword into the London Stone, now in Cannon Street, and declared himself the new Mayor of London. After a huge, ugly battle on London Bridge, resulting in hundreds of casualties, Cade met to discuss a possible pardon for him and his fellow rebels. However, he soon learned that the government was going to betray him. They had deemed him a traitor and there was a reward for anyone who could bring Cade in, dead or alive. During a suspicious fight in East Sussex, the man known to hundreds of thousands of people as Jack Cade was killed. His body was quickly taken to London where it was quartered and his head was rammed upon a pole on London Bridge. Twenty or so of Cade's followers were rounded up and put to death, despite being pardoned. John Aylmer, John Mortimer, a rebellious man, undercover and known by secret authorities as Jack Cade.

Michael Thompson was also rebellious as well as undercover, and was known to secret authorities as Jacob Ramsay.

II. PRAGUE

Michael and Rebecca opened the door to their hotel room in Prague. They were staying in The Golden Wheel, a fourteenth-century hotel on Mala Strana.

"I'm going to take a quick shower, do my hair and make-up and we'll go out to dinner," said Rebecca, kissing Michael as she flung her coat on the bed and headed for the bathroom.

Michael removed his overcoat and crawled onto the bed. He retrieved his small Paperchase notebook and the hotel pen and wrote what he and Rebecca had done that day. His scrawling handwriting told of him and Rebecca visiting Prague Zoo and how he saw 'the man with the spider tattoo again'. He had previously seen him on the plane a couple of days earlier. The little notebook contained many a scribble, with a mixture of peculiar sightings, restaurants visited and obscure diary entries.

Rebecca held Michael's hand tightly as they paced across the snow-covered Old Town Square in Prague, in the Czech Republic. Suddenly a man confronted them.

"Hey! Hi! You speak English? You want to come to my bar?" said the young Czech man.

"No thank you," replied Michael as he and Rebecca continued their walk, passing him.

"I can give you a two-for-one drink offer all night!" called out the man.

"I'd rather have a glass of red," replied Rebecca, quietly and cold-breathed to Michael, hurriedly, tightening her grasp upon his hand.

"It'd be bad free drinks, I bet anyway," Michael said to her.

"I can give you a free entry to our Jazz Room!" called out the man, louder than before, still optimistic that the couple would turn back around and follow him.

"The place we're going to is meant to have live music," stated Rebecca to Michael, quickening her pace.

"We have dancing midgets!" shouted the man.

Michael turned around, alarmed and somewhat intrigued by the Czech man's statement. He was then tugged forward by Rebecca, who frowned at him.

Within the restaurant of a hotel upon the square, five or six old-timer jazz musicians played their music in a corner as diners ate their meals overdone in garlic gravy.

Michael and Rebecca sat close to the music. They toasted one another with their glasses of warm Chilean red wine.

She smiled at him. "I can't believe you were actually tempted to go to that bar and see dancing midgets," she laughed, touching his smirking face.

"You have to admit, I think it would have been interesting," Michael said.

"Curiosity killed the cat," Rebecca smiled.

"Curiosity killed the midget."

"Maybe the midget killed the tourist in the cellar bar," said Rebecca, raising an eyebrow as she sipped her wine.

"This is extremely garlicky," remarked Michael, changing the subject.

"Mm, I know. Why do they do that? Is garlic their main export?" Rebecca asked.

"I thought it was prostitutes," Michael observed, tucking into his tender chicken breast.

Rebecca shot him a look, withholding a smirk and chewing her own breast of chicken.

"Did you write in your book today?" Rebecca asked, sipping her wine.

"Yeah. When you were in the shower."

"Did you say you saw the spider man again?"

"I did! What if he's following us?"

"You've seen him twice! Once on the plane and once at the zoo. People can do the same things on holiday, you know?"

"What if he owns a cellar bar with midgets as waiters and-" Michael stopped when Rebecca leaned in close and kissed him on the lips.

"Sshh. I love you. Eat your garlicky dinner."

"I love you, too," Michael said.

12. BORN TO BE WILD (PART ONE)

Michael drove past Greenwich Park, with Blackheath on his right-hand side as headed towards Charlton Village.

"Born to be wild!" he sang out, tapping the steering wheel. There wasn't even any music playing from the stereo. Perhaps the song had just finished. Either way, he was in a very happy mood.

Michael pulled his car into the school car park and switched off his engine.

In the kitchen, Michael and his colleagues, Paul, Helen, Catherine and Patricia, sat at a table.

Everyone was looking at Patricia, curiously.

Patricia proudly beamed. "I wanted to announce to you all together that I am officially seeing somebody."

Catherine jutted out her chin and fixed her tiny eyes on Patricia. "Is this really a topic suitable for breakfast conversation, Patricia? Is it really a conversation to be having in school, actually?" She stuck her chin out even further and nodded as she sought acknowledgement from the other members of staff, who she hoped would agree with her.

"I'm seeing Norman," Patricia stated.

"Who?" Paul said, with a frown.

"Norman? Police Officer Norman?" said Helen.

"But I had my eye on him," chirped Catherine. "You lucky dog."

"Yes, Norman Clarke, our Safer Schools Police Officer," replied Patricia. "Right."

Michael exchanged a look with Helen and Paul across the table.

Both had gritted teeth, trying to smile and show genuine happiness for Patricia.

Patricia released a sigh of relief and stood up. She towered over her colleagues.

"Okay. Done it. I'd prefer it if this information doesn't leave here." With that, she left the room.

"Well, if that's not a conflict of interest, I don't know what is," remarked Michael.

"I think that's an unfair thing to say, Michael. I find you quite mean," protested Catherine. She wiped a tear from her cheek and walked out the room.

"What the bloody hell is she crying for?" asked Paul.

"What are you thinking, Helen?" Michael looked at his boss, who seemed a million miles away.

"I'm thinking lots of things. I'm thinking it's not only too soon for Patricia to be seeing someone, especially as she's still undergoing bereavement counselling, but that the someone who is seeing her is our Safer Schools Police Officer. You're right, Mike, it's a conflict of interest. Let me think on this one for a bit. It might not be anything to worry about, but gut feeling is telling me otherwise."

Helen wasn't too keen on Norman. She had tried to have him replaced by another officer. Someone who wasn't so easily swayed. Someone whom the children both respected as a force of law and were comfortable being around.

Norman was neither.

Michael walked along with two cups of tea. He stopped in the doorway to Helen's room as she looked up from her desk and her computer screen.

"Thanks, Mike," she said, as he placed one cup on her mouse mat.

"Everything ok?" he asked, seeing her frown at the monitor.

"Just looking at flights for Thailand."

"What do you think about Patricia then?" asked Michael.

"Hmm, I think it's a match made in ego land." Helen turned on her chair to face Michael. She sipped her tea and tightened her mouth as she looked at him.

"It could be dodgy."

"How do you mean?" she asked.

136

"Well, he's not exactly John McClane or Inspector Morse, is he?" Michael said.

Helen chuckled. "No. No, he's not."

"He wants to prove himself. Loves the fact that some staff members think he's quite powerful. He's all about status."

"As is Patricia."

"As nice as she is," Michael said.

"Exactly. Which is why we all have to keep her in check every now and again," Helen continued. She frowned at Michael's face which was scrunched up, looking pained. "What's the matter?" she asked.

"I don't know. It's just a feeling, really. A hunch, intuition, I don't know, I just sense danger," he replied.

"You think Patricia's dangerous?"

"Not intentionally, no, but irrational and misguided. That's what makes her dangerous, but hey, it's extremely early days."

"Yes, we should be happy for her that she's found love, despite it being far too soon," said Helen.

"I love our cynicism," Michael smiled.

"Let's hope it's just that."

Paul stood outside his room in the corridor and rang the brass hand bell. The sound echoed through the corridor. Paul looked at Michael at the other end of it and saluted him, accompanying it with a smile. "Halfway through the day, sir."

"Not halfway close enough, Mr J," Michael said, as several children spilled out from another class.

Sinatra Umbundo stepped into the corridor from a set of double doors. He was late. The first face he saw was Paul's.

"Late again, Sinatra. Everything okay?" asked Paul.

"Whatever, man," Sinatra replied, scowling and glancing up the corridor to see Michael.

Their eyes locked. Sinatra's expression was full of hurt.

"Stay away from me, snake." Sinatra stared at Michael as he passed Paul and went into his classroom.

In the classroom, Paul stepped half in and half out. He saw Sinatra slouched on a comfortable soft chair, checking his Blackberry messenger. "Wrong class, Sinatra. No maths today. You've got art."

"I'm done with that shit," Sinatra said, firmly.

"Bit grumpy today, sir. Woke up on the wrong side?" Paul enquired, keeping the door open with his body.

"My whole life is the wrong side," Sinatra answered.

"Okay. Well, c'mon, into art. It's nice and calm in there."

"I don't do calm. Fuck calm."

"No swearing, sir, and off the phone," Paul sighed.

"This is bullshit. It's fucked up," Sinatra grumbled as he pushed himself up from the chair and walked towards the door.

The art room had a host of pupils' work pinned to the walls. A few pupils were sitting around one big table in the centre of the room. A mixed bunch.

The white, violent schizophrenic

Lee Mace sat at the table, simply sketching a tag on an A3-sized piece of cartridge paper.

Anna, the quiet Russian girl, pretty and always clean and fresh, sat opposite Lee Mace. She wrapped some wool around a circular cardboard disc, occasionally tutting as she glanced up at the boy opposite her.

Olga, the outspoken, punky Polish girl sat next to Anna. Her beehive hairdo was firmly fixed with hairspray and her dark eye make-up was as much a stand-out feature as were the bright pink lacy knickers poking out at the top of her black Juicy Couture tracksuit bottoms. She, too, was wrapping wool, green wool, around a circular cardboard disc.

Abdul Rah-Maan, the kind, pleasant Afghan, sat next to Lee Mace, cutting out a circle from a square of cardboard.

Michael held up a woollen pom-pom that had been made using two cardboard circular discs and different coloured wool. It had sticky plastic eyes attached to it and a sort of monster appearance. A character.

"So, this is what we're aiming for." Michael looked up to see Sinatra in the doorway.

Paul was behind him. "We've come to join you, sir." Paul sat at the table and exchanged a look with Michael.

"Sure, no problem. Okay, Sinatra, you'll find on the table in front of you a piece of cardboard with a couple of shapes drawn on it. Circles. Cut the circles out, with the hole in the middle, and then I'll show you what to do after that," Michael instructed.

"I don't understand," said Anna.

"What? What don't you understand?" Paul mimicked her accent.

Anna smiled, trying hard to disguise it. She adored Paul and had great affection and admiration for him. She saw him as a father or even grandfather figure. Her own grandparents were back in Russia. She and her mother had fled a violent set of relationships in Moscow. Anna had witnessed severe domestic violence. Attacks on her mother by a dangerous, alcoholic father, who had once stabbed himself in front of her and beaten her beloved grandfather at the airport after chasing Anna and her mother all the way there.

The grandfather had driven them both there to catch their plane to London, when her biological father found out. In a drunken rage, he drove through the night and cast his angry eyes upon Anna and her mother, walking through to the gate, being waved at by her grandfather.

Anna had turned to wave back, only to see her father running towards him. Her eyes widened with shock and pain glazed over them when she saw her father punch her grandfather on the back of his head, striking him down to the ground.

Her father, wild as they came, stared at Anna, not taking his eyes off her as he sent a hard, swift kick to her grandfather beneath his feet.

Anna saw the grey-haired man in a heap as she was dragged round a corner by her mother. The last image of her grandfather. The last memory of home.

Paul had a couple of girls of his own. He was a quiet, caring, humble, kind, sensitive and an incredibly fun-loving man.

"I don't understand what pom-pom is," frowned Anna.

"Pom-pom. You are pom-pom," replied Paul in an Eastern European accent.

"Nyet," she said in Russian. "You are a pom-pom," Anna continued, pointing to a pile of coloured wool upon the table.

"Oi, mate, Abdul. D'you know the Taliban? D'you wanna join them?" said Lee Mace, randomly whispering loud enough for Paul and Michael to hear.

Both looked up to give him a disapproving stare as he glanced up to see if he had been heard.

"Taliban? I join Taliban? No. Taliban are very bad. I know Taliban. I know they are bad," Abdul replied in his broken English.

"What's everyone doing this weekend then?" Michael asked, changing the subject.

"Yeah, what does everyone like to do?" Paul joined in.

"Weed. Smoking weed," confessed Lee Mace.

"Films. I will watch films. Harry Potter," replied Anna.

"I will be sleeping! My God, I have to get some sleep. Probably buy some make-up, see some friends, maybe a boy! Oh, don't! I am so excited for the weekend. Can I leave now, sir?" gushed Olga, excitedly.

"I'll probably be banged up. Right, sir?" Sinatra said, with a glare at Michael, who tilted his head, confused, but somewhat suspicious and a little concerned.

"Actually, I think I have to deal with my boyfriend. Well, he thinks he's my boyfriend. Bloody Albanian men," sighed Olga.

Anna rolled her eyes.

"Albania? You seeing someone from Albania?" asked Sinatra.

"Yeah! I am actually," smiled Olga.

"Is he in OTR?" Sinatra enquired, curiously.

OTR stood for On the Run. It was a gang formed around 2002 in the borough of Bromley, south-east London. The gang started various street battles with other Albanians, brandishing their weapons consisting of guns and knives and showing their tattoos off on the internet. Tired of killing and causing severe injury to one another, the OTR was said to have split, with other members and loyal, younger, highly impressionable Albanians forming their own gangs under the OTR umbrella, with names such as Real Albanian Gangsters and ASA Albanians spanning from north-west London to Greenwich. Their role wasn't to fight their fellow countryman, but to 'clean house' by claiming the streets of other gangs. As the majority of their members were older than your average gang member, they'd drive around in their cars packing automatic weapons, entering other boroughs, namely Greenwich, and 'sort out' other gangs. All the gangs were extremely dangerous, each with their unpredictable, unstable, volatile members. However, OTR was considered to be one of the worst out there.

"I like to wrestle. Wrestle fight. Fighting," said Abdul, motioning a wrestling action with a smile and recollecting a stirring memory of back home.

"Fucking Talibanna," muttered Lee Mace.

During break-time, the staff team assembled in a hall. Catherine stood watching a couple of kids playing table tennis, while Paul and Michael kept an eye on the rest sitting at a table, checking their mobile phones.

One dealt out some playing cards for a game of Black Jack.

A dinner lady, preparing for lunch, arranged tables and chairs.

Michael noticed Abdul in a corner of the hall, practically facing the wall. He looked upset.

Michael gestured to Paul. "Is he okay?"

"Dunno. He seemed all right in your class. Well done for covering that, by the way. Not just an oily rag, eh?"

"What, like you?" Michael teased.

"Eh, I'm just a rag. I'm not lucky enough to have any oil," smirked Paul, patting Michael on the back.

The two had a great working relationship. A surrogate work father for Michael and the son Paul never had. If only Michael enjoyed sport, like Paul did, he'd be perfect. They were practically inseparable at break-times. Playful banter was mixed easily and smoothly with serious work and home issues. Through rain or shine, windy or uncomfortably hot summer days, Paul and Michael were usually the only members of the staff team to be found outside.

Paul would often be seen in a black beanie hat, with his hands firmly shoved into his pockets, reeling off accounts from days of old when he was a mountaineer and how frostbite affected his hands and fingers considerably. He was a well-travelled, handsome man who had retired twice already. He was a true lover of work and his workmates.

Patricia entered the hall, looking taller, more upright, and she stepped up to Paul as Michael made his way to Abdul.

"Hello, miss," said Paul.

"Yes, I'm fine. Busy. Very busy." Patricia looked across the hall to fix on Michael and Abdul. "What's going on there with Abdul? Anything I should know about?"

"Nope," Paul frowned.

There was an air of some sort with Patricia. Perhaps it had always been there, but she held herself differently and looked at people differently, too.

"How was Abdul in class?" she asked.

"Okay. Talking about the Taliban a little. People joining it, I think, and a bit about wrestling," Paul said, recounting the lesson before.

"Really? Well, that's concerning." Patricia scrunched up her face.

"Not really," shrugged Paul, seeing Patricia turn and exit the hall. He turned his attention to the pupils playing Black Jack.

"Join in this game, sir," said Sinatra, pulling out a chair for Paul to sit next to him. Paul sat down with them.

Michael crouched next to Abdul in the far corner of the hall. He noticed Abdul's eyes were glassy and tearful.

"Are you okay, Abdul?"

"People think I am a rich man. The miss who interviewed me, she said two times to me that she think I am rich."

"When?" Michael frowned.

"I fly here by plane and she and other people think I am rich. I did come here by plane, but I had to walk to Iran to get to the plane. From Afghanistan to Iran, I walk. With a hundred people. All strangers to me, with bullets and guns and Taliban around me. I had to say goodbye to my mother and my Baba. I miss, you know miss? I miss my mum and dad." Abdul released a tear and immediately wiped it away. "Myself I hurt."

Michael placed a comforting hand upon Abdul's shoulder.

"You're safe now. You're safe here," Michael stated.

"Thank you."

"I mean it. I'm here to help you. All of us."

Abdul managed a smile and nodded his head. He stood and stretched, arched his back and made his way to the table where the pupils were playing Black Jack.

Sinatra glanced up to see Abdul sit down and looked back further to see Michael had followed him.

"I wouldn't trust him, man. Guy's a snake. I swear down that guy's a fucking Fed snake."

"Now, now, language, sir," Paul cautioned, eyeing his cards.

It was later that day, in Patricia's office with the door closed. PC Norman Clarke sat down with her. They sipped tea together.

He was leaning on the corner of the desk with his side practically becoming one with it.

She leaned one elbow on the desk, exposing tremendous cleavage from her enormous bosom. She crossed her legs and revealed a stocking-clad thigh. Being in Norman's company aroused her. It was no doubt the uniform as Norman had little power in his role to turn anybody on.

"Mm, good tea," observed PC Norman.

"Mm, you're not wrong." Patricia gently blew her hot beverage.

"So what's new today?" PC Norman's voice was ever so camp. It sounded similar to the cartoon character Henry's Cat, voiced and created by Bob Godfrey. Actually, it was somewhat unfair to the genius of Bob Godfrey as that would suggest Henry's Cat was boring. It was, by no means, boring, however, there was more than a mere hint of a whining nature when Henry's Cat, narrated by Godfrey, said "Ohhh." That was how PC Norman sounded. He had a monotonous, droning whine of a voice.

"Well, you know the Afghan boy?" asked Patricia.

"What's his name? Shaheen?" Norman sipped his tea.

"No, he's Iranian. He'll be moving on soon, but the Afghan lad is Abdul Rah-Maan."

"Oh. Yes. Go on, I know. I think I saw him outside when I was coming in. He pushed another boy. Might have been playing."

"No, probably not playing. Not when you hear this. He was in a classroom and talking about joining the Taliban and how he liked fighting," announced Patricia.

"Was he? Was he? Well, that's alarming."

"Isn't it?" Patricia agreed.

They sipped their tea.

Michael helped Paul unplug the laptops from the wall in his classroom, and together they placed them inside a lockable cupboard.

"Another day gone," Paul remarked, squatting to insert another computer on a shelf in the portable storage unit.

"Indeed. Odd one, as usual." Michael reached up to a plug socket and flicked the off switch.

"Don't bother unplugging it, we'll leave the leads in."

"Really? What's the point in the charging unit?" Michael asked.

"They don't bother elsewhere and well, why make it more difficult for ourselves?" Paul said as Catherine and Patricia entered and sat down.

"Shall we meet in here then?" asked Catherine. Her chin jutted out and her head nodded, in her usual wobbling fashion.

"I guess so," chuckled Paul.

"Who have you got there, Pat?" asked Catherine, who fixed on a green card file in Patricia's hand.

"Billy Ray."

"Cyrus?" chirped Paul.

"No." Patricia became incredibly serious.

"Okay," Paul shrugged and exchanged a look with Michael as they sat down. "It's nearly that time, sir," Paul continued, slouching in the comfortable chair. He rested his eyes and he placed his hands upon his belly.

"I'm whacked," said Michael.

When it got to around the two-thirty mark during the day, Paul and Michael were truly exhausted. It wasn't to say that the other staff members never felt the same, but the two thoroughly expressed it.

The days took their toll when dealing with the draining issues of the vulnerable, day in and day out.

"Before I get talking about this new referral, I'd like to discuss the Abdul issue," began Patricia.

"What Abdul issue?" asked Paul.

"Abdul said in a class today that he wanted to join the Taliban and how much he likes fighting," continued Patricia.

"Er, not really. Somewhat of a false truth," Michael sighed.

"I don't believe it is," snapped Patricia.

"How do you mean, Pat?" Catherine was confused.

"Abdul is dangerous and so I took it elsewhere," stated Patricia, with Michael and Paul frowning.

"Could you explain what happened? I'm feeling a little left out here," said Catherine.

"Nothing bloody happened!" Paul cried out.

"Oh, so an Afghan man saying he wants to join the Taliban is nothing happening, is it? Okay, okay, I'm wrong, forgive me, I'm wrong," blurted Patricia, causing more frowning and exchanging of looks between the other staff members.

"Nobody said they wanted to join the Taliban," Michael pointed out.

"You've taken it the wrong way, Pat," said Paul.

"Why didn't anyone tell me?" asked Catherine.

"Because there is nothing to tell!" Paul was flustered.

"Yes, yes there is!" Patricia was becoming angered and highly stressed by the situation.

"Patricia, I don't understand. Why are you doing this? We've never reported anything like this before," said Michael.

"Well, we've never had anyone like Norman before. He impresses me," she said, utterly content with her reply and folding her arms.

"So, what is Norman intending to do, because trust me, I know how this kind of thing pans out. Norman takes this false information to his superiors," Michael said, passionately.

Patricia interrupted, "It isn't false information!"

"It is false information. Once again: Norman takes the false information to his superiors, who will subsequently take it to a higher level. What next? The boy's house is checked, the people who made the initial nonsense into a concern are checked, and then what? The boy is questioned. We're questioned. The police leak the damn thing to the press in order to keep terror and fear in the public eye and an ever-present, constant threat in people's minds. Bloody hell, Pat, what have you done? It's not an episode of 24 you know!" Michael exclaimed, surprising Paul and Catherine, who were with him on that.

"Well, excuse me for raising the issue of a possible terrorist threat!" Patricia flung her arms into the air and stood up. She headed for the door and left the room.

Paul, Catherine and Michael looked at one another in disbelief.

"What the bloody hell has she done?" groaned Paul.

"She's nuts, I knew it. She's all about status and this relationship is a wrong one. That poor, poor boy." Michael rolled his tongue around inside his mouth, filling out his cheeks and gums, thinking.

"I don't know what to say. I have to bring this matter up at the Senior Leadership Team meeting this evening," said Catherine.

"Helen needs to know about this," added Paul.

"I'll deal with it." Catherine stood, jutting her chin out and nodding.

At the police station near to the school, Police Constable Norman Clarke was in his inspector's office, with the latter nodding his head and filling in a form of some kind.

"So I believe this issue to be a very credible threat, sir," said PC Norman.

"And you trust the information coming from the source?" asked the inspector.

"Yes. She's a very reliable and highly professional member of the teaching team," Norman replied.

"I'll fax this document to Special Branch and then it's down to them to carry out the investigation. When I receive a reply, I'll let you know."

"What could the reply be, sir?" asked Norman.

"Various details. Probably a date for them to visit the school and speak with those concerned," the inspector told him.

He took the document to a fax machine.

"Understood, sir."

"Is there anything else, Norman?"

"No, sir. That's all."

"Yes it is. Thank you." The inspector turned his back on Norman as he toyed with the fax machine on a filing cabinet, simultaneously stirring a cup of tea.

Norman tilted his head and got up from the chair. He walked the three steps to the door and grasped the door handle, turning back to the inspector.

"Cheerio," said the inspector, pressing the green 'send' button on the fax machine.

Norman fixed his eyes on the document as it slid into place and reeled down into the rollers. He opened the door and stepped out of the office, closing the door as he left.

"Bloody idiot," sighed the inspector, sipping his tea and returning to his chair.

Rebecca and Michael sat at their small dining table. They clinked their wine glasses, toasting one another.

"Cheers, my love." Michael leaned over and kissed his girlfriend on the lips. Together they took a sip of their French Bordeaux.

"Mm, that's a good one," Rebecca said, tucking into her fajitas, which Michael had prepared before she came home. "Thanks for cooking, Mikey."

"That's okay, my beauty. You cook nearly every day."

Rebecca told him about her new job. She had been there two months now. It was a far cry from the daily tears she'd endured at the recruitment firm where she was previously with the Botox-obsessed, coked-up boss.

Rebecca was now well away from that line of work and was working for an extremely successful corporate benefits company. A young, mixed team now surrounded Rebecca. Their boss regularly praised them for their hard-working and loyal approach to the business.

Michael could not get his head round what exactly the business was. All he knew and cared about was that Rebecca was now happy in her job and was no longer coming home stressed or calling him on the phone in floods of tears. He had once been equally as happy in his own workplace, until an all-round, combined foolishness of a select few people took centre stage.

"Are you okay?" Rebecca asked, looking closely at Michael's face as she gently pressed her fingertips against his frowning forehead.

"Huh? Uh, yes, no. No, not really, babe," he answered.

"What's up?"

"Just work." He sipped his wine.

"You can tell me, you know. I know the types of children you deal with each day. I know you hide the strain of it sometimes," Rebecca said, moving her hand to stroke his cheek.

"The place, it's just suddenly turned into some sort of castle of unhappiness. I can't believe what has happened. This new Afghan boy we have, Abdul, he's nice and polite and says please and thank you and is just genuinely respectful. This stereotypical chav boy, Lee, was winding him up, poking fun at him, saying 'Do you know the Taliban?' and 'Do you wanna join them?', with Abdul saying 'Taliban, I join, no. Bad.' Patricia got wind of it and goes off on one, as all her mind takes in is 'I join the Taliban.' She then tells her new boyfriend, PC Goon. It's just mental. She's undermined everyone."

"I'm sure it'll be fine and Helen will put her back in her place," Rebecca soothed, trying to comfort him with her reassuring words.

"Well, she didn't consult her either."

"I don't know what to say, Mike. I don't know how I can make it better," Rebecca said, calmly and with a helpless expression on her kind, beautiful, pale face.

Michael and Rebecca sat on their sofa, both with laptops, feet on the coffee table and television on.

Michael's iPhone sounded out. He eyed the screen which read 'Jacob Ramsay'. He retrieved the phone and took the call.

"Hello?"

"Hi Jacob. How you doing, mate?" sounded the familiar Scots accent of Detective Malcolm Crowe.

"Hey. I'm good. You?" Michael replied, exchanging a look with Rebecca who pretended not to listen.

"Yeah, great, great. Wondered how you are and if you wanted to meet up this week."

"Erm, I'm unsure. I was thinking I might ease off for a little while. To take a break. You know?" Michael said quietly, coming across a touch nervous.

"Oh, oh right. Okay. No problem. Well, we were just seeing if you wanted to catch up. You give us a call when you feel you can make it, okay buddy?" said Crowe.

"Cheers. That sounds good. I'll be in touch."

"Cool. See you, mate."

Michael lowered the phone and thought for a moment. Out of the corner of his eye, he saw Rebecca looking at him.

"You should have told them about the boy at school and the Taliban thing with Patricia's policeman boyfriend," Rebecca observed, closing her laptop.

"Completely forgot. I'll speak to them. Maybe I'll call Dad." Michael said, turning to look at her.

"Call him now or you'll leave it too late," she ordered, as Michael slid his phone into action again, scrolling into his favourites list. He found 'Mum and Dad'.

Michael's father was at the dining table with his own laptop and a scanning device. A lot of old photographs and negatives were strewn across the table. He squinted through his gold-rimmed spectacles at an old fashioned black and white photograph of himself as a sixteen-year-old police cadet when his old Nokia mobile phone rumbled upon the table, vibrating and sounding out the familiar ringtone. He took the phone and depressed the green button to take the call.

"Hello Mikey, you all right?" Edward said.

"Hey, Dad. I have to tell you about something that happened at work. It's crazy."

Michael told him about Abdul, Patricia and her boyfriend, PC Norman.

"What a goon! Well, play it out. See how it unfolds. He may not have reported it at all. He does seem the type of twit who would do such a thing. Can you not call your undercover contacts and have them stop it from going further?" Michael's father asked.

"I was going to ask you the same thing," Michael admitted.

"I'll have a word with Simon next door, and maybe Geoff," Edward replied, as he slid a negative into his machine.

"Mad Geoff?"

"Yes. He knows a few top blokes in that area. He's a great contact to have and he always pops round. Surprised we haven't seen him this week actually."

"Okay. Thanks."

"Oh, I bought this great thing the other day in Aldi. It's a scanner that scans negatives. Found some really old ones. I've got loads! I'll email you a few pictures," Edward promised.

"Oh, brill. Okay. I'll keep you posted on what happens at the school."

"Listen, if it gets too much and it's keeping you awake at night, you go sick. You're a loyal member of that team, Mike."

"I know. I'll speak in the week," Michael muttered.

"See you later. Bye, Mikey."

"Bye Dad." Michael ended the conversation and put his phone beside him on the sofa.

It was nearing the end of the Senior Leadership Team meeting at the referral unit's main site. Helen and Catherine were there, as well as PC Norman, two other female Deputy Heads in their late fifties, a sixty-year-old female Assistant Deputy Head and the Head Teacher, Josephine Golding, a tall, black woman in her late forties.

Michael thought she could kill kittens with her ever-present glare.

She came across as a soulless woman and had a divide and rule approach to her so-called management style, whether it was with the children or her staff. She never praised anybody or anything. Never a 'please' and certainly never a 'thank you'. In fact, at the beginning of every inset day, without fail, she would always state how disappointed she was with staff and pupil behaviour, yet, simultaneously, buoy herself up at how great she had made the school look. Gaining an outstanding OFSTED inspection and other great-on-paper tick-boxes.

At their last inset day she had reeled off a speech about how a cup of cold coffee had been placed on top of a set of staff lockers and had been knocked, spilling the drink into two separate lockers. She wasn't complaining that the coffee had spoiled staff belongings, but the fact that the coffee had stained the newly purchased lockers. After spouting her disappointment, Josephine Golding would then expect new staff members to stand up in front of the entire workforce and introduce themselves.

One new teacher actually stood up, said her name, followed it with, "I think I have made a mistake in coming here," and put on her coat and left, never to return.

Josephine was either behind her closed office door or standing at the end of a corridor, arms folded, with a completely hostile body language package or stance and glaring look, just staring at teachers, who struggled with unruly pupils. Pupils who wandered aimlessly, sparked up cigarettes, kicked doors and banged on class windows. Josephine stared at loyal, creative and hard-working staff, some of whom put up displays to make the place look relatively attractive. She would give them and the display a look of utter disapproval, often accompanied with a sigh, loud enough to be heard at the other end of the corridor. Josephine sometimes released a tut that could be heard at the opposite end of the school, due to the echo created by the wide corridors and cold, solid walls.

She wasn't even a Head Teacher, in title anyway. This was a self-appointed title. Her correct job title was Centrally Funded Alternate Provision Manager. It didn't quite have the same ring as Head. She was a devious, calculating woman, yet also incredibly insecure. She was a bully.

"Lastly, I'd like to express my concern about a situation that's arisen in our staff team and a young, innocent pupil," said Catherine. She nodded her head as she looked at each person in turn.

PC Norman reclined on his seat, leaning back, knowing that what was about to be said was definitely going to include him. He was nervous, yet bizarrely smug with it, too.

"I know what you're going to say, Catherine, and I've allowed PC Norman to deal with this matter," said Josephine Golding, in her nasal tone.

"How do you know about it?" asked Helen, curiously.

"What do you mean, how? PC Norman told me," Josephine snapped.

The other Deputy Heads turned to Helen and Catherine, each with a knowing expression and an equal smugness.

"Patricia undermined me, Josephine. She undermined Helen and the rest of the staff team. She totally undermined me as a manager," Catherine informed her, passionately.

"Patricia did what we all would do, Catherine, and that was to report a possible threat," answered Josephine.

"A possible threat to whom? There is no threat."

"That's right. Michael Thompson said it was a nothing conversation that was completely taken out of context," Helen said, supporting Catherine.

That angered Josephine and, strangely, the rest of the Deputies.

"And you believe Michael Thompson, do you?"

"Yes. Yes I do," Helen declared.

"You put too much trust in him. He's just a Learning Mentor!" Josephine said.

"Exactly," chimed one Deputy.

"He's not just anything at all, Josephine. In fact, he's a very good Learning Mentor and an extremely loyal member of my team. He set up the place with me." Helen frowned and wondered why her colleagues were so anti Michael.

They were so sycophantic and probably disliked one another, yet were as devious and backstabbing as each other. They took as much money as they could. Each was nearing retirement and striving to gain those management points that added to their pension.

Helen was different. She had a life outside of school. She was a seasoned traveller and had always said to Michael, "Work to live, not the other way around." Helen had shielded her close colleagues within her team from the ever bitter and distrusting Josephine. Despite being open with them, she would never disclose what a deceitful game player she really was as she didn't want her team to be filled with any form of hate for the woman. It was unhealthy. Helen in fact, took the full brunt of Josephine's angry, negative state of mind.

"I don't know what the fascination is with him," Josephine went on, looking at some paperwork before her.

"There's no fascination, Josephine. Michael's a talented, good thinking and kind young man. He goes above and beyond what is expected of him. I don't know why you dislike him so much," defended Helen.

"So what about the boy? What about Abdul?" chirped Catherine.

"What about him?" PC Norman leaned in.

"Yes, what about him?" sided Josephine.

"Well, it is a nothingness," Catherine shrugged.

"It certainly is not. I don't call a potential terrorist a nothingness, do you?"

"A potential terrorist? Says who?" Helen cried out.

The other deputies were alarmed, tilting their heads in a timed fashion, giving a sense of robotic motion.

"Patricia had reported what she felt to be a concern. If a member of staff is offended or concerned by something, then it is concerning and offensive. Plain and simple. It is council policy to report this particular incident."

"There wasn't an incident, Josephine!" called Helen, interrupting her Head Teacher, infuriating her even more.

"Yes, yes there was and that's the end of the matter!" Josephine raised her tone.

"It's a silly, unprofessional and unkind thing to do." Helen stood up for what she believed.

"It's the right thing to do!" shouted Josephine.

The other Deputies and PC Norman nodded their heads as Helen winced with pain, placing a hand across her chest. She scrunched up her face.

Michael's father leaned against a work-surface in the kitchen. He spoke on a cordless telephone, pushed on his gold-rimmed spectacles and pinched a biro between his fingers, ready to write something. His eyes searched the kitchen top and he tightened his face, disappointed in trying to locate something that wasn't there.

"Hello Geoff. Thanks for getting back to me. I spoke with Michael and he said the boy's name was Abdul Rah-Maan, that's right. Yes. Does it match what you've got?" asked Edward, as he thumbed some letters and envelopes. He examined one and flipped it over to press his pen down hard onto, trying to write an address. Edward rested the envelope on a copy of the Yellow Pages, sighing, shaking the pen and then breathing on the nib before he pressed it down hard again to write. "Thanks Geoff. Mike can't get through to his contacts at the moment, so I'll pass this onto the bloke down the road who's their guvnor. See what they can do."

A little later, Josephine and Helen were in the same meeting room, alone.

"I will not be spoken to that way and I do not like Michael Thompson," Josephine announced, watching Helen pack a couple of folders into her bag.

"You don't know Michael Thompson."

"What does he actually do? I don't get the appeal. I don't trust him," she continued.

"You don't trust anybody, Josephine!"

"Will you stop? You and your bloody, goody two-shoes team. Can't do anything wrong, can they?"

"Well, it was them who won you your outstanding OFSTED, Josephine. It was Michael's class that OFSTED inspected and gave great approval to. A class he doesn't even teach! He's not even a qualified teacher, yet OFSTED adored his lesson! They even wanted to steal the curriculum and timetable that he was an integral part in developing. That's only a fraction of what Michael does." Helen defended her wonderful colleague. A colleague she regarded so highly and dearly.

"I don't bloody trust him and I think he's a waste of money. He's on a lot of money, too."

"Oh, Josephine, he's not on a lot of money at all!" What a load of nonsense.

"Helen, he is on a lot of money!" Josephine yelled.

"What, twenty-one grand? I think he's worth triple that. Can you honestly say you're worth ninety-two thousand?" Helen bravely said, receiving a horrid scowl.

Josephine pointed her forefinger at Helen. "Yes, I do! Yes I am worth that! And more! I'm moving Michael to another department," she yelled.

"No you're not."

"I am! There's too many in your team as it is."

"There's not enough in my team, as it is." Helen was in total disbelief that this conversation was actually occurring.

"Helen, don't cross me. This is how it is. I'm moving Michael. There'll be a change to your beloved curriculum and I'm sanctioning everything PC Norman puts forward to me about this Afghan terrorist and that's the end of it. I'll not have anything else said on the matter."

Helen was shocked. She winced again, clutched her bag and made for the door. "I think you're a bloody pathetic fool, Josephine." Helen gripped the door handle and left the room, leaving Josephine fuming.

Josephine marched round the table for the door, flinging it open and yelled at Helen who had descended the stairs already.

"I want the SEF done by the end of the week! Do you hear me? I want it done by the end of the week!" she screamed and slammed the door.

The SEF was a Self-Evaluation Form. It detailed the heart of a school and was used by inspectors before they turned up to inspect it. It was a document that was meant to help a school focus on what was required for them to reach a better status. It took ages to complete. Josephine never did her own paperwork. She used other, more talented and professional staff members to get where she wanted to be in her professional life. She would step on and stamp on and crush anybody to reach her goal. It was said the only creature that would survive a nuclear war was a cockroach. Josephine Golding was a bloodsucking, venomous, poison-spreading cockroach. She was bitter, paranoid and extremely dangerous.

Edward had an A5 envelope in his hands as he walked down his lane, the unmade, pot-holed filled road to the house next door but one. He went up the driveway and to the front door. He pressed the doorbell and waited several seconds, then twice flapped the letterbox. There was still no answer, so Edward slipped the envelope through the letter box, turned and walked back to his bungalow again.

Helen sat behind the wheel of her Fiat Punto. It was a puke-coloured car that was waiting at the traffic lights. It was dark and the red of the lights shone upon her face as a tear escaped her eyes and she began to cry. She wiped the tear on her cheek away with the back of her hand, sniffed and then suddenly sobbed.

"I hate her. I bloody hate her!" she cried out.

Sitting at a dark wood dining table within a semi-detached house, somewhere in Plumstead, was Abdul, the Afghan pupil. With him were his Pakistani foster parents, Mr and Mrs Ahmed; the latter was serving some rice onto Abdul's plate. She served him a Chicken Karahi dish. The yellows, reds and browns were warm and extremely appetising to look at.

Abdul smiled with joy. He bowed this head to Mrs Ahmed.

Mr Ahmed smiled at Abdul. Mr Ahmed placed his hands together and closed his eyes. "Bismillah hirrahman nirrahim." It roughly meant, "In the name of Allah, the most merciful the most gracious," and was sometimes said by Muslims before a meal.

"How was school today, Abdul?" asked Mr Ahmed, as he poured a glass of water from a glass jug into a crystal tumbler.

"It was okay, Uncle." Abdul lowered his head, shoveling some of his food into his mouth, hoping not to be questioned about school any further.

Mr Ahmed knew something was wrong. He turned to his wife, who raised her brows and shrugged her shoulders. He said something to her in Urdu, to which she replied, accompanying it with another shrug.

Abdul looked up and tightened his mouth, saddened and disappointed.

"Please, I am okay. Do not worry about me," he said.

"You understand Urdu, Abdul?" asked Mr Ahmed.

"I know Urdu, Punjabi, Pashto, Dari, Kashmiri, Farsi, Balochi, English and a bit of Arabic," answered Abdul.

157

"What do you want to do with your life, Abdul?" asked Mr Ahmed. He repeated the question in Urdu.

"In life, Uncle?" he replied, also in Urdu.

"In your working life," Mr Ahmed said, once again in Urdu.

"In a working life, I would like to be a journalist," Abdul said.

"More rice, Abdul?" asked Mrs Ahmed in English, serving a large spoonful onto Abdul's plate.

"Thank you, Auntie." Abdul managed a pained smile.

"With your language skills, you could be a banker or a broadcasting journalist. You could help the BBC, Abdul," said Mr Ahmed, in Urdu. He looked at Abdul, head lowered, trying his hardest not to make any eye movement except to focus on his food.

Abdul didn't even divert his eyes to look at his glass of water as he reached for it.

Mr Ahmed frowned curiously, with a look of sadness for the boy. "How was your schooling today?" he asked.

"Good, sir. Good," Abdul replied.

Walking down the hallway a little later, Mr Ahmed stopped and tilted his head to see a silhouette behind the front door, outside. He walked to the door and put the chain on as he opened it, leaving just a two-inch gap, enabling him to see who was on the other side.

Standing on the doorstep was a white man, in a suit. He was about forty years of age, with short, greying hair.

A woman, of around thirty, stood behind. She wore a black trouser suit and white blouse. She was also white and a little short, with an unwelcoming, plain face.

The man smiled and held up a warrant card, flashing his Metropolitan Police badge and identification. It said he was Detective Sergeant Jason Greer.

"Evening Sir. I'm Detective Sergeant Greer and this is Detective Constable Jackie Mosley."

"What can I help you with, sir?" asked Mr Ahmed.

"It's just a routine house call, sir. We're making door to door visits in your road and would like to ask you a few questions relating to burglaries in the area," explained Detective Greer.

Mr Ahmed nodded his head, thinking about what had just been said to him. He closed the door and unlocked the chain. He re-opened the door once again, wide enough to stand in the doorway.

"If you don't mind, sir, it might be better and less awkward if we came in," said Greer, clutching a leather bag under his arm.

"Yes, very well. Of course," replied Mr Ahmed, opening the door wider still to let the detectives inside his home. He led the detectives down the hall to the living room.

Detective Greer exchanged a look with Detective Mosley. She appeared awkward and somewhat uncomfortable. Her eyes diverted, briefly, to the bag under Greer's arm.

The bag had a camera inside it and was filming from one end as the detective walked. It was a spy camera. It captured the hallway and then the living room. The camera bag captured Mr Ahmed gesturing to the sofa, and Detective Mosley as she sat herself down.

The bag was placed on the arm of the sofa and filmed the remainder of the living room, which was half lounge and half dining room, the same dining room that just a few moments ago Abdul had been sitting in.

"May I get you any tea? A drink of water perhaps?" Mr Ahmed offered, towering above the detectives.

"Tea would be nice. Thank you," said Greer.

"I'm fine, thank you," replied Mosley.

Mr Ahmed nodded his head and passed the two detectives as he left the room.

Greer eyed the door and looked at Mosley.

"One in the plant pot in the dining room, another under the coffee table."

Mosley stood and took a couple of steps to the dining part of the room. She retrieved something from within her jacket. A business-card holder, however it did not contain business-cards. Inside was a listening device. A bug. She placed it into the plant pot, which housed a Kentia palm. She gently touched the leaves.

"Come on, Jackie."

"Tom, it's a Kentia palm. I have one just like it. Well, this is in great shape. Mine's not so good."

The tiny, circular, contact-lens-sized listening device lay upon the soil of the houseplant.

Detective Mosley straightened as Mr Ahmed stepped back into the room. "I was just admiring your palm, sir."

"Yes, my wife is the plant lover. In Pakistan, we have a property there with much larger palms. The leaves must be three metres in length," Mr Ahmed told her, lingering in the doorway.

"Really? That's amazing," Detective Mosley said, with genuine interest.

Greer wasn't so impressed. He just wanted to get out of there.

"Do you take sugar, Detective?"

"Ah, yes, yes please. Just the one."

"Sweet enough, eh Detective?" Mr Ahmed said with a smile. He formed a wider grin as he exchanged a look with Detective Mosley, who returned the smile. He nodded, looked at his plant and turned to step back out of the room.

Mosley looked at Greer, who tilted his head to her.

"Are you finished now, Mr Titchmarsh?" said Greer, sarcastically.

"I prefer Monty Don." She shot him a look as she made her way to the sofa.

Greer placed a similar listening device under the coffee table. "Activated?"

"Activated," he replied.

Mr Ahmed returned with a cup and saucer, placing it down upon the coffee table.

It was then that the contact-lens-shaped listening device dropped from underneath the table and onto the floor.

Greer noticed it instantly, glistening on the carpet.

"One sugared tea, Detective," smiled Mr Ahmed as he turned his back briefly on them, pulling his trousers up slightly as he sat down opposite Greer, who took the opportunity to quickly lean down and retrieve the bug.

He returned it to the underneath of the table, pressing it harder to stick better this time.

"Thank you."

"So what is this about burglaries, detectives?" Mr Ahmed inquired, looking at both Greer and Mosley in turn.

"Yes, well, we've received several calls concerning suspicious-looking large vehicles in the area, sir. These large vehicles have been parked in this road and the road parallel to it. Their registrations have been logged, but aren't listed on the DVLA database, meaning they don't match the vehicles they're on."

"What do you mean by large vehicle, Detective?"

"The ones reported have been noted to be transit vans and lorries."

"Like a removal truck?" Mr Ahmed asked.

"Yes. Just like those," nodded Greer, as he retrieved and then opened a folder. He showed Mr Ahmed some photographs of a lorry and a transit van, with several registration plates listed underneath the picture.

Mr Ahmed looked at the picture with interest, but not with any particular recognition of what he was seeing. "I have not seen any of these vehicles before. As for the licence plates, I don't know. Do you have any faces?"

Greer turned the page of the folder that revealed six male faces. They were all white men in their late thirties. Something was quite odd about each of them. A couple were blurry, like an image capture from a CCTV camera. The rest were mug shot style photos.

Mosley arched her neck to eye the pictures, as did Mr Ahmed, who once again formed the same expression as he did when he looked at the previous vehicle photographs.

"I'm sorry. I do not recognise these men," he shrugged, as Greer smiled and closed the folder.

"That's perfectly fine, sir. Like I said, it was just a routine house call. Door to door enquiries."

"I understand, detectives."

"While we're here, is there anything you would like to inform us about, a report of any other crime? Are you satisfied with the police service?" asked Greer.

"I'm satisfied, sir, yes. I must admit that I do not have much contact or communication with the police. Never any trouble," he smiled and chuckled to himself. He smiled at Mosley, who returned the look, with a warm, genuine sense of charm for the man. He turned to see Abdul enter the room.

Detectives Greer and Mosley also turned to see him.

Abdul froze in the living room as he stood between the houseplant and the dining table.

Mr Ahmed spoke to Abdul in Urdu. "Abdul, are you not comfortable in your room?"

"I was looking for the Play Station game, Uncle," Abdul replied, also in Urdu.

"Quickly then, Abdul. As you can see, I am busy with guests. They are policemen," Mr Ahmed said, once again in Urdu.

"Policemen?" Abdul frowned.

"Yes." Mr Ahmed turned and smiled at the detectives.

"Everything OK, sir?" asked Greer.

"Yes, he is my foster-child. Abdul, these are detectives. Looking for burglars."

"Burgers? Like McDonalds?" replied Abdul, confused.

Mosley smiled at the young man.

"Not burgers. Burglars," corrected Mr Ahmed. He said the word again in Urdu for Abdul to understand.

"Is this boy the only one in your care, sir?" asked Greer.

"My wife is the main foster-parent, Detective, but yes, Abdul is currently our only looked-after child, however we have had many. Abdul, come introduce yourself."

Abdul managed a smile, despite being reluctant. He just wanted to get his Play Station game and return to his room to play it. He took three steps toward the detectives, who both stood and extended their hands to him. Abdul looked at Mr Ahmed, who nodded his head, permitting him to shake their hands. He did so, accompanying it with a smile and a brief nod of his head.

"Hello. My name is Abdul. Abdul Rah-Maan."

"Hello Abdul. I'm Detective Greer."

"I'm Detective Mosley. Hello Abdul."

"Where are you from, Abdul?"

"I am from Afghanistan. Kabul, sir."

"Kabul?"

"Yes."

"When did you come here, Abdul? To the United Kingdom?"

"He is quite new to this country. His father was a journalist in Kabul," stated Mr Ahmed.

"Interesting. And Abdul, how are you finding life in London?"

"Finding?" replied Abdul, confused by the word.

"Do you like life in London?" Mosley asked.

Abdul received a look from Greer. "Yes. I like London, but I cry for home and my family."

"Thank you, Abdul. You can play your game now," Mr Ahmed waved him away, turned and smiled at the detectives.

"Do you go to school, Abdul?" asked Greer.

That caused Mr Ahmed to scrunch up his face. He thought the quizzing of Abdul was over. He straightened, rolled his aching neck, which expressed that he was fine with further questioning for his foster-child.

"Yes. I go to school."

"Do you like it?"

"Sometimes. The teachers are nice."

"And the pupils? Are they nice?"

"Sometimes nice. Sometimes not nice."

"Like all schools, detectives." Mr Ahmed, chuckled and gestured Abdul to leave, with a nod of his head, which he did.

"Goodbye. Thank you," Abdul said, turning as he took a copy of 'Call of Duty Black Ops' from a shelf near the house plant before he left the room.

"A nice boy," stated Greer.

"Yes. Very polite. Very grateful," answered Mr Ahmed.

"Is Abdul ever in trouble in school?"

"No. Never in school, sir."

"Out of school?"

"Not to my knowledge, sir. No."

"We've been aware of some Afghani gangs in the area."

"Really? Where are the gangs, detectives?"

"They're quite prominent in Woolwich market. A market stall is run by an Afghan man. He heads a group of younger Afghanis. They sell mobile phone covers and unlocking services, sometimes hats and cigarette lighters. They're known to bully customers as well as the people who work for the main man who owns the stall. If Abdul lives in this area, he's more than likely to know about the stall," Greer told a greatly concerned Mr Ahmed.

"I will pay more attention to Abdul's whereabouts, Detective, however I state to you that Abdul is a good boy. He comes straight home from school. I would know if he was at the market."

"What about at weekends?"

"He goes to cricket or visits Croydon. Is Abdul in trouble with the police, Detective? I thought you were here to discuss burglars."

"Yes, yes of course." Greer closed his folder and stood, towering above Mr Ahmed, who was still in his chair.

Mr Ahmed stood up and clutched his own hands. He smiled warmly at each of the detectives.

"Well, it was nice meeting you and thank you for your time," said Greer.

"Please look after those plants," Mosley said. She smiled which made Mr Ahmed more at ease.

He smiled at her, warmly.

Walking down the street, Mosley and Greer made for an Audi.

She shook her head as she eyeballed the file in Greer's hand. "Who were the faces in the file? I've not seen those before."

"Photoshopped images. They're created. Computer generated. What do they call them? Sims. Not real people. Nobody is real anymore."

"And the vehicles? None of them had registrations or they were all obscured."

"They're just vehicles. We'll monitor the boy. He did seem a bit nervy and the foster dad just wanted to get rid of him."

"He's lost his family, Tom."

"All the more reason for him to become hostile."

"I don't see it. Not with him. He appeared to be a normal teenager."

"We're in a high state of terror alert, Jackie. Nothing is as it appears," replied Greer, as he unlocked the car and opened the driver's door. He clambered inside behind the wheel.

Mosley snorted as she rounded the passenger side.

Abdul lay on his single bed. He stared up at the ceiling in the lilac painted room. His mind was elsewhere and eyes were glassy. He had a pained expression and his mouth was tight with fear and anger combined. One of his shoulders was bare, as he had rolled his T-shirt up over it. Abdul scrolled his thumb on the metal roller of a cheap cigarette lighter to ignite a flame. He rolled his thumb off and the flame disappeared. He did it again. Almost like a light switch - on /off - on /off - on /off. Was it out of boredom or was it some kind of distraction? In between the fingers of his other hand was a craft knife. The blade was out as far as it could go as he pressed it into the upper forearm that gripped the cigarette lighter. He dragged the blade across his tanned skin, cutting and slicing. It left a line on his arm like a bloody snail trail. Abdul, without looking, took the lighter and heated up the blade for several seconds and continued to harm himself, pressing the blade down hard upon his bicep. It made another scarring cut upon his flesh. He winced with pain and released a tear, all the while staring continuously upward at the ceiling. Abdul never blinked once. There was a knock upon his bedroom door, which caused Abdul to blink suddenly. He took his attention immediately away from his trance-like state and instantly sat up. He rolled his shirtsleeve back down to cover his bicep, but there wasn't enough material to cover the new cut in his arm. There was another knock on the door.

"Abdul," came the voice of Mr Ahmed.

Blood trickled down Abdul's arm. He leaned across the bed to a cabinet and opened a drawer into which he tossed the cigarette lighter. He was about to put the craft knife in as well, but hesitated. Instead, he closed the drawer and noticed a school exercise book upon a desk.

Another knock upon the door sounded out.

"Abdul, I am coming in," announced Mr Ahmed from the other side of the bedroom door.

Abdul slid himself off the bed and strode to the desk where he flipped open the exercise book and put the knife just inside the front page. "One minute, sir. One minute please," he called out, as a droplet of blood fell onto the white plastic of the desktop. Abdul's eyes widened with fear. He slid the exercise book over the blood and grabbed a hooded top from the back of a chair, pulling it on just as the bedroom door opened.

Mr Ahmed was in the doorway. He looked at Abdul, standing to attention, arms by his sides, as if awaiting instruction, like a soldier. "Is everything all right, Abdul? Why did you not answer the door when I knocked?"

"I did not hear you, sir," answered Abdul.

"You did not hear me? I knocked twice and called out your name."

"I was thinking, sir."

"Thinking? What were you thinking?" Mr Ahmed asked.

"Home, sir. Always thinking of home."

Mr Ahmed nodded his head, understanding Abdul's reply. His eyes searched Abdul's room. The muted portable television depicted the Channel 4 soap Hollyoaks.

He fixed on the exercise book and Abdul followed his eyes to it, side-stepping to block Mr Ahmed's view.

"Why, sir? Why they come really?" Abdul asked, causing Mr Ahmed to frown suspiciously and look at Abdul closer.

"Why do you ask this question? Are you in trouble?"

"No, sir. No trouble. No trouble."

"You do not think chori is important enough for police to investigate and ask us questions?" quizzed Mr Ahmed.

"I don't know."

"Yes, I think you do know," stated Mr Ahmed, in a more serious tone.

"Uncle, I not bring police here."

"Who do you speak with at school, Abdul? Who do you tell about yourself? What teachers do you trust?"

"I do not understand, Uncle." Fear broke into his voice.

"Police detectives do not just appear at my front door and only my front door. Do you understand? I see them leave and get back into their car. They do not go to the next house and ask about chori. They just leave. These police are not in uniform, Abdul. They are special. They do not wear uniform. They are like a spy, Abdul. Do you understand?" Mr Ahmed said, passionately.

"What is this word? I do not understand."

"A spy, Abdul. Jasoos. Jasoos." Mr Ahmed repeated the word in Urdu and Abdul shook his head in an instant, fear was in his eyes.

"Jasoos? No. No, Uncle."

"Yes. Have you brought jasoos to this house? To speak with me? To look at my family? To come into my house? The house I work hard for? Abdul? Answer me!" Mr Ahmed shouted and took a step nearer Abdul. He raised his hand to strike him.

Abdul cowered and turned a shoulder to Mr Ahmed, who held his hand upward, in a karate style chop fashion, above his head.

"Please, Uncle!" Abdul cried out, holding his hands to his face, to shield himself from a potential chop to his neck. He opened his eyes to connect with Mr Ahmed's, which stared wild at Abdul, thinking, hesitating and wondering if this boy had brought trouble to his door or if it was a coincidence.

He lowered his hand and nodded his head.

"No more television. You will polish Auntie's silver and brass and then shine all the shoes. Do you understand?" Mr Ahmed barked his order, firmly, in Urdu.

Abdul lowered his head and stared at the carpet. His eyes followed Mr Ahmed's brown leather slippers as they pivoted, in military fashion, and stepped to the bedroom door.

The door opened and Mr Ahmed's brown leather slippers stepped out.

The door closed leaving Abdul to continue to stare downward at the bedroom carpet. He took a deep breath and slowly looked up. Tears streamed down his cheeks. He looked around the room. It was a nice room, but it still wasn't home. Abdul's home was approximately 3,547 miles away. From London to Kabul, Afghanistan. The home he shared with his mother, his father, his older sister and younger brother, aged four.

Abdul's father was a businessman. A part-time journalist, he also had his own company in Kabul and it often required him to be away. Travelling to other countries. He had several shops. They sold tobacco mostly. Sometimes car tyres and spare parts. A peculiar general store, with the occasional newspaper thrown in.

Contrary to popular belief, Kabul is a thriving city. A safe city. It even has a university and Abdul's sister was enrolled there.

Abdul missed them all, especially his younger brother. His brother was just two years old when Abdul left for the UK. He shed tears of sadness when he remembered him. He shed tears of hopelessness when he thought of his mother, for when his father was away on business and when she was without a man in the house to look after her and his sister and brother. He slowly removed his hooded top and pulled it over his head as to gently slide his arms from the sleeves. Abdul winced with pain as the recently cut skin he sliced a heated knife into had scabbed over and caught upon the cotton, causing it to bleed and weep again.

"Abdul!" bellowed out the voice of Mr Ahmed from downstairs.

"Coming Uncle!" Abdul hollered out as he unbuckled his belt and slid off his jeans. He picked them up from the floor and folded them tidily, quickly placing them on the chair by the desk. In his briefs, he opened a drawer and retrieved a pair of grey jogging bottoms. He sat himself on the bed and pulled on the tracksuit pants, sliding them over his feet, his shins, his knees and to his thighs. He stopped and his eyes fixed upon his thighs. Both had dozens of self-harming scars upon them. Slash marks lined across his thighs, from his knee up to his groin area. They were not as fresh as the scars on his arms, however they looked truly awful. Some might think he had ran blindfolded through a barbed wire fence and continued on and on through several more.

Abdul pulled the jogging bottoms over to his waist and stood up. He took a deep breath, retrieved the matching hooded top and pulled it on once more, stepping to the door. He gripped the door handle, paused for thought and set foot outside to the upper landing of the house, closing his bedroom door.

Sinatra Umbundo sat on the edge of a single bed in his bedroom, playing GTA 5 on his X-Box. His Nokia phone beeped and indicated a text message. Sinatra paused the game and retrieved his phone. He read the text: FEDS SHOT DED KILLAZ. Sinatra widened his eyes and lowered the phone. He was in shock.

An alarm sounded out and Michael opened his eyes to the shard of sunlight that shone through the white blind against the window of his bedroom. He looked at Rebecca, who lay beside him as the Samsung mobile phone alarm sounded again.

Rebecca stirred and reached for the phone on the bedside cabinet, next to a glass of water. She snoozed the alarm and put her head back on the pillow.

"Is it waking up time?" Michael yawned.

"Mmm," she answered, still with her eyes closed, nestling her head deep into the pillow as Michael leaned over and kissed her.

Michael slid himself out of the bed, working his feet into his slippers. He retrieved his glasses from his nearside cabinet and grabbed a blue toweling dressing gown from the back of the bedroom door. He pulled it on.

Both were pleased that it was Friday.

Michael entered his open plan living room and kitchen. He flicked on the TV then the kettle and made his way into the bathroom. Staring at himself in the bathroom mirror, Michael began to work his electric shaver around his stubbled cheeks.

The showerhead spurted water onto Michael's face. He stared, blankly, at the white tiles ahead of him and sighed.

Back in the bedroom, Michael grabbed a maroon dressing gown from the back of the door and tossed it onto the bed where Rebecca was still very much in a cozy, half-sleeping state.

She opened her eyes and slowly sat up, twisting herself out of the duvet as she put on the gown.

Rebecca slotted her size three feet into her slippers and shuffled along toward Michael, wrapping her arms around him, placing her head upon his chest, with her eyes closed.

"I need to get ready. I've got a meeting at Gatwick at ten," said Rebecca, opening her eyes and straightening.

"Do you want any lunch?" Michael asked her.

"Just some fruit," she replied, stepping out of the room.

Michael made two cups of tea. He placed one of the mugs on the dining table and the other on the coffee table, in front of the TV. He cut a length of a baguette and began to make himself a ham roll. He smelt the ham, closing his eyes as he did so. He loved the smell of its smokiness. Taking three slices, he placed them inside his roll, and then poured some pineapple juice into two glass tumblers, placing one, once again, upon the dining table, next to the mug of tea, and the other upon the coffee table, again next to the second mug of tea. It was very much a daily routine, even the making of the ham roll. Michael was, without a doubt, a creature of habit. He wrapped his roll in tin foil, placing it into a Sainsbury's carrier bag. From the fridge, he removed an apple and two clementines. He rummaged around in a cupboard and pulled out a bag of McCoys crinkle cut Thai Chicken flavoured crisps.

He knew they were bad for him and no doubt high in fat, but they were certainly one of his favourite types of crisp, though his taste salty snacks would sometimes vary: Walkers' Worcester Sauce flavour as well as Wheat Crunchies. Michael came across quite childlike when shopping in the supermarket with Rebecca.

She encouraged the behaviour by asking if he'd like a chocolate biscuit of some sort to take to work for his lunch, which he often agreed to.

He rummaged deeper inside the cupboard and retrieved a KitKat, which he added, together with the crisps, to the Sainsbury's bag.

The bathroom door opened and Rebecca stepped out, looking cleaner, refreshed and more awake as she entered the open plan living room and kitchen where Michael was spreading strawberry jam onto two slices of toast. She gulped her pineapple juice down, taking an Akai berry and a couple of other vitamins.

"I'm running out of these," she admitted, shaking a practically empty plastic container of Akai berries.

"They're well expensive though. Do they work?"

"Mm, I think so. Andy swears by them."

"Well if they taste like the bottle smells, then I'd swear by them too," quipped Michael, smirking at Rebecca, who grinned back at him, downing some water and an Akai berry.

It was seven thirty-when Michael began to eat his toast while he sat on the sofa, watching Daybreak on ITV and checking his email on his MacBook. The news was on and depicted the Foreign Secretary in crisis talks with the UN about a possible threat from Iran due to the uprisings in Tunisia, Egypt, Libya and Syria.

On 17th December 2010, a report alleged that a policewoman, in the town of Sidi Bouzid, approximately 190 miles south of Tunis, in Tunisia, had confiscated a vegetable cart.

The cart belonged to a twenty-six-year-old man called Mohamed Bouazizi. His vegetable cart was unlicenced, and had been for several years. Having been caught before, Bouazizi knew he could pay his fine and move on. The fine before was ten dinar. Ten Tunisian dinar was equivalent to around four pounds fifty pence. When he tried to pay his fine, the policewoman spat in Bouazizi's face and then slapped him. He was naturally insulted, stunned by the officer's behaviour and then received verbal abuse from her too as she mocked his dead father. Bouazizi set out to complain to the officer's superiors, but was ignored, so he left. However, within the hour he returned to the headquarters, drenched himself in petrol, from head to toe, soaking his clothes right through, before setting himself on fire. It wasn't long until people heard about the incident and they began to protest in the town, leading to a demonstration in some of the streets of Sidi Bouzid.

Police used tear gas on the many protestors. Public outrage quickly grew over the incident, leading to protests, and on the nineteenth of December even more police were called in.

Three days later, a protestor electrocuted himself by scaling a pylon. Another protestor soon followed suit, claiming financial difficulties and that the country's solidarity scheme was to blame.

It was another two days later, on the 24th December, when police shot dead a man named Mohamed Ammari, also injuring many other demonstrators.

The demonstrations escalated in scale and people protested against high unemployment and the rise in food costs as well as the political corruption and lack of freedom, especially in speech. There hadn't been such protests by the people in more than thirty years and many, many people were dying because of what they believed.

The people wanted President Zine El Abidine Ben Ali to go and on the 14th January 2011, twenty-eight days later, he resigned. He had been in power in Tunisia for twenty-three years.

It was just eleven days after that, on the 25th January, when an uprising in Cairo unfolded. Protestors, millions of them, demanded an end to Hosni Mubarak's Presidency. They wanted justice. They wanted a non-military government. They wanted freedom.

The city of Suez was witness to most of the violence.

Mubarak and his loyal Central Security Force imposed a curfew, yet it was widely ignored. There were thousands of supporters on both sides, for and against Mubarak. Even the military, who were ordered to use live ammunition on the demonstrators, refused to do so.

Despite hundreds of dead and thousands injured, on the 11th February, Egyptian Vice President Omar Suleiman announced the resignation of President Hosni Mubarak. Two days later, the Supreme Council dissolved Egypt's parliament and suspended the Constitution, taking up power. On the 23rd March, the Egyptian Cabinet introduced a law that criminalized protests and strikes. That new law stated that anyone who organized or called for a protest would be fined or sentenced to jail.

During that time in March, protesting against governments spread across to Bahrain. On the 14th March, military troops from the United Arab Emirates and Saudi Arabia were sent into Bahrain, ordered by the Gulf Cooperation Council to protect the oil.

Similar revolutions were threatened in Jordan, Yemen and Syria, with some protestors calling for a 'Day of Rage' in Damascus. A 'Friday of Glory' was called for amongst the online community in March, followed by a 'Friday of Martyrs' in April, where once again thousands took to the streets.

April 8th, known as the 'Friday of Resistance', became the largest protest yet on the streets of Daraa, as well as at the port of Latakia and the cities of Edlib and Qamishli.

It was on the 25th April 2011 that the Syrian government sent in tanks to Daraa. Around thirty or so protestors were reportedly killed as the tanks rolled in, assisted by snipers upon rooftops. Phone lines were cut. Water supplies and power, too.

The border to Jordan was closed.

The President of the United States, Barack Obama, accused Iran of secretly assisting Syrian President Bashar Al-Assad in cracking down on the protestors, condemning the use of violence as "outrageous".

Inspired by the protests in Tunisia and Egypt, a much more large-scale revolution was fast developing. In Libya.

In February 2011 civil war practically engulfed Tripoli. The Libyan leader was Colonel Muammar al-Gaddafi, a man who implemented Sharia law as well as putting in place surveillance cameras in schools, government buildings and offices and also factories. Not as a safety measure, but to monitor the people more closely out of distrust. He had public executions broadcast on television and with the majority of the country's wealth, brought in by its huge oil reserves, arms were bought and terrorist groups were formed. He announced to the world that there was no problem in Tripoli or the rest of his country, stating the West and Israel had engineered a rebellion. On 17th March 2011, the United Nations Security Council passed Resolution 1973. That created a no-fly zone and allowed the use of "all means necessary" to assure all civilians within Libya were safe. In late March, French jets destroyed five enemy tanks. The enemy, in that instance, was the Gaddafi regime.

The operations were called Ellamy and Odyssey Dawn,

The United Kingdom and the United States launched over a hundred Tomahawk cruise missiles, targeting Libyan air defense systems. The country had now escalated into civil war.

China, India, Russia and Turkey condemned the strikes by international forces.

Revolutions throughout the Arab World spread fast and furious. Were they engineered by Western and Israeli agents? Who had armed the rebels and was it true that the intended target all along was none other than Iran? Was there a plan to overthrow the sixth President, Mahmoud Ahmadinejad? There was certainly mention of it on the news channel that Michael was watching. It spread across the internet and social media websites, such as Twitter and Facebook, but Iran was a far cry from Michael's world.

In Israel, Prime Minister Benjamin Netanyahu made a speech, calling for the West to act against Iran. "If the international community was applying special pressure on Libya and warning its leader and soldiers against violating civil rights, the same warning must be aimed at Iran's leaders and their henchmen. At the same time as Gadaffi is massacring his opponents in Libya, the regime of the ayatollahs in Iran is systematically executing its opponents, I believe that a firm reaction will send a very clear message of encouragement and hope to the Iranian people, that no one has forgotten their struggle for freedom and liberty."

Former British Prime Minister Tony Blair contributed to the situation that occurred in Iran, saying, "I think it's very important that we stand up now for those people who want to protest for freedom and proper democratic elections in Iran. I think a change in Iran's government would be possibly the single most dramatic change in the whole of the region because you would then have Iran playing a constructive part. You would have Iran not trying to destabilize other countries in the region, and arming militia-type groups."

President Obama also stated, "My hope and expectation is that we're going to continue to see the people of Iran have the courage to be able to express their yearning for greater freedoms and a more representative government, understanding that America cannot ultimately dictate what happens inside of Iran any more than it could inside of Egypt."

The Middle East was changing fast and dramatically. The media reporting of the many uprisings was just as fast and furious. Propaganda was clearly evident and it was difficult to know what was real or not.

At seven forty-five, Michael placed his plate, complete with toasted crumbs, into the beige plastic washing up bowl and stepped to the bathroom to brush his teeth. As he exited, Rebecca quickly entered and carefully she inserted her contact lenses.

She turned to Michael and smiled at him. "You ready to go?"

"Yep." Michael turned back to the living room to retrieve the two plastic carrier bags containing their lunches for the day.

"Oh, I got you a present!" she gasped.

"A present! Really? What?"

"Stay there and close your eyes." Rebecca excitedly ran to the bedroom and in seconds returned to find Michael doing exactly as she had asked.

"Open your hands out," she said.

He did so.

She placed something onto the palms of his hands. She leaned in and kissed his lips. "Open." She stepped back as Michael opened his eyes, looking down to see a roll of silver gaffer tape in the palms of his hands.

He beamed a smile. "Gaffer tape! Yay!" he said, like an overjoyed child.

"Now you can fix your glove box," she smiled, referring to Michael's car glove box that had recently broken.

"I'll get some scissors!" He turned, leaving his loved one smiling with love and bemusement.

"Oh, it's so easy making you happy, my love," she laughed as he opened a kitchen drawer and located a pair of orange-handled scissors.

Rebecca stepped outside, into the crisp day with glorious sunshine.

Michael made his way to the passenger side of his car and unlocked it, opening the door for her.

"I'm not coming to work with you today," she reminded him with a smile.

"Huh? Oh, for some reason I thought it was Saturday and we were going shopping," Michael replied, closing the car door.

"I'll call on my way home," Rebecca promised, kissing him on the lips as she gently held his fingers.

"Okey doke. I love you," Michael said.

"I love you, too." Rebecca looked deep into his eyes. Her own sparkled and her skin caught the sunlight as she let go of his fingers and turned away to walk to Loughborough Station, just a minute around the corner from their home in Luxor Street.

He watched her become a dazzling silhouette, disappearing into the brightness and rounding the corner at seven fifty-six. Clambering inside the car, Michael placed his beige canvas workbag behind his seat and slotted the key into the ignition. He reeled off a length of the silver tape that his true love had given him, and cut the strip with his scissors. He stuck it across the top of the locking seal. He cut a shorter strip and stuck it down the seal along the side before sliding his fingers down, flattening it free of air bubbles and pressing the tape firmly. Michael put the tape and the scissors on the passenger seat and twisted the ignition key, bringing the car to life.

The radio came on halfway into a Pink song which he flicked off to LBC, the talk radio station, as he shoved his vehicle into gear, pulling his seatbelt on and maneuvering the car out from the curb and to the end of the street.

It was six minutes past eight and Michael was driving towards Dog Kennel Hill, heading into East Dulwich, Grove Vale, East Dulwich Road, Nunhead Lane, passing Peckham Rye Park. He hit the lights at Evelina Road.

Nick Ferrari, the presenter on LBC, was discussing the situation in the Middle East and whether the United Kingdom should once again stand shoulder to shoulder with its US cousins across the pond and intervene with the uprising in Iran.

"Definitely not," Michael said to the radio as he pulled to a stop at a set of traffic lights.

The travel report kicked in at around eight-sixteen, just as Michael drove over the many humps of Drakefell Road. There must have been around fifteen or sixteen or more. Along one section, on that bright morning, it was like driving blind due to the intense sunshine streaming through the windscreen, and then he hit a speed hump.

At eight-eighteen the radio station took a call, just as Michael pulled into Malpas Road and onto yet another stretch of speed humps. If he judged it right, he could drive straight over them, lining his wheels so they were evenly spaced either side of the mound in the road. Michael stopped at yet another set of lights, this time at the crossroads at Lewisham Way. He listened to the foreign caller on the radio, a young -sounding man who had spent most of his life in south London.

"Yeah, hi, this is Fariz, yeah. Mornin'. I wanna talk about da trouble dat's 'appening in da Middle East and Iran. Well, I'm from Iran. I support the protests and all that, yeah, but I fink people underestimate what the regime is capable of, yeah, cos when you protest, yeah, you've gotta be so brave and make sure you're not followed back to your house, yeah, cos dey will get you. The soldiers will get you or da people who are paid by da government will get you if you're seen to be a protestor and are recognised. Trust me, yeah, I know. I have friends who have gone missing before. My own mother, yeah, she was a teacher and she spoke out about how fings were, yeah, but... I'm trying not to get too emotional. It's hard for me. Dis situation has to be dealt wiv so carefully. Yes, da Iranian regime has to change, but it's how to change it and who is gonna do it and who is gonna replace it. Lots of factors at play here, you get me?"

"I get you, init," mimicked Michael, as he made a right, heading for the aptly named Friendly Street as another caller chirped in. He had a heavy accent. Older than the previous caller. Perhaps from India. "Hello sir. Yes, I think this whole situation is bad news for us. What with Egypt, Libya, Syria and now with Iran. It will only be bad news. More terrorism. More fear. More extremists. More radicals. More fanaticism. What do you replace it all with anyway? Another democratic puppet that the West puts in place? It's as if we are re-living thirty years ago. It's the Ayatollah Ali Khamenei all over again and the revolution back in 1979 and the demonstrations against the Shah in 1977. It is the same situation and the same outcome will occur. I tell you. It is all engineered. The entire play out. The US is behind all of this, I guarantee."

"Probably right," Michael chipped in as he found himself at the traffic lights at Blackheath Hill. He flicked over to another radio station and listened to the remainder of 'Suicide Blonde' by INXS. Michael sang along to the song as he tapped his fingers on the steering wheel.

Michael's car passed Wat Tyler Road and headed onto Shooters Hill Road, slowing to let a group of schoolgirls cross over. They were from St Ursula's Convent School.

Michael continued up and turned left into Charlton Way, with Greenwich Park on his left hand side.

The green lights shone brightly at the crossroads of Maze Hill and Vanbrugh Park, enabling Michael's car to drive straight over, passing the large houses on either side of him, and then Blackheath High School on his left. He grinned when he saw a pug being walked, slowing his car to take a better look. His smile was caught by the young thirty-something walking it.

There was a police presence at Mayhill Road as Michael drove past on Charlton Road. That was, of course, where an acquaintance of Sinatra Umbundo had been shot dead. Michael raised his eyebrows, fixing on several black African women holding bunches of flowers as they walked past a police officer standing at the entrance to the road.

"Wonder what went on there?" Michael said to himself as he continued his drive along Charlton Road.

He slowed at the set of traffic lights where the Cherry Orchard Estate was situated. Michael's eyes fixed on another's as he followed somebody crossing the street in front of him.

That certain somebody's eyes were clearly fixed on Michael also. It was a Groundhog Day situation. A revisited moment in time as Michael watched Sinatra Umbundo cross the very street, in front of his car, where Michael had been previously with the undercover officers.

Sinatra's gaze was well and truly fixed. Glued. Wide-eyed and concentrated on Michael like a wild animal. He was eating a box of fried chicken with a handful of fries.

"Fried chicken for breakfast. Staple diet," Michael mumbled to himself as the lights changed from red through to green. He shifted gears and passed Sinatra, who was already on the other side of the road. Michael took another glance, seeing Sinatra's stare holding firm.

"What's with the staring, man?" said Michael, driving past Charlton House and rounding into the Village.

In Cemetery Lane, Michael drove to the junction of Charlton Park Lane. He glanced at the cemetery briefly as he awaited a break in the traffic. "There'll be another one joining you lot soon," he sighed.

At eight thirty-two Michael's car headed towards Plumstead Common and Winn's Common. The road was surprisingly clear for that time of day and particularly that time of the week. Driving down the tree-lined Winn Common Road made Michael feel he was in a different place entirely, albeit briefly, until he entered into the narrow and steep road of Riverdale. Michael slowed to let an oncoming police car, heading uphill, pass him.

Plumstead Police Station was situated partly in this road, and officers, plain clothes and detectives, lined their own vehicles down the street. Michael knew this because a former pupil of his used to live down that very road and often moaned to him about how none of his family could get a parking space due to "all the bloody copper filth parking their cars in front my house".

As soon as he arrived at work, PC Norman immediately approached Michael. Norman the policeman stood tall and extremely upright, with a stern expression upon his face.

"Michael, come this way a minute," requested PC Norman, turning his back on Michael and stepping up the corridor away from him.

"Pardon me?" Michael frowned and glanced past the officer to the open door of an office at the end of the corridor. He saw Josephine Golding, the head, sitting inside.

She turned her head, ever so briefly, catching Michael's look and closed the door.

Michael stared at PC Norman, several steps ahead of him. The man glanced back round and gestured with his head for Michael to follow him. The look was highly authoritative and unfriendly.

"What's going on?" asked Michael, reaching another classroom door where PC Norman now stood.

Norman quickly opened the door wide and shoulder-barged Michael into the room.

"This is him. Michael Thompson," announced PC Norman, closing the door, with Michael finding himself inside the classroom.

The classroom had a long, boardroom-type table in the middle, with about fourteen chairs around it. There was a whiteboard at one end and some children's artwork on the walls. A water cooler was present in one corner, too.

On two of the chairs sat a man and a woman. They were smartly dressed and in their late thirties. In front of them, on the table, was a green cardboard folder, an A4 notepad and a school file on a pupil.

The woman was nearest Michael. She gestured to a seat and Michael frowned, glancing back to the door and then at the two unfamiliar people sitting before him.

"Hello. I'm Michael and you are...?" he said, extending his hand and taking one step toward the man and the woman, both of whom exchanged a look with one another.

The man edged an inch or two up from his chair to lean forwards and shake Michael's hand.

The woman did the same, not looking at him, and neither made any real effort to acknowledge Michael. She gestured to the chair once again, but Michael remained standing.

He looked at them with a pleasant expression, yet still wondered what was going on. He made an instinctive guess, but could it be true? His heart was pounding inside his chest.

The two exchanged a look again and the woman sighed.

"I'm Detective Paula Stevens and this is Detective Ben Jordan."

Detective Jordan jutted his head up, in an all too street-style manner. He was slobbish and actually wearing black tracksuit bottoms, a shirt and a black blazer.

"Okay - so... Do you have any identification?" Michael asked, receiving a deep sigh in return from Detective Stevens.

She glanced at her colleague who nodded his head, as if to give the go ahead.

"My father was in your line of work, and several of my close family, too, so I've been raised to ask these things. Thanks," Michael continued as Stevens and Jordan flipped their small, black wallet-type Warrant Cards, revealing a glimpse of passport-sized photographs of each of them and the Metropolitan Police badge. Michael eyed it closely and then looked up at each of them in turn. He straightened, gaining courage and exhaled. "Just a second."

With that, Michael suddenly darted out of the room and raced down the corridor.

PC Norman was at the opposite end and bolted after him. "Hey! Where are you going! Get back here!"

Michael's heart pounded with every step. The floor was slippery from the fluid that the cleaners used. His shoes slid as they made contact with the wood. He glanced around and saw PC Norman setting foot after him. Michael raced down some steps and through a tiny wooden door that led to a spiral wooden staircase. The building was certainly an old one. A modern school would never have had such nooks and crannies. Michael fumbled for his keys, nervously, unlocking a door to a hidden room. He locked it behind him and bounded up another set of stairs, working his way to a far corner of an upper classroom, well away from any pursuing foe.

PC Norman curled his lip as he looked around an empty corridor. He tried a door, but it was locked. He shook it, angrily, craning his neck to work out exactly what was behind it and where it led to.

Michael thought fast. He pulled his phone and dialed the one and only number he could ever think of calling in a situation such as that one: his father's.

Edward's mobile rang and vibrated on the dashboard of his jeep. He was parked on his driveway, washing the vehicle down. The sound of the phone alerted him and he straightened like a meerkat to listen. His eyes fixed on the phone. He picked it up.

"Hey Michael. Everything all right?"

"Dad, I arrived at work and PC Goon shoved me into a room," blurted Michael.

"Hold on. Slow down. What do you mean?" asked Edward.

"I mean exactly that. He barged me into a room and there were two detectives waiting inside, wanting, I guess, to quiz me about an Afghan boy we have."

"Detectives?" Edward leaned into his jeep and reached under the driver's seat. He winced as he stretched, pulling a second cell phone from underneath. A piece of red electrical tape was attached to it. "Did you get the detectives' names?"

"Yes. One man, Ben Jordan. One woman, Paula Stevens," Michael answered.

Edward pressed a button on the second cell phone. "And where are you now?"

"I'm in a room. I ran off, but the Goon is on the lookout for me."

"OK. All right. Don't worry." Edward lowered the phone and clambered into his jeep, closing the door for privacy. He brought up the second cell, adopting a completely different tone of voice.

"Two-nine-five-two-nine-three-three-six-six-two." Edward paused for a beat. "Five-seven-seven-zero-nine-one." Edward had coded in. He continued. "ID check on IC9. Ben Jordan. Male. Paula Stevens. Female." Edward waited for a reply. "Benjamin Jordan. IC3. Paula Stevens. IC1. And? Out."

Edward lowered the second, red-taped phone and brought up his original cell to speak with Michael again. "Michael? OK, listen. The two detectives are MI-5."

"What? Why? Dad." There was panic in Michael's voice.

"Listen. It's OK." Edward tried to keep his son calm.

"No, it's not OK. They're military intelligence."

"As was I."

"Dad, it's different with you asking me questions. You're my dad!"

"Now, you don't have to be in there if you don't want to, but you've done nothing wrong. Any time you feel uncomfortable, you just walk out or you give them my number, do you understand?" Edward said firmly.

"Yes," answered Michael.

"The two detectives are from an organisation called Prevent. It's an anti-terrorist division. Get the case number off them and give it to me once you're done. Don't worry, Mikey. It'll be OK."

Michael composed himself before leaving his hiding place and entering the room again. He managed to avoid PC Norman.

The two detectives frowned.

"Are you all right?" Detective Jordan asked him.

"I had only just got into work before being shoved into this room so I had to sort some things out," said Michael. "So, where are you based? Where are you from?"

Detective Stevens admitted they were from Prevent.

"Right," said Michael. He relaxed, knowing his father had checked them out successfully.

"We're here to ask you what you know about the suspect known as Abdul Rah-Maan and the leak to the Daily Express newspaper."

Michael scrunched up his face and looked past Stevens and to Jordan, who was resting his head with a clenched fist nestled into his flabby cheek, his elbow propping himself up. He looked back to Stevens.

"I don't know what you mean. The leak? What leak? What suspect?" Michael responded, receiving yet another sigh from Stevens.

"Do you have knowledge of anyone by the name of Abdul Rah-Maan?" she said, abruptly.

"Yes. He's a student here," Michael replied.

"Good. Then we want to discuss the incident that occurred in this school."

"What incident? When?" blurted Michael, receiving again a deep, long sigh from Stevens, who slid a file in front of him, stubbing her manicured, maroon-painted fingernail to a date upon a piece of paper. Michael noticed the words, 'During a lesson, Afghan pupil Abdul Rah-Maan was discussing the Taliban in an alarming manner.' Michael looked up at the Detective and sneered.

"Is something funny? Terrorism is a serious, serious threat to this country and it isn't anything to laugh at," she frowned.

"You are the police, aren't you?" Michael asked.

"Of course we're police," she snapped.

"There was no incident here and I really think this is a complete waste of your time. You've been misled, detectives."

"I want to make it clear that you understand that we are in a high state of terror here in the UK," she continued, in a progressively aggressive manner.

"That's debatable. I do, however, understand what you're saying. I do. I also understand that the boy you've mentioned, Abdul, is simply that: a boy. He's a boy who misses his family considerably. He's a boy who is alone here in London, living in foster care. He's a boy who cries when he tells me about how he walked from Afghanistan to Iran in order to be able to travel to the UK. His family sent him here," Michael stated.

"He was discussing the Taliban," said Stevens.

"No. He was answering a question. The question was 'do you know the Taliban?' This question was from a white, working-class boy who is a bully and a racist. He asked if Abdul knew the Taliban," Michael replied, firmly.

"So it's this white boy who we should be questioning?" Jordan remarked, looking up, but still resting his head on his knuckles.

"You shouldn't be questioning anybody! Like I said, this is a big misunderstanding. I was there, in the class."

"You weren't the teacher at the time?" asked Stevens.

"No. Do you know what this school is? At all?" Michael asked each of the detectives, who both sat up and folded their arms.

"It's a school, but go on," said Stevens, in a cocky manner.

"Not exactly. This provision, on this particular level, this department, assesses students. The students come to us via a panel within the borough. They could be excluded kids - expelled from school. They could have moved into the borough and are therefore seeking a new school, closer to where they live. They could have even moved into the country. From ages eleven to sixteen. All races. All abilities, both genders and from any country. We even get asylum seekers, young offenders and the occasional attempted murderer, thief and rapist. The most high profile children in the borough come through these doors. Abdul Rah-Maan is one of those children who came from another country. Afghanistan. He doesn't know anybody. He keeps himself to himself. Don't you think if he wanted to join the Taliban then he would have probably stayed in his own country where it would have no doubt been a whole lot easier to do so?" Michael said passionately, as he reclined in his chair, searching with his eyes for some kind of relaxed realisation in the expressions of the officers opposite him.

"Are you sympathising with terrorist views?" asked Jordan.

Michael was in utter disbelief. He shook his head and curled his lip. He told them about Abdul and how he came to be here in the UK. He told them how good and respectful and polite he was in class and to him and the other members of staff.

"When the complaint was brought to our attention, it was noted that Abdul can be violent and verbally abusive," stated Stevens.

"Not at all. Never. Who made the complaint?" asked Michael.

"PC Norman and another member of staff," responded Jordan, glancing at another piece of paper, in front of him on the table.

Michael sneered again. "And what dealings would PC Norman have with Abdul? None. He doesn't. He's hardly ever here and when he is, he's downstairs with another member of staff, who no doubt was the one who made the complaint. Am I right?" Michael was on a roll.

He watched the detectives exchange further looks before finally showing some genuine interest in him and what he was saying.

"A Patricia Hayes made the initial complaint it says here," said Detective Jordan.

"Exactly. I'm unsure whether you know this, you probably do, but PC Norman is in a relationship and currently living with Patricia Hayes. A recently bereaved woman," Michael told them.

Detective Stevens briefly closed her eyes as if the hammer had fallen. She opened them and turned to her colleague, both forming an expression that clearly read: a) What the hell was going on here then? b) Typical Special Policeman turned typical Police Constable based in a school. c) What a waste of time. d) All of the above.

"That explains it," muttered Stevens under her breath.

"What you say in this room to us is of course taken in the strictest of confidence, Michael. You do understand that, don't you?" said Jordan, leaning in.

"I understand. Yes."

"You said that your father was in this line of work. What did you mean by that?" asked Stevens.

"Whatever line of work you're in," Michael said firmly, "he was too."

The detectives exchanged a look. Stevens slowly got up from her seat and discreetly made a call in one corner of the room.

"Have the two of them been seeing each other long?" Jordan asked, showing more interest in Patricia and PC Norman's relationship than the originally intended reason for them being there.

"It's hard to gauge. She's changed, or maybe she hasn't changed. She told her once trusted colleagues she was about to enter into a relationship with our school's police officer. She asked what we thought and we congratulated her on finding somebody again," informed Michael, honestly.

"Why would she ask her colleagues what you all thought about it? What would it have to do with any of you?" inquired Detective Stevens.

"Because we've each helped Patricia in our own unique way."

"How do you mean?" asked Jordan, curiously.

"Her husband committed suicide. It seemed an incredibly random act. My parents helped her considerably."

"How?" Stevens questioned, quickly.

"I can't say exactly how, but my father, being my father, knew a lot of people and had a lot of experience when it came to coroners and coroners' courts and, therefore managed, to get a 'death by misadventure' verdict that enabled Patricia to acquire her deceased husband's pension. His position in his job came with a lot of money. It wasn't just my parents who helped her out. So many close colleagues did. Helen, my Deputy Head, was wonderful. She'd visit her, without fail, every Sunday. She'd call her every night. She promoted her at work but now, suddenly and bizarrely, Patricia is this cold, calculating, egotistical power-tripper, who now believes she's-"

"-Sherlock Holmes?" interrupted Jordan.

"There are two of them we're talking about, Ben," sniped his colleague, Detective Paula Stevens.

"Sherlock and Watson."

"Clouseau and Kato, more like," she scoffed.

"It's as if they get off on each other's power," Michael explained.

"Imaginary power perhaps," added Jordan.

"So, do either Patricia or PC Clarke have any direct dealings with Abdul?" asked Stevens.

"Patricia interviews parents and new pupils. She'll make telephone calls home if they're late or absent. She'll go on various review meetings if they're involved with the Youth Offending Team or are in the care system."

"But she isn't in the classrooms?" Stevens probed.

"No," replied Michael, firmly.

"And you are?" she asked him.

"Yes, naturally. I monitor behaviour. I mentor and counsel the children, as well as provide support in the classes that may require it. The turnover for students is fast. You could have a great set of children who are high achievers one week or month, and then the next, they'll be the complete opposite and you'll get a set of criminals. It could flip again and you'll get a new cohort who are extremely needy and require one-to-one teaching or youngsters who just cannot be in a classroom with any other child. Like I said before, one minute a refugee, the next minute a sex offender. One minute a child with autism, then the next a boy soldier from the Democratic Republic of the Congo. I'm in a team that has to continuously adapt to the changing dynamics of the client group, and we do it incredibly well and have done for many years. It's a tight team, too. We know one another. We trust one another and we certainly know when a child is cause for concern or not, and when we do, we take the appropriate action. Abdul is not a cause for concern," Michael declared with true passion and conviction, staring directly at Stevens and Jordan.

"I see. I read in a recent report dated two days ago that Abdul was swearing aggressively at a young girl and at Patricia," she observed to Michael as she eyed some paperwork.

"The children are never out of our sight or hearing. From nine in the morning, through to break-time, lessons and lunchtime, and until they go home." Michael leaned over to see the report in front of Stevens. "It says here this particular incident occurred at break-time. I don't think so. It's made up. Fabricated. It's completely untrue because I play badminton with Abdul every break-time. He hates missing the opportunity to play with either Mr Jones or myself. This report was written up by Patricia who wasn't even in the dining hall at the time."

"Why would she make it up?" asked Jordan.

"To back herself up! To add weight to her complaint. To not make herself look stupid in front of the people that she reeled this pathetic story off to. To make Abdul appear to be a bad boy and justify her claim that he was a terrorist," continued Michael.

Jordan and Stevens exchanged another look.

Michael's time in the room entered into its second hour.

The three of them discussed in more detail the ins and outs of the workings of the school and the types of children Michael encountered. The detectives finally got back round to quizzing him about Abdul before bringing the meeting slash interview to an abrupt end.

Detective Paula Stevens closed the folder that she had been writing notes in. She felt disappointed the meeting hadn't gone entirely her way. Whether it was solely to do with Michael rightfully justifying his view, giving facts on PC Norman and Patricia, or if it was simply down to the fact that Michael's father used to be in a similar line of work to them, if not of higher rank. It was unclear.

"Well, I don't think we'll be taking this any further," she said, looking at Michael, who instantly appeared satisfied with the decision.

"Did you want to speak with anyone else? Another member of staff who deals with Abdul?" Michael offered.

"Would they say anything different?" answered Jordan.

"No. They'd say pretty much what I have said."

"Apart from the 'my father was in the secret intelligence service'?" Stevens said, neither mocking, nor being sarcastic. She was serious and perhaps slightly concerned.

"Yes, apart from that," admitted Michael.

"Then there's no reason to speak with anyone else. There's no incident to follow up," Jordan said, with an out-of-the-blue smile.

"Can I have the case number, please?" Michael asked.

Detective Stevens sighed and nodded to Jordan, who jotted a number down and passed it to Michael.

"So... Is that it?" Michael asked, warily.

"Yes. If you do happen to come across anyone in the future who you feel is a potential threat or cause of concern, then please give us a call." Detective Stevens slid her card to Michael. It had her name and the familiar Metropolitan Police logo on it, a couple of telephone numbers, as well as an email address.

Michael pocketed the card and nodded his head. He stood up and tucked his chair back under the table. He looked at them and lingered, wondering whether they would say anything else to him.

They didn't. Their heads were lowered over a diary of some sort and Jordan was leaning in closer. His face was hidden by his bulky frame and Stevens' shoulder.

Michael waited for a couple of seconds. He waited two more for any sense of a head movement or body shift. Nothing. He raised an eyebrow and turned. He opened the door and stepped out into the corridor.

Paul Jones, Michael's colleague, was in the doorway to his classroom and gestured to him, silently with his head, to step inside. He followed it with an empathetic smile. Warm, kind, like his father. The door closed to Paul's classroom and he sat himself down on a comfortable soft chair.

"Take a seat. There's a cup of tea underneath the chair for yer," said Paul, watching Michael slump himself down on a similar chair next to him. He sighed deeply.

"Man, how long was I in there for?" relaxed Michael, reaching underneath his chair to retrieve a mug of tea.

"Nearly two hours. How'd it go? Did they water-board you?" Paul asked, sipping his tea with a smirk.

"Ha, no, but I felt it was coming when I first sat down and they started to quiz me. They said 'We're here to ask you what you know about the suspect known as Abdul Rah-Maan and the leak to the Daily Express newspaper."

"The Daily Express?" Paul echoed, with a frown.

"Yeah. I'm like 'what?' and going straight in with calling him a suspect. Poor, poor boy." Michael drank some tea.

"Indeed, sir. Indeed. Are they going to pursue this nonsense or not?" asked Paul, with a tightened, pained expression, watching Michael closely reclining into his chair, tired.

He shook his head. "No. As soon as they learnt that Patricia and Norman were in a relationship, they pretty much realised that the whole thing was a waste of their time, or at least that's the impression I got."

"Did they ask about them then?" Paul wanted to know.

"It kind of steered that way. They had to know how the whole thing evolved into this stupid mess."

Outside, in the corridor, Detectives Stevens and Jordan stepped out of the room they had been in. Josephine Golding trotted down the corridor to talk to them just as Sinatra Umbundo stepped out of the boys' toilets.

He lingered in the corridor, outside the door, but within earshot, as he buckled his belt.

Josephine didn't pay any attention to him. She was too wrapped up in her own ego and fixed her eyes on the officers before her. "Detectives. I hope your time spent here was of value and you managed to unearth the hard-line facts that we do indeed have a possible terror threat here in our school, not to mention a serious action of gross misconduct from a staff member," gushed Josephine in her usual harsh, self-righteous tone.

Sinatra tilted his head, listening. He shuffled back towards the wall, into a darkened part of the corridor.

Detective Stevens formed a hundred-mile-an-hour smile. It was more of a mouth twitch really. She sneered as she looked at Josephine. She towered above her, in a more powerful manner.

Josephine frowned, awaiting an answer. Jordan coughed and looked into the shadows to fix his attention on Sinatra, who noticed that he'd been clocked.

Sinatra entered a classroom.

Jordan turned his head to Josephine. "We've come to our conclusion and we won't be pursuing this matter any further," he announced, stepping past Josephine to a set of double doors just as PC Norman and Patricia exited another door together, smiling.

Their smiles instantly disappeared when they cast their eyes on Josephine, who looked angry and embarrassed.

"What about the boy? What about the staff?" Josephine blurted.

"The boy is fine."

"And the staff?" Josephine asked.

"Well, you have loyal staff, some of who have powerful connections. I'll leave it there."

Detective Stevens walked away from her, making after her colleague. She snorted as she looked Patricia and Norman up and down.

Patricia frowned and glanced at Norman, then at Josephine as Stevens exited via the double doors.

"I wanna talk to you two. Now. In the office, now," commanded Josephine.

She turned on her high-heeled shoes and clip-clopped up the corridor, toward the small office.

Sinatra adjusted his belt and lowered his jeans below his backside, exposing a pair of black boxer shorts. He stood bow-legged by the classroom door.

"Sinatra, sit down please and pull your trousers up. I don't want to see your backside," scolded Catherine Riverdale, sitting at the desk.

"Why are there police detectives here, Miss? Have they come for the Afghan students?" asked Sinatra, trying to come across as innocent as he possibly could, but was clearly fishing.

"What do you mean by that? There aren't police here and why would they be after Abdul? That's quite a racist thing to say?" responded Catherine sharply.

"Why is it racist? Did I say Abdul? No. You must be thinking the same as what I was, otherwise you wouldn't be calling me racist, init, so you is as racist as well, but anyway, we'll leave it, yeah, so just tell me: why are the police here?"

Catherine frowned, jutting her chin out as she looked around the class, fixing on Abdul who had already honed in on the conversation.

"Police? Police are here? For me? Why for me?" Abdul cried, becoming tense and fearful and very defensive.

"Nobody is here for you, Abdul. Continue with your work please," Catherine insisted.

"It's time to go home. I'm going home, yeah," Sinatra said. He straightened and gripped the door handle.

"Yes, home time now, Miss. Home time, but tell me why police are here. Why they here for me. I am good boy."

"Sshh, no police are here," Catherine repeated.

"What you lying for? I saw them. Dat other teacher even said 'detectives' to them and asked if they'd found the threat in the school. Who's da threat?" Sinatra said, forcefully.

Catherine was confused, unaware that the detectives had questioned Michael, let alone for nearly two hours.

"Have you seen Michael at all?" she asked Sinatra, who had already opened the classroom door and set foot outside.

"Why would I see him? Have you not? Where's he been anyway? Has that snake been wiv da Feds? I bet he has, you know. That snake. I betchoo he has, man," Sinatra said angrily, bouncing out of the room and into the corridor.

"Michael is with police? Why he talk with them? He tell things about me? Is he jasoos? You speak my name, Miss. Why police here? They come to my house and now they come to my school. What's happening? You tell me what's going on," pleaded Abdul.

"I don't know, Abdul. Calm down."

"I am calm. You be calm. I am calm! I go home now," he said, following Sinatra out of the room and into the corridor.

"I wouldn't trust that fucking snake, Abdul man. Seriously yeah, he's a snake," Sinatra said, bopping alongside Abdul as they made through the set of double doors and down some concrete stairs.

"What you mean by snake? Why he snake? What is this?"

"A snake, man. You can't trust him," explained Sinatra.

"No trust Michael?"

"No."

"Michael no trust because he snake?" Abdul asked.

"Yeah."

"Shit man fuck. Michael snake. Fucking snake man," Abdul muttered in his thick accent as he rounded the corner of the short set of concrete steps

"I will not be made to look a fool, Patricia. At the end of the day, I'm the one who will end up looking stupid and getting my knuckles rapped for this mistake that you and Norman decided to cook up," spouted Josephine Golding, the Head Teacher, spinning round on her chair in the small office at the end of the corridor.

"But, I-" stuttered Patricia. She felt ashamed, like a naughty schoolgirl. She was sitting on a softer, much lower chair than Josephine, which made her feel even more insecure and a lesser important human being.

"We'll stick to the original story. He was a threat. Staff and pupils felt uncomfortable and what Michael heard was wrong," Josephine said, pointing her forefinger at Patricia, whose eyes had started to well up fast and wasn't handling the telling off well at all.

"What... what will happen to Michael?" she asked, quivering, with her left leg and knee jittering.

Josephine noticed this and Patricia placed her hand upon her knee to settle herself, but this just caused her hands to shake instead.

"I'll be moving him next week. He can go downstairs to the basement floor and deal with the nutters there. Bit of luck he'll give up and hand in his notice in a couple of weeks," she said in her monotonous voice, just as the telephone sounded out. She sighed and took the call.

"I have a call from a journalist saying they're from the Daily Express. They're asking for the Head Teacher who sanctioned Special Branch to quiz a pupil who said the word 'Taliban' in class. What shall I say to her?" came the concerned secretarial voice on the other end of the line.

"You bloody tell them no comment and hang up the bloody phone!" shouted Josephine, slamming the receiver down hard and panting. Her eyes were wide and expressed extreme anger.

"What was that?" Patricia calmly asked, like she was asking "Mummy, is everything all right?"

Josephine turned slowly to Patricia, looking wild and untamed. "I will not be brought down by your fucking mistake, do you hear me?" hissed Josephine through gritted teeth to Patricia, who started to cry, nodding her head.

"Yes. Yes. I'm sorry. I'm so sorry."

"He did this. He did all of this. Michael has connections. He brought the press to our door." Josephine's mind raced. She breathed heavily.

"But he wouldn't have known about any of this," Patricia trembled.

"Quiet!" ordered Josephine.

"I want everything to come through me. Is that understood?" Edward said into his phone whilst he sat inside his car on the driveway of his home. "The Head Teacher who gave this the go-ahead. She'll be checked out too, am I right? I want reports of all the monitoring activity. What her husband does for a living. Is he in debt. Where her kids go to university and all the pubs they go to. I want pictures and video. Is that understood?" his voice was highly authoritative. A man concerned, yet in control.

"You poor boy," said Catherine Riverdale.

She looked at Michael as she and Paul sat with him around her classroom table, clutching another cup of tea.

"This place has gone to pot," Paul sighed, as Helen entered the room. Her face said it all. Her eyes were glassy as she just stood there, looking at Michael, who got to his feet and the two embraced one another.

194

Helen hugged him tight, like a work mother. She adored him. She once expressed to another colleague a few years back that Michael would be the ideal son in-law for her. Helen held his arms and stepped back to look at him.

"I've just found out. I'm sorry. This would never have occurred if-"

"I know. You don't have to say," interrupted Michael.

She leaned close to hug him again, disguising that she was in fact whispering into his ear. "Work-related stress. Get signed off for two weeks."

The two of them locked eyes.

He nodded his head, understanding what she had told him, taking it in. "Thank you."

Michael entered an empty classroom elsewhere within the school. He dialed his father's mobile phone number.

"It's disgraceful, Michael. This woman, this head, should be reported. She can't go around sanctioning things like this. The bad thing is, Mikey, is that the boy, the Afghan lad, he'll have a link to terrorism whenever he's asked his name by police and they do a check on him."

"You're joking? No way! That's awful," Michael exclaimed.

"Yeah. His name will flag up and the officer who checks him will have to call his superior and then they'll inform him or her on what's what. Bad eh?" stated his father.

"Really bad. Listen, I've got to go now. I'll call you later on," Michael said, hanging up the call.

Sinatra and Abdul walked upon the pavement, outside the school.

Sinatra offered a bag of Haribo jelly snake sweets to Abdul, forming some kind of bond with him in doing so.

Abdul delved his hand into the bag and pulled a green and yellow snake, holding it up to his face.

"A snake! Mike the snake. Look, sir. Look," he said, suddenly widening his eyes and biting the head off the jelly snake. He chewed it ferociously, showing his yellowing teeth to Sinatra as he did so.

Sinatra laughed, but it was put on. However, the fake chuckle was soon masked by Sinatra's attention being pulled elsewhere, beyond the chain-link fencing to the school car park.

"Look. It's his car, man. It's the snake's car," he said, as he pointed at Michael's Golf that was parked in the car park, shadowed by a tree and an out-building of some kind.

"It is the car of the snake? Really?" said Abdul, still continuing to chew on the jelly candy.

"Yeah, man. Come wiv me, yeah. Abdul, come on, man." Sinatra led Abdul through a break in the fencing and into the car park. Sinatra looked around as they made their way to Michael's vehicle.

They were instantly blocked from any security camera view because, unfortunately for Michael, he hadn't managed to get his usual parking space today as for some reason the car park was quite full.

"What you do to the car?" Abdul asked, smiling.

"I don't know. I wanna do somefin, yeah?"

"You want to break car?" asked Abdul, as he rounded the car and crouched down beside the right side rear wheel.

"Where you goin', Abdul, man?" Sinatra whispered, shuffling low, holding his jeans with one hand as he stooped round to where Abdul was.

He was kneeling beside the tyre and had unscrewed the tiny black cap to the valve. He skimmed the palm of his hand across the rough ground and located a small stone. More like a piece of gravel really. He put it inside the cap, then found another and did the very same thing.

"What you doin', Abdul?" asked Sinatra as Abdul replaced the cap, pushing the stone into the valve and releasing air from the tyre as he screwed it back.

"We will see him drive and psshh! Over the hills? The hills, in the road?" struggled Abdul, excitedly.

"Hills? What hills, what the fuck are you talking about?"

"The hills that make the car slow and then the car drive and then the car hits the hill and goes slow."

"Oh, speed humps. Yeah, so what?"

"Yes, speed... hump? Yes. He drive. The snake. He drive his car over the hills, the humps, and each time hump, pssh, air goes from wheel, yes? You understand?" explained Abdul, trying his hardest to tell Sinatra that whenever Michael drove his car over a speed hump, more air would squish out from within the tyre. He was adamant about the fact and was acting as if he had tried and tested that action before. Perhaps he was a rogue back in Afghanistan. Maybe it was what all the kids did back there.

Michael had thrown buds at windows. He had even played Knock Down Ginger by ringing on a doorbell and running away. Children from the dawn of time had played a prank of some sort on an adult.

Was Abdul the same? Could he just be playing?

Those particular boys, despite their curled, smiling mouths, whisked up by a frenzied adrenaline rush, did, however, feel angry. They were angry with Michael. That was the difference. That was what set the action apart from the prank category. The action was meant to cause angst, distress, unnecessary chaos and possible harm.

"So he could have a flat tyre?"

"Flat tyre, yes. Yes, flat tyre, pssh," Abdul panted. He straightened, but lowered his head, concerned he could be seen over the car roof or through the window. Not that there was anybody around.

"Let's bounce, man. Let's go," Sinatra said, tugging Abdul's shirt.

"Yes, let's see the snake on the hill humps. Joking, yes?"

"Jokes, man, jokes."

Michael sat with a child. A thirteen-year-old girl called Majestic.

She was white, with a huge amount of wild hair that twisted out, round and upon her head, this way and that, with a fringe that had been hair-sprayed to her forehead. She had a necklace that dangled down her turquoise hooded top, a top that had 'Go Deep Go Hard' printed on it in neon pink. The necklace glistened her name, 'Majestic'. She toyed with a Blackberry phone that pinged every few seconds as they sat at a desk in a classroom.

Michael sighed and looked up at a clock. It was half past two in the afternoon and it was a rarity that Majestic was there at all, let alone at that time.

Some pupils were taught in an afternoon as they couldn't cope with mornings, however even then they didn't take part in much either.

"Sir, yeah? I'm not gonna do any bloody stupid work, so you can make an aeroplane out of it or somethin' cos I'm not doing it," Majestic sighed.

"Is that what you wanted to say, Majestic?" Michael said, frowning at her.

"No, but I saw you had some work looking shit in front of yooz, so thought I'd say something," she said in her squeaky tone.

"You did write an interesting story the other day, Majestic. Did you not want to type the rest of that up?"

"No. Anyway, Miss sent that fucking story to my dad and he grounded me cos of what I wrote in it. It was my story. If I wanted my dad to read it then I woulda given him a copy of it. Sending it to my dad. Oh my days, I can't believe it!" she said, giggling strangely, covering her mouth.

"Well, the story was really graphic, Majestic, so I think that's probably why Miss told your dad about it," Michael explained.

"No, she didn't! She didn't tell him about it, she just fucking sent it and said, like, 'this is Majestic's story which made us feel concerned' or some shit like that. I mean, it's English, it's what the lesson is all about, making up fucking stories."

"Choose different language please. Try not to swear so much."

"Well, she fucking makes me swear. Sorry but she does. Interfering bitch," Majestic said, giggling and covering her mouth as she did so once more. She was very conscious about her lower teeth as they weren't straight at all and one in particular was chipped. She was an attractive little girl, but far too young to have experienced the type of things she had seen. "Anyway, I dunno what was so crazy about it. Miss got a yellow highlight pen and marked some of the words and shit. I think she's the crazy one. Maybe she's a lesbian. Do you think she could be, sir? Here, look, I got my story, look," Majestic said, tapping a few keys on a laptop in front of her.

"No, it's OK, Majestic, I've read it." Michael really didn't want to hear any of it, but it was too late.

"Look yeah. Dis is the highlighted shit in my story that Miss was so worried about. 'I went to a shubz and met bare buff boys from Turnham. They all had fizzies and showed me dem. A few minutes later they took me inside the house and put their cocks in my mouth and one jizzed on my head which really pissed me off cos it took me like free hours to get my hair ready and shit. One boy slapped me in the face and pulled my jeggings down-'"

"Majestic, I don't want to hear anymore," interrupted Michael.

Majestic continued, despite Michael's effort to interrupt. "'I was being abused but I secretly liked it as well. Den one boy found my bandanna and figured out I was from Deptford gang and slapped me again, so I ran out. They could see my pussy though but I didn't care cos I just wanted to get back on tha bus and get fucking out of there. I fucking hate Turnham.'"

"Majestic. That's enough, please. I said I've read it."

"Oh my God, it's just a fucking story. I didn't fink you should be worried about it," she giggled.

"It just sounds a little bit too real, Majestic."

"Don't people say 'write what you know about' or shit like that?" Majestic replied, tilting her head. She was serious and somewhat confused.

"So what were you going to say?"

"Oh yeah. Do you believe in ghosts? I do. In my room, the candle flickers and it's den dat I know I have to sing, so I sing my ghost song to make da ghosts let me sleep. I fink I first found out about da ghosts when I was in primary school and it was den dat I first went a bit off the rails and started getting into trouble," she explained, trying her best, in her matter of fact way, to explain the reasons behind her odd behaviour.

It was actually when an elderly uncle of hers died a few years back that Majestic started to go off the rails. Why her previous schools or social worker hadn't picked up her over-sexualised behaviour and language was beyond anyone's guess.

Michael had figured that the elderly uncle must had been abusing Majestic.

Even Majestic's father had said to Michael that, "Majestic started going mental when her uncle died. She weren't the same."

A primary school teacher reported in her file that Majestic was far too sexualised for her age, at that time eight years old, asking female teachers, "When you touch your fanny, does it feel good?" The response from

Majestic's mother was, "All little girls say things like that. What the fuck is wrong with you teachers? Don't you have kids of your own?"

Michael decided he would contact the member of staff who dealt with the procedure for Child Protection.

"Shit, it's well late, I'm gonna go. See you tomorrow, sir," Majestic said, getting up off her chair and speedily making for the door. She walked in her usual waddling manner and exited the room.

Michael exhaled and shook his head.

"Man, what a mess," he murmured to himself, as he scooped up some paperwork and closed down the laptop.

It was a quarter to four and Michael inserted his car key into the ignition and started up the engine. He pulled on his seatbelt, shoved the vehicle into gear at the same time and gently rolled out of the school car park and onto the street. After a few turns here and there, Michael found himself on the very road that Abdul had mentioned. The one with the hill humps. Speed humps to everyone else.

The car rolled up and over one and down with a thud. The heavy vehicle's bulk came down hard on its rear tyres and pressed its weight on them. It wasn't long until the car approached another hump as Michael ascended the steep road and, once again, the car slammed down. Twice more.

Michael could have driven much, much slower, at a snail's pace, but that would have held up the cars following close behind him, and the bottom line really was that he just wanted to get home and out of the area.

Slam! The car bounced down hard off the hump and indeed, as predicted by Abdul, the right hand rear tyre was becoming flatter with every concrete hump he passed over.

As Michael reached the top of the road and turned onto Winn Common Road, he began to notice that something didn't seem right with the car. He frowned and turned down his stereo, catching sight of the silver gaffer tape on the passenger seat. He scrolled his window down to listen as he drove slower. He passed through the width restriction in the road. Highly concerned, he didn't even notice Abdul and Sinatra standing on the grass at the top of the street as he drove pass them. He pulled his car over across the road into the layby area, switched off the ignition, unbuckled his belt, flicked the locks up and exited the car. He bent down to the right-hand rear tyre and saw that it was considerably flat. Frowning, he inspected the cap and unscrewed it. It practically came off as soon as his finger and thumb touched it, and when it did, the tiny gravel like stones dropped to the ground. Michael's eyes danced and diverted to the stones and then looked at the plastic cap to the valve.

"Muthas. They let my tyre down. Chav fuckers," he muttered, sighing as he figured out what to do. He sighed again and pressed his fingers against the side of the tyre, seeing exactly how flat it was, wondering if he could continue and drive the vehicle all the way home, without any trouble. He decided against doing so as it would probably damage the wheel.

"Dammit," he said, straightening to stand. He pulled his iPhone and saw the time was ten to four. He scrolled to his favourites to locate 'Bex'. He pressed her name and brought the phone to his ear, sighing. He rolled his tongue around inside his mouth, filling out his cheeks and gums, thinking as he looked at the deflated tyre and awaited Rebecca to pick up.

The ringing went straight to her voicemail.

"Hi, you've reached Rebecca Samson. If you'd like to leave your name, number and message, I'll get back to you as soon as I can. Thank you." Beep.

"Hey baby, it's me. Just calling to say I was on my way home from work but I've got a flat tyre. I found a few tiny stones in the valve cap. It's bound to be a pupil at work or something..."

HOOT! A car horn sounded, passing Michael's car, which caused him to stop speaking.

"Yo, hang up da phone. Do it, man," came a voice.

Frowning, Michael's tone changed as he turned again and completed his message.

"Yeah, I'll hopefully not be too late, my love. If I can't manage to change the wheel, I think there's a garage down the road from work or near this common. Speak later. Love-"

"I said, put da phone down!" said the voice again, more aggressively.

The phone was smacked out of Michael's hand and hit the ground.

13. RESOURCEFUL

Rebecca sat on the sofa, in the flat she shared in Luxor Street with her boyfriend, Michael. Her knees were nestled up close to her chest and her two phones were tight in her grasp: her work iPhone and her personal Samsung. Her MacBook Pro was open and split with her Hotmail and her work Outlook Express setup. Her mascara was smeared slightly from her eyes down her cheeks. She had been crying and she was still sniffing. Her thumb scrolled to the name 'Mikey' on her iPhone and she brought the phone to her ear. It beeped and went straight to the automatic default voicemail.

"Hi, my love. It's gone seven, nearly eight and I'm wondering where you are. I've emailed you and can't get through to that or your phone. Just worried, that's all. I don't think you said you were going out tonight. Love you."

She hung up the call and lowered the phone. She wiped a fresh tear from her left cheek with the back of her hand.

She heard a car engine outside. Rebecca straightened and peeped out of the window to a see a dark-coloured Audi. She then noticed a dark blue transit van had pulled up behind the Audi. The windows of both vehicles were too dark to see anyone inside. She shrugged, disappointed by the view. She'd been hoping it was going to be Michael's silver VW Golf. She took her Samsung and scrolled through to another set of names.

A ring sounded out. It was quite loud and was instantly answered.

"Hello Bec, how are you!" came the familiar voice of Michael's father.

"I don't know really. I'm a bit concerned as Mike's not come home from work yet," replied Rebecca, holding back tears. Her hand was trembling.

"He hasn't? Blimey, he's late. OK, did he say he was going out at all?" asked Edward, calmly.

"No. He would have texted me or called or emailed. I know sometimes his phone signal dips in and out, but he'd always manage to get through to me if that ever happened. I'm - I'm worried that something's happened and I can't help thinking he's..." she blubbed, releasing a flood of tears, unable to fight them back any longer. She clutched a paper tissue and brought it to her nose, wiping it.

"It's OK, don't cry. I'm sure he's fine. Don't cry, Rebecca. When was the last time you spoke or had word from Mike?" Edward asked her.

"He - he called me when he was on his way home, saying he had a flat tyre," Rebecca answered, trying to compose herself.

"And what time was that, do you think? Do you remember?" Michael's father held the phone tight against his ear, entered his living room and sat at the wooden dining table. He flipped open an A4 notepad and reached for a ballpoint pen.

Michael's mother, Violet, looked up from the leather Chesterfield sofa, concerned.

"What's wrong? Are they OK? Tell me they haven't broken up!" she said, frantically, receiving a wave of Edward's hand, signaling her to be quiet as he made a face at her, mouthing the words, "No, shut up."

"Mike called me at three forty-nine this afternoon," Rebecca sniffled.

'15:49 - called Rebecca Samson (live-in girlfriend),' Edward jotted down fast upon the notepad. "What time does he leave work?" he asked.

"Sometimes he can get away at half three, but I think his normal time to finish is three forty-five," Rebecca said.

'15:45 - leaves work (Plumstead),' Edward wrote. "That's right, I remember now. So, did he say to you where he was when he called to tell you about the tyre?"

"He left a message on my phone, so I - I didn't get to speak with him." Rebecca started to sob again, breathing with quick jerky breaths, almost hiccup-like.

"Rebecca, it's OK. You're OK, Rebecca. You're calm, you're doing fine," Edward said to her down the line as Violet got up from the sofa, rounded the dining table and, pulling out a chair from underneath, sat next to her husband.

She eyed the notes written on the pad and wondered what was going on.

"He - Mike said he was going to go to a garage near a common where he was at. I don't know - I..."

"Do you still have the message on your phone?" Edward asked coolly.

"Yes. It's saved. I have it," Rebecca answered.

"Good. Now, did you hear anything else in the background of the message at all, Rebecca? An unusual sound, another person's voice, traffic noises?"

"I - I heard a car beeping and I think someone else's voice, but it was quite faint. I - I don't know." She felt as though she had failed with her not knowing. Rebecca really disliked failure. Sure, nobody does, but her especially. She was a winner, whether at work or playing a board game. She did her best and her best was to win and succeed.

"That's fine. Thank you. You're doing great, Rebecca. You're really good. Now, keep your phone charged and what I'll do, I'll make a few calls and Violet or myself will call you in a short while, all right?"

"Yes," Rebecca said, composing herself once more.

"Do you have any wine at home?" Edward asked.

"Erm, yes, yes. Half a bottle, surprisingly," she replied, caught slightly off-guard.

"Haha, well, you get yourself a glass, make sure your phone isn't on silent mode and plug the charger in now if it's nearby. Is the charger near you?" Edward asked her.

Rebecca turned her attention to the iPhone charging lead which rested on the arm of the sofa and pulled it to her iPhone. She inserted it into the bottom of the phone.

Bleep. The iPhone began to charge.

"Yes. It's charging now," Rebecca informed Edward, Michael's patient, caring and highly professional father.

"Great. OK, don't leave the house, make sure you eat and don't answer the door to anyone," Edward softly commanded.

"OK."

"Speak to you later, Rebecca. Don't worry. Love to you. Love to you. Bye."

"Bye," she replied, laying her charging phone on the arm of the sofa. She sniffed and wiped her eyes and nose.

Edward placed his Nokia mobile phone on the wooden dining table, next to the notepad and jotted down another piece of information.

'Sounds on message: 1) Car horn. 2) Person(s).'

"What's happening, Ed?" Violet asked.

"Hold on, wait a minute," Edward replied as he continued to write further notes. 'Flat tyre: near a Common? May go to a garage nearby.'

"Right. Rebecca said that Mike's not arrived home yet. She's very upset and concerned."

"Well, of course. He should be home by now," Violet stated, looking at and reading Edward's notes.

"Don't use the phone and if anyone calls, can you be quick to let them go, please?" Edward requested.

"Of course. Of course. What are you going to do?"

"I'll give Geoff a call first and then I'll pop down to Simon's."

"Don't you think you should call Carolyn?" Violet said.

"Oh no! Not yet. I don't think it'll get to that. Goodness me! First things first, Vi. That's the last thing to do. Crikey," he blurted.

"Oh, sorry. I just-" Violet humbly replied.

"It's all right," he said, retrieving his pad and mobile phone.

He stood up and passed his wife, who suddenly began to sob. Edward turned and lowered himself to put an arm around her, kissing her cheek. "Hey, it'll be all right. Make some ginger tea, eh?" he said, comforting his nearest and dearest. His most cherished for nearing forty years.

She nodded her head. "I can't help it. He's-"

"Sshh. It's all right. I'm going to phone Geoff in the other room," Edward finished and headed off.

"Edward! How are things?" answered Geoff. The tall, large-framed white man was slumped in a leather armchair in his living room, with a laptop on his big, bare thighs and his legs stretched out. He rested on the extended foot and leg rest that flipped out from the base of the chair. Geoff was in his late fifties

205

and was wearing shorts and a West Ham football shirt. His mobile phone was in one hand. He muted the television.

"'Allo Geoffrey. Hope I'm not disturbing you," responded Edward, on the end of the line.

"Of course you are, Edward. You interrupted my surfing the net for hot babes and watching mindless Jason Statham films. Course not, what's up?" Geoff quirkily replied.

"Right, I just had a call from a very upset young lady."

"Blimey, what have you been up to?" Geoff joked.

"The young lady is our Mike's girlfriend, Rebecca," Edward explained.

"Right. Go on." Geoff took on a more serious tone.

"Mike's not arrived home yet and it's just gone eight o'clock."

"What time does he usually get home each day?" Geoff asked.

"A little before five."

"Let's say five, then. And when does the youngster leave work in darkest Plumstead?" Geoff inquired.

"Quarter to four," Edward said. "He called his girlfriend four minutes after leaving work saying he had a flat tyre. Said he was near a Common. What would that be Woolwich or Plumstead Common, Geoff?" Edward asked, his own voice now expressing slight concern.

"Mm, left his work at three forty-five, made a call at three forty-nine - four minute drive, taking into account traffic - more likely Plumstead Common, Winn Common, around there," calculated Geoff.

"Yeah, I thought so, too."

"Give me Michael's car reg and leave it with me," Geoff commanded Edward, who reeled off the details and then ended the call.

It was at four twenty-one that afternoon when a uniformed police patrol vehicle drove down Winn Common Road, the very road where Michael had discovered his flat tyre. The police vehicle swirled its blue lights as it pulled into the layby and in front of Michael's parked car.

Three white children, from ten to thirteen years of age, ran across part of the Common, heading for some residential flats as the two male police officers exited their car and walked towards Michael's VW Golf.

Two other kids were inside the car with the passenger door and driver's door wide open. The kids looked up to see the officers approaching.

One was a teenage girl, fifteen, mixed race, full make-up. She sat on the back seat, resting her elbows on the headrests of the driver and passenger seats. She widened her eyes, as did the white boy of seventeen trying to remove the car stereo with a screwdriver and making a real mess of the dashboard.

"Are you the owner of this car, mate?" asked the officer, standing by the driver's side, on the paved area.

"Nah, it's my mate's, init," scowled the young man, sighing, yet he continued to do his best to pull the radio out.

"What's your mate's name then?" asked the police officer.

"What? Oh, I dunno his real name, init."

"Do you want to describe him for me?" the officer asked.

"What?"

"I knew we'd get busted by Feds," the girl complained.

"Shut up, man!" the young man snapped.

"Your mate who owns the car. What does he look like?" asked the officer, patiently but firmly.

"He's er - tall. Like a man. He's hench. Black, yeah."

"What's hench?" asked the officer, which caused the girl to giggle, immaturely.

The young man smirked. "Hench. You know, big init. Shit, man," he said as he tossed the screwdriver to the floor of the passenger side and looked at the officer. He then glanced through the windscreen at the other policeman in front of the car.

He was speaking into his radio. "Do you want to step outside the car, please? And you, love. Come on," the officer commanded.

"I have a registration to a silver Volkswagen Golf," said the second officer, speaking into his radio, eyeing the number plate of Michael's car.

The young man clambered out of the car, along with the girl who clambered through the centre between the driver and passenger seats instead of flipping the seat forward and getting out that way, the normal way. They straightened, annoyed they were interrupted, especially by coppers.

"Look, the car door was open, yeah. Nobody was around yeah, like for ages, yeah, so I took my opportunity init."

"What's your name?"

"Hello Geoffrey. What's the update?" asked Edward, sitting in an office-type room that housed a desk and a standalone PC with a landline telephone.

"At 16:23 two uniforms called in a check on a plate which came back as Michael's car," Geoff informed him from his comfortable, reclining armchair, reading from his own A5 notepad.

"OK. Go on."

"His car was on Winn Common Road, in a layby and was having its stereo removed by a couple of teenagers. They've put a 'Police Aware' notice on the windscreen of the car."

"Right. Any report of Mike?"

"Hold on, I'm not finished with the car yet," Geoff replied.

It was 18:07 and the grass of Winn Common was being churned up by dirty swirling circles from tyre tread marks from a silver-coloured Volkswagen Golf. It slid this way and that. It was Michael's car and the driver was a spotty, white, sickly-looking fifteen-year-old boy, tracksuit clad and with three equally pasty-faced youths inside. He crunched the clutch dreadfully, shifting through the gears awfully as he drove the car over the grass and towards a mass of bushes.

"Shit!"

"Ah man!"

The youth struggled to control the vehicle and tried to steer. He grappled the wheel as if he had caught a Great White shark with a regular fishing rod on the back of a tiny rowing boat.

The car slammed into the undergrowth and suddenly sank into the ground, due to the dip on the bomb-crater-like part of the Common.

The youths jerked forward and winced with pain.

The driver's head whipped forward and his forehead made contact with the steering column. The rear passengers were flung into the front seats and headrests.

Their shoulders smacked one side, really hard.

The front passenger, bizarrely, was the only one with a seatbelt on, which locked the moment the front of the car hit the low level ground that forced it to a sudden stop.

It was 18:26 and the bright blue lights of a fire engine swirled around fast, accompanying its siren, as it headed down Winn Common Road to where a silver Volkswagen Golf burned amongst the mass of bushes in the large dip of the Common. It was Michael's car and it was on fire: a fire that burned ferociously.

The fire spread to the petrol tank.

BOOM!

The silver Volkswagen Golf exploded into a ball of flame and continued to burn as the fire engine closed in.

"It was at 18:18 when a sixty-one-year-old Tibetan woman telephoned for a fire engine to put out a burning car. Once the fire had been put out, the reg came back as Michael's," continued Geoff, speaking on the telephone to Edward, who was nodding as he sat at the desk in the office-type room.

"Still no sign of Michael?" asked Edward.

"No. It is possible that he went to a garage and when he came back, the car was being broken into. I mean, it's wise not to get involved with kids round there," Geoff posited, trying to come up with a plausible scenario.

"Yeah, but the police station is just down the road from where he left the car. He would have gone inside and mentioned his police connections. Any report of that at all?"

"Nothing, Edward, no. Listen, I'll put a call out and description and have it attached to the pick-up of the yobs who the uniforms took in earlier on, as well as the car fire call. It's likely your boy's phone battery has died and he's on the bus home," Geoff said, in a comforting manner.

"Maybe, Geoffrey, but Mike would get a taxi or get in touch with me. OK, I'll wait for you to call if you hear anything more and I'll give his girlfriend a ring to see if she's heard from him. Thanks Geoff."

"No problem. Keep me posted, Edward."

"Will do. Cheerio, Geoffrey," Edward hung up the landline phone. He sighed and closed his eyes briefly, tightening his mouth, thinking, biting his lower lip as he stared into space. He turned to the door to see a worried-faced Violet in the doorway.

"Where is he?"

"I'm going to call Rebecca to see if he's home," Edward announced, taking up his mobile phone again. However, it buzzed in his hand, signaling the name. "Geoff?"

"Just been told that the chav kid who was trying to nick your boy's car stereo is still in custody," said Geoff on the other line.

"Oh right," replied Edward.

"D'you want me to put a word in to keep him overnight?"

"Oh, yes please."

"Will do. Bye Edward," Geoff said, hanging up the phone.

"Nothing too important. I'll tell you in a minute," Edward told Violet as he pressed a button on the phone for Rebecca's number. It didn't even ring twice before she answered.

"Hello?"

"Hello Becky?"

"Yes, Ed, it's me. It's me. Hello," she said, with keen anticipation for news of her boyfriend. Her love.

"Is Mike home?"

"No. No he's not. Oh, oh, no, he-" her voice quivered.

"It's OK. Hold on. We'll get him back to you, d'you understand, Rebecca?" Edward said, with positive passion.

"It's nine o'clock at night. He would have told me if he was going out or was stuck somewhere!"

"I know. I know, and I'm sure there's a very simple explanation as to why he's not turned up yet. Now, do you want us to come round and be with you or did you want to come here and stay?"

"I - I have to be at work. I have to go to Bath tomorrow to see a client. I can't be late for the train. What if he's not back? What do I do?" Rebecca asked, worrying that Michael's absence would interfere with her work.

"Rebecca, you continue going to work and living your day to day life, do you hear? Like you said, it's nine o'clock. We'll play it by ear and if he's not back tonight, I'll get in touch with some people I know, OK?" Edward said, firmly, keeping Rebecca focused.

"Yes. Yes, OK," she sniffed.

"Now, did you get that glass of wine?" Edward asked her in a different, more relaxed tone, but still playing the role of a good cop. It caused Rebecca to form a slight smile.

"Yes. Yes I did," she said, eyeing an opened bottle of Piccini, a Tuscan Chianti Reserva and the filled glass of red.

"Right. Well, you watch something relaxing on TV and any news that I receive, I'll give you a call. Text us if Mike arrives home."

"I will. Thank you, Ed. Thank you."

"Speak soon. Love to you, Rebecca."

"And to you. Bye."

Rebecca reached for her glass of wine. Her eyes became more and more glassy as her quivering lips touched the rim of the glass to take a sip of the Chianti. She swallowed and clutched the glass, staring blankly ahead into nothingness. She began to rock her body back and forth.

"Please be all right, my love. Please be all right. I love you so much. Please be all right."

The front door to Edward and Violet's neighbour's house opened and Simon found Edward standing on the doorstep outside.

"'Allo Ed, what's up?" asked Simon.

"Sorry it's late, but I wondered if you could get in touch with your gang unit," Edward asked politely.

"What's that? Erm - why?" frowned Simon, stepping outside and pulling his door to.

"My son, you know, Mike, hasn't returned home after his day at work. I've been in touch with the local Met and his car's been found abandoned. Some joyriders burned it out. It's all on the PNC," Edward said.

"Right. So, what can - what can I do?"

"Your gang unit patrols the area where Mike was last and where his car currently is. It's on Winn Common, in Plumstead. I was thinking if your boys could make a few inquiries, speak to their snouts, they might unearth something new," Edward said, in a rehearsed manner, bordering on the desperate.

Simon sensed the urgency and nodded his head, understanding Edward's thinly disguised angst. "I'll give them a call. I got the envelope by the way and passed it on. What's the make of the car?"

"Thanks for that. A VW Golf. Silver."

"And where was it last?"

"Winn Common. Where he left it. Where it was also found on fire."

"OK."

"He called his girlfriend at ten to four this afternoon to tell her he had a flat tyre," Edward briefed him.

"Ten to four. OK."

"His phone's no longer ringing and that was the last we've heard."

"Local garage, tyre fitter or something like that?" asked Simon, fixing his look constantly on Edward.

"No. I called all the ones in Plumstead and Woolwich, and the ones that border Welling and Erith, asking if anyone of Mike's description had come in regarding a flat tyre. No reports at all," Edward shrugged.

"OK and what - what was the name of his code? What's the listed name that Mike goes under as an informant?"

"Jacob Ramsay," answered Edward.

It was midnight and Rebecca was in her pink pyjamas and a black vest, lying on the sofa with a thin, grey airline blanket loosely draped over her. She was lightly sleeping, with her glasses on her chest and her hands still gripping her phones. It was dark in the living room and the only light that was being cast was from the glow of her MacBook on the coffee table.

Her Samsung mobile phone rang, making her jolt and widen her eyes, forming the briefest of smiles of joy which disappeared in similar split second time when she saw that it was Michael's mum and dad on the display.

"Hello?" she answered, wearily.

"Hello Rebecca. It's Ed. I'm not waking you, am I?"

"I was just on the sofa. Have you heard anything?"

"I was calling to ask if Mike's returned home yet," asked Michael's father, quietly.

"Oh. No, no, not yet. I don't know what to do." She had cried herself out of tears and simply shook on the sofa. Her body shivered and trembled as if she had just been plucked from an icy lake.

"It's all right. We'll find him. You go to bed. Get some rest for work tomorrow and if either of us hear anything new, then we'll contact one another, does that sound all right?"

"Yes," Rebecca whispered.

"Remember, don't answer the door to anybody unless it's Mike and you know it's his voice."

"I won't," she promised, obeying Edward's comforting voice on the other end of the line.

"I'll speak to you tomorrow. Night Bec. Night. Love to you."

"Night," she said softly, as the line went dead, with Rebecca trembling further. Her lips quivered and suddenly she found more tears. They streamed from her eyes and down her cheeks as she wailed. She sat up and rocked herself in the dim light of the room. "Where are you, baby? Where are you? Please come home. Please. Please. I love you. I love you so much. Don't leave me. Please come home," she sobbed.

Edward's eyes were glassy. Sitting at his desk in a white towelling dressing gown, he pondered his next move and put his gold-rimmed glasses on. He unscrewed the cap to a bottle of still Evian water and swigged a mouthful, gulping it down before wiping his mouth with the back of his hand. He pressed the tip of his forefinger to the corner of his eye, sliding away some sleep that had built up within. He yawned and turned around to see Violet, also in a white towelling dressing gown, holding a fluffy pink hot water bottle against her stomach.

"Has he come home yet?" she asked, with a pained expression.

"No," he answered softly.

"Have you heard back from Simon?"

"No. He's quite unreliable really. How he's a DCI I just don't know," Edward digressed.

"Yes, I know. As you always say, Ed. So, what are we going to do? I want to know where my son is!" she said, raising her voice.

"Do you think I don't? Bloody hell, Violet! Goodness me."

"All right, Edward!"

"Crikey, I'm doing all I can."

"No you're not. No, you are not."

"Oh Violet, please. I have to go through the correct channels first," he explained, calmly.

"Like you always do - tip toe, tip toe, ever so softly," Violet said, criticising her husband.

"Oh don't. Please."

"Oh, I was just wondering if you knew where my son was. Doesn't matter if you can't find him. It's all right," she said, mimicking him and suddenly letting loose her tears.

"Violet, it will be all right," Edward said, reassuring her.

"I can't help it. He's such a good son. He's just like you, always helping people and never taking from anybody. Always putting himself last all the time. Where the bloody hell is he?" Violet sobbed, turning to walk away, but stepping back to continue. "And that poor girl. Is Rebecca OK on her own? I don't like her being on her own and worrying all night. That dear, dear, sweet girl. Oh God," she cried and turned away.

Edward pulled on a pair of jeans and then a pair of thick black socks. He buckled a brown leather belt around his waist. He removed his dressing gown and retrieved a dark green polo shirt from the back of the chair, which he put on. He stepped out of the room and grabbed a dark blue fleece from a hook in the hall and entered the kitchen to see Violet sitting in a chair in the corner, clutching a mug of boiling water with a slice of lemon floating in it.

She looked up at him as he put on a pair of brown leather shoes.

"I'm going to where Mike's car is in Plumstead."

"Not on your own, you're not," she commanded.

"Oh I'll be all right!" he snapped back, lovingly.

"Come here and let me tie your laces."

"I can't get down there. Thank you," he said in a different, much more gentle, child-like manner, shuffling a couple of steps to her.

Violet tied the lace to one shoe.

"Give Jason a call. He'll go with you," she said, tying the other lace.

"I'm not waking him up now. I'll be fine."

"He'll want to go with you. You call him and meet him there," she instructed, letting him straighten his legs and sigh.

"Right. I'll give him a call," Edward agreed, stretching out his hand, clutching his mobile phone and scrolling to a name that read "AAJASON'.

A Blackberry phone vibrated on the dashboard of a black Suzuki Vitara jeep. The vehicle pulled to the curb of a residential street.

A male hand shifted the gears into neutral, pulled the handbrake up and took the call.

"'Allo Dad, what's up?" boomed a deep sounding voice. It belonged to a very tall, tanned, dark-haired, handsome man behind the wheel. His name was Jason Thompson and he was Michael's middle brother. He was forty-two years old and always used to play with Michael when they were younger. He once shared a room with his brother and was always there for him, like he was at this particular time, when Edward told him briefly of the situation at hand.

"I'll be with you in five minutes," Jason said, as he shoved the vehicle into gear, released the handbrake and roared up the street into the night. Jason had once been a police officer himself, but was too young and immature to handle the responsibility, not to mention the decent wage. An incident embarrassed his father and Jason was due to be sacked, however Edward wangled it so Jason was able to resign before the damage set in too deep for those of a higher rank to realise. He'd have made a good copper now, though, probably a better spy than anything, but having spawned several young children over an equal amount of years, he had found himself in a more stable and less dangerous occupation.

The black Vitara jeep rolled onto Edward and Violet's driveway and to a halt, under a tree. It caused security lights to flare up which illuminated Jason inside.

He exited the car to be met by Edward.

"You all right?" Edward said, hugging his tall son.

"Yeah, cool. How's Mum?" he asked.

"Oh, you know. Worried."

"Of course. Shall we go in yours then?" Jason said.

"Yeah, OK," replied Edward, leading the way to his own car, another Suzuki jeep, but a dark metallic grey.

"Where do you think he is then?" Jason asked his dad, buckling his belt and adjusting the seat back as far as it would go as his father drove.

"I don't know," Edward muttered.

"If it's those bloody kids he works with... I keep telling him to get shot of that job. What's he do there anyway?" moaned Jason.

"The children tell him their problems. All sorts of stuff."

"Why Greenwich? It's nuts. It's not like it was when we were growing up round there." Jason reminisced of youth long gone.

"Oh, I know. Mike's told us all about it. I don't like him doing it either," Edward stated, as he continued to drive, heading through the streets of Crayford, a town not too far from them.

Violet sat at the desk in the office-type spare bedroom. The landline handset was in the grasp of one hand and a crumpled Kleenex was in the other, moistened slightly by tears she had previously cried.

"Hello Carolyn, it's Violet. I'm sorry to be calling you at such a late hour, but I just didn't know what else to do. I'm so sorry. It's Michael. Mike. He hasn't returned home from work to his girlfriend and she's terribly worried. We all are. Edward's been in touch with some of his police contacts and - and - and they informed him that Michael's car was found, broken into and then set on fire." She couldn't contain her emotion and began to cry. She tried to compose herself quickly. She coughed and straightened. "I'm sorry, Carolyn. I'm sorry. I know. I know. It is completely out of character, otherwise I wouldn't call to ask if you're able to check anything at work. Is it possible? We hate putting on anybody - well, you know we don't, but I don't know what else to do. Is it possible, do you think?" continued Violet, in a desperate, pleading tone. "His mobile phone number? Michael's? Yes, just a moment. I have it here," she said, reaching to the side of the desk to locate a piece of grey cardboard with rows of names and telephone numbers written on both sides of it. Neighbours. Family. Emergency numbers. Gas. Electricity. Water. Violet flipped the board round and found Michael's name and his mobile number. His girlfriend, Rebecca Samson, was listed underneath. "I have it. Oh, our mobile, too? And his girlfriend's? OK, I have them, Carolyn. Are you ready?"

Edward and Jason turned into Winn Common Road, the last place where Michael was known to be.

Jason's eyes were everywhere as the car drove down the tree-lined, pitch-black street. Only a handful of streetlamps were visible and did a poor job in illuminating even the smallest of areas around them. Jason pointed at the windscreen, looking at something up ahead and to the left, in the darkness.

"Up there, Dad. Keep going and pull in," he instructed.

Edward pulled the car to the side of the road.

"Hold on a minute," Edward said, and retrieved a couple of mini Maglite torches from the glove box. He handed one to Jason.

"Inward or outward spirals? Parallel, grid or zone?" Jason questioned, with a smirk on his face, reeling off the five different searching techniques that a crime scene investigator might decide to take.

Edward managed a smile and a chuckle, patting his son on the shoulder. "Let's just see what the situation is first, son."

They both exited the jeep and twisted their torches on, shining a bright ring on the ground in front of them. Edward rounded the vehicle and went to the boot, which he opened.

Jason was already stepping on the grass and turned to see his father retrieve a fishing tackle box from the jeep. Jason aimed his light this way and that, like a farmer cutting crops with a scythe.

Edward accompanied Jason and directed his light ahead of him, picking up Michael's burnt-out VW Golf. His eyes glazed over and he tightened his mouth, saddened to see such a sight. He stopped and stared at it for several seconds.

The rear window was smashed. Three of the rubber tyres had melted.

The driver's window had been smashed, too. The passenger windows were blackened by fire. The windscreen was cracked. The driver's side mirror dangled. The ground and bushes around it were charred black and wet.

"Dad?" Jason said, breaking his father's gaze.

"Yep?" he answered, turning to see Jason holding up a reel of silver gaffer tape with his torch.

Edward frowned. "What's that? Electrical tape, something like that?"

"Yeah, and it's dirty. Take it with us?"

"Oh yeah," replied Edward, watching Jason literally take one lengthy stride to the pavement.

Jason dropped the tape near the jeep and stepped back onto the grass to shine his torch around further. "There's another set of tracks over there, Dad," he signaled to his father, gesturing for him to look further down the road, but still on the grass.

Edward shone his light to combine the two beams of his and Jason's torches. He squinted his eyes for a better look. He turned his head to the burnt-out vehicle amongst the bushes, shining his light to cast it downwards at the ground, searching for tread marks.

"Mike's car made this set of marks," Edward noted, as he followed a twisted path with his torch.

"So what's the other one? Fire engine?" Jason asked.

"No, the fire engine would have come from that direction. Erith station is just up there. Probably would have been them. What's the other one? East Greenwich? I don't know. Either way, a fire engine would have entered the way we came and driven across. There. That's their tread." Edward pointed, casting his beam at a set of dead straight tyre marks in the ground.

"And those?" Jason inquired, curiously, as he aimed his light further down ahead.

"They're not Mike's and nor do they belong to the fire engine," Edward stated, pulling his digital camera out of his fleece pocket.

"Do you want my light?" asked his son.

"Please," answered Edward, kneeling down and opening his fishing tackle box. He retrieved an L-shaped photomacrographic scale and placed it on the ground and on part of the tyre track. He held the camera vertically, in a portrait position, and waited for Jason to cast his beam down to the ground and then took a picture of the set of car tyre marks within the mud. He stepped to a more defined patch and crouched to snap another photo, with the scale in place.

"How do they look?" Jason asked, curious to see what his father had taken.

"Good enough," replied Edward, showing Jason the display. He nodded in approval at the clearly visible tyre markings.

Edward lowered his head and then received an arm around his shoulders from Jason, who patted him on the back.

"We'll find him and he'll be fine," Jason said.

"Yeah, I know. Here, press this in would you?" Edward asked, taking a polythene bag of some sort and handing it to Jason. "Do what it says on the bag."

The bag was a Crime-Cast, a plaster casting mixture.

Jason broke the small water bladder that was housed inside and gently shook and kneaded the dough-like mixture inside the bag. Meanwhile Edward unfolded an adjustable aluminum frame which he set over a hardened tyre mark.

"How's it doing?" asked Edward, looking up at Jason's peculiar expression as he inspected the squishy bag.

"Weird. What is it?" he asked, handing it down to his father, who sprayed the tyre track with a tiny spray.

"It's a casting mixture."

"And that?"

"Hair spray. Keeps any stones or loose stuff from moving around. Fixes it all in place," Edward told him, tearing open the bag and pouring the mixture over the hardened tyre track within the metal frame. He carefully squeezed it all out and scraped the mix across to each corner and side of the frame.

Jason watched his father keenly and curiously, wondering what else was in that box of tricks of his. "Where'd you get all this stuff?"

"The internet," Edward said, glancing up with a smirk.

"I thought you got it all from work."

"I'm retired," answered Edward.

"You never retire from a job like that," quipped Jason as Edward gently lifted up the plaster cast and took out a brush from his box, dusting off any dirt.

He squinted to look as he brushed away to reveal the tyre track in Jason's beam, cast by his torch.

"Cool." Jason was impressed by the indentation on the cast.

"Not bad, eh?"

"Shall we check the car then?" Jason said, stepping to the darkness with his light source leading the way.

Edward closed his box and followed him, putting the camera into his pocket and pulling out a VW car key.

"Will that fit?" asked Jason.

"Should do. It's Mike's spare key," replied Edward, unlocking the boot of the car and opening the lid.

"Why didn't he change the wheel?"

"Don't know. He's done it before, shrugged his father, thinking to himself, glancing around and then looking back inside the waterlogged boot. He shone his light inside. Nothing was unusual at all. Apart from a couple of damp Sainsbury's shopping bags, it was empty.

Jason lifted the cover to reveal the spare wheel. He exchanged a look with his father, whose lips were firmly pressed together, tight, angered, flustered, but still very much controlled.

Edward exhaled a deep breath and rounded the driver's side, shining his torch into the vehicle. It was a sad, sorry mess; a melted dashboard and steering column.

"Whadya think, Dad?" Jason asked, once again watching his experienced father open his CSI supply box and pull on a pair of nitrile gloves. They were blue, and were latex and powder free.

He poked his head inside the vehicle and his eyes scanned around the car. He looked to the door and then switched on his torch. He twisted it so that it ejected a UV light. Evidence couldn't hide from ultra violet light. It could pick up fingerprints, body fluids, fibres and even blood. Edward put on a pair of orange goggles and shone his UV beam into the car.

Jason shuddered. It was becoming cold, especially as he was standing still, watching his father in his element, doing whatever it was he seemed to do best. Detective work. Finding evidence. Doing what was needed to find people. People like Michael.

Edward narrowed his eyes as he shone the UV light over the inside of the driver's door. The light picked up some spatter around the door handle. Edward tightened his face, almost expressing pain and hurt. He took a bag of transparent sticks of some kind. It was a bag of Heme Stix, used for detecting blood. They consisted of two glass ampules inside a plastic tube. Edward took a cotton bud-like swab from his box and moistened it with a pipette filled with water. He rubbed a stain on the door handle with the swab and then removed the cap from the Heme-Stix vial, breaking the head of the swab into the vial.

"Is it blood?" asked Jason, watching his father again, exhaling his warm breath into the cold night air.

"Could be cherryade," quipped Edward, who then pressed his finger and thumb together against the lower part of the vial, breaking an inner glass ampule. This liquid was brown in colour and when broken allowed the swab to become wet. He then snapped the clear ampule that was attached to the cap and shook it well. A blue-green colour appeared.

"It's blood," said his father softly.

"Whose blood is it? Mike's? Is it Mike's blood?" Jason blurted. There was panic in his voice as he watched Edward put the vial into the box and then retrieve another swab.

Edward rubbed the swab under the inside door handle again, all around the plastic. He retrieved a white postcard-sized blood testing card and dripped water from his pipette onto each of the four circles printed on the top of the card. Each circle was labelled, the first with 'Anti-A', then 'Anti-B', followed by 'Anti-D' and 'Control'. There was a small chart underneath which allowed for information to be written in for the person's name and blood type, etc. Edward put the swab onto the first circle and then repeated the process with three more swabs, which he had rubbed from the door handle. The water and blood on each circle reacted with whatever solution was housed within the card itself. Edward tilted the card in different directions, thus allowing the blood to spread to the edges of the circles. It revealed a different pattern in each one. He put the card down flat on the floor of the car and then retrieved a laminated card, which depicted the various blood types. He held the laminate to the four circles of blood on the cards, squinting with his aimed torch to see more clearly. The circle labelled 'Anti-A' depicted a speckled, marbled pattern. The 'Anti-B' was a full block of red. 'Anti-D' was also speckled and the 'Control' circle was the same solid red as 'Anti-B'. Edward matched the blood he'd found to the illustrations on the laminate. He identified the blood type as A positive. A+. A rhesus positive.

"What is it?" asked Jason.

"It's A positive," answered Edward.

"Same as me," remarked Jason.

"Same as you, same as me and same as Michael," his father stated. He stood and placed the bloodied card inside a plastic evidence bag, along with the swabs, before zipping it up and putting it inside his box. He joined his son and retrieved the plaster cast of the tyre mark from the ground and the aluminum frame, which he folded and placed back inside the box.

"At three forty-nine, Mike called Rebecca and left a message on her phone. At four twenty-three this afternoon Mike's stereo was being pinched. Couple of coppers called it in. At six-eighteen, the car fire was reported. Now, from when he made the call at three forty-nine to when the coppers found the chav nicking the radio, we've got thirty-four minutes. Where was Mikey in that time?" questioned Edward not only to Jason, but also to himself, thinking hard. He removed his gloves and popped them into another evidence bag.

"What are the options?" asked Jason.

"Eh?"

"On what to do?"

"Well, the idiot who tried to take the radio is still in a cell down the road."

"They're still holding him?" Jason said, surprised.

"Yeah. Good ole Geoff, eh?" Edward said, faking a slight chuckle.

"Yeah," laughed Jason.

"We could pay him a visit."

"And then?"

"See what turns up from him. If it's nothing, then I'll pass the photos of the tyre marks to someone," Edward explained.

"Oh, and who's that?"

"D'you remember Carolyn?"

"Carolyn?"

"Carolyn Wright."

"Oh, the spook!" Jason quipped.

"Yes. MI-5 Carolyn."

"Mum's friend. Her daughter went to school with Mike?"

"That's right, yeah," replied Edward, turning and leading Jason away from the car.

On the pavement, Jason crouched down to tie his shoelace, placing his torch on the ground. It beamed along the pavement as he twisted the cotton lace into a bow. However, the torch started to roll away, making the light fade. It dropped over the side of the curb. Jason sighed and shuffled and reached down to the curb to pick up the torch, just as he saw his father, Edward, opening the driver's door of the jeep. Jason clutched the torch and his eyes followed to the end of the beam. He frowned and straightened and began to walk several steps down the pathway. He bent down to the curb again and retrieved something else, scooping it up with his torch. He walked back to the car where his father stood, watching him.

"Whatcha found now?"

"It's an iPhone case. It's Mike's."

"How'd you know that?" asked Edward.

"The front corner is split. I bought it for him and he told me on the phone the other week that it had split. Cheap rubber." He pointed a forefinger to the split front left corner.

"OK, bag it up, and the roll of tape as well," instructed Edward as he clambered inside behind the wheel.

The weatherproof structure, known as a randome, covered antennae and microwave activity. The ones upon Menwith Hill, the RAF base in Harrogate, Yorkshire, looked like gigantic golf balls. The RAF base provided communications and intelligence support to the United Kingdom, Australia, Canada, New Zealand and the United States, collectively known by the abbreviation AUSCANNZUKUS. It was the home of ECHELON. In the simplest of terms, ECHELON intercepted internet and telecommunications, aiding in political and diplomatic matters, the apprehension of drug cartels, the uncovering of terrorism plots and, no doubt, a whole lot more besides.

It was earlier that day, at 16:01, a particular cellular telephone call was flagged up on the ECHELON computer system, which brought it to the attention of one of its data analysts working at the base.

"Yo. Get 'ere quick, yeah. I done somefin and joo gotta get 'ere wivda car, man."

"Whasup blud?"

"I've shanked da Prime Minister and now I'm gonna kill the Queen, init? Just get to da fuckin' Common, man. Wynn Common init."

Two distinct male voices were detected. The telephone conversation was intercepted the moment the words "Prime Minister" were spoken. Specific technology was even able to record the call from the very beginning, despite the fact that "Prime Minister" was only mentioned nine seconds into the conversation. The caller ID was flagged. The words 'shanked' and 'shank' were known to be gang terminology for 'stabbed' and 'stab'. When the system analysed the word 'shanked' at lightning speed and reworked it with a more fitting 'stabbed', the caller ID was flagged again when the computer noted the sentence: "I've just stabbed the Prime Minister." And again when the mention of the Queen was made, and finally once more when the sentence "I'm going to kill the Queen" was put in order. Each lined was flagged with the same caller ID, along with their mobile phone network, bank payment details, including all direct debits and standing orders, home address, driving licence, car registration, car make and model, car insurance, credit card payments, employment and tax records. The caller ID linked to that particular cellular phone, and to all the listed details, was one Michael Thompson.

At 17:22 that cellular phone belonging to Michael gave out a signal, and despite the device not technically being in use, it was still continuing to transmit, therefore intelligence services and their high-tech systems could listen in, which was exactly what ECHELON was doing automatically.

"I'm not getting muddy. It's filthy down there."

"It's just for one night. He can stay there until we figure out what to do."

Again two male voices were detected. One was the same as before, the second was of a different pitch and tone.

"I'll do it, then. Get out my way, yeah."

"This isn't good for you. It isn't good for us! Bad things will happen, do you not understand!" and again, the data analyst collated the information received, including the area, and noted the transmitting signal that began to fade in and out and then die out altogether several minutes later. The data analyst attached it to the caller ID, which was Michael Thompson.

In Plumstead Police Station, Michael's father flashed a badge of some sort and spoke with the Duty Sergeant, who had already been informed that Edward may turn up. It was arranged for Edward to speak with the youth who had broken into Michael's car earlier that day.

"I ain't talking to no-one until I see a solicitor. Get me a solicitor!" yelled the youth from his cell.

Jason, who was also present with his father, fortunately was dressed in trousers and a white shirt. He'd had an interview that afternoon and, to his father's approval, believed he could pass off as a late-night solicitor.

Edward and Jason lingered by the front desk, waiting.

A Pakistani gentleman was also by the desk. He placed a large, bulky Filofax on the front desk surface and explained that he had found it at the train station and was handing it in as lost property.

Edward listened in.

The Duty Sergeant behind the desk sighed and said that he would go and get a form and wouldn't be a moment, despite the gentleman saying he couldn't hang around and just wanted to hand it in.

"I'll deal with it, sir. You go home and get some rest," Edward said, stepping up to the man and taking the Filofax from him.

The Pakistani man nodded, smiled in a bemused way and exited the police station.

"Shove it under your arm," Edward whispered to Jason, grabbing a pen off the front desk as the Duty Sergeant reappeared.

"Oh, has he gone? Bloody lost property. Waste of time. Right, the youth told me that he's not speaking to anybody until he sees a brief," said the Duty Sergeant.

"Tell him we've got one here," replied Edward, gesturing to his son, standing tall, next to him.

The Sergeant eyed Jason up and down and raised his eyebrows.

"Okey doke. Sure."

A dark-coloured Audi pulled up outside Michael's home in Luxor Street. Two white men, in their late thirties and casually dressed, were behind the wheel and in the passenger seat. They looked out of the window and up at the top floor of a house. Michael's house. A moment later, a dark blue transit van pulled in behind the Audi.

"Shall we let them get started then?" said the driver of the Audi.

"No. I think we should wait. It's too early," replied the male passenger.

In an interview room, in Plumstead Police Station, Edward and Jason sat at a table. The Duty Sergeant led the youth who'd tried to steal Michael's car stereo inside.

"Take a seat, son," instructed the sergeant to the youth, who swaggered to a seat and with a carefree, I-don't-give-a-damn attitude, pulled a chair out and slumped on it.

"You my brief?" the youth said to Jason.

"I only have a couple of questions. Before you broke into the car-" Michael's father was quickly interrupted by the youth.

"I told you people yeah. The car was already open. Like, the door was already open. What's wiv yooz, yeah?" he moaned.

"OK. When you got to the car, did you see anyone else nearby?" questioned Edward.

"Nobody was around. Just me."

"I don't care if you're protecting your friends. I'm not here for any of them. I just want to know if you saw anyone in or around the car."

"I dunno, man. Is dis allowed?" he said, looking at Jason, who nodded his head to him.

"Did you see anyone near the car before you got there?" Edward asked again.

"Yeah, all right. Fuck sake. I did. Let me go now. Pricks."

"Language," warned the Duty Sergeant.

"Who did you see?" asked Edward.

"Some black kids, init. I ain't racist, but I did."

"Black kids. How many?" Edward asked.

"I dunno. Two. Anuva kid who was mongrel or somefin."

"What do you mean? You mean he was handicapped?" Edward asked, curiously.

"No. Just actin' like a fuckin' nut. He was spinnin' round and shit. Fucking Taliban," muttered the youth.

"What was that?" Edward leaned across the table.

"Oh, what now? Was I not being - what's the word? Politically right or somefin? Wankers."

"Forget about any of that. What did you just call him? The other boy, the mongrel. What did you call him?" Edward probed, hoping to gain some possible positive information.

"Taliban. All right - all right, Af-gan-iss-starrrn," the youth said sarcastically.

"And he was acting strange?" Edward was curious, desperate for more detailed information.

"They're all strange. Listen yeah, da Taliwacka was wiv a couple black kids, probably Cherry yoots, and took the geeky looking librarian bloke wiv 'em. Can I go now please?"

"What geeky bloke? Who was the other one? Who?" pressed Edward.

The Duty Sergeant tightened his face, tapping his wristwatch.

"I dunno. Some bloke. Looked like you but younger. Probably a Fed just like you. Dat's it now yeah. I'm not talking. Fucking take me back to my cell," ordered the youth, standing up from his chair and making to the door. He stared at the Duty Sergeant with an impatient expression.

"I'll take him back," said the Sergeant to Edward, standing and opening the door. He then escorted the youth out of the room.

"Now what?" Jason asked his father, who rolled his tongue around inside his mouth, filling out his cheeks and gums, thinking, just like Michael did.

Earlier that day, at precisely six-thirty in the evening, in a grimy, eerie flat set within an equally uninviting estate in Thamesmead, a forty-two-year-old, well-built Nigerian man placed a polythene wrapped brick of cocaine into a black holdall. It was a kilo slab and it accompanied eight more identical blocks held within. Each one of the kilo slabs had a street value of two hundred and eighty thousand pounds. The total value of the eight kilo slabs of cocaine contained in the sports bag was over two million pounds. The bag was zipped up and the man gripped the handle tight and straightened before striding out of the dark room and into a narrow hallway. The walls, stained yellow by cigarette smoke, had stacks of Reebok shoeboxes lined up against them. Some brand new trainers were exposed on the top boxes and another Nigerian man, in his late thirties who wore jeans, a crisp white shirt and a long black leather jacket, inspected a pair of running shoes.

"I want a pair in a size twelve," said the leather-jacket-wearing Nigerian to the first man, who carried the sports bag.

"I do not have a size twelve. Are you crazy? They are a pair of running shoes, not a pair of skis, you eed yot. What you are looking for is in the next box. Come. The others are waiting to leave," replied the man with the sports bag.

His friend opened the lid to another shoebox.

He pulled out a Beretta 92A1 pistol. That handgun contained fifteen rounds, weighed 950 grams, and had an effective range of fifty meters.

He assessed it in his hand, gripping it and nodded his approval. "It is for me? What do you have?"

"What I always have, plus three hundred of what you have there under my bed. Come on. It is time to go," instructed the first Nigerian man. He edged his companion to the front door, but his friend stopped him and gestured for him to turn around and look back up the hall.

He did so and noticed a little Nigerian boy, about six years old, who was wearing a Manchester United football kit, eating a bag of Walkers salt and vinegar flavoured crisps and looking sad, with big, brown doughy eyes.

"Watch your television programme or put on Toy Story 3. You like that movie film. Daddy will be back later. Maybe I will bring back a new DVD for you off the Chinaman, yes? Go to your room now, you hear me?" ordered the first Nigerian man to the little boy, who lowered his head and shuffled his feet, covered with dangling ill-fitting football socks, out of the hallway and into another dark room.

"You are leaving him on his own?" asked the second man.

"What, you want him to come with us? Are you crazy?"

"He is six years old!"

"But nearly seven. Let's go," replied the man clutching the sports bag that contained more than two million pounds' worth of cocaine. And with that, the two Nigerian men exited the flat.

In a brand new, blue BMW 7 Series sat two Nigerian twin brothers, aged twenty-two. One had a scar on his left cheek and a milky white coloured pupil in his left eye. Either he was blind in that eye or it was simply discoloured for some reason. The scar and the milky white eye were the only differences setting the two brothers apart, as they were dressed identically, in dark blue jeans, black roll necks and black bomber jackets.

The scarred one sat in the passenger seat, while the other brother gripped the steering wheel. The Nigerian brother with the scar turned his head and saw the two older Nigerian men making their way from the flat to the car.

They opened the rear passenger doors and slipped themselves inside the vehicle, just as the engine started up.

"Amala?" said the twin without a scar. Amala was a Nigerian slang term for cocaine.

"Meguski, where were you earlier? I try reaching you onda phone?" replied the cocaine-handling man. Meguski was Nigerian slang for a fool.

"He was acting big man widdat aboki area boy," responded the scar-faced brother, looking with his milky eye at his brother at the wheel, stating he was acting like a boss to a local foolish boy.

"Joo always awoof wid dat arrow," remarked the cocaine handler in his Nigerian slang, saying the man was always doing free stuff for the daft boy.

"Amebo. Gossip. Amebo," said the driver being mocked.

The doors closed and the car pulled away, out of the gloomy looking estate and out of Thamesmead, a part of south-east London widely known as Little Lagos.

At nearly the same time, at 18:45, a very similar situation was also taking place, but this time on the Conaught Estate in Woolwich.

A group of five Somalian men in their mid-twenties made their way to a new Ford Focus. Some wore jeans, some wore tracksuits, and all wore black hooded tops. One carried two Adidas track bags, while the remaining four carried bulging, thin synthetic Nike gym sacks.

They each clambered into the Ford.

The Somali man with the two track bags sat in the passenger seat and unzipped one of the bags, a red one. He pulled out a Mac 10 machine pistol. He checked the magazine. It was full. He placed the weapon back inside the bag.

In the back seats, three of the wiry men each pulled out a varied amount of weaponry themselves. One had an Uzi, while the other two had Glock pistols.

The driver put on his seatbelt and started up the car. He checked his mirrors and shoved the vehicle into gear, released the handbrake and drove off like he had only recently passed his test; either that or he was just extremely cautious and really didn't want to be pulled over by the police. As he drove, the passenger with the two track bags pulled on his own seatbelt and then gently patted the other bag, a blue one.

It was nearing 2:00 and the landline telephone rang. Violet picked up the receiver and quietly answered. It was her friend, Carolyn, who told her that she couldn't divulge too much information, especially not on the telephone.

Carolyn informed Violet that a call was made from Michael's mobile phone at 16:01 the afternoon of the previous day. She said that some statements made in a conversation had been brought to the attention of a division within the Security Services and been linked with Michael's name and address.

"So they knew of Michael's disappearance?" Violet gasped, in hope.

"Well, no. There wasn't any official reporting or notification of Michael being missing until four hours later, when Michael's girlfriend phoned to inform Edward," replied Carolyn.

"Oh, I see. So what happened?"

"Like I said, Violet, I can't say too much and I haven't heard what was recorded from the mobile phone conversation, but what I can say is Michael's phone is being monitored and, no doubt, his home as well."

"By your people?" inquired Violet.

"Yes," replied Carolyn.

"And do you know where the conversation took place? Can you work out things like that?"

"The 16:01 telephone call signaled from SE18: Winn Common Road in Plumstead," Carolyn informed Violet, who jotted it down on a pad beside the landline phone.

"Yes?"

"There was another signal from a different area: SE10, Maidenstone Hill, at 17:22. The signal has been noted to pulse," Carolyn continued.

"Pulse? What does that mean?" Violet asked as she wrote down what she had been told.

"It means the signal is fading in and out. That's all I have. I'm sorry, Violet. I'll let you know if anything significant at all comes up relating to Michael, but please don't worry. I'm sure he's all right."

"Yes. Yes, I know. I hope so. I just hope so. Thank you, Carolyn. I'm so grateful. Thank you. Goodbye now." Violet hung up the receiver as her body jerked forward. She released a sudden sob and a slight wail. She sniffed and exhaled a deep sigh as she looked at the pad that she had just written on. She took up the telephone again.

Edward and Jason sat in the jeep, parked not too far from Plumstead Police Station. Edward sighed and Jason looked at him, feeling lost.

"What do you think we should do, Dad?" he asked.

"I don't know, boy. I just don't know what to do."

"If we had the Afghan kid's address, would we go there?"

"It's too late to go visiting now I think, but anyway, like you said, if we had the add-" Edward paused as his mobile phone rang out. He retrieved it and took the call from his wife.

"Ed? I've just spoken with Carolyn."

"Oh Violet. Why? I said not to yet. What did she say?"

Violet told Edward what her friend, Carolyn from MI-5, had said to her on the phone about the intelligence collected from Michael's phone earlier on.

"OK, so where was the last signal transmitted from? Did she tell you that?" Edward asked, flipping the glovebox open and knocking Jason's knees as he fumbled for a notepad and pen.

"A place called Maidenstone Hill in SE10," Violet replied.

"Maidenstone Hill? Doesn't ring any bells," Edward frowned, twisting the key to the ignition to start the engine.

"Carolyn said the signal was pulsing."

"OK. The phone could be in a tunnel or amongst trees or high-rises maybe. Violet, I've just remembered something. Are you in the kitchen or bedroom?"

"I'm in the bedroom, but I've got the walk-around phone. Why?" she replied, in a more curious, softer tone.

"Can you go into the kitchen to where the phone goes? I need you to get a pencil from my drawer."

Violet entered the kitchen and walked to the corner of it, her every move instructed by Edward.

"Yes, got it," she responded, opening a drawer and retrieving an HB pencil.

"Can you get some grease-proof paper now please?" Edward asked.

Violet thought about the question for two seconds and then opened another kitchen drawer, pulling out a roll of grease-proof paper.

"What shall I do now, Ed?"

"Roll it out and place it over the top of the Yellow Pages."

Violet moved some paperwork off the Yellow Pages and reeled out a length of grease-proof paper before laying it across the top of the phone directory. She tore off the section.

"All right, Ed. I've done it. What now?"

"Hold the paper down firmly and rub the pencil across it, like Mike used to do with coins and brass rubbings," said Edward, patiently.

Violet skimmed the pencil across the grease-proof paper, back and forth, back and forth, some lines harder than others, but all of them picked up the trace of indented letters and a number being revealed from underneath. "It looks like part of an address," Violet said, with surprise in her voice.

"That's good. What can you read, Violet?"

"Gurdon something. I don't know if it's a road or a street or what," she sighed, with instant disappointment.

"That's fine. What's the number?" he asked her.

She told him the number that she had just unearthed.

Edward thanked her for that and then told her to go to bed.

Jason retrieved an A-Z of London from the back of his father's seat, looking up a street called Gurdon.

"It's set back from Woolwich Road," Jason said.

"OK, now look up Maidenstone Hill," replied Edward, shifting into first gear and releasing the handbrake. He drove off as Jason looked up another street.

"It's off Blackheath Hill."

"Which end?" Edward asked.

"Bottom end."

"We'll go there afterwards as it's on the way to the address Mum gave us," Edward stated, driving the vehicle into the night.

Mr Ahmed stepped out of his front door. He was wearing a pair of pale blue pyjama bottoms, a white vest and a maroon dressing gown that flapped open in the night air. In one hand he held a bag of recycling which he put into a wheelie bin. He slid his hand into the gap between the drainpipe and the wall of the house, retrieving a pack of hidden cigarettes. He flipped the pack open and took out a disposable lighter and a cigarette, which he lit. He sat himself on the doorstep and took a long drag of his cigarette, exhaling the smoke, which drifted and disappeared into forever. He frowned, seeing a set of headlights reflect on the side of a car parked opposite and then disappear. Not a sound of an engine, not a glimpse of any more light. Mr Ahmed shrugged and took another pull on the cigarette. He glanced upwards and suddenly started coughing, instantly alarmed, edging himself backwards and up to the next step as he was cast in shadow.

Edward towered above him, staring down, with Jason looming behind him at the garden gate.

"Where's the boy? Where's Abdul Rah-Maan?" Edward asked firmly and directly to a frightened Mr Ahmed. "Are you afraid?" Edward continued, sensing Mr Ahmed's extremely noticeable fear. "Take a deep breath. Breathe out and swallow," commanded Edward to Mr Ahmed, who did exactly as he was told.

"What - what has - he done?" Mr Ahmed stuttered.

"Is Abdul inside the house?" Edward asked.

"Are - are you police?"

"Yes or no? Is Abdul inside the house?" Edward became more assertive and tense.

"Yes. Please - what?"

"Where?"

"Upstairs."

"Which room? Is he asleep?"

"The first room. At the - top. He should - he should be sleeping," Mr Ahmed stammered, frightened by Edward's abruptness.

"What time did he go to bed?"

"Early. After dinner. Around six. He was tired. Preoccupied with something. Please. Tell me. What has Abdul done?"

Edward thought fast, taking in the brief information Mr Ahmed had just told him, staring down at him, intimidatory. "How's his English?"

"English good. Farsi good. Urdu good," Mr Ahmed said, mentally exhausted already.

"But Abdul bad," Edward replied, lowering his left arm, discreetly pointing his forefinger to the ground. The finger was blue, with the hand housed in a Nitrile glove. He darted past Mr Ahmed and into the house.

Jason advanced to the step, with Mr Ahmed staring from the door back to him and about to get to his feet.

"Sit down," Jason ordered Mr Ahmed, who shivered at the sight of the menacing six-foot-plus Jason.

Edward ascended the stairs of Mr Ahmed's home, speedily, yet quietly. He weighed up the environment upon reaching the top and grabbed the handle of the bedroom door with his gloved hand.

Blood seeped from Abdul's stomach as a razor blade ran across his skin, pinched by his forefinger and thumb as he lay on his bed. His teeth were gritted with absolute pain in his face and tears streamed down his cheeks. The blood trickled down one side and onto the bed linen. His eyes quickly diverted to the blood on the sheet, flustering him more and he reached for a box of Kleenex.

Edward barged into the room. He locked eyes with Abdul. In two strides, Edward had reached the boy. Abdul tried to scream out, but to no avail.

Edward covered Abdul's mouth with a cupped hand, grabbing and twisting Abdul's hand that held the razor blade in one swift motion.

Abdul's arm was bent awkwardly up behind his back, with his hand forced in a direction that caused additional, more extreme pain.

Edward looked into Abdul's wide, fearful brown eyes.

"Abdul. Abdul, where is Michael? Main Michael ko dhuund raha hoon." Edward spoke in both English and Urdu. He was an inch from Abdul's face and pressed his gloved hand against his mouth. "Kya aap Urdu bool sakte Hain?" Edward continued, asking Abdul if he spoke Urdu.

Abdul frowned, extremely confused and scared.

"I will break - your - neck. Nod your head if you understand," Edward said calmly.

Abdul nodded his head quickly. Tears escaped his glassy eyes.

"Michael, your teacher. Do you know who I am talking about?" Edward asked, with Abdul once again nodding his head.

Abdul wriggled his head free to gasp and speak frantically. "Aap ka taaluq kahan se hai?" Abdul asked where Edward was from in Urdu.

"Mera naam Edward hey. Mera taaluq hifaazat se hai," Edward said in perfectly clear Urdu. He told Abdul that his name was Edward and he was from security. He quickly secured Abdul once more.

He struggled like a frightened rabbit as Edward put on the pressure more forcibly.

"Rokna jidojehed. Stop moving. Stop," instructed Edward, pressing his hand harder against Abdul's face. His fingers were just under his nose, a nose that breathed in and out ever so quickly, snorting in an animal like fashion. "You were with Michael today. Yes?"

Abdul nodded his head to this question and twisted his face away once more, gasping.

"Koi baat nahi! No problem. No problem, sir," Abdul blurted.

"Where is Michael?"

"Mujhe andazah nahi. I have no idea," Abdul panted.

"Michael? Kidher? Where? Kidher?" Edward mixed his Urdu and English.

"Mujhe nahi malum!" Abdul cried.

"Ssh. Yes you do know. You do know. Jaldi Karo! Hurry up. Michael? Kidher? Where is he?"

"Aaj. Shaam main. Bura." Abdul squirmed, edging away on the bed.

"Today? This evening was bad? Why?" Edward quizzed.

Abdul shook his head.

Edward fixed on the razor blade on the bed, by the pillow.

"Mujhe yeh dena! Give me this," Edward snapped, pinching the blade with one hand and grasping Abdul's face with the other, holding the razor blade closer to his eye. "I will count. Shumaar. When I reach three - shumaar tin - you'll be blind aap nabeena. Samajna? Understand? Eik. One. Michael. Where? Kidher? Do. Two. Michael. Where? Kidher? Kidher?" Edward squeezed Abdul's extremely fearful face hard, nearing the sharp metal razor blade closer and closer to his left eye.

He closed his eye, but Edward worked his thumb up his cheekbone and applied more pressure and dug it to his lower eyelid, pulling it downwards to expose a glimmer of white from his eyeball. He moved the blade a fraction closer, millimeters from making contact with his eyeball.

"Dad!"

Abdul's eyes widened to see Jason standing in the bedroom doorway behind them, with Mr Ahmed just a step in front of him.

"Tin," Edward continued.

"Yeh kya hai?" cried Mr Ahmed, startling Edward into turning around and seeing Jason and Mr Ahmed.

"Get him out of here!" Edward called out to Jason in a soft, but angry tone as Abdul jerked himself further up the bed, making Edward flinch and lightly cut Abdul's cheek.

"Yeh kya hai? What is this? What are you doing? Who are you people?" Mr Ahmed demanded, advancing.

"The door. Get the door!" Edward said to Jason, who turned to see someone approaching from another room out on the landing.

He closed the bedroom door, holding it firmly shut with his foot and body, preventing anybody from entering.

"Dekho!" Mr Ahmed cried out, on seeing Abdul's bleeding abdomen.

"Shut up. He did that to himself. He's a self-harmer."

"Meri tabiyat kharab lag rahi he," Abdul whimpered.

"Oh you'll feel sick in a minute," Edward promised, sitting up on the bed, glancing back and forth from Abdul to a bemused Mr Ahmed.

"You speak Urdu?"

"Sirf thori si. Just a little," Edward replied.

"Mujhe daktar ki zururat he!" cried Abdul, touching his cheek and seeing blood on his fingertips.

"You need a doctor? You'll need a doctor when I finish with you. Where - is - my - son? Mayra baita, Michael? Kidher?"

"Why would Abdul know your son? Who is your son? Please. Maybe I can help you. Abdul?" insisted Mr Ahmed, highly confused.

"Raja? Raja?" came a female voice from outside the room, making Mr Ahmed's head twitch.

"Barae meherbani kuch deyr intizar kijiye!" Mr Ahmed called out to his wife to give him a moment.

"Raja?" called the woman again.

"Shab bakhair! Goodnight!" he said loudly, turning round to Edward and Abdul, and glancing back at the imposing Jason just behind him.

"My son deals with this boy at his school. My son went missing this afternoon and this boy has information regarding his disappearance," said Edward.

"But - but how do you know this? Abdul?"

"I have significant information placing Abdul at the scene of where my son was last positively known to be."

"He is scared. I am scared. You are making him frightened. Look at him," pointed Mr Ahmed.

"I haven't even begun, sir."

Edward looked around the room and noticed something poking out from under a book. He tossed the razor on the size and reached for the knife. It was the craft knife. He began to roll out the blade which caused Abdul to gasp and Mr Ahmed to shake his head.

"Dad," Jason said calmly, intervening and trying to defuse the tense situation.

Edward looked at the terrified and trembling Abdul, quaking and shivering with fear upon the bed, tight in the corner, his knees against his chest. He looked back at Mr Ahmed, who was equally as fearful. He looked up at his son, Jason, highly concerned as to what his father was capable of doing. He looked at the ejected blade of the craft knife in his grasp. He lowered his head and sighed, briefly closing his eyes, thinking. He swallowed and took a deep breath. He tightened his mouth and turned his attention to Abdul once again.

"You will tell me everything I need to know in order for me to find my son or I will personally see it that you are put on a plane back to Afghanistan within hours. Do you understand me?"

"Kya aap ahistah keh saktay hein?" answered Abdul.

"Speak slowly? You want me to speak slowly? Af-ghan-is-stan - to-mor-row. Do - you - under - stand - me?" Edward stated precisely, taking on more of an interrogator role as he tightened the blade held in the craft knife.

"He doesn't know," Mr Ahmed interrupted, as Abdul looked up at him.

"Don't look at him. Look at me. Abdul. What happened when you left school today?" Edward said firmly.

He didn't even wait for the reply as he suddenly grabbed Abdul and dragged his body to the chair, sitting him down on it. He twisted Abdul and the chair round to face the edge of the bed. He sat down opposite Abdul.

They were now face to face.

Abdul looked at the knife and then up at Edward.

"I don't want to hurt you, Abdul. You didn't come to this country to be hurt. You came here to be safe. You can continue to be safe, Abdul, if you tell me what you know about my son."

Abdul gulped. His bottom lip quivered. His chest rose and fell quickly with fearful, pained breaths.

"Bara dam. Big breaths. Eik, do. One, two. One two," Edward commanded, mixing his Urdu and English together again.

Abdul took instant note and breathed more deeply and calmly. "I - I left my school with Sintra and-" Abdul began.

"Sindra?" Edward interrupted.

"Sintra. Yes," Abdul continued in his thick pronounced accent, but obviously he meant Sinatra.

"Sandra? Does she go to your school?" Edward inquired.

"Sintra. Sintra. Not a girl. A boy. Yes. He goes to school with me," corrected Abdul.

"And what is this boy like? Is he white? Black? Is he Afghani?"

"Africa. He is from Africa. He - Use Angrez main kya kehte hain? Torh diyaa?" Abdul asked Mr Ahmed in Urdu.

"In English? Broke? Yes. Broke. What broke?" Mr Ahmed asked. He now expressed his own keen and flustered curiosity.

"What broke? Did you break something? What broke?" pressed Edward.

"Sintra. He broke. He broke the wheel of the car. The wheel goes flat," continued Abdul.

"This boy made the tyre go flat. The car tyre?"

"Yes. Yes, the tyre. The tyre on the wheel."

"This boy, Sandra? He did this? He broke the wheel?" Edward quizzed. He never took his eyes off Abdul, who hesitated in responding to the question, glancing to his left at Mr Ahmed.

Abdul lowered his head, glassy-eyed, He released more tears. "No. Not just him. Me. Him and me," admitted Abdul.

"Then what?"

"Michael drive and the wheel. The tyre goes flat. Sintra and me see him on his phone," Abdul said as he described his time with Michael.

HOOT!

A car horn sounded out. It passed Michael's car, causing him to stop speaking and look up.

Michael frowned as he saw Abdul in the middle of the street, on the other side of the Common. He curled his lip and turned, surprised to see Sinatra next to him on the pathway. He turned again to see a group of white youths on the Common in the distance.

One was the youth who was later caught trying to steal his car stereo.

Michael briefly noticed the youth looking and then walking away elsewhere.

"Yo, hang up da phone. Do it, man," commanded Sinatra.

Frowning, Michael's tone changed as he turned again and completed his message to Rebecca's answerphone. "Yeah, I'll hopefully not be too late, my love. If I can't manage to change the wheel, then I think there's a garage down the road from work or near this common. Speak later. Love-"

"I said put da phone down!" shouted Sinatra, aggressively, as he suddenly batted Michael's phone out of his hand.

The iPhone made contact with the ground, bouncing in its rubber case and then completely out of it, sliding upon the pavement.

"What do you think you're doing!" Michael blurted out loud to Sinatra.

"Be quiet, man!" shouted Sinatra.

Abdul, who had now crossed the road, looked at the flat tyre and laughed, pointing at it.

Michael frowned at Abdul, trying to weigh up the situation as quickly as he could.

"Yes, I have a flat tyre. It's not funny. Did - did you two have anything to do with this?

"I said, shut up! Shut up, fool." Sinatra edged closer to Michael, totally in his personal space, causing him to step back to his open car door. "You're a Fed. I see you, man. I see you wid da Feds," hissed Sinatra. He pointed his finger toward Michael's face.

"Get your hand away from my face," insisted Michael, calmly, putting his hand up to gently move Sinatra's hand away.

Sinatra's chest inflated, angered by the contact Michael had just made with him. He clenched his fist and held it upwards, alarming Michael and causing him to take a defensive stand.

"You going to hit me? Oh my days. Oh my fucking days. I can't believe you were gonna hit me. Come on. COME ON!" Sinatra yelled as he suddenly delivered a two punch combination to Michael's face. One fist hit Michael's chin, making him stagger backwards and into the driver's open door. The second fist made contact with Michael's nose, instantly making it bleed. His head whipped round to one side.

"Please. No fighting! No fighting!" Abdul screamed.

Michael touched his nose, and felt the blood on his fingertips. He cupped his bleeding nostrils with one hand as his eyes flickered and his body swayed. As he tried to straighten, he lost his footing, caught totally off-guard. He set one foot forward and slipped on the fallen iPhone. His foot slid and his leg buckled, and as he fell, his hand gripped the side of the door where he left blood on the inside of the door handle. He fell awkwardly to the concrete pavement and it was then that he received a sudden, swift kick to the head from Sinatra. Michael's head cracked against the metal door, knocking him out cold.

"You fucking undercover pig Fed. Get up. Get up, man," Sinatra scoffed, as he towered above Michael's unconscious body.

"Sintra. Sintra, no!" replied Abdul, with fear in his eyes, grasping Sinatra's arm, angering him further.

"Don't touch me, man. Get your terrorist hands off me, blud. GET OFF!" Sinatra yelled, shaking loose Abdul's grip. He fixed on the iPhone and picked it up. He pulled his own mobile phone and scrolled through some numbers in his address book, dialing one on Michael's iPhone. It rang immediately.

"Yo. Get 'ere quick, yeah. I done somefin and joo gotta get 'ere wivda car, man," Sinatra said.

"Whasup blud?" came a male voice on the other end of the phone.

"I've shanked da Prime Minister and now I'm gonna kill the Queen, init? Just get to da fuckin' Common, man. Wynn Common, init."

Sinatra hung up the phone. He looked at Abdul with wild eyes and then down at Michael, whose nose was still seeping blood. He pocketed the iPhone and glanced inside the car, catching sight of the silver gaffer tape on the seat, as well as Michael's beige canvas school bag. He reached in and grabbed them both, then clenched his fist, pushing it against the car door, closing it. He stooped to grab hold of Michael's arms and pulled him upwards. He looked at Abdul and called him to come over, with a simple but aggressive gesture of his head.

Abdul stepped over to Michael and slid his arm under his limp body, aiding Sinatra in propping him up and onto his feet.

Together, they stepped onto a large grassy area with a few trees and bushes. The grassland dipped and sloped into a massive, crater-like space.

"I must go home, Sintra," said Abdul, with concern in his voice and on his face.

"My name is Sinatra. Sin-ah-tra."

"Santra. Yes. Yes."

"Fuck sake. Listen, yeah. You wait. You wait here, yeah. You wait here, Abdul, or I'll fucking kill you, yeah," Sinatra threatened.

His own mobile phone rang and he retrieved the call, crouching down beside a bush, hiding from the view of the road and residents who lived nearby. "What, man?"

"Yo, where you at, blud?" came the voice on the other end of the phone.

"I'm in the pit, man. Where we found that bike, yeah?"

"All right. I'm there, blud. Later." The call ended.

"Who is coming, Santra? The police?"

"Shut up, Abdul, man. No. Not the police. Listen, yeah, don't you dare talk to anyone, yeah? Nuffin happened today. We didn't do anything, yeah? D'you hear me? Abdul?"

Abdul looked at Michael's slumped body amongst the undergrowth. He looked up at Sinatra whose eyes stared past him. Abdul turned around to see a Peugeot had pulled up fast onto the grass and had stopped near them. He squinted to see the driver was a black man, of West African origin. Nigerian, twenty-two years old.

The driver exited the car. He was dressed in dark blue jeans, black roll neck and a black bomber jacket. He was the man from Little Lagos and he paced across the Common to a discreetly hidden Sinatra and Abdul, who had crouched down.

The man loomed above them both.

"What's da emergency, blud?" he said to Sinatra, who parted a section of a bush to reveal Michael's body sprawled on the ground underneath. "Is he dead?"

"Dunno," answered Sinatra.

"What the fuck, man. Are you fuckin' stupid?" said the driver, noticing the gaffer tape in Sinatra's hand and then looking at Michael. "Tear some tape off and stick it over his mouth, yeah."

Sinatra picked at the end of the tape with his fingernails and reeled off a short length, which he bit off with his teeth. He stuck it across Michael's mouth.

"What shall I do wiv dis?" Sinatra asked, holding up the roll of tape.

"Who gives a shit? Throw it, man," replied the young Nigerian man.

Sinatra tossed the gaffer tape across the grassland.

"I'll open the boot, yeah, and we can stick him in my car. I'll take him to wherever you want but that'll be it. You're on your Jack Jones, you get me?" said the young man.

Sinatra nodded his head as the young man stepped to his car, unlocked the boot and returned to Abdul and Sinatra.

"Get him up then. Pricks," ordered the man to Sinatra, who once again gestured Abdul to help and together they propped Michael up and followed the young man to the rear of the Peugeot vehicle.

The white youth Edward was later to question at the police station walked across the Common with a girl. He saw Sinatra and the young man heaving

Michael into the boot of the yellow Peugeot. He noticed Abdul with a peculiar expression on his face conducting a very odd dance. He looked away and edged to the end of the road to watch Michael's car.

The boot lid of the Peugeot closed shut on Michael and the young man looked at Sinatra and Abdul.

"Get in. He can bounce," replied the young man with a glance at Abdul.

Sinatra looked at Abdul. "Go home, Abdul. Swear down you won't tell nobody, man. Like I said, I'll kill you. Go home, Abdul. Go home," Sinatra ordered as he rounded the car and opened the passenger door to clamber inside.

Abdul watched the other young man slip inside the car, behind the wheel and start the engine.

The car reversed, then disappeared up the street, towards Woolwich Common.

"Why didn't you tell anybody about what had happened?" Mr Ahmed asked Abdul.

"Oh come on! Why do you think?" chirped Edward.

"Please. No trouble. I'm begging you, sir. Please. I beg you," Abdul cried, reaching out to clutch Edward's hands.

Edward moved himself backwards, still on the bed, but edging away from Abdul's pleading, guilty hands. "Where did they take Michael?"

"I don't know, sir. Please believe me," Abdul pleaded.

"Kidher?" Edward said more assertively.

"Mujhe nahi malum!" cried Abdul. Tears streamed down his face.

"You do know! Not good enough! Where did they take my son?"

"He does not know, sir. Please. Look at him. He has told you all he knows," insisted Mr Ahmed.

Edward thought hard and turned his attention to him, rising to his feet and grabbing his arm.

"You're coming with me," Edward said to Mr Ahmed, glancing round to Abdul, still fixed to the chair. "You stay here. Samajna? Understand?" Edward continued, sending a burning stare into Abdul's eyes.

Abdul nodded with fear as Edward grasped Mr Ahmed tight and gestured to Jason to open the bedroom door.

He did so, quietly.

"Where are we going?" asked Mr Ahmed.

"Quiet," replied Edward, escorting him down the stairs of the house.

"Please do not hurt me. I am a father, too."

"I'm not going to hurt you. Move," commanded Edward, stepping out of the house and up the garden path.

"Then why do you need me?" asked a fearful Mr Ahmed.

"Because if you stayed here, you'd call the authorities, that's why. Come on. Walk."

"Why not take Abdul? He is the cause of this situation. You could take both of us. Abdul may call the police," stuttered Mr Ahmed to Edward, who brought him to a halt beside his jeep.

"Do you really think Abdul will call the police? He's a terrified young man, scared out of his skin who won't dare move from the seat where we left him. That's why I left him there and that's why I'm taking you with me. Shut up and get inside," Edward said firmly, opening the rear passenger door and shoving Mr Ahmed inside.

"Maidenstone Hill?" Jason said, going to the driver's door.

"Yep. You drive," replied Edward, tossing the car keys to his son and clambering inside the back, next to Mr Ahmed.

Jason got behind the wheel and adjusted his seat, scrolling it back for his long legs to be comfortable. He started the car, shifted into first and turned the car into the adjacent street. He switched the headlights on.

Abdul rocked back and forth on the chair. His arms were folded and held tight into his stomach. Tears rolled down his cheeks and he stared at the craft knife lying on the bedside cabinet.

Mr Ahmed sat on the back seat of the jeep next to Edward, as Jason drove down Blackheath Hill.

"Slowly," Edward said, looking out of the window.

"And you think your son will be here?" Mr Ahmed asked, curiously.

"Ssh. I said, be quiet, sir."

"And if he is not? What then?"

"I'll do whatever it takes to find my son. Now be quiet," Edward snapped, flustered by Mr Ahmed's questions.

"And will you be taking me with you on your journey until you find him?"

"He said, shut up! Bloody hell! Just shut up!" yelled Jason.

"There. On the right. Pull in," Edward indicated.

The pale, slim seventeen-year-old-young man called Jack, who was Sinatra's secret boyfriend, crouched by a garden gate. Shaking, he looked at his hands in the light of the street lamp. His palms were blood-stained. His lower lip and jaw trembled with fear. His face was suddenly illuminated as he shielded his eyes with one of his bloodied hands. A car's headlights shone, picking Jack out as he stooped, knees against his shoulders, squinting and saluting a red hand to the oncoming vehicle which had Jason behind the wheel of it.

"Lights off and pull in," commanded Edward to Jason.

"D'you seem him?" Jason asked, doing as he was told.

"Yes. Stay here. Do you hear me?" Edward growled, pointing at Mr Ahmed and then exiting the rear of his jeep. He stepped onto the pavement and trod the few paces to overshadow Jack. "Oi. Look at me. Look up."

Jack rolled his eyes upwards and then arched his neck to lock eyes with Edward, still continuing to shiver.

"What's your name?"

"Jer - Jer - Jack."

"You're covered in blood, Jack. Whose blood is it?"

"Ev - ev - every - everyone's," replied Jack.

Edward frowned as Jack lowered his hands. He noticed patches of blood on the pavement, as well as droplets. He turned and stepped to one side, away from his own shadow, to see more blood, this time a footprint consisting of blood and mud. He looked at the car parked nearby, smeared with blood and a clearly visible bloody fingerprint. Edward flipped out a ruler, laying it near the print and retrieved his digital camera, framing the footprint within the screen as he took a clear photograph of it.

"Are you hurt?" Edward asked.

"Just - just my heart," Jack answered, staring blankly ahead of him into the metal of the car door facing him.

"What happened here? Was somebody stabbed?"

"No. They - they were all - they were shot." Jack's voice became more controlled with every word.

"Shot where? Have the police been here?" Edward asked, becoming frantic.

Jack sneered and looked up at him.

"I haven't called them yet."

"Well, maybe someone else has," Edward suggested, bemused by Jack's slightly cryptic sentences.

"I hardly think so."

"And why don't you think so?" asked Edward firmly, crouching down and putting his staring face closer to Jack's.

Jack did a slow burn of a look to meet Edward's eyes.

"Because only I saw it happen."

Edward suddenly grasped Jack's neck with his gloved hand, digging his thumb into a pressure point at the end of his jaw, applying it harder, causing immense discomfort to Jack as he arched his back, twisting his body.

"Show me where," ordered Edward, rising to his feet with Jack. He saw a shadow on the ground and turned to see Jason.

"You OK?"

"Ahmed?"

"In the car. I've locked the doors."

"Take my camera and match the picture I've just taken to the shoe print I made a cast of," Edward said, handing his digital camera to Jason.

"You're - you're hurting me," Jack whined, awkwardly leading Edward round the side of the house.

"Good. Keep walking."

"I - I can't. It hurts. I feel like being sick."

"Then be sick. Move." Edward was jerking Jack forward when he suddenly threw up over himself.

He coughed and dribbled spit and vomit as he stepped into a dark pathway that ran along the side of the house.

Edward pulled his UV torch and switched it on, shining his light, picking out a path.

"Who else lives here?" Edward asked, warily.

"Nobody. Just me and sometimes - sometimes my sister."

"And where is she now?" Edward looked around his new surroundings, consisting of overgrown bushes, unkempt trees and overhanging branches. His UV light caught traces of blood on some leaves. He was cautious.

"She's with her boyfriend."

"And where does he live?"

"Crissake! I don't know!"

Jason scrolled through the images on the digital camera as he sat in the driver's seat of the jeep. There were several pictures of Edward and Violet. In a country pub. At a beach eating fish and chips. Edward and Michael in the garden of their home. Michael and Rebecca, smiling, with a glass of wine, in the same country pub.

Mr Ahmed peered curiously at the photographs. The next image was the plaster cast taken of the shoe print from the Common, then the new image of the muddy and bloody shoe print from the pavement outside.

Jason flicked back and forth from the bloody footprint to the muddy one from the Common. They looked identical. He turned to Mr Ahmed. "In the back, behind you. There's a plaster cast. Can you get it please?" asked Jason.

Mr Ahmed didn't bat an eyelid as he complied, turning round and reaching over the back seat into the boot, pulling out the plaster cast of the shoe print. He eyed it, briefly, then handed it across to Jason.

"Cheers," said Jason, holding it upright and switching his eyes left to right at the cast and the digital image of the bloody print outside. They were indeed the same.

"They're identical," commented Mr Ahmed.

"Yeah."

"Very clear. Was the bloody shoe outside here, on the street?" Mr Ahmed asked.

"Yep."

"And the plaster cast? Where was this taken?"

"On the Common," Jason replied.

"What does it mean?"

Jack led Edward to the back garden. It pained him to do so, but he arched his neck to jut his head forwards as he gestured to a metal grate. "There. In there."

Edward looked to where Jack was pointing to and frowned. "What's down there?" he asked, receiving another sneer from Jack as he released his grip on him.

"You mean you don't know? You go acting like a scary James Bond CSI man, taking pictures of footprints and putting a Vulcan Death Grip on me, and you don't know what's down there?" Jack said, gaining confidence, but in a campish manner.

"Why should I know?"

"Because this is Blackheath. Doesn't everyone know?"

"Stop wasting time and tell me what's down there!" Edward said more forcefully.

"Go down there and 'ave a look yourself, old man."

Edward jabbed the end of the torch into Jack's side and then applied a thumb and wrist lock on him, forcing him, awkwardly, downwards.

"You first, you cocky little sod. Go on." Edward shoved Jack towards the metal grate.

Jack bolted his head round, suddenly with a face full of tears, and yelled at Edward. "Don't push me in here! It's not here, is it? It's there! Look! Are you blind? It's there! There's the hole!"

Edward diverted his eyes to a small, dark, tunnel-like entrance beside Jack, near a clump of bushes and crumbling brickwork. The metal grate must have previously covered this entrance. It was around two feet across and perhaps three feet high.

"You first," ordered Edward, as he shone his beam across the hole.

Muddy steps, made of rock and chalk, led down into pitch-black darkness. The steps were slippery. Wet with water. Wet with blood. "Who's down here?" called out Edward to Jack, who was several steps ahead of him, caught in Edward's flashlight. Edward stopped and glanced back. A glimmer of the night sky shone twelve or so feet behind him. He fumbled for his mobile phone in his fleece pocket and illuminated the display with his torch. The phone was losing bars of signal. He thought for a moment as he paused and looked back to Jack, who was gaining distance. "Wait! It's too dark. Wait for my light!" yelled Edward, setting foot, carefully, to descend further into the cavern: Jack Cade's Cavern. The beam of light from Edward's torch shone across a more level and certainly less dangerous pathway.

A chamber was picked out, then another, then two more. They twisted deeper into nothingness.

Edward zigzagged his torch, widening the beam to see more. He noticed Jack round a corner of the underground chalk cavern going into one of the chambers.

"Slow down!" Edward called, sighing and taking just one step before stopping still and staring.

The walls were crumbling pieces of heavily bloodstained chunks of chalk. Light from Edward's torch brightened the floor of the cave to spot two men.

Their bodies were twisted in a blood-soaked heap.

One man had been shot in his neck and the left side of his head.

The other had been shot in the back, arms and both thighs. The men were of Somali origin.

Edward slowly rolled his eyes upwards, along with his beam to cast light onto Jack, who was standing in the opening of the chamber ahead. His glassy eyes glistened in the glow.

"Jack? Jack, are there more bodies in there?" Edward asked calmly.

Jack slowly nodded his head once. His jaw was tight.

"Are any of them alive?"

Jack slowly shook his head.

Edward lowered his head, looking elsewhere with brief despair. He gasped a breath of momentarily dashed hopes. He looked up at Jack, wondering what kind of devil hell was beyond him in the next cave. More bodies for certain, but was his son, Michael, amongst them? Shining his light downwards, he stepped past one of the dead bodies and over another, looking upwards to the chamber entrance to where a warm, orange glow seeped out from within.

Four roadwork lights delivered an orange bloom, illuminating the large, solid, chalk-walled chamber. Benches, carved into the rock, faced one another on either side. Two twisted pillars and a bar in one corner. The place was a magnificent, secret gem of a meeting place, concealed deep under Blackheath.

Edward appeared at the chamber's arched entrance and stopped instantly. With Jack standing opposite him, he eyed his surroundings and took in the cold stench of death before him. It was all around him.

The body of another young Somali man lay awkwardly just two feet in front of him. His entire clothing wet with blood. His eyes were open and stared like a waxwork figure.

A fourth Somali man was seen, tangled and twisted, with two darker-skinned men, half on the ground and half upon one of the carved-out benches. The Somali, with his eyes closed, clutched his shot gut with one hand and gripped a Mac 10 Uzi machinegun pistol in the other.

The other two men were Nigerian.

One wore dark blue jeans, a black roll neck and a black bomber jacket, with one milky eye staring blankly upwards and a scar running from this eye and down his cheek. He, too, had been shot and was incredibly blood-soaked. His body contorted and entwined with his fellow Nigerian national, slumped over the bench, with one arm missing.

The wall was spattered with blood and riddled with bullets.

Edward was pained by what he saw. He turned his horrified eyes to one of the pillars in the middle of the chamber.

At the base of it was one more Nigerian, half soaked in his own blood and half covered in a pink and red powder. Bullet shells, blood, cocaine and death were contained within this underground lair.

"What the hell happened here, Jack?"

"I - I was trying to study. I - I need to study. I can't concentrate if I hear just the slightest sound. It disturbs me. It's like - it's like being woken from a dream. Maybe this is a dream. Yes. Yes this is a dream..." Jack's voice trailed off.

"Jack!" Edward shouted, jolting Jack from his momentary trance-like state.

"I had my headphones on the second time. It just sounded like drilling was happening under my house."

"Jack. Jack, please. Tell me what happened," Edward asked, calmly.

Jack sat in his living room reading a book on childcare, in between flicking through a copy of Heat magazine, tutting at the snippets of D-list celebrity gossip he feasted his eyes upon. He checked his white Baby-G wristwatch. It was 17:15. He twitched, turning his head as he heard a car engine outside. Placing the book and magazine down, he knelt on the sofa to peer out of the window. He saw a couple of figures outside, but they were gone as soon as he had time to crane his neck further sideways to see.

"Are they going down the side?" he said to himself, curiously, sliding off the sofa and striding out of the room.

A door opened and Jack stepped out from the kitchen to an outside pathway. The same pathway that Edward and he had now walked down. Rugged, overgrown with weeds, but when Jack went for the first time that day it was much lighter outside, giving a somewhat fantasy, Secret Garden vibe. He looked to the right and jolted with fright to see Sinatra shuffling his feet down the pathway from the street.

"Babe? What are-"

"Shut up, man. Ssh," Sinatra said, aggressively.

Jack frowned and then fixed on the Nigerian man from the Common walking a couple of feet behind him.

"What's going on?" Jack asked.

"Who he?" asked the Nigerian.

"He's ma boy. Chill bruv," replied Sinatra, passing Jack as he pushed back a branch to step further to the garden.

"I'm just taking him out and then it is all for you to deal with. Understand?" barked the Nigerian.

"Sin, deal with what?" Jack was confused.

"Go back inside, man. It's cool, init blud. Seriously, just go back inside da house, man," insisted Sinatra.

"No. What are you doing?"

"You not pleased to see me? Oh my days," scoffed Sinatra, acting up.

"You two lovas can kissy kiss make up later. Sinatra. I get da man for you now. I have to go," said the Nigerian, stepping out of sight to the street.

"What's going on?" asked Jack, with a hurt expression looking at Sinatra who pushed on through to the garden. Jack followed him, frowning to see Sinatra pushing back bushes and branches, as if to search for something.

"Where is it?"

"What are you looking for?"

"Nuffin. There it is," Sinatra said, breaking a branch and tugging some of the bush apart to reveal the metal grate that covered the cave entrance.

"Why do you want that? Oh my God!" Jack said, catching sight of Michael being shoved forth into the garden, down the pathway, by the Nigerian. Jack looked him up and down, seeing the silver gaffer tape across his mouth and a piece of black electrical tape over his eyes.

Michael's wrists were tied behind his back with plastic ties and he mumbled, poking the tape out with his tongue and blowing it out enough for him to speak.

"Where are you taking me?" Michael yelled out.

"Shut the fock up and move!" shouted the Nigerian, barging him forward.

Michael stumbled a couple of steps and then received his beige canvas bag in his back, knocking him down.

"All yours. What are you doing down there, arrow boy?"

Sinatra scowled at the Nigerian who was shaking his head at him, then tilted his look as he squinted to stare at the metal grate concealing the cavern below.

The Nigerian turned and set off back to the street. He stopped to look back at the metal grate and paused for thought. He nodded his head and pointed a forefinger at the grate as he smirked. He sneered and continued until he was out of sight.

Jack curled his lip and looked at Sinatra. "Who the hell was that?"

"I may not be able to see you, but I can hear you. I'll identify all of your voices," Michael said, getting to his feet again. He swallowed and cocked his head to try and hone in on every sound around him.

Sinatra continued to scowl. He paced past Jack and entered the house via the kitchen side door.

Jack sighed, glanced at Michael in the garden and then walked after Sinatra, who returned with a tool box, slamming it down on the ground and alarming Michael.

Sinatra located a screwdriver and unscrewed part of the metal grate. Some of it came away with ease, however he struggled to extract the screws from the other half. He gripped the grate and pulled and pulled. He strained hard. His biceps flexed and he gritted his teeth as the grate finally came off the brickwork it was attached to, sending Sinatra rolling backwards into the bush.

"Help me up, man," Sinatra snapped, staggering out of the bush, with Michael's iPhone dropping from his pocket.

"I'm not getting muddy. It's filthy down there," complained Jack, eyeing the phone on the grass as he took a step forward.

"It's just for one night. He can stay there 'til we figure out what to do," Sinatra said, picking up the phone and brushing and blowing off the dirt. "I'll do it then. Get out my way, yeah," he continued.

"This isn't good for you. It isn't good for us! Bad things will happen, do you not understand!" Jack cried, not fully comprehending the situation.

Sinatra put the phone back into the pocket from where it had previously slipped out. He looked at Michael and then at Jack, welling up with tears before making his way into the house.

Jack rested his hands against the kitchen sink, tight-lipped, flustered and feeling emotionally betrayed.

"Why don't you ever tell me what's going on with you!" Jack shouted. He stepped out of the kitchen and outside to the path, catching sight of Sinatra disappearing, with a flashlight, into the darkness of the cavern. He frowned and ventured into the garden, crouching down by the hole in the wall. "Sin? Sinatra, what the hell, man."

"This is fucking nuts, blud. I'm the Don. I am the Don!" Sinatra's voice echoed and he laughed, twirling around with his flashlight in the cavern below ground.

The light caught Michael standing in the darkness. His jaw trembled. He managed to speak through a gap in the gaffer tape.

"Sinatra, I know it's you. Please. Just untie me. This is a serious issue. You'll get done for kidnapping."

"Kidnapping? I don't think so," Sinatra said, stepping away to shine his light elsewhere, exploring.

"I do think so, Sinatra," Michael contradicted him, firmly, twitching his head and hearing a rock or a stone tumble down the steps from the darkness behind him.

Sinatra's flashlight whipped round, shining on Michael and the area around him, picking out the chalk walls and glimpses of the chambers, as well as Jack, who peered from the set of rocky steps.

His face was frightened, yet concerned. "Sinatra, let the man go."

"Who is that? Yes. Yes, let me go! Listen to him, Sinatra. Listen to your friend," Michael pleaded.

"Are you mad? You need to be taught a lesson, bruv," scoffed Sinatra, chuckling to himself.

"Where am, I Sinatra? I need to tell people I'm OK," Michael called.

Sinatra suddenly pulled Michael into a chamber.

"ARE YOU CRAZY!" yelled Jack, feeling his way in the pitch black, crawling on his backside and gently easing himself down the muddy, chalky steps.

The beam from Sinatra's flashlight was like a firefly bouncing around the chamber and Jack used it as his guide, making his way towards it. He peered into the chamber's entrance.

"Sinatra, please. This isn't it a joke now. You have to understand how serious this is for you." Michael's voice trembled as he stood near a pillar in the large and impressive chamber.

"Serious for me? Are you mad? It's serious for you, prick."

"What are you planning to do, Sinatra? Jesus! How long are you going to keep him here for? A few days? A week? Are you going to feed the poor man?" Jack called from the chamber's rocky arched entrance.

"Ah yeah. I didn't fink about dat. Are you hungry, Michael? I've only got some gum. D'you want dat?" Sinatra asked, delving into his jean pocket and retrieving a pack of Wrigley's Juicy Fruit.

"Sinatra, chewing gum is not food," Jack stated.

"I'm being kind, man!" Sinatra removed a stick of gum and unwrapped it. He gently peeled off the silver gaffer tape from Michael's mouth.

"Open your mouth, man. Michael, open your mouth."

Michael warily opened his mouth as Sinatra popped the stick of gum between his teeth. He began to chew.

"I'll be back in a minute, man," Sinatra told Michael then joined Jack.

"What the fuck are you doing, Sinatra?" Jack whispered.

"Just scarin' him, man," he replied, casually, pulling the iPhone from his pocket and slotting it inside Michael's workbag. He slung the bag into the darkness and edged Jack out of the chamber.

Michael stood alone, against the pillar, in the dark, deep underground. "Hello?" his voice echoed and his body shivered.

"I dunno where to park, man," moaned one of the Somali men driving the Ford Focus into Greenwich Park.

"We're nearly late. Just park anywhere," responded the Somali in the passenger seat, clutching his Adidas track bags. He looked at his cheap digital wristwatch: 18:55.

The four Nigerian men walked through a chalk tunnel, deep underground.

The twin brothers gripped Maglite torches, while the man carrying a bag of cocaine and another man, with a Beretta pistol, held roadwork lights, casting orange beams ahead of them.

"I always forget the way," noted the man with the Beretta.

"Me too. Every step looks the same," chirped the man with the milky white eye.

Jack and Sinatra sat on the sofa in his small living room. The television was on and the movie Harry Brown was playing on the DVD.

"Dis film is crap, man," commented Sinatra, sighing.

"It's seven o'clock, Sinatra."

"So?" Sinatra replied, scowling and turning the sound up on the TV.

"Turn it down and talk to me," Jack said, placing an arm around Sinatra, with him edging away.

"Get off me, man. Stop being gay."

"Stop being gay? Are you serious? Why are you pretending to be so tough? This isn't you, Sinatra."

"Isn't me? What you saying, isn't me? How do you know what is or isn't me? Fool." Sinatra kissed his teeth and zapped the TV sound up some more.

The orange glow of the roadwork light shone on the pale skin of Michael's face. He must have sensed the bright beam as his head twitched. Perhaps it was the sound of footsteps that echoed into the chamber.

"Whoa! What the fock is this!" gasped the Nigerian with the milky eye.

"Who's there please?" asked Michael, in fear.

"Shit man. Who is he?" said the cocaine carrying man.

"Please. I've been kidnapped. Can you call the police or something? Please. Anyone."

The Nigerian with the cocaine in his sports bag laughed out loud. He formed an intense frown.

"Call the police? I think not. Who are you, and why are you worth kidnapping?"

"I work in a school."

"Shut up!" spouted one of the men. He was the twin without the scar. The one who'd helped Sinatra.

"I've heard your-" Michael was soon interrupted when the five Somali men entered the chamber from another tunnel.

"You are late," said the Nigerian with the cocaine.

"I've been down 'ere once, init. Joo fink I can remember deez caves and da layout anshit?" replied the Somali with the two track bags.

"Who the fuck is he, man?" came one of the men, waving his Glock pistol in Michael's direction.

"Never mind who he is. Do you have the money?" asked the cocaine-carrying Nigerian to Mister Track Bags, who scoffed and sneered at the question and exchanged a look with each of his fellow Somali friends.

"Of course, man," retorted Mister Track Bags, raising his blue bag.

The four Somali men suddenly pulled their weapons and started firing, rapidly. They darted around the chamber, like springboks, as they blasted bullets into the chalk walls.

The Mac 10 machine pistol sounded like an electric drill as it spat out bullets. The Glocks sounded like loud bursts of air. Each one released a flash of light in the darkness of the cavern.

Michael was illuminated by the gunfire. He pressed tight against the pillar, gritting his teeth, frightened as hell. He lowered himself down to the ground, rubbing his right shoulder to his right eye, peeling off the black electrical tape that covered it. Widening his eye with fright, he wished he had left it on as he witnessed the onslaught that took place around him.

The two gangs were killing each other.

Screams of pain, adrenaline and fear combined were released by all as bullets raced this way and that, embedding into the chalky walls and piercing and puncturing skin and splitting bone.

One Somali fired his gun whilst diving for the sports bag that was packed with cocaine, but he was soon riddled with bullets, forcing him off his feet and backwards over the stone bench.

Jack and Sinatra exchanged a look, frowning at one another.

"Is that drilling going on?" Jack asked.

"I think it's coming from underground, you know," replied Sinatra, muting the television and standing, listening to the faint sound of an echoed popcorn-sounding drum that rumbled underneath the house.

"Has somebody got fireworks?"

"It ain't November yet, man?" Sinatra pointed out as he exited the room and grabbed his flashlight from the side. He set foot outside to the path.

"Wait! Sinatra, I'm scared." Jack suddenly fled after him.

It was darkening outside as Sinatra strode to the plant-covered cavern entrance. "I'm gonna 'ave a look, man," he said to Jack, against the background of short claps of thunder which escaped from within the hole.

"Let me get my coat. It's getting cold. Wait there." Jack turned back into the house.

Sinatra's light beamed along the way as he hot-footed it down the steps into the depths of the cavern. The noise became clearer and more identifiable as gunfire with every step he took. He swallowed, amazed at the sheer sight. A bizarre curiosity ran through him. He blinked every time a shot was fired. A lot of shots were being fired. He heard a muffled yelling, whistling and echoing through the tunnels. It reminded him of when he was younger, much younger, and back in Angola. It both terrified and excited him.

BANG! BANG!

The noise was deafening. Blood spattered the white, uneven chalk walls. Bodies were strewn about the place, twitching. They jerked and oozed blood. Jaws hung loose and limbs dangled like worn out toys. The dead were amongst the dying.

BANG!

A gunshot sounded off and started a three second silence until it ended with the sound of the bullet casing pinging on the ground with a metallic noise.

A shuffling and a groan sounded out.

Michael squinted with his one free eye, searching through the gunsmoke, chalk dust and cocaine particles, which drifted in the air. They caught the light of the orange roadwork lamps. He quaked with fear as he looked at the contorted mass of bloody bodies around him. He caught sight of a silent figure, lurking in the tunnel beyond the entrance.

It was Sinatra. He signaled Michael to be quiet by placing a forefinger to his lips as he crept into the cave, not knowing the sight that would soon shock him.

Michael slowly stood, relaxing just slightly at the sight of a known face, but was still wary of him.

Sinatra was horrified by the dead bodies strewn around the cavern, but was also somewhat in awe of the sight of guns and drugs as he passed Michael. He turned and stood in a darkened arch of another chamber, taking in more of the view of the dead.

"Gangsta. This is gangsta."

BANG! BANG! BANG!

Michael blinked with each gunshot as Sinatra was blasted three times in the chest, sending him back and down into the darkness.

The last bullet shell spun in the air, twisting round and around, reflecting the light in its brass casing. It landed with a ping at Michael's feet and his eyes diverted and fixed upon it. The eyes rolled upwards to meet another pair.

A pair that belonged to the Nigerian who'd first aided Sinatra.

The Nigerian man winced with pain and was bleeding heavily from a gunshot wound to his thigh and left side. He looked at Michael. "You're coming with me," he said to Michael, limping forward and pressing the black electrical tape down over his right eye to fix it in place again. He turned and staggered to the Adidas track bag, unzipped it and saw bundles of fifty and twenty pound notes. Hundreds of thousands of pounds in tight bundles, secured with red elastic bands. The type a postman would use. He grabbed the bag, slung it over one shoulder, then scooped up Michael's beige canvas bag. He glanced to the darkness where Sinatra lay dead.

"Fuck. Stoopid. Arrow boy," he said to himself, limping round, having done a full circle. He struggled to reach for the bag of cocaine. Some of the kilo bags had split from the gunfire, but he managed to take six bags that he placed into his own. He moaned with pain.

Michael seized the opportunity. He sensed he wasn't being watched so closely and lowered himself to pick up the bullet shell by the ends between his finger and thumb, not actually touching the rounded outer casing at all. Despite his wrists being bound, he removed his chewing gum and stuck it to the pillar. He then stuck the bullet shell to the gum, just as the Nigerian straightened and turned to him.

"Time to go."

"Where are you taking me?" asked Michael, as he was shoved by the man into the cavern and toward the steps. His head turned as he walked. His eyes weren't taped up securely enough. He could see Jack, standing still as a rock, trembling with absolute fear, in a darkened corner by the steps.

"Move," barked the Nigerian, prodding him up the rocky stairwell and out of sight.

Having listened to Jack, Edward closed his eyes. He reopened and sighed, looking around at the dead Nigerians and Somali men who littered the cave. He saw Sinatra being cradled by Jack and then a sparkle of brass caught his eye in the orange glisten of a roadwork light. A single bullet casing, fixed to the pillar with gum. Edward frowned. He covered his mouth as to not to breathe on it and pulled an evidence bag from his fleece pocket, gently easing the gum off the rock with the bag so it fell into it, along with the bullet shell. His eyes then fixed upon a Beretta handgun on the ground near him.

Jason looked ahead as his father approached the vehicle and opened the boot.

Mr Ahmed was almost falling asleep in the backseat. He turned around with a jolt to see Edward rummage in the back of the boot.

Jason exited the car and joined his father.

Edward had a peculiar wooden box with wires and a clamp of some sort. It was the size of a shoebox, but a little taller. He had already prised the bullet shell from the gum and was coating it with some kind of carbon powder, clamping it into the middle of the box. He reached deeper into the boot for two car batteries that were joined together. He attached them to the box via a set of wires. It was like he was about to jump-start the box in a weird kind of way.

"Stand back," he said to Jason, who did so, just as Edward clamped the metal pincer to the battery.

BANG! A short, sudden burst of a thousand or so volts was sent to the bullet shell casing.

"What the bloody hell!" cried Mr Ahmed.

Edward blew the shell and formed a satisfied look.

"I think Mike just helped us out," Edward murmured.

"How - how d'you mean?" asked Jason, exhaling his warm breath into the cold night air.

"There was a shoot-out in a cave underground. Ssh - don't say anything. I'll tell you more later. The boy I just found said Mikey was taken away by a Nigerian bloke. I'll get a fingerprint off this shell and it'll lead us to him, I'm sure of it," Edward said with pure conviction.

"I thought you couldn't get prints off bullet casings," frowned Jason.

"Not usually, but this way you can. A forensic chap called Dr John Bond found a way. Thought I'd try it myself, and he was right. You can. Even years after the bullet was fired," Edward continued as he located a print and took it off the casing, backing it on a plain white postcard. "Take a picture of that on your phone, would you please?"

"Bloody heck. Are you a real life spy?" asked Mr Ahmed, no longer feeling scared, but somewhat excited to be in Edward's presence.

"Not anymore," Edward replied, looking at Mr Ahmed.

"I feel honoured to be in your presence, sir," Mr Ahmed said humbly.

"Don't be," Edward responded, concentrating on the image of the print as Jason took a clear, decent picture of it.

"I apologise for my rudeness earlier," Mr Ahmed continued.

"Are you able to email it to someone?" Edward asked Jason.

"Course," Jason confirmed.

"Let me give Geoff a call. He's on a late shift."

Behind the wheel, in the jeep, Edward retrieved his mobile phone and spoke to Geoff, informing him that he had a fingerprint to check immediately against the police database for an identity and any known associated addresses.

As Geoff already knew the situation and the natural urgency surrounding it, he obliged without question or hesitation, receiving the emailed fingerprint from the projectile casing and scanning it into the database for any known offender.

Olafemi Kuku. Twenty-two years old. Nigerian born. Lived in Thamesmead, South East London. A persistent offender since he arrived in the United Kingdom at the age of eleven. Despite previous known addresses and aliases, it was the Thamesmead address which Edward took particular note of and together, with his son Jason, he drove to that address.

The Nigerian man known as Olafemi sat in the back of a minicab, driven by a Nigerian man in his forties. Next to Olafemi was Michael, complete with his tied wrists and taped eyes. Olafemi Kuku was indeed the very man who, previously, was involved in a bloodthirsty gunfight deep underground in Jack Cade's Cavern.

"OK to walk?" asked the driver, looking up into his rear view mirror at Olafemi.

"Yes. Two minutes. OK?" replied Olafemi.

"OK," said the driver and with that, Olafemi opened the door, wincing as he limped to a money transfer store a few feet from where the car was parked.

The face of a fifty-five-year-old Nigerian man peered out of the window of the money transfer store and nodded to acknowledge Olafemi who was standing outside. The man unlocked the door and let Olafemi inside the darkened shop.

"Olafemi. What is so urgent? What is the emergency?"

"I need a passport," Olafemi commanded, wincing.

"A pail? Come back in two days," snapped the man, annoyed. A pail was Nigerian slang for passport.

"I need it tonight. I know you can do it. I have money. Lots of money. Do it for me. I need to leave tonight," said Olafemi.

"Just a passport? How will you leave the country? Do you have transportation? Where is your private jet?" chuckled the man, already moving to a back office. He opened a cupboard filled with British passports.

"No planes. A boat maybe."

"A boat? I can sort you out a ship. How old are you now?" quizzed the man, looking through a number of passports. He flipped the back page and eyed up several photographs that depicted African men.

"Twenty-two."

"Twenty-two? How about thirty-seven? This one?" said the man, showing Olafemi a passport picture of a Ghanaian man in his late thirties who looked similar to Olafemi.

"Perfect," Olafemi agreed, nodding his head, giving approval to the ready-made passport.

"All right then, Mr Mynah Lampitey?"

"Lampitey? You are giving me a name from Ghana! What is wrong with you?" snapped Olafemi.

"No, what is wrong with you? Take it or leave it."

Olafemi snatched the passport from the man, scowling at him. "How much?"

"A thousand pounds."

"No problem." Olafemi pulled a bundle of cash, which must have been twenty thousand pounds at least. The top note was bloodstained as he fingered the money to count.

"This will do fine," said the man, taking the whole bundle from a weak Olafemi.

"There is much more than a thousand pounds there!"

"Inflation. Go home. Wait for my call. I will get someone to take you to a boat."

"Thank you."

"Just stay out of trouble when you get back to the UK again, do you understand me, Olafemi?" ordered the man, sincere and stern as he looked Olafemi up and down.

"I understand, Uncle," replied Olafemi, respectfully. He turned and left the store.

Detectives Cole, Crowe and Blake drove through the night on a dual carriage way, heading towards Plumstead High Street.

"McDonald's tonight?" suggested Crowe, cheerily.

"Not tonight, mate," replied Cole.

Blake's attention was drawn elsewhere as she stared out of the back passenger side window and across the carriageway to a row of shops, silent, closed and deserted. Except for the sight of Olafemi who clambered into a minicab that quickly pulled away. She turned her head back in a double-take and fixed on the lone white passenger who was in the back with Olafemi.

"I swear I just saw Jacob," she exclaimed to the other detectives.

"Jacob? Oh, Ramsay?"

"Yes."

"You've got him on the brain, especially since the boss mentioned he had gone missing this eve-" Crowe's voice trailed off and he glanced at Blake on the backseat.

"Where'd you see him?" asked Cole.

"Back of a car. Couple of black guys inside," she replied.

"Dammit. Can't turn around," replied Crowe.

"We'll have to go up there, mate," Cole said

Blake sighed and glanced round out of the back window to a totally deserted street. There was no sign of anyone or anything, and especially no cars.

Edward drove toward Abbeywood, passing through Plumstead.

Jason looked at his father, tense behind the wheel, staring and thinking.

Mr Ahmed was asleep in the backseat. His seatbelt prevented him from sliding across, but he still looked uncomfortable nonetheless.

Michael was shoved into a hallway of a dark, dingy flat with brown décor on an estate in Thamesmead.

Olafemi left a blood-smeared handprint on the wall as he barged past Michael and frantically staggered into a room. In his distress and discomfort, he slung a sports bag onto an unmade double bed, opened a chest of drawers and pulled out several boxes of brand new Calvin Klein underpants, tossing them into the bag. He closed the drawer and opened another, finding a pair of new Levi jeans. A crisp white shirt hung on a wire hanger in polythene from the door handle. He packed each into the bag.

He stuffed four bundles of elastic-band-wrapped cash from the Adidas track bag he had collected from within the cave into his own bag under the clothes, along with the six kilos of wrapped cocaine. He laid them on the top and painfully exited the room.

A scared Michael turned as he heard the man step near to him and dropped the sports bag on the floor and pass into another room.

"What are you going to do with me? If you're going, please, just go, but please, leave me here. Please, I've not seen your face."

"Shut up," replied Olafemi from the other room.

A cell phone rang and Michael's ears pricked up and his head turned toward the direction of the telephone ring.

"Yes, I have money! Come up. The door is open. Come up," Olafemi said, impatiently before hanging up the call. He gulped down a glass of water and washed his bloodstained hands in the kitchen sink.

An overweight, tired Nigerian man, in his late forties, exited a dark Vauxhall car and glanced up at the flats in the Thamesmead estate. It really was a concrete jungle with a maze of meandering walkways that formed eerie, jagged shadows. He sighed and heaved his bulk towards a stairwell.

Michael shivered in the hallway and swallowed, swaying slightly with fear and tiredness combined. His head twitched to the door as it opened and the bulky Nigerian man entered.

His eyes locked onto Michael, hands bound and eyes taped, bag draped over his neck. He frowned and walked past him, peering into the kitchen, his eyes diverting immediately to a pool of blood on the floor.

Olafemi rested against the kitchen sink. The blood was escaping from his leg at a rapid rate. He slowly looked around to meet the eyes of the other man, looking him up and down from the doorway with disgust.

"We are going here." The overweight man handed a folded strip of notepaper to Olafemi.

"OK." Olafemi placed the paper on the side by the kettle and winced with pain.

"I have eshin waiting to take a passenger. Where is the money?" the man said in a thick Nigerian accent, then announced he had a car outside.

"There is kishi in the bag outside. Take the akata I have in the hall. He is going to come with me," said Olafemi. In Nigerian slang kishi meant money and akata was white man.

"I was told one passenger only. Fashi," said the man. Fashi was a Nigerian slang term for forget it.

"I will be out in a minute! Just take the white man!"

The man in the doorway looked at Olafemi, turned and stepped back into the hall to where Michael was. He looked at the small sports bag and picked it up, noticing the cocaine that was laid on the top. The overweight Nigerian held the sports bag on one hand and grabbed Michael's arm with the other, then led him to his car. He opened the rear passenger door and shoved Michael inside. As he heaved his own bulk into the car, he looked at the cocaine in the bag again. He turned to Michael and wondered if he should go with the money and drugs and leave Michael behind or if it would benefit him to take him. He looked up at the flats, sighed, impatiently tapping the wheel like a drum with his big, thick forefingers. He started the engine, formed a devilish smirk, pulled the car away out of the estate just as another vehicle's headlights flared up and entered.

Edward pulled his jeep into the estate and saw the car with the overweight Nigerian driving past them, the man shielding his eyes from Edward's headlights. Edward turned his head to look at the man as he passed them. He quickly took a mental note of the car registration.

"I can call up some more people, Dad," Jason suggested to his father.

"No. It's OK, son," Edward said, opening the door and tucking in his shirt as he stood outside.

Jason noticed a Beretta pistol in his father's waistband, which was soon covered up when Edward zipped up his fleece. He frowned, worried.

"Careful," Jason warned softly.

"If I'm not back in five minutes, just wait longer," Edward smirked, trying his best to lessen his son's worry and tension.

He carefully pulled on a pair of clean gloves. Edward ascended the concrete stairwell and exhaled deep, sighing breaths every other step. He was by no means as fit as he used to be. Getting back into the game after so many years of being inactive was taking its toll. It was simply the stress of the situation and his pure anguish that was driving and pushing him. He reached the right level and walked past a couple of flats coming to an open door: the door to Olafemi's home. Edward tightened his mouth and entered the hall just as Olafemi exited the kitchen.

Their eyes locked, both staring for different reasons.

Olafemi, caught off-guard and confused as to why a once-well-built white man was in his hallway. Edward, wary, yet satisfied that he had already located the man who had taken his son from the cave.

"Olafemi Kuku?" Edward asked, brief and hard.

"Wahala? Comot!" Olafemi yelled aggressively at Edward to get out.

Edward bounded forth, clenched his fist and punched Olafemi hard in the throat, making him double over and choke for breath. Edward noticed his gunshot in his side and grabbed hold of the bloody wound. He forced him into the kitchen and slammed him into the work-surface.

Olafemi wheezed. His face filled with the pain Edward was causing him as he clutched his injured side and pushed him backwards over the kitchen sink, creating further discomfort.

"Olafemi Kuku?" repeated Edward.

"Wetin!" Olafemi said "what" in Nigerian Pidgin English.

Edward scanned the draining board. He picked up a fork and pressed it hard to Olafemi's Adam's apple.

"I no sabi. I don't understand. Talk English or you'll be breathing through a pen for the rest of the night," Edward said.

"I don't know you! What do you want?"

Edward dug the fork harder against Olafemi's skin and clasped a dishcloth, which he covered Olafemi's face with.

Olafemi tried to blow the cloth off, but Edward began to pour water from the kettle over the cloth on his face. Makeshift waterboarding. He coughed and spluttered as the water entered his mouth and nose.

"Listen well. Where is my son?"

"I no. I no sabi." Olafemi struggled to speak, even in his own native tongue.

"Yes, yes you do know. You do know!" Edward insisted, pouring more water onto Olafemi's face.

Olafemi spat and spluttered some more, choking and practically drowning.

"Please - please. No more. I speak," gasped Olafemi.

Edward removed the dishcloth from Olafemi's face and angrily stared down at him. Olafemi took two deep breaths. His eyes rolled to the kettle and the piece of folded notepaper given to him by the overweight man. With all his energy he reached across, grabbed the piece of paper and stuffed it into his mouth.

"What are you doing? What is that? Gimme that!" yelled Edward, seeing Olafemi chewing and trying to swallow the paper. He suddenly cranked Olafemi's head back further, down into the sink and rammed his hand deep into Olafemi's mouth, right into his throat.

Olafemi gagged. His body jerked, violently.

Edward's hand worked its way further down. His knuckles were clearly visible as they poked out of the skin of Olafemi's neck. Edward retracted his hand, his finger and thumb pinching the piece of paper moistened with blood and vomit as he took a step back from Olafemi, letting him drop to the kitchen floor, spewing up.

Olafemi found it incredibly difficult to breathe.

The paper was torn between Edward's fingers and he laid it flat on the worktop, piecing it together like a jigsaw, trying to read what was written. The ink had smudged considerably, but the numbers and letters were just about identifiable. The number BSQU45T226 was written down.

Edward turned and scowled at Olafemi.

"What is this? What's this number?" Edward stared at it some more. The letter 'U' stood out to him.

Olafemi sneered as he slyly opened a cupboard door and placed his hand inside. He smiled a bloody grin.

"An airplane," Olafemi said.

"No, no, it's a freight container. This is a number of a container ship. You bloody bastard."

"It's for me - and this is for you," Olafemi blurted. He dribbled blood down his chest.

Edward turned and saw Olafemi's hand inside the cupboard, about to pull something out. Edward pulled the Beretta pistol from the top of his jeans and took aim.

Olafemi suddenly coughed and choked.

Edward gripped the handgun tight with his gloved hands, aiming it at Olafemi's head, but he had choked on his own blood and slumped sideways.

Olafemi had died from his blocked airway. Dead from his wounds. Dead from who cared what? Dead.

Edward lowered the gun as he watched Olafemi's arm lower from the cupboard. Olafemi's fingers were limp as they lost the grip of a .38 revolver.

Edward looked at the number on the soggy paper and the gun in his hand. He headed out of the kitchen and into the hall. He made out of the flat and onto the balcony walkway where he suddenly threw the Beretta pistol into the middle of the dark waters of Southmere Lake.

Jason and Mr Ahmed looked up quickly as Edward clambered back inside the jeep, exhausted and out of breath.

"Dad! Did you find him? Did you find the man? Did you find Mike? Are you OK?" Jason gasped.

"Sir? Is everything all right?" asked Mr Ahmed.

"I found the man," Edward said wearily.

"And?"

"And he's dead," Edward sighed.

"Did you kill him, sir?" asked Mr Ahmed.

"No. He killed himself," Edward replied, placing the piece of paper, now wrapped in cling-film on the dashboard.

"What's that? Where's Mike?" asked Jason. He had become quite frantic.

"I think he's on a ship," Edward told him, extremely tired. He was mentally and physically exhausted.

"A ship? I used to work in shipping. It was a long time ago, sir. But how did you learn of this fact?" inquired Mr Ahmed.

Edward turned, showing him the piece of paper taken from within Olafemi's throat.

"This is the owner's code. These letters reveal the country where the ship was registered and this means it is a freight container. This is a serial number and here tells me it is an open top container vessel," informed Mr Ahmed.

He studied the piece of paper and looked up at Edward and Jason, who were both impressed by his knowledge and grateful for his assistance.

"Thank you, but it's not enough," Edward sighed, wearily.

"But it is, sir. It is. Tilbury Docks is just forty minutes away. We have time to get there. How long do you think it has been since your son was taken there? It cannot be too long ago, sir."

"That bloody car! I knew it. I knew it was dodgy! It has to be him."

"Who? Who, Dad?"

"The car. The car that left when we pulled in," spouted Edward, starting the car and speedily driving out of the estate.

The A13 was practically deserted. The occasional heavy goods vehicle rumbled along the inside or middle lane, as did the dark Vauxhall car driven by the overweight Nigerian man.

Michael trembled on the back seat. Tears streamed down his cheeks.

The car was nearing Tilbury Docks, in Essex.

Edward, shifted gears like Robo-Cop. He drove himself, Jason and Mr Ahmed along the A13 into the night.

Together, they too headed for Tilbury Docks.

Hundreds of coloured containers were stacked on one another in dimly lit rows, stretched across like a grid. They looked like Lego bricks, but were a million times bigger. These were corrugated metal freight containers. Their names ranged from Intermodel containers, ISO container and Sea-Can. Each had its own ISO reporting mark. The huge steel boxes were currently at home in Tilbury Docks. Some were being lifted by cranes onto a container ship.

Some had cast sharp-edged shadows, and standing in one particular shadow was the overweight Nigerian.

He spoke Portuguese to an unshaven, tanned European man.

He was a dock worker. The Nigerian showed him the kilos of cocaine in the bag, and he nodded his head in approval. The docker was in his mid-forties and rubbed his stubbled cheeks, thinking as he glanced back at the cargo ship being loaded. He looked back to the Nigerian man and placed his hands on his hips.

"Mostre-me o homem," he said in Portuguese.

The overweight Nigerian man reached into the pitch black nothingness and pulled Michael in to where the two men stood.

The tanned docker puffed his cheeks out and exhaled a deep sigh as he looked Michael up and down.

"Dá-me dois minutos." His Portuguese continued as he told the Nigerian to give him two minutes and, with that, he rounded a container and disappeared into the darkness.

"Am I going to die now?" Michael asked in a surprisingly calm manner.

"I don't know what will happen to you," replied the overweight Nigerian.

"Why?"

"You are no longer anything to do with me," shrugged the Nigerian. He glanced up to see the tanned dock worker return with a Middle Eastern docker of similar age.

"You speak English? French?" asked the new arrival.

"English," replied the Nigerian.

"OK. How many pounds of cocaine do you have?" asked the Middle Eastern man.

"I have six kilos in total," said the Nigerian.

"Six kilos? Six kilos multiplied by two point two is thirteen point two pounds," stated the man, quickly and impressively.

"And him?" asked the Nigerian.

"Wait. For the cocaine I can give you twenty AK47 assault rifles with ammunition."

"AK?"

"AK47. Standard Chinese model 47. The standard folding butt model comes in at one dollar shy of six hundred dollars. I will also give you one hundred thousand dollars in cash," said the Middle Eastern man.

"One hundred thousand? In dollar? It is not enough," scoffed the Nigerian man.

"You wanted guns and you wanted money."

"Yes."

"You also want me to take this man off your hands."

"Yes."

"So it is a deal. Take it or leave it."

"This man can help your cause. You know that he is worth more than the deal you are offering me," declared the Nigerian man.

"OK. OK. Two hundred thousand dollars. Final offer."

"Deal." The Nigerian extended his right hand for the man to shake.

"Deal. OK. Hold on," the Middle Eastern man shook his hand then disappeared around the container.

Michael shook with absolute fear, too frightened to speak let alone shout out for help, but who would have heard him? The noise of the engines and cranes and clanging of metal hooks against corrugated steel containers would have certainly overpowered any other sound, especially that of a scared yell. Michael knew this. Shouting wasn't an option.

"Bring your car up more," instructed the tanned, original dock worker. He grabbed Michael tight as the Middle Eastern man returned.

The Middle Eastern dock worker cranked open the end doors of the container next to him and slung the sports bag into it. He then gave a brief look at Michael, spun him around and, in one swift motion, he slit the plastic binds that tied his hands together and shoved him inside the container. He slammed the door and bolted it tight. The sound of steel hitting steel echoed like rolling thunder.

The lid to a wooden crate that contained ten standard Chinese AK47 assault rifles was fixed tight. The box was pushed across the folded back seat of the Vauxhall, which joined a second crate already housed inside. A grey blanket was draped over the crates and the boot then closed.

The dock worker handed the overweight Nigerian man two hundred thousand dollars in cash before he worked his bulk back into his car.

The number BSQU45T226 was peeled off the top of the door to the steel container just before it rose into the night. A crane lifted the container up and across the docks and loaded it onto a ship.

Edward, Mr Ahmed and Jason stood by an Indian security guard at the checkpoint barrier to the docks.

The guard looked at the clipboard and occasionally glanced Mr Ahmed up and down, puzzled at seeing him in his pyjamas.

"I have just begun my shift and the other guard left fifteen or so minutes ago."

"We have an ISO 6346 number," stated Mr Ahmed.

"Just a moment," the guard took the number from Mr Ahmed and entered his booth.

Edward peered through the booth to see the guard flip through sheets of paper on another clipboard. He watched him run his forefinger down a list and then watched him step back outside.

"That particular crate was loaded over three weeks ago."

"I don't understand. It has to be here," said Edward, desperately.

"The ship that the crate was loaded on, what was its destination please?" asked Mr Ahmed.

The man looked at the clipboard again.

"It says the destination is to be confirmed," said the guard.

"No destination? That's bloody ridiculous," blurted Edward.

"It is quite common," replied the guard.

"Call the Coast Guard," ordered Edward.

"Pardon me?" The security guard was confused.

"Get the Coast Guard on the phone. I want to report a kidnapping."

"A kidnapping? I have contact details for the Maritime and Coastguard Agency for a minor injuries unit. They're five miles away,"

"Minor injuries? Are you nuts?" yelled Edward.

"Dad? We have a number that isn't here."

"Then why not? Listen, do you have any ships bound for Nigeria?" Edward sighed, clutching at any thought he could.

"Nigeria? Erm," the security guard pondered and shook his head. He ran his finger down his list again and flipped the pages on the clipboard and looked up to Edward and his desperate expression. He was confused by his inexplicable situation, yet felt his frustration completely. He shook his head again.

"Are any ships heading for Africa?" Edward asked softly.

"No, sir. I'm sorry. I'm sorry I cannot help."

Edward's face tightened. He turned around, pinching the bridge of his nose and rubbed his eyes and he suddenly began to cry. His shoulders jerked twice as the tears flowed and he leaned his body against the wing of his jeep.

Jason shared his father's pain. He couldn't bear to see the rock of his family crack like that. If his father hadn't any other clue then what on Earth could he do? He looked at Mr Ahmed then back at the security guard, who helplessly shrugged.

"Sir, can you tell me when the last ship left the dock and its destination port please?" asked Mr Ahmed.

"The last ship left here around twenty minutes ago. The destination was the port of Genoa, Italy," replied the man.

Jason glanced at his father who stared into the night. Tears welled up in his eyes.

Edward's mobile rang which broke his trance.

"Geoff? Geoffrey? What's up? Any news?"

"Just calling to ask the same thing, Ed. Where are you at?" Geoff asked.

"We're um... we're at Tilbury."

"What you doing there?"

"There was a possible lead. I've got another plate to run."

"Go on," urged Geoff as Edward told him the registration number he'd got a glimpse of when the overweight Nigerian had driven past him.

Geoff told Edward he would get back to him as soon as he could, and ordered Edward to go home and get some rest.

Edward dialed up his friend, Carolyn. Fortunately for him she was still working in her office at Thames House, between Millbank and Horseferry Road in London, otherwise known as MI-5.

Carolyn was an attractive blonde in her late fifties. She wore a grey suit and clutched a telephone receiver in one hand and a mug of hot chocolate in the other. She told Edward that the line was a secure one as he informed her of what he knew about Michael's disappearance. She understood his anguish. She had also known Michael since he was a baby and naturally felt the need to help as much as she could, but also, like Geoff, ordered Edward to return home and get some rest.

"Go home, Edward. Comfort Violet. If anything comes up, I'll call you."

"Anything, Carolyn. Anything to do with the docks, shipping, cargo, anything. Please," Edward pleaded.

"I will. Ed, I learned one of our cars was observing Mike's house. It's since been recalled because his voice didn't match any of the spoken words that were flagged when a call was made from his phone. I've noted his disappearance and attached it to any signal that it emits."

"Thank you. Thank you," he said.

Rebecca was fast asleep on the sofa. Her mascara was smudged and smeared from the corner of her eyes and down her cheeks. The blanket covered just half her body. Her two phones flashed on the coffee table and one arm of the sofa as their batteries charged. A glimmer of daylight slid through a gap in the blind. It shone on her beautiful face. She didn't stir.

14. THE BUBBLE

The Bubble was a nickname for the auditorium within the headquarters of the Central Intelligence Agency in Langley, Virginia. It was a few miles out from Washington DC. That particular building could hold nearly five hundred people, but on this day, it was holding just two.

Deputy Director of the CIA James Monroe crossed his legs as he sat on one of the chairs in the Bubble. He had been sworn into the position eighteen months prior, having previously been Director of Intelligence. His prime role back then was being chief of the CIA's division in the Middle East. He rubbed his cheeks, polished his glasses with his tie and looked at the man sitting on the chair behind him.

The man who filled the shoes he had stepped out of to gain his more senior level. The new Director of Intelligence was Frank Moses. Among his responsibilities was intelligence analysis on key foreign issues.

"What do you have, Frank?" DD Monroe asked.

"We have confirmation that our man boarded the ship in the port of Genoa, Italy," replied DI Moses.

"And the ship was definitely on its way to Iran?"

"Yes. It was the only ship we knew at the time that would be in Italy. Italy obviously still trades with Iran, Jim."

"Yes, yes. I know all that. Listen, what happened to our asset? Is he to be trusted?"

"Hundred percent," replied DI Moses.

"What was the route of the cargo ship?"

"It left the United Kingdom and travelled via Gibralta. Eight days later, it arrived in Italy. After a day in the dock of Genoa, it was bound for the Iranian port of Bandar Abbas where it arrived seventeen days later," continued Moses.

"What was the last intel from the asset?"

"Two same-day communications from the asset. First com gave intel stating a crate of AK47s had been sold dockside to a Nigerian male prior to leaving

Great Britain. Second was in Badar Abbas saying there was a change of plan and there was a friendly hostage situation."

"Meaning?"

"There's been no further communication since."

"In twenty-eight days?"

"Yes," answered Moses.

"How reliable is he?"

"The asset? Very."

"Could he be dead?" asked Monroe.

"Possible, but not likely. He's a highly skilled operative. Probably just gone dark."

"Twenty-eight days is a long time to remain dark, Frank. What about this friendly hostage situation? Could he mean he, the asset, is being held hostage?" quizzed Monroe.

"I'll get word from other agents who confirmed sightings of the asset when he arrived at Bandar," replied Moses.

"I wanna know what happened the moment he left that port, Frank. I wanna know who that hostage is because it cannot overshadow the mission."

At the port of Bandar Abbas in Iran, the container ship from Tilbury had docked and was being unloaded. The sun was scorching down and hundreds of people were milling about the place.

The boot of a gleaming black Mercedes S Class slammed shut and an Iranian man extended his hand to another.

"Siamak?" said the Iranian man who held his hand out for another to shake.

"Yes. I am Siamak," replied a tall man with jet-black hair. He was a handsome Iranian man, with deep-set eyes and a kind face. On that day, he wore fashionably ripped blue jeans, brown cowboy boots and a green Abercrombie and Fitch t-shirt.

"Watch the car. I will be two minutes, OK?" said the first Iranian, who rounded the vehicle and became lost amongst a crowd.

Siamak glanced back at the cargo ship and the boot of the Mercedes. He exhaled, discreetly pulled out a cell phone and began to sing under his breath the Frank Sinatra song 'I Guess I'll Have to Change My Plan'. He sang softly, giving a perfect Sinatra impression. He slyly switched his phone off and slid it into his pocket.

A tech guy brought up a visual on a large, central screen within an operations room. The Director of Intelligence, Frank Moses, loosened his neck tie, folded his arms and formed a pained, tired expression as he looked at the surveillance photograph of an Iranian man in his early thirties.

"Remind me," said Moses to the analyst tech.

"Hamid Golzar, Iranian. A former pro-Ahmadinejad rebel, who's started out on his own. He has access to pretty much everything: guns, chemicals, hostages, kitchen sink, you know. He's a radical. He has strong links with Libya and Syria, not to mention Al-Qaeda and Hamas, but also the new ones the world will be hearing about in a few years: Boko Harem and ISIS. Our friends at MI-5 confirm that their missing national could have been taken aboard the cargo vessel that was bound for Italy, sir."

"This would match the intel from the asset," Moses responded.

"Yes, sir."

"And he's since coded in?"

"Yes. Emmett Smith briefed us on what occurred when he arrived in Iran," reported the analyst.

"I'm listening," said Moses.

Rebecca, Violet and Edward were having dinner in their home. Chicken casserole with mashed potato. The only one who managed to eat entire mouthfuls, and not just simply spread food around the plate, was Edward.

"I don't understand why we're not allowed to put the story out to the press. It doesn't make sense," protested Rebecca, sniffing.

"I'm waiting to hear why, Becky," said Edward in a comforting tone, however unsure and baffled he was.

"Even the local newspaper said they'd help, but now they're saying they can't. It's been over a month! Why!" Rebecca began to cry.

"The Home Secretary has issued a D Notice," stated Edward.

A D Notice was short for Defence Notice. The system was set up in 1912 and was a voluntary suppression of particular categories of information on the advice of the government. D Notices were sent out to national and provincial newspaper editors, as well as those behind radio and TV companies, advising them not to report on a certain subject. The rationale behind the censorship was that an adverse group could unearth intelligence secrets or assets sensitive to national security. The five Defence Advisory Notices in the United Kingdom, were:

DA-Notice 01: Military Operations, Plans and Capabilities.

DA-Notice 02: Nuclear and Non-Nuclear Weapons and Equipment.

DA-Notice 03: Ciphers and Secure Communications.

DA-Notice 04: Sensitive Installations and Home Addresses.

DA-Notice 05: United Kingdom Security and Intelligence Special Services.

One of the listed D Notices, for reasons as yet unknown to Edward, was connected to his son. All he knew was that he was not allowed to inform Michael's employers that he was missing. Not allowed to discuss with any form of the media, be it print, telecommunication, online or social. Not allowed to pursue any line of investigation himself. It was like a super-injunction that prevented him from gaining any new information on the whereabouts of his son, or from informing those close to him who cared for Michael and simply called him a friend. Of course Edward had told Michael's boss, Helen. She had to know. She adored him as a colleague and as a friend, which Edward knew well.

The conversation with Helen was a difficult one for both her and Edward. She wanted so much to tell the rest of her team, but knew details would leak out. She was extremely angry with Patricia, who was completely unaware of the traumatic situation that she was partly to blame for. Helen was kept up-to-date by Edward.

Edward emailed her regularly, even his findings when he received laboratory results from a lab in Oxford to whom he had sent the chewing gum and blood samples for them to extract and test for DNA, clarifying that it was a one hundred percent match to Michael.

Edward's Nokia mobile phone rang and made everyone at the table jolt when its familiar tone sounded and the plastic casing vibrated on the wooden dining table. He took the call and frowned when he heard that it was Mr Ahmed, the foster parent of Afghan pupil Abdul Rah-Maan.

"Hello, sir. I hope I am not disturbing you."

"No. Not at all, Mr Ahmed."

"First I will inquire on whether you have any news of your son."

"No. Nothing yet."

"For that I am sorry. My family continue to pray for you and the safety of your son, Michael," Mr Ahmed replied.

"Thank you. That's very kind," said Edward.

"I do, however, bring more sad news, sir. I telephone to inform you that Abdul was found dead this afternoon. He accidentally severed an artery in his thigh while he was cutting himself. Because of his self-harming."

"That's terrible news. I'm sorry for the person who discovered him. It couldn't have been a pleasant sight," replied Edward.

"It was my wife. Abdul had not had any food with us and so she went to see him in his room. There was a lot of blood."

"I'm sure there was. I hope your wife is OK."

"A little distressed, but we are not really surprised, sir. Abdul naturally blamed himself for what has happened to your son and did not gain the answers he wanted about him from his school. Because they think your son is unwell, I suppose."

"Yes, that's correct. They're not allowed to know."

"I understand. Well, I am just calling to tell you this and I am here if you need to speak with me or if I am required by any authorities."

"Thank you," replied Edward, quietly. He closed his eyes, saddened by what he heard. He released a deep sigh.

Rebecca jolted again for as soon as Edward put the phone on the table, it rang and vibrated again. Edward instantly took the call.

"Carolyn? What's new?" Edward asked, speaking in a different tone, with his wife and Rebecca turning keenly to listen.

"I can't disclose too much just now, but the US agencies believe they have information which could lead to Michael's whereabouts," Carolyn, Edward's MI-5 contact and family friend, informed him.

"The US? Why would they know anything?" Edward asked, curiously.

"The US?" Violet whispered.

"America? Is Mike in America?" Rebecca frowned.

"We need you and Rebecca to come to us," said Carolyn.

"OK. When?"

"As soon as possible. When is it convenient?"

"We can get to you within the hour," Edward said.

"OK. I'll let security know. See you then."

Edward hung up the phone and told Violet and Rebecca what Carolyn had said.

A confused and slightly more hopeful, yet still very anxious Rebecca nodded her head. She wiped her cheek with a white cotton napkin.

"You like the Rat Pack?" said the Iranian man, as he drove the Mercedes out of the Iranian port. He glanced into the rear view mirror at Siamak.

"What was that?" replied Siamak, in Persian Farsi.

"Frank Sinatra. I heard you singing it," said the Iranian in English, with an American twang. "When we stop, come sit up front with me." "Your English is good." Siamak eyed the surroundings as the car drove through the streets.

"American teachers! I also spent two years in London. The London School of Economics. Not bad, huh? I heard Gadaffi's son was also there, but not when I went," noted the man, smiling. He held up a dirty, creased green school exercise book. "In here is a copy of what was written in the man's own notebook. His name. Where he's from as well as some other names. Muslim names. Evidence of espionage, you know? Man, I had to stop my guys from kicking the shit out of him before they wrapped him up. I tell you though, ma man, when I saw the coded messages in his book, I just had to put my cigarette out on that spying dog's body, you know? I like our country. I'm loyal to my country, like you are, ma man. I don't want Western spy bastards starting a revolution like they have in our other Muslim lands. I tell Hamid this and man, he is as angry as he is excited to have this dog, you know?" he chuckled and continued to focus on the road.

Rebecca sat in the passenger seat of Edward's jeep as he drove through London, heading for Albert Embankment. Both of them had a thousand and one thoughts racing through their minds as they stared dead ahead.

"Do you think he's dead?" Rebecca asked calmly before bursting into tears.

Edward pressed his lips firmly together. Of course the thought had entered his mind, but not that night. "No. He's alive and you keep believing that, OK?" he said, firmly. His eyes glazed over as he concentrated on the road.

15. LUXOR STREET

The Black Mercedes travelled through the Iranian streets and passed the day to day hustle and bustle of usual street life. Cafés and markets, shops and general businesses.

The Iranian driver turned and gestured with his hands left and right out of the window and towards the windscreen. He looked at Siamak on the passenger seat next to him.

"No revolution. No demonstrations. No displays of ill treatment. Not one single person holding up a board saying 'Down with the USA'. Everything the same as it always was, so why on bastard Western news channels do they show pictures of fires, crowds of civil unrest and a call for our leader to be removed? I tell you why. Because it is fake. It is fake and we have to prepare for an invasion, my friend. I've studied this. It's propaganda and is a total psy-op. It's a psychological operation. Seriously. Why remove Mahmoud Ahmadinejad? We have schools and we have great surgeons and doctors and teachers. We also have the oil, my friend. It's another oil war and a chance to put in one of their loyal Western puppets again. The person in the trunk will change things. He's, how you say? A bargaining tool."

Siamak managed a smile, looking out of the window, squinting at the brilliant whiteness caused by the sunshine beyond.

It was daybreak over the Iranian sands of Kavir-e Lut. The desert blanket rolled on for what appeared to be forever in the south-eastern Province of Kerman. The crescent-like hills, known as barchans, and the leafy heaps called nebkas were natural relics. It was a tranquil place, yet very much a place of loneliness.

The gleaming black Mercedes S Class scrolled across the invisibly marked-out road. The heat rippled upwards where the ground met the sky and it distorted everything in sight. The vehicle's bonnet soaked up the rays of the sun. The bluest of skies reflected within the tinted windows, making the occupants feel there was another world beyond the glass: a safer world; a happier world.

The Mercedes slowed to a halt as an older, beaten-up white Mercedes model blocked the route ahead.

An Iranian man, in his early thirties, stood by the rear of the white Merc. The man had three days' worth of stubble on his face. He was a dirty, sweaty man in crisp, modern clothing. He wore a blue and white chequered scarf around his neck. His jeans were either Armani or fake Armani. He narrowed his eyes and put on a pair of shiny gold aviator-style sunglasses, which he kept in the breast pocket of his white cotton shirt. The shirt was absolutely spotless, as if it had just been removed from its packet, or taken off a coathanger at the dry cleaner's. How could somebody have a shirt that clean in a place as scorching hot as this? He wiped his brow with the back of his right hand as his left clutched an AK47 assault rifle.

This was without a doubt the most successful rifle ever produced. One could roll a tank over an AK or even sink it in water and it would still manage to shoot accurately, without fail.

The Iranian man who held this weapon was called Hamid. The boot of the black Mercedes popped open and Hamid scrunched his face up and almost pouted. His eyes narrowed to a squint once more and he glanced around behind him, thumping twice upon the side of his own vehicle.

A second, similarly-dressed Iranian man clambered out of the driver's side of the white Merc. It was Siamak and he adjusted his shirt collar, with the car keys just dangling from one hand as the other shoved a Desert Eagle pistol down the front of his jeans. The gun's handle was clearly visible and looked threatening as he joined Hamid at the boot of the car.

They exchanged a look as Siamak unlocked the boot, turned around and propped his Ray Bans atop his head.

Hamid slung his rifle over his shoulder as Siamak raised the lid.

The two of them ventured a few sandy feet away from their white vehicle and passed the driver's side of the black, more modern one and went to the boot at the rear. Together they reached into the darkness of the boot and struggled as they pulled out a body wrapped in brown parcel paper. They staggered, turning around with the package, wincing at the weight, as they heaved the bulk into the boot of the white Mercedes with a slump.

The first man, Hamid, hot-footed it back to the black Merc and closed the boot lid, gently tapping the glistening metal. The engine purred and the black vehicle smoothly made a turn, leaving the area. It went back the way it came from, with Hamid and Siamak standing in its tracks in the scorching sun.

The men watched the black shape shimmer in the heat as it slowly disappeared out of view.

Siamak climbed into the driving seat of the white Merc and Hamid shuffled into the passenger seat next to him, slotting his AK47 between his knees.

Siamak inserted his key into the ignition and turned it, bringing the car to life. He lowered his sunglasses, released the handbrake, slammed the car into drive and did exactly that: he drove. Across the sandy terrain, which rose, dipped and weaved without a glimpse of shadow.

Hamid fumbled inside his jean pocket and pulled out a pack of Wrigley's Spearmint gum. He brought the pack to his mouth and took hold of a stick between his teeth, as if it were a cigarette. He offered the pack to Siamak, who simply waved his hand, declining. Hamid shrugged and unwrapped his stick of gum, throwing the wrapper to his feet on the floor.

The old Mercedes travelled smoothly across the desert sands of Kavir-e Lut. It was a terrific view. It was like a pre-historic, mechanical beast meandering along in the sunshine, as if it were a daily occurrence. Only Libya and the US possess similar deserts to those of Iran.

Unfortunately for the body wrapped in brown parcel paper, housed within the boot of the car, this was not the US. This was Iran.

There were some ruins in the distance. It looked like an ancient industrial ghost town.

Siamak looked out of the windscreen at the ruins. His mind raced with a thousand and one thoughts. He hadn't seen this place before.

The sun continued to beat down, although it was now later in the day. The white Mercedes, with an open boot, was parked near the ruin. It had either been bombed out, abandoned due to old age or both; neglected, rotten, like the men within.

Hamid leaned against the rear of the vehicle. He looked up to the blue sky and squinted. He eyed the hunks of twisted metal nearby, glanced inside the boot and plucked out a pack of Bahman branded cigarettes. Pleased with his find, he slammed the boot lid down to a close and retrieved a shiny silver Zippo lighter from a front pocket to his jeans. Hamid tapped out a single cigarette, placed it between his tightly pressed lips and flicked a flame from the Zippo. He lit the cigarette and took a long drag from it, exhaling his white transparent smoke into the blue sky, like a rogue cloud.

The faint sound of screaming and shouting echoed off the hardness of the metal that lined the walls within the dark, eerie and cold chamber of the bombed-out underground ruin. The sounds were like screaming ghosts that wailed through the labyrinthine corridors. Heavy breathing and loud footsteps accompanied the occasional flickering shadow exposed by electric lights which were mounted every so often along the walls.

Siamak was illuminated briefly by the wall light. He was struggling to hold the feet end of the body parcel, having unintentionally slammed it into the wall of the corridor several times. He looked up at the body parcel's head end and shrugged.

Hamid looked at the bulging parcel with satisfaction. He signaled men with a quick wave of his hand and the brown parcel tape was ripped this way and that, with one lengthy piece being torn at ease. It suddenly exposed the face of a young white man, whose mouth was gagged with silver tape.

The partially unwrapped man was in a kneeling position, within a generator room. The man was Michael Thompson. Michael was weary and had stubble on his face. His hair was unkempt and, along with his face, was in need of a wash. The brown paper was pulled away, revealing Michael's ill-fitting clothes, consisting of a pale blue shirt and jeans two sizes too large. There was blood that stained the collar as well as the front of the shirt. Michael was also bloodied around the nose and forehead.

A bigger-built Iranian man continued to unwrap the man, with Siamak standing slightly behind, by a metal grille, clutching an AK47 assault rifle.

Michael's eyes darted around. He squinted and tried to adjust to his new surroundings.

Another Iranian set up a Sony DSR-570WSP broadcast quality 'green friendly' camcorder on a tripod.

Michael looked at his bound hands. He breathed through his nose, heavily, in and out, in and out, deep, but with discomfort. It was like he had a cold as, with every breath, a bubble formed from one nostril. It was reminiscent of a frog's throat expanding as it breathed. However, Michael did not have a cold: his nostril bubble was filled with blood. He swayed back and forth, until the man doing the unwrapping, Hamid, took a step back and stared at him for a couple of seconds.

Hamid suddenly punched him, hard, in the side of his face. If it wasn't for the metal clanking noise of a sliding gate behind him that kept him awake, Michael would surely have been knocked out.

Michael's head was forced to look forwards.

Hamid ripped the silver tape off Michael's mouth and then slapped him around the face.

"Why were you in Luxor?" Hamid said, in his strong Middle Eastern accent. "Luxor. Did you spy for the British in Cairo? Did you engineer the uprising against Mubarak?" He slapped him again. "Answer me, you fucking spy dog! Did you start the revolution for the CIA? Are you CIA man in Luxor?" The questioning Hamid turned to Siamak and waved him over.

Siamak joined him, frowned and then Hamid took hold of his rifle. Hamid suddenly slammed it into Michael's chest, forcing him down to the concrete floor. The angry Iranian stepped over to Michael, towering above him.

Michael opened his mouth to reveal his bloodstained teeth and gums. "I've never been to Luxor. Luxor is Egypt. I live in Luxor Street. It's off Cold Harbour Lane, in Lambeth. The Borough of Lambeth. In London. I live in Luxor Street," he said in his British accent.

Hamid grabbed Michael's hair and yanked his head back. He stared wild into his eyes. "You will take off your clothes and put these on. D'you understand?" He shoved his head away as he released his grasp on his hair.

Michael's eyes searched the floor and fixed on a neatly folded orange jumpsuit.

"Orange is the new black," he sarcastically muttered.

Hamid cut his silver tape bindings and released his hands and feet. Michael shifted himself across the cold, concrete floor on his hands and knees, like an injured animal, to where the orange jumpsuit was. He reached for the suit, but Hamid trod on his right hand. Michael winced with pain and gritted his bloodied teeth.

The big, black Caterpillar boot was lifted, leaving a red mark on the back of Michael's hand.

He grabbed hold of the jumpsuit and pulled it close to him, like a comfort blanket.

"OFF!" yelled Hamid, making Michael jolt when he heard his sudden shriek.

Michael was self-conscious as he unbuttoned his shirt. He revealed his slim and incredibly bruised torso. His chest had cuts and cigarette burn marks across it. He stood up and lowered his jeans. He didn't need to unbutton them as they were too large. He clutched the orange jumpsuit and conserved his modesty, never looking up, but he was fully aware of his dangerous audience.

Hamid stepped forwards and snatched the jumpsuit from Michael. He threw it across the room and sniggered a peculiar laugh that was followed by two chuckles elsewhere in the room.

Michael shivered. He stood naked, with his hands covering his genitals.

Hamid stepped up to him and looked him up and down. "Who beat you?"

Michael tried hard not to make eye contact.

"Who fucking beat you? People cannot wait for me. They probably kick you on the boat when you travel here. You fucking dog!"

Michael rolled his eyes to meet the Iranian's.

"You fucking dog. Do you hate me?"

"I don't know you," replied Michael.

"Do you need to know someone to like or hate them?"

"I would like to get dressed before I start educating you." Michael swallowed and looked around his surroundings.

"Mazhabeto gayidam. Do you not understand?" said Hamid, as he spat in Michael's face.

Michael looked up from the floor as the spit remained on his left cheek, just below his eye.

"It means I fucked your religion. Do you understand? Mazhabeto gayidam! I fucked your religion!" he yelled and spat at him again, but nothing was left his mouth. He just made a raspberry sound, which caused Michael to sneer.

"It makes no sense. How would you do that, exactly? How could you possibly have sexual intercourse with my religion? You don't know if I even am religious," said Michael, in a foolishly brave manner. He shivered and stepped onto the jump-suit, crouching slowly and pulling it up and fastening it.

Hamid curled his lip and stared with disgust at Michael.

"Cooney sag," muttered Michael, under his breath, in Persian.

Hamid bolted and shoved his angry and incredibly surprised face close to Michael's.

"You know my language? You call me a faggot? Sag mazhab! Sag mazhab!" yelled Hamid."

"I have the religion of a dog? Am I correct?" asked Michael.

"You are a spy, yes?"

"No," Michael replied.

"Yes! You are a CIA spy from Denmark!"

"Denmark? I've never been to Denmark. I've never been to Denmark!"

"Liar!" Hamid punched Michael in the face. "You live in Denmark. You insult Muhammad."

"No. I live in..."

"In hell! You live in hell."

Michael was about to respond, but sneered again instead.

"You find my words funny? You live in a funny hell? Yes?"

"It could be considered by some to be hell. What do you expect? It's South London," Michael quipped.

He felt as though he was in a half-sleep, like when he woke up in the morning. A dream-state, but not quite.

The Iranian curled his top lip, confused by Michael.

A guard handed him a scruffy, green exercise book. It looked like a child's school book, which had endured every possible weather condition. Gone were the days of "my dog ate my homework", this was more like "a terrorist organisation kidnapped my maths book, Miss." Battered, torn, dampened, dried out, faded and dirty. Hamid waved the book in front of Michael's face, aggressively and extremely annoyingly.

Michael scrunched up his face up and moved his head away.

Hamid pointed a dirty forefinger at an inkblot on the front cover of the book.

"I have this. This says you live in Denmark. It says you live in Luxor. It says you're a lying, fucking dog."

"It says all that?" mumbled Michael.

Hamid opened the book. "Here! Look! Your name! Ja... Jac... What is this word? Read this word to me." He put the book close to the man's face and Michael looked at the childlike block capital writing, penned in black biro.

"It says Jacob. The word is Jacob. It's a name."

"And this word. What is this word?" Again, the dirty forefinger waggled and pressed down into the book against another poorly practiced word.

"Ramsay. It's another name," said Michael.

"Say them together. The two words. Fucking say them."

"Jacob Ramsay."

"Jacob Ramsay. That is your name. Your name is Jacob Ramsay."

"No," replied Michael.

"Yes. Your name. It says so in the book."

"Then give me a red pen and I'll correct the book."

"A red pen? I stick a red pen in your fucking eye, you fucking dog! Your name is Jacob Ramsay. You live in Luxor and Denmark. It says so here. Look." Hamid once again pressed his dirty finger hard onto the paper and smudged the ink that said the words, "NAME: JACOB RAMSAY. ADDRESS: LUXOR ST NR DENMARK HILL".

Michael darted his eyes left to right, across the words. "Luxor Street. S and T stand for street. N and R must stand for near. Luxor Street is near Denmark Hill. Listen to me. I live in Luxor Street, in London, not Egypt. I've never been to Egypt. Luxor is the name of a street. Denmark is the name of a street.

I have never been to Denmark. These are names of streets in London. The United Kingdom," explained Michael, frantically.

"Liar! You are lying, bro. You are a fucking lying, spying dog who spy in Egypt! You were in Egypt and started the revolution to get Mubarak out. You spy in Egypt and spy in Denmark and your fucking name is fucking Jacob Ramsay."

"No, it is not!"

Hamid punched Michael in the face.

Michael was punched in the face again and again. His nose and lips split and he fell to the ground with Hamid towering above him.

Hamid pulled him to his feet for Michael to stand once more.

Michael's lips bled and his eyes were glassy. He had a vacant expression and had the face of a heartbroken man. Beaten, distressed, weakened and messed, pale and bloody, dirty and muddy, angered yet hopeless. Don't give up, just don't give up, he told himself in the whispered voices of his loved ones.

Siamak rubbed his stubbled cheeks as he looked on with another Iranian man.

Hamid held the collar of the orange jumpsuit with his left hand and slapped Michael around the face with his right palm. He slapped him again and his eyes blinked and rolled to meet Hamid's.

"My name is not Jacob Ramsay."

Hamid dragged a metal chair along the cold, concrete ground in the bunker-type room where Michael was being held captive. The noise was equal to someone clawing their nails down a school blackboard. The metal legs squealed as they scraped across the stony floor. It just added to the eerie feel of the medieval, industrial style of the place.

It was days later.

Michael had newly-formed black eyes, featuring brilliant blues and yellows around his eyelids and cheekbones. He was forced to sit on the chair as an Iranian, with the Sony DSR-570WSP camcorder, moved his tripod to within a few feet in front of him, adjusting the equipment, setting up to film.

The interrogating Hamid stepped out of the shadows and dropped a smouldering Bahman cigarette butt to the floor. He stamped it out with the toe of his Italian-made brown leather shoe. He folded his arms, looked at the camera and then at Michael. He brought forth the stained and tatty exercise book from within his back pocket. He unrolled the book and opened it, pointing his dirty forefinger at some handwritten, scribbling, scrawling text.

"Arsenal is a football team, yes?" Hamid said.

"Yes. It's a football team," replied Michael.

"Arsenal Football Club. The Gunners?"

"Yes. The Gunners," Michael responded, wearily.

"They are successful?" asked Hamid.

"Very."

"They are a good team?"

"Yes. They're a good team. They're in the Premier League," said Michael.

"Why are they so good?" enquired the Iranian.

"They have lots of money and a good manager."

"Who is their manager?"

"His name is Arsène Wenger," Michael replied.

"Is he British? It is not a British name."

"He's French."

"French? You know him?" Hamid was curious.

"No," Michael sighed, weary of Hamid's questions, weary of life.

"You know football good?"

"No, I don't know football good," mocked Michael, with a slight touch of sarcasm.

"But you know Arsenal and the football manager good. You are telling me good answers, so you know it good," said Hamid, who stepped closer to Michael, creating a shadow in front of his feet, where he sat.

"It's pop culture," explained Michael. "Everyone knows a little."

"Pop? Pop music? We are not talking about pop music, bro. We are talking fucking football."

"No, not pop music," Michael sighed and looked up to see the Iranian just a foot in front of him. "Pop culture. It's short for popular. It means-"

Michael suddenly received a slap around his face, from Hamid, cutting short his explanation.

"I know what fucking popular means, bro. I fucking know what it means. You fucking understand? I know what fucking popular means.'

"Then you should fucking know what I was fucking saying in the first fucking place, then you wouldn't have to fucking ask me so many fucking times." Michael wished he had responded that way, but he didn't, as it would have no doubt resulted in him being dragged to the middle of the room and shot in the head, or beheaded, or worse. Could there have been any worse than that? There was always something worse. Always. Michael was being tortured, traumatised, terrorised under extreme interrogation by people unfamiliar and foreign to him in a place equally as frightening and terrifying as those tormenting him. He wasn't thinking of a 'this could be worse' situation. This was the worse situation.

Hamid rubbed his cheeks with the forefinger and thumb of his right hand, rolled his tongue around inside his mouth, filling out his cheeks and gums, thinking as he looked at Michael. He looked at the exercise book and narrowed his eyes at the writing, as he had done many times before, perhaps finding it difficult to read. He showed it to Michael.

"What does this say?"

Michael looked at the book. He knew it was a pathetic copy of some of own writing from his Paperchase notebook, but he didn't have the energy to work out why. He squinted, however his squint was merely due to his bruised eyelids, which made it hard to see anything at all.

"It says "Woolwich"."

"Wool..."

"Wool-itch. Woolwich," corrected Michael.

"Woolwich is an army place, yes?" quizzed Hamid.

"How do you mean? What do you mean by army place?"

"Army place. Army place! Where army live. Where army work. Is Woolwich where army live and work?"

"Yes. Yes, Woolwich is an army place," answered Michael.

Footsteps sounded. They circled and stopped behind his chair. Michael swallowed and gulped, but he was swallowing hardly anything at all. His mouth was so dry and he was ever so tired. Weary, drained, tired of speaking, tired of breathing, tired of hurting.

He saw a flicker of silver, twisting in the dull fluorescents. A shadowed figure grasped Michael's right hand, yanked it back behind him and sliced his palm with the shiny blade of a butterfly knife.

Michael winced with pain, twisted in his chair, but the arms of another shadowed figure held him tight as the slicing man unscrewed the cap off a small bottle of Bell's whisky and poured it onto Michael's open wound. He yelled out in extreme discomfort.

Hamid grabbed an oil-stained cloth and suddenly rammed it into Michael's mouth. He locked his eyes onto a can of oil, reached for it and dragged it in one swift motion. Hamid poured the oil down onto the rag in Michael's mouth. The brown, goopy liquid seeped into the rag and down into Michael's throat.

He gagged and choked. Michael leaned forward and the cloth fell from his mouth to the floor.

"America will create more bad guys. You know that, don't you?" said Hamid.

Michael breathed heavily, in and out, ever so fast. He wrapped his bloody hand with the dirty cloth and pressed it tight. His eyes were wide and raging.

"It's about pipelines. America and their eff sake oil, huh, ma man? You know there is plan for Arab pipeline to go from Saudi Arabia? It was meant to go through Syria, but they cannot run it because of Assad. He is Iran and Russia's friend. You just wait, ma man. You just wait. Wait for the Big Apple Americans to create a new bad man. Already I hear of this. Bin Laden, Al-Qaeda, Islamic State International or the Incredible Hulk. All fucking bullshit, ma man. Just an excuse to attack Assad and lay down pipes for oil."

"I don't know what you're talking about. It has nothing to do with me," said Michael.

"But you're wrong, bro. It does. You know Israel wants to take over Syria. It's all their plan, ma man. Israel want a Palestinian gas reservoir. It has a trillion cubic feet of gas. I know this. It's why they attack Gaza, ma man. To take their gas," Hamid chuckled. "All gas and oil, bro. Did you know Russia is main provider of gas to Europe? Effed up world, ma man." Hamid lit a cigarette with a cheap plastic disposable lighter and took a long drag from it. "You are in the army, you lying dog."

"No!"

"YES!" screamed Hamid. "Woolwich is an army place. You have been seen every day in Woolwich army place. You are in the army."

"I don't understand. Who saw me? Woolwich is a town, not just an army place!" responded Michael, trying to explain through quick, painful, tired breaths.

Hamid flicked open the exercise book and waved it around, as if it were a flag on Coronation Day. "It says everything in here. Everything you do. Every place you go. You go to Woolwich Arsenal. Explain to me what arsenal is, you Christian bastard."

"Arsenal is-"

"Yes, you know. You know it is a place for guns. It is a place for army. You know that Woolwich is army place."

"It's the name of the town. Woolwich Arsenal is the name of a town in London. South-east London," explained Michael dully.

The shadowed slicing figure grabbed Michael's hair, yanked his head back and exposed his bare neck and pulsing jugular.

Michael gritted his bloodstained teeth that exposed his bleeding gums.

Hamid the interrogator edged his face nearer to Michael's and eyeballed him, curiously.

"You know why I ask you about football and Arsenal football team?"

Michael couldn't answer as his jaw had been gripped by the dirty hand of the shadowed figure, behind him. He could only breathe heavier.

"I ask you about Arsenal football because why? Why do you think I ask?" Hamid smiled and formed a satisfied expression, as if he had just got one over his teacher or a parent or smart-arsed his way, cockily, through a TV quiz. "What does Arsenal football have on their clothes? What is their symbol?"

Michael breathed faster and louder while his Iranian captor and his big grin stared close at him. "It's a big gun, like the old American cowboys have, bro. You know that," said Hamid, as he slapped Michael's face and nodded to the unseen, silhouetted figure holding his head, instructing him to let loose his grip. Michael rotated his jaw around and rolled his eyes upwards.

"Arsenal Football Club's also known as The Gunners. It's because of the history of where they were founded, in Woolwich. It was an ammunition laboratory in 1695 and in the eighteen hundreds... eighteen hundreds, it became a military academy. It's not an army base really anymore. It was sold off. There are houses there now, but the place is still called Woolwich Arsenal. I have to drive through Woolwich Arsenal to get to my workplace. I am a teacher, not in the army. I'm not in the army."

"Yes, you're in the army," spouted Hamid, straightening.

"Listen to me! You're misinformed! I'm not in the army! I'm not in the army!"

Hamid gestured to the unseen shadowed figure by waggling his finger in a quick, waving flick.

Suddenly, Michael was rocked backwards upon his chair and dragged into the darkness behind him.

A high-pitched squeal sounded out. It was the gate to a six by six cell within the underground industrial base in Iran being opened. Droplets of water rolled down the rusty iron bars where they eventually joined a larger, stagnant puddle that filled the cracks and holes of the concrete floor.

A glimmer of electric light illuminated Michael's bruised and bloodied face. He sat on a plastic crate that had once contained bottles of Coca Cola.

Hamid crouched and peered through the bars at him.

"Are you hungry? We can get all food, you know? Pizza, Italian pasta. Iranian food. Koobideh or khoresht. It's not a problem." His manner was in stark contrast to how he had previously behaved. It was if the violence was simply part of his job and this was his home-life; a more caring side. "I'm not a monster. You are my guest as well as my prisoner. Think about it. You tell Siamak what you would like, okay?"

Hamid held his curious stare on Michael for a few seconds. He studied him like he was a creature in a zoo. He straightened and stepped into the darkness, only to be replaced by a tall man with jet-black hair: Siamak.

Siamak was indeed a handsome Iranian man. For some reason he oozed kindness and warmth. "My name is Siamak. I'll be your guard for the night."

Michael sneered and slowly formed a half smile. He frowned and looked closer through the bars.

"Did I say something funny?"

Michael rolled his eyes upward to meet Siamak's. "I'll be your guard for the night?"

"That is correct," answered Siamak.

"Was that a joke in English?"

"Not quite," Siamak replied.

"But almost?" asked Michael.

"Almost? Almost in what way?" Siamak asked again, intrigued, like a pupil in a class at school.

Michael coughed. "Almost in the way an entertainer says 'I will be your host for the night'".

"I understand your joke. I'll be back in five minutes, okay?" Siamak turned away.

"Your name? Sia..." Michael called out.

"Siamak."

"Siamak. What does it mean?" asked Michael, seeking any information he could to feed his mind and keep it active.

"It is Farsi. It means 'a man's whose horse is black' or 'black-haired man'. Something like that."

"Your English. It's very good," stated Michael.

"I don't know about that, but my mother, she's-"

"SIAMAK!" the distant yell of the Iranian torturer sounded out from elsewhere within the darkened base.

"I'll see you in a while," continued Siamak, who turned away and stepped into the darkness.

His footsteps sounded on the wet concrete and became more and more faint until there was silence once more.

Michael stared at one of the bars that made up the cell door. The middle bar, a rusted, vertical pole, separated half of the cell. To the left hand side of the bar, Michael had a view of a corridor ahead. It captured shards of orange from poorly-wired electric lighting. To the right hand side of the cell bar, it was black, the complete unknown. A cracked toilet was loosely positioned in one corner.

There was clear evidence of others having been there. Dried excrement was present around the toilet bowl.

Michael had forced himself not to use it at first, making himself wait to let it dry. He remembered the first time he'd seen it. He'd cast his eyes on the dried poop that was suddenly punctured by a claw, with a rat appearing from underneath, deep within the toilet. The rat didn't last long as a Desert Cobra slid through and killed it. Michael had hurt his back on the cell bars when he'd jumped away from the snake.

One of Hamid's guys had laughed, grabbed the snake through the bars and walked off with it, into the darkness.

A droplet of water made contact with the middle bar, which caused Michael to jolt suddenly. He blinked and was suddenly taken out of his mesmerising trance. His eyes darted around and then fixed on the water drop that rolled down the bar. He jumped again as Siamak appeared once more.

Siamak crouched down looking concerned as he stared into the cell at Michael.

"How are you feeling?" he asked.

"Like I've just been tortured," Michael replied.

"Not a joke this time, huh? I'll get you some food. A kebab. Good lamb. Seriously. Rice, too. It's uh, Basmati though. Not Iranian rice."

"Why are you being nice to me?" asked Michael.

"Nice? I am being respectful. Am I not polite?"

"Yes, you're being polite. It's being nice."

"What is your name?" asked Siamak.

"Is this good cop, bad cop?" asked Michael.

"What is good cop, bad cop? Is it a movie thing?"

"Kind of a movie thing, yeah. When a suspect is being questioned and a cop isn't getting anywhere. They offer the suspect coffee," explained

Michael. He was exhausted, yet felt more relaxed around Siamak.

"Or they give him a donut," interrupted Siamak.

"Yeah, or a donut. The cop's questions and good nature don't get the result he intended, or perhaps it does, I don't know, but whatever the case, another cop steps in and takes a more hardline approach. A threatening and often violent method. The good cop does the good things and the bad cop does the bad things. It's certain to gain a positive result. If you're using both methods, it limits the odds of failure dramatically."

"I understand this technique. I've seen it many times. So what is your name? Hamid says your name is Jacob."

"Who's Hamid?" inquired Michael.

"The bad cop," said Siamak.

16. THE BIG CHIZ

Michael sat in the damp six by six cell and looked up at Siamak, the peculiarly kind-natured kidnapper.

"Hamid is on his way to speak with you. He is angry," warned Siamak.

"I think I've experienced angry Hamid before," responded Michael, cockily.

"No. Not this angry Hamid, but listen to me. OK? I'm here to-" Siamak was seriously concerned for Michael, but quickly turned around when the sound of echoing footsteps were heard.

Siamak was indeed the most mysterious out of all the Iranian captors Michael had seen during his time there. Siamak expressed kindness and empathy openly. He didn't want to set himself apart from the rest of his comrades, but did so nonetheless and it was much to their distaste and dislike that he did so, whether he could hide his compassion or not.

"Here to what?" asked Michael, who started to breathe heavily. He assumed a sudden expression of sheer panic as Hamid, the Iranian torturer, appeared at the cell gate, wide-eyed and furious.

Hamid's dirty fingers clasped Michael's tiny notebook: pocket-sized and spiral-bound, with a black plastic cover. The Paperchase notebook, with the paper that consisted of sections of blue, red, grey and green tiny squares. Twelve by seventeen to be precise.

Michael adored them. He had a stationery obsession. It was hardly a vice, however, if it was this little book which had enraged Hamid.

"You are the spy in Europe. Open the gate," Hamid instructed, snapping his fingers at Siamak. "You stayed with another infidel. A female crusader. I read your words."

Hamid tapped the notebook on the cell bars as Siamak opened the gate.

Michael looked up. He was overshadowed by Hamid who had now crouched and was tapping him on the forehead with the book.

"These are your words yes?" Hamid asked as he thumbed open the book and pointed his stubby forefinger at some poorly written scrawl.

Michael didn't have to look at the handwriting. He knew it was his book. He rolled his eyes upwards to meet Hamid's.

"Yes. They are my words. It's like a diary."

"A diary. Yes. A diary telling me of your sins," Hamid said, firmly.

"If you call going to Prague with my girlfriend a sin, then I must duly confess, but let me tell you this: you'd best start rounding up the thousands of drunken British louts who stagger along the streets of Prague on their stag weekends, because if I'm a sinner, by God, those guys are the devil's army." Michael shouldn't have spoken. He was so weak.

Hamid moved himself round to sit next closer to Michael. He read from the book and squinted at the terrible handwriting. "You are the devil? Is that what you say me?"

"Say me? No. I tell you," corrected Michael.

"There is not just one devil. There are many," said Hamid. He shuffled closer, as if he was Man Friday sliding up close to Robinson Crusoe to view a treasure map or share some food, or even a young Tarzan learning from his elder ape family member. A peculiar fascination took place. Hamid pressed his thumb against the squared paper notebook. "Look. Here. You arrive in Czech and, look, I read. 'I arrive in Czech and see the man with the spider tattoo on his... neck who I... saw on the plane.' The man with the tattoo. Like a spider. You know him. He is your contact. Is he your handler? You see I find you out. Look. I read again." He thumbed to the next page and squinted as he ran his dirty forefinger under the handwriting. He continued to read in his broken English, like a student, wanting praise after he had done so. 'I... see the man with the spider tattoo again after breakfast when I check the internet. Bex is... in the room, doing her hair.' What is doing?" asked Hamid, curiously.

"Doing. She's doing her hair. Combing, brushing, straightening. Making hair look beautiful. Presentable," responded Michael. He was tired and sick of his captor.

Hamid stared at him for a few seconds, like an artist's model. Hamid despised the Western World. He tried his best to remain as faithful to his Middle Eastern roots as he could. He detached himself from watching satellite television. He kept only to IRIB, the Islamic Republic of Iran Broadcaster, however he didn't always. He had friends and once a really good, close friend.

A man he trusted and confided in. Hamid liked cinema and once expressed in confidence to this close male friend that his favourite film of 2004 was 20 Angosht, translated as 20 Fingers. It dealt with divorce and homosexuality and was, naturally, extremely controversial. Hamid's friend disclosed the information to a fellow group of male Iranian friends, much to Hamid's embarrassment. "The film won Best Feature in Italy!" Hamid exclaimed, only to receive a collaboration of ignorant laughter. He felt an embarrassment he hadn't experienced before. He felt shame. He felt angry. He felt betrayed. Hamid never disclosed anything to this friend again. This was because he drugged his coffee and led him down a narrow alley at night where he then bashed his skull in with a rock until he was dead. After he had done so, Hamid injected his friend with heroin and then tossed the hypodermic needle beside the body, and spat on him. He walked back home, collapsed with exhaustion on his bed and closed his eyes. He tried to remove the violent images in his mind that prevented him from sleeping. He twisted onto his side, scrunched up his eyes and pulled the pillow over his head, as if there was a noise outside he didn't want to hear.

Of course there wasn't a single sound outside. It was silent. However, inside Hamid's mind there were a hundred and one different noises. The sound of his dead friend's final conversation with him. The sound of his dead friend's footsteps, echoing within the alley way. The sound of his dead friend's head being struck by the first blow of the rock. The sound of his dead friend's body falling to the cold, hard ground and the heel of his shoe scuffing and scraping as his leg slid this way and that upon the floor. The sound of his dead friend's gasp as he winced with pain. The sound of his dead friend's skull cracking like an ostrich egg. The sound of his dead friend moaning with sheer pain. The sound of his dead friend's skin upon his forehead splitting open and tearing around his hairline, like a row of stitches being ripped along a seam. The sound of his dead friend's final moan. The sound of his dead friend's blood and brain squelching each time the rock was brought down on his head. The sound of the rock connecting with the cold, hard ground as there was no longer any brain matter or skull for it to travel through. The sound of the rock echoing upon the stone floor. It was probably the sound of a stray dog that barked which distracted Hamid from continuing and so he stopped to turn his attention elsewhere.

On his bed, he twisted back round to stare upwards and started to cry. Hamid didn't know if he was crying because he had, in its simplest form, killed his best friend for mocking his preferred film choice, or if was he crying because he had killed his best friend for simply exposing the truth: that Hamid was, in fact, homosexual. An extreme reaction by any means, but for Hamid, it was his way of dealing with it. He felt he had eliminated this fact by murdering the one man who knew him.

The one man who loved Hamid had mocked him and thus brought about his demise.

Hamid vowed he would never again be taken advantage of or mocked. When his friend's body was found just a short time later, despite the horrific sight of the corpse, the death was of no surprise to the authorities. It was just another very violent, drug-related crime. Injecting drug use (IDU) in Iran, to Hamid's advantage, was rapidly escalating. "You wish to hurt me, Jacob?"

"How many times do I have to-" Hamid slapped Michael across his face.

Hamid grasped his hair and slammed his head twice against the concrete wall. He pressed his head to the brickwork and held it there.

Michael grit his teeth.

"You wish to hurt me now, Jacob?"

Michael breathed heavily and rolled his eyes upward to meet Siamak's, who stood in the cell gateway with a tightened expression of his own.

Hamid broke his own wide-eyed, mad stare and turned briefly to look up at Siamak. Michael took his chance. He shoved his left elbow into Hamid's throat and pushed upwards on with his other hand on Hamid's knees, making a stumbling dash out of the cell.

Hamid made a delayed reach for Michael's clothing and tried to clutch at anything, but he lost balance and toppled over onto his side.

"SIAMAK!" screamed Hamid, as Michael hesitated briefly then barged Siamak out of the way.

Michael, bizarrely, hesitated again, just for a split second, to decide on which lengthy corridor to flee down.

"SIAMAK!" yelled Hamid as he got to his feet.

Siamak collected himself and turned to see Michael running down the corridor dead ahead. Hamid straightened and stood in the cell gateway. He held onto the bars and glared at Siamak. Then he caught sight of Michael disappearing into the darkness. He smirked. Hamid shrugged, stepped out of the cell and leaned back against the bars, next to the open gateway.

Siamak stood on the other side.

The door was between them.

Hamid signaled to Siamak and made a cigarette gesture with his two fingers to his mouth.

Siamak thought briefly, nodded his head and retrieved a packet of Bahman cigarettes. He handed the pack to Hamid. In the darkness of a damp, abandoned generator room, Michael trod cautiously. He glanced behind him to look into the sheer blackness. The light source was a lone flickering fluorescent tube. He passed a block of piping as he stepped with his bare feet into cracks within the concrete, which were filled with dirty water puddles. He reached a metal fence and his fingers gripped round the squared links. Michael looked beyond the fence to another dimly lit corridor running parallel to the one he'd chosen. He gripped tighter, with his face practically reflecting the tension in his fingers. He was disheartened. The place he found himself in was simply a fenced-off generator. He'd picked the wrong corridor. He lowered his head, then glanced up briefly and turned back to retrace his steps. He did a double-take, looked twice and squinted through the grille that prevented him from walking any further. Michael stared and then swallowed. He stumbled back, with absolute shock. What on Earth had he seen?

Hamid exhaled his cigarette smoke into the dark air. He looked ahead and smiled, seeing the weary Michael trudge back towards him from the depths of the corridor.

Siamak was surprised to see him, but not Hamid, who knew it was a dead end. Hamid stepped aside. He pointed at the other corridor.

"Next time, choose that one, but be quick, asshole, because next time, I will shoot you. Do you think you can run faster than a bullet? Do you think you are Superman?" Hamid sneered, as Michael stepped back into his cell. Hamid narrowed his eyes as he watched Michael pass him. He looked at his thinning body. He looked at his bottom and then raised his eyes.

Michael released a deep sigh and turned around to face the cell gate, which closed and locked.

Hamid held the notebook once more. His fingers gently held it and the burning cigarette sent smoke into a desperate, dark and depressing nothingness. "Are you playing with my mind, Jacob?"

"Are you playing with mine?" Michael replied.

"You are not like the spy heroes from movies," Hamid chuckled.

"Oh."

"You are quite easy to defeat. Do you think I will destroy you?"

"Maybe."

"Maybe? There is no maybe. I will."

"Maybe," Michael replied again.

Hamid narrowed his eyes again. That one repeated word had stirred him. It caused him to rethink Michael. He wondered whether Michael was the easy nemesis he made him out to be or if he was really playing with his mind? He put his cigarette between his lips and thumbed open the book again, locating a desired page.

The smudged ink and dirt-stained paper was difficult to read for any average English reader, but for a non-English speaker, reading Michael's poor handwriting and, indeed, in the darkness was a mean feat. "You have dated the time you were in Eastern Europe. In Prague. Five Al-Qaeda were arrested. Your government told the world they were Al-Qaeda, but they were not. I know this. They were taken and have not been seen. You were there. In Prague. When they were. I know this. It is true. They were Turkish. Not Al-Qaeda. What is Al-Qaeda anyway? Do you know? Can you tell me? Is it made up? An American and British creation? If I want to join, where do I go? ANSWER ME!" Hamid screamed, causing Siamak and Michael to jolt. Hamid gripped the bars and rattled them, like a caged animal. "Do I type into YouTube or the Google? Huh? How do I join? Is it like a youth club? I think not."

Despite Michael being inside the cage, he was safe. He stared, scared of the raging Hamid on the other side of the bars.

Siamak gently touched Hamid's left bicep.

Hamid turned his head slowly and held his stare on Siamak. "I am hungry, Siamak," said Hamid, in Farsi.

Siamak glanced at Michael, standing in the shadows. He looked back at Hamid and nodded his head, turned and walked away into the pitch-blackness of the second corridor.

Hamid watched Siamak go and turned to look at Michael. He pouted as he looked him up and down. He leaned his back against the wall, facing the cell. "My cousin was one of the men taken in Prague. They say it is a good country for terrorists to pass into Europe. What do you say?" asked Hamid.

"'They?' Who are 'they'?" replied Michael.

"'They.' 'They' are America, ma man. They are the man. They are fucking Justin Beiber, like you, my man. They are the Clinton and Bush Administration. They finance Mister Obama. They are fucking Simon Cowell and the American Idol Pop bullshit. They are everything, my man. What do you call the ones in charge of everything?" questioned Hamid.

"I call them The Big Cheese," responded Michael.

It made Hamid smile.

"The Big Chiz? What does this mean?"

Michael thought to himself and smiled too. He loved facts, especially historical ones.

The Big Cheese was a term that was apparently recorded in the first quarter of the nineteenth century, in London, England. It meant first-rate, pleasant or simply good and even advantageous. Ironically, it derived from the Hindi or Persian word chiz, which simply meant 'thing'.

It was in 1886 that the Scottish Orientalist, Sir Henry Yule, made an entry in Hobson-Jobson, a famed Anglo-Indian Dictionary. Yule wrote of an expression 'the real chiz'. He cited an expression among Anglo-Indians, penning the phrase, 'My new Arab is the real chiz.' The real thing. Those who returned to England from India began to use the word chiz. With the majority of people naturally not used to it, chiz soon turned to a word more familiar sounding: cheese. It was inevitable that such a term travelled further, importantly to the United States of America where the phrase 'the real cheese' evolved into 'the big cheese', describing an important person.

"It means the most important person," stated Michael.

Hamid nodded his head. "I think I know this phrase. Is it like 'top banana'? Or 'big fish'? Is it good English?"

"Yes, it is good English," replied Michael.

"And big fish and top banana. Is it the same as big cheese?"

"It is the same. Yes," Michael answered wearily.

"Where does this come from? Calling somebody big cheese?"

Michael knew exactly where it came from. He was an intelligent man. His mind was full of trivia and odd, unusual facts. His answer could either help and go smoothly for him, continuing the casual banter back and forth, or could spin wildly out of hand. He was humble, modest even, with friends. Surely it was a simple answer. What harm could it do to inform his captor? He straightened and took a step towards the light and the cell bars, closer to Hamid. He took in a deep breath.

Hamid was taken aback by Michael's movements, despite them being slow.

"The big cheese. It comes from the Persian word 'chiz', meaning a thing. An Orientalist known as Sir Henry Yule first wrote it down in his set of dictionaries. An orientalist is really a term for Oriental Studies. It's an academic field of study that embraces Near Eastern and Far Eastern societies and cultures, languages, people, history and archaeology and all that stuff. The word 'chiz' was brought back to England and people began to say 'this was the real chiz'. It meant the real thing. The real deal. The only thing. Nothing to compare it to. The biggest thing. The big thing. Chiz changed to cheese. The big cheese. As with everything, the big cheese went to America." Michael held his stare on Hamid who, although he didn't fully understand every single word that he was being told, was intelligent enough to realise that the man before him was knowledgeable, and knowledge was, after all, power.

Hamid formed a nervous smile and tilted his head.

Despite Michael's weak, dirty and exhausted physique, and not least being caged inside a small, dark and wet cell in an underground base of an abandoned industrial building, somewhere amongst the sands of Iran, he held - for the briefest moment in time - the power.

Hamid moistened his dry, uncomfortable lips with his tongue and swallowed, thinking as he backed against the wall.

"Is America missing you? Is Lady Gaga missing you?"

"What does your heart tell you to believe? That I don't know America and America doesn't know me, or something else?" replied Michael.

"I think America knows you," said Hamid.

"I don't," said Michael.

Siamak listened and watched. He looked at his wristwatch. Siamak loomed into the darkness.

17, THE LIST

The Iranian captor known as Hamid smoked a cigarette as he stood outside the abandoned industrial structure, concealed beneath the sands of Iran. Hamid thumbed through Michael's tiny notepad, trying to understand the handwritten words scrawled inside.

The relatively good Iranian called Siamak stepped outside. Hamid glanced round and offered him a cigarette and he took one.

"What are you reading?" asked Siamak.

"The Englishman's book," replied Hamid. "It has a list of names. Arab names. Written inside. He's a spy, you know?"

"Are you so sure?" asked Siamak.

Hamid turned around, sharply. "Yes. I am sure. This infidel is of impure blood and will kill us given just the slightest chance. He is playing us, Siamak. You are a fool to be kind to him. I believe he has engineered the revolutions in the Middle East. Egypt. Tunisia. Libya and us. Here. In Iran."

Siamak lit his cigarette, took a long drag from it and exhaled his smoke into the clean, blue skies above.

"Say, for instance, that he is innocent," he suggested.

"But he is not," interrupted Hamid.

"But imagine he is. Just grant me this story," said Siamak. "Imagine he is innocent of crime. Not of sin, but crime. What if we are mistaken?"

Hamid looked him deep in the eye and exhaled his smoke. "He is not. Believe me. He is against Islam," he said.

Within the dark and wet cell that contained Michael, a shadow was seen. A puddle was disturbed. Michael's eyes diverted quickly to see a rat scurry across the damp ground and into the darkness.

"That thing was as big as a cat," he said to himself.

He was bearded now. He had been there for weeks, maybe a month or more. His eyes rolled around, this way and that, and followed something. A fly perhaps. His eyes narrowed and squinted. He wondered where his glasses were when he touched the bridge of his nose and twitched. He scratched his beard on one side of his face and twitched again. He suddenly jumped and shrieked. "Argh!" He stumbled backwards into the cold, concrete wall, looking downwards. Michael scrunched up his eyes, tight and then re-opened them wide, looking more awake and less trance-like and more conscious of his whereabouts. He gasped as he saw the face of Hamid, staring at him through the cell bars on the other side.

"Are you going crazy?" Hamid asked.

"Should I be?" replied Michael.

"I don't understand," said Hamid.

"Neither do I," responded Michael. He twitched again.

"Do you miss Justin Bieber? You have shaved head now. Do you miss your life?" asked Hamid.

"Right now, this is my life," Michael said.

"Are you playing word with me?"

"I'm not playing word with you, no," replied Michael, sarcastically.

"But you fucking are," insisted Hamid.

"But I'm fucking not," argued Michael.

Hamid formed a smile. He pointed a finger at Michael and brought forth the notepad. "Do you know that your American leader says Osama bin Laden is dead?" said Hamid.

"I thought he died years ago," Michael sighed. He was tired of Hamid's questions.

"Ha! Yes, yes he died years ago. Of kidney failure some say. I ask you, how many times can Osama die?" asked Hamid.

"I don't know. I'm not an expert on him," said Michael.

"Some say he had a code name," stated Hamid.

"Oh."

"Yes. The CIA gave Osama bin Laden the name of Tim Osman. It is a Western name, yes? Not Arab name."

"I guess not," Michael answered.

"Your book has a list of names. Arab names. Muslim names of brothers. Can you explain this of your book?" asked Hamid.

"Show me."

Hamid turned the pages and held the notepad up close to Michael's face through two of the iron bars.

Michael squinted as he jutted his head closer, trying to read in the darkness. Scrawled inside the book were several names: Guled Omar-Ali, Shaheen, Abdul Rah-Maan, Rabee and Nasif Farah.

Michael rolled his eyes upwards to meet with Hamid's. "What do you want to ask me about them?" he said to Hamid.

"Did you kill these Muslim brothers? My Muslim brothers. Did you murder them?"

Michael shook his head, calmly. "No. As far as I know, they're very much alive."

"This one. This one here. Why is his name marked?" Hamid pointed his dirty forefinger at the underlined name of Abdul Rah-Mann. "Is he a bomb-maker? Do you think he is a terrorist? Al-Qaeda? Let me tell you something. There is no Al-Qaeda, bro. It was made up by your governments, just like your news. You make up everything. You fake your news, bro. Your news is like a Hollywood movie, you know? Do you know that? Your fucking news is shit, bro. It's all green screen and Photoshop. Your movie director Stanley film the fucking moon landings, bro. You know that? I know that. Even Spielberg was considered for fucking Argo, my man. You know that? CIA is Hollywood, my man. Did you think up the crazy idea of telling your American leader to say to the world that bin Laden is dead? I tell you, bro, I know people in Pakistan do not believe this. It is bullshit," Hamid chuckled and formed a smile as he stepped back, eyeing the notepad and looking up at Michael. His paranoid, distrusting mind was filled with conspiracy theories. Although he rarely watched television, he did read a great deal, whether it was underground newspapers that preyed on the young and impressionable or websites claiming the bizarre and outrageous. Hamid believed the Twin Towers were empty on the day of September 11th 2001 and that a missile was used to strike them both and not two passenger planes at all. He believed every news network was in on the conspiracy. He believed major terror attacks were staged events, carefully orchestrated by the powerful elite of the Western world and it didn't stop with the War on Terror either. Hamid believed natural disasters, like tsunamis and earthquakes had also been staged. However, he often became confused and flustered when he discussed which earthquakes were a special effect of the West and which were real but used by the West as a special 'weather weapon', like HAARP.

"I don't know. I've not seen or heard any news. I've been here," said Michael, exhausted.

"So, answer me, ma man. This name, why you have him marked this way?"

Michael touched his front teeth and rubbed one of them. He rolled his tongue around inside his mouth, filling out his cheeks and gums, thinking, as he looked up at Hamid. "He is someone rare."

"Rare? What is rare?" asked Hamid, with extreme curiosity

"Not ordinary. He surprised me," replied Michael.

"Like a clown?"

"No, not like a clown. He is nice. Warm. A nice person. Not violent," answered Michael.

"Like a gay?" Hamid said, with a frown.

"I don't know about that. I don't think so," said Michael.

"So how is he surprising you? Does he jump out of a box?"

"No. He's not a bloody clown, don't you understand me! Listen, he was a nice boy who you could actually have a conversation with."

"Are you gay man, too?" asked Hamid, aggressively.

"No, I am not gay man, too," Michael snapped, becoming more rapidly in tune with his environment again.

"I don't believe you, bro," said Hamid.

"Well, you don't have to, bro. I mean, you haven't believed me so far, have you, so hey, why break a habit, Hamid?"

Hamid frowned, not understanding Michael's fast-paced dialogue. "You need to slow down your words, you fuck."

"Listen, Hamid. The cussing and cursing doesn't suit you and I'm sure your Lord and Saviour, not to mention your mother, wouldn't like you speaking that way, especially to guests, so how about a little respect?"

Hamid formed a scowl and stared angrily at Michael through the vertical, solid, iron bars. He suddenly reached through and grasped Michael's bald head, pulling him forwards against the cell bars. Clang! He stepped up close, still clutching the front of his head tightly.

Michael snarled as he looked up at Hamid, who was close, practically eyeball to eyeball.

Hamid pointed at him.

"Tomorrow, you go on internet. You'll be like a movie star. Many people watch you, bro." Hamid released his grasp and Michael straightened. He looked up at him and stepped back into the shadows. Hamid lowered his eyes to his hand and spread his fingers, gently moving them. He let the hair drift to the ground below and into the darkness.

Michael listened to Hamid's footsteps as they echoed down the corridor and into nothingness. He sighed and twitched.

"Psst. Hey. Mister. Jacob," called the kind Iranian known as Siamak through the cell bars to the man.

Michael looked up and scratched his bearded face.

"I liked your story of the Czech Republic. The midget talk made me laugh," said Siamak.

Michael half smiled and lowered his eyes to the wet, concrete floor.

"Do you love her?" Siamak asked.

Michael rolled his eyes to meet Siamak's. "Of course. Yes, very much," his voice croaked. He coughed. He coughed again and cleared his throat and wiped his mouth, freeing it from spit. He looked up at Siamak once more. Michael's eyes were hollow, bordering on soulless.

"Please. Do not lose hope in seeing her again," said Siamak, as he whispered through the bars.

"Don't lose hope? Are you joking?" replied Michael.

"No, no I am not making joke. Please, listen, how do you say, for what it is worth..."

"For what it's worth? Seriously, for what it's worth? I was sold. I was sold and do you know what for? Do you? DO YOU!" shouted Michael, causing Siamak to jolt backwards and blink.

"Please, please be quiet. I am not allowed to speak with you. It is not good at this time. We must be quiet."

"We? And for what it's worth. Do you know how much I was worth that day? Apparently I was worth an iPhone and a good scaring. How much are you worth? Are you worth more than that? I thought I was. What is a human being worth?"

Siamak tightened his mouth. He understood Michael's pain and anguish. He widened his eyes, forced a smile and tapped the bars with his knuckles.

"Hey. Hey, do you like music?" he asked.

"What?" answered Michael.

"Music. I can get you music. What music do you like?"

Michael scoffed. "'Born to be wild', can you get that?"

18. BORN TO BE WILD (PART TWO)

Rebecca sat down at a table next to Edward. They were in a boardroom type office within MI-5.

Carolyn stood by the open door. She waited until a young, handsome man stepped through and entered the room. She closed the door and seated herself next to Rebecca, comforting her with a warm smile.

The young, handsome man, on this night, was dressed smartly, with a casual edge. He had a brown leather belt in his blue Chinos, with a pale blue shirt and sleeves rolled and neatly ironed to the elbows with a harsh crease. He flexed his toes within his pair of new, soft brown leather shoes as he clutched a Styrofoam cup of coffee. His dark hair was shiny and strong, bodied like a stallion and his chiselled features were striking. He weighed up the room and the people within in it and then gave them a welcoming smile. This smooth-faced man was in his early forties and was American. A New Yorker. His name was Harry Stamper and he sat down opposite Rebecca and Edward. Stamper opened a black leather folder to reveal a notepad and an expensive-looking pen, as well as several notes. He looked up and offered a smile again.

"Hi. Thanks for coming down. I'm Harry Stamper, CIA Station Chief here in London."

Edward nodded his head and extended his hand across the table for Stamper to reach across and shake firmly.

"Harry Stamper. Hi," he said, shaking Rebecca's hand gently. He nodded his acknowledgement of Carolyn, seated at the end, next to him.

"Right, we're listening," said Edward confidently, opening his own notepad and an old Bic ballpoint pen. He was old school and Stamper knew it.

"OK. I'm not gonna beat around the bush here, guys. Mr Thompson, I've been informed of your background and experience in the field as well as your evidencing the situation so far," reeled off Stamper.

"Not to mention my personal involvement," added Edward.

"Sure. Of course." Stamper gritted his teeth and toyed with his cup.

"You can get to the point now," said Edward.

Rebecca was confused and on edge. Her hand jittered upon the table and, without looking, Edward gently cupped it as he stared at Stamper.

"We'd prefer that what I have to tell you remains in this room."

"Who do you mean by we?" asked Edward.

"We? By we I mean the United States of America, sir. Narrowed down, I mean the Whitehouse. OK, you'll be aware that there is a current crisis spanning across the Middle East. We're calling it the Arab Spring. News stations across the globe are being fed the name. Are you familiar with that news, Miss Samson?"

Rebecca straightened in her chair and glanced at Edward, not expecting to be asked any questions just yet. She coughed and looked at Stamper. "I don't really follow the news. I usually get home too late to watch it on TV. I see the front pages of the papers when I'm on the train to work. Michael watches the news. I get most of what's going on second-hand, from him," Rebecca said, nervously.

"But you are aware that there is an uprising in various countries across the Middle East? Namely Syria, Libya and Iran?" questioned Stamper.

"Yes. Libya especially as it seems to be more focused on than the other countries," replied Rebecca.

Edward frowned. "I'm not here to discuss your politics and what you - the Whitehouse - are calling your engineered uprisings. I saw it when Hilary Clinton covered her mouth in that odd photograph when you killed bin Laden for the umpteenth time and she called it her Spring cough. Obviously an in-joke bypassed by the MSM."

Stamper was caught off-guard. "MSM? Mainstream media? I got it. Right. Sure. Is this where the two of us sit down in leather armchairs, talk about what's real and not real and smoke cigars?"

"I don't like cigars," Edward said, eyeballing Stamper.

Stamper swallowed and frowned. "OK. We've received intelligence that a man of your son's description is currently being held in Iran."

Rebecca gasped.

"What's the strength of this intel?" inquired Edward.

"Strong, sir. Strong. Due to matters of National Security, yadda yadda yadda, I can't disclose too much. What I can tell you is we have a friendly agent presently stationed in Iran who has confirmed the sighting and is, to our knowledge, still in close proximity to your son."

"Al-Qaeda?" asked Edward.

"Al kinda," quipped Stamper.

Rebecca couldn't have been any more confused than she was in that room. She shook her head, close to tears. She felt emotional pain in her heart and circled the worst of the worst thoughts in her mind. Her eyes diverted to the comforting arm Edward placed around her. He gripped her shoulder tight as he looked ahead, once again, at Stamper.

"What are your game plays?" asked Edward.

"Excuse me?" replied Stamper.

"Your scenarios. To get my boy out of there. You know what I mean."

"We... erm..."

"Because if you haven't got one then I'm going to have to put a quick plan of action together to get him out myself, and I know that we, the Whitehouse we, wouldn't want me to do that. Now, given your employment status, you'll know my history. Both you and Carolyn know that I'm more than capable of putting a team together, probably from MI-9 and heading to-"

"MI-9?" asked Stamper, curiously.

"You know full well that MI-9's focus is the Middle East. With your type of security clearance, it's without a doubt you'd know I dealt with that particular department on more than one occasion. So, what are your game plays?" pressed Edward again. He leaned on his free arm resting on the table and stared at Stamper.

Stamper puffed out his cheeks and sighed. He knew he wasn't a match for Edward. "Our asset boarded a cargo vessel in the port of Genoa, Italy. On board he discovered information that a friendly national was being held against his will in one of the containers that was previously loaded onto the ship at Tilbury Docks here in the UK. We had been following regular arms and drugs shipments that subsequently led us to Iran. Your son, Michael, was an opportunist moment. Simple as that. He was a major find for a certain Iranian rebel group and they seized the day. They paid a Nigerian UK national two hundred thousand dollars and several AK47 assault rifles in exchange for your son."

Rebecca gasped again and Edward clutched her shoulder tighter.

Carolyn gently touched Rebecca's other hand, trying to control her own emotion.

"The asset's cover appears to be slipping. This means we are required to get him out of there before information is extracted from him by hostile forces," continued Stamper. "We can get a drone out there super-fast. A Predator is in the vicinity as I speak."

"No. No drones. Wait. You have a man on the inside? If your man's cover wasn't about to be blown, then my son wouldn't mean a bloody thing to you. Correct?"

"Correct, sir," confirmed Stamper, lowering his head, regretfully, trying not to meet anyone's eyes.

"So you're going to get your man out and, at the same time, get my son out with him. Correct?" stated Edward.

"Correct, sir."

"So when are you going to fly me to your base in Turkey?" asked Edward, with a smirk.

Stamper exchanged a look with Carolyn, who shrugged her shoulders. She formed a half smile and discreetly wiped a tear from the corner of her eye.

Stamper gathered his thoughts. He coughed and turned to Rebecca. "So, Miss, I'd like to ask you just a couple of questions."

Rebecca looked at Edward for guidance and when he nodded at her with a pleasant and reassuring smile, she turned back to Stamper.

"OK."

"If we were to play out a certain noise or a sound or a phrase for Mike to hear, could you name something that he would instantly recognise?" asked Stamper.

"He would recognise anything. Could you be more specific?" asked Rebecca, slightly confused by the question.

"Sure. In his current, presumed fearful state of mind, what sound could possibly relax and comfort Mike?"

"I don't... I don't know."

"You don't have a favorite word? Favorite movie quote maybe? How about a song that reminds him of you?"

Rebecca smiled a relaxed, beautiful, love-filled smile. She rolled her amazing eyes upwards to meet with Harry Stamper's.

Siamak smiled and threw a warm, friendly look at the bearded Michael through the cell bars. Michael frowned and suddenly thought differently once again of the kind-hearted Iranian stood before him.

Siamak released a deep sigh. He looked at Michael with the most serious of expressions.

"Listen to me real good," he said in a sudden change of accent. American. East coast.

"Who are you?" asked Michael curiously, as echoing footsteps sounded along and throughout the corridor. The sound loomed nearer, closer.

"Sshh. I'm-" He cut short his words and bolted his head round to see four Iranian men.

"We need to talk, Siamak," said one of the men, in Farsi.

"In a minute. I'm speaking with the prisoner," Siamak turned his head away, but gained an ever-growing feeling that things could turn sour any second.

"Speaking with the prisoner is one of the things Hamid wants to discuss with you. He is starting to distrust you, Siamak," said the Iranian man, who placed a hand upon Siamak's shoulder.

Siamak turned around. "Do you distrust me, brother?" he glanced at the hand and looked into the Iranian's deep-set brown eyes.

"He has started to doubt your loyalty," the Iranian said.

"And what do you think, brother?"

"I don't know what to think, Siamak. There are reports of revolution across the whole of the Middle East, in our neighbours' countries. I have family in these countries and cities. I am OK with Ahmadinejad. I do not want America here. I do not want war, Siamak, but I will fight to keep the unwanted out, whoever they are. He will benefit us," continued the Iranian man as he gestured to Michael, who was fully aware that he was being mentioned.

Siamak looked at each of the men around him.

Each one had an AK47 assault rifle slung over one shoulder. Each one also had a pistol either in his grip or tucked into his belt.

One man had a cool-looking shoulder holster. It housed a 357 Magnum.

Siamak curled his lip and frowned at the man, who smiled a glistening, gold-toothed grin. He glanced at Michael and wondered if he should go with the men, which would surely mean the end of him. He pondered taking on the four men, but then what would await him after that? He glanced at Michael again, safe, for the moment, behind the bars.

"OK. Let's go." Siamak formed a pleasant smile for the Iranians, who nodded, pleased with him, relaxing them.

They turned to head back up the corridor. The Iranian with the 357 Magnum pistol glanced round at Siamak to see him bending down to tie his bootlace. He turned back round again.

Siamak discreetly removed a tiny tracking device, around half the size of a pager, from his pocket. He slid it into the shadows of Michael's cell.

Michael's eyes diverted to the sound of Siamak sliding the plastic device across the concrete ground and coughed, to disguise the faint noise.

Siamak depressed a small button upon the device, ejecting a red LED light. His eyes raised to meet Michael's. Michael placed his bare foot gently over the flashing red light, watching Siamak get to his feet.

In the geosynchronous equatorial orbit, in outer space, a glistening spy satellite, the size of a school bus, strayed with a twist.

Within an aircraft hangar at Izmir Air Station in the Izmir Province of Turkey, an ODA SF team was being briefed on their next mission by the 18A Detachment Commander, the Captain.

ODA stood for Operational Detachments-A. A twelve-man team made up this United States Special Forces Company. The company included the Chief Warrant Officer, an 18Z Team Sergeant, the Master Sergeant, 18Bs Weapons Sergeant, as well as the 18Ds Medical Sergeant, Engineer, Operations and Intelligence Sergeants.

"This is an operation consisting of the infiltration of a hostile base and the extraction of two friendlies," stated the Captain.

"CIA intelligence has confirmed there is no threat of NCB," added the Assistant Detachment Commander, thus informing the team there was no known nuclear, chemical or biological threat.

A UH-60 Black Hawk helicopter awaited the team outside the hanger.

The Medical Sergeant looked out of the hanger towards the Black Hawk to see a Major of the Special Forces Company hand a man a set of black combat gear.

The sunshine was so incredibly bright that it was hard to make out faces, until another helicopter passed nearby. It blocked out a section of light that enabled a clear view of the two men beside the Black Hawk.

One of the men was Harry Stamper, the other man, being given the black clothing, was Edward Thompson, Michael's father.

"Sir," the Medical Sergeant gestured to Stamper and Edward outside.

"CIA London Station Chief Harry Stamper. The second man is the father of our other friendly. Name's Edward Thompson. British. Knows the game. We'll leave it at that, gentlemen," issued the Captain.

"Looks like he's coming with us," muttered one of the team.

"And you'd be right. It's been assured Mr Thompson won't jeopardise the mission. He wants to be there when we ID his son," continued the Detachment Commander.

Edward, standing by the helicopter, turned and looked at the Special Forces team in the hanger. He knew they didn't want him there just as much he would rather be back home in England, but what mattered to him more than anything else in the world was that his son, Michael, was safe and happy in his heart and mind. He could not rest until he knew this for himself.

"I know a lot of favors had to be pulled in order for you to be with us on this operation, Mr Thompson. I know your background and respect you for what you've done for your own country and in working with ours. I just ask that you respect us and do what any of us say, do you understand that Mr Thompson?" the Captain stated, buckling himself up.

"Yep. Understood," replied Edward, dressed head to toe in black combat gear and sitting inside the Black Hawk.

The rotor blades whirred round and around and the beast itself began to rise off the ground. It left the base with the Special Forces team housed inside.

Siamak entered a larger area of the underground industrial base in Iran when Hamid confronted him. Hamid stepped away from a video camera, managed by two other Iranian men.

Before Siamak could weigh up what was going on around him, Hamid had acknowledged several of his men who quickly pulled their weapons and aimed them at him.

"What are you doing, Hamid?" cried Siamak in Farsi when the butt of an AK47 rifle was suddenly cracked round his head. It knocked him to the ground and it was then that he received a kick to the face from Hamid.

"You are not to speak with our lying infidel again, Siamak. You will remain here until I am one hundred percent certain that you are one of us, and at this moment, I feel you are not," said Hamid in Farsi. He was flustered and stressed. He towered above Siamak, who clutched his bloody nose and lip.

"I am with you, Hamid! I am with you!" Siamak yelled.

"You spend too much time with that spy!" Hamid shouted back.

"Because I want to know more about him! How can I learn if I do not speak to him?"

"You treat him like a baby, Siamak!" Hamid cried out.

"He is a human being! Allah is kind, loving and merciful. How can we not be the same!" Siamak shouted back and received another kick, this time to his ribs. He even heard a crack. He winced with pain as Hamid ordered two of his men to go to the cell and collect the hostage infidel.

Michael looked up as shadows loomed towards him. He backed away in his cell as it was quickly opened and he was suddenly dragged out. His toes scraped the hard concrete, cutting the skin of his feet as they slid across the jagged ground, scattered with shards of metal, glass, pieces of gravel and coarse sand.

"Where are you taking me? Please! I'm not a spy! I don't know any spies! Please listen to me! Please!" Michael screamed as he was dragged along the corridor and into the darkness. He widened his eyes as the Iranian men pulled him round into another dimly-lit section.

The men shouted in Farsi at Michael as they passed the grille that had prevented his ill-conceived escape plan not so long ago.

Michael had feasted his eyes on what he saw when he'd fled his cell that time: several large plastic barrels and a wooden pallet stacked with rocket shells. "What are they? Where are you taking me? Please!" Michael screamed again as he was pulled through a metal doorway and along a grilled bridge of some sort. He saw a stairwell and another metal door. His shins and knees scraped the ground as he was dragged, painfully, up a set of metal steps that then led him into a large room. He was suddenly placed upon the chair that he had most certainly been seated upon before. He breathed, frantically, and scanned his new environment, casting his eyes upon a beaten and bloody Siamak, sprawled on the ground in a heap opposite him, near cables and wiring.

Siamak moaned with pain. One eye was swollen shut. He looked past the video camera and fixed on Michael on the chair in front of it.

"You're making a mistake!" Michael screamed.

An Iranian stepped over to Siamak and reached into the cables and wiring. He retrieved something and straightened. He turned and made his way back to Michael.

"No. No, please," Michael shivered with fear as he saw the Iranian man grip an electric drill.

The Iranian squeezed the drill trigger and the lengthy bit rotated fast. In no time at all, he had shoved the metal point down hard into Michael's right thigh and drilled through his skin. Pieces of combined cloth and flesh spiraled out into the darkness.

Michael opened his mouth to scream, but there wasn't a sound. He either had no energy to do so or the scream was simply drowned out by the noise of the drill. His throat was gripped to keep him still, but he managed to lower his eyes to the drill retract. It was like drilling for oil as the metal drill bit was removed and out spurted a fountain of blood. The drill whirled again and was suddenly inserted into Michael's left thigh. It was messier as it churned into his flesh half an inch down.

The Iranian man stepped back, threw the drill across the room and spat at Michael, who edged himself off the chair and fell forward.

Michael clawed the ground, pulling himself just two feet across the floor, leaving a bloody trail behind him. He was quickly dragged up and shoved back onto the chair. A sheet dangled behind him, with Arabic characters painted across it. The paint was still wet and dripped down the sheet. The Iranian flag was also present. A spotlight illuminated Michael, who squinted and shielded his eyes, but his hand was suddenly grabbed and forced back behind him. It was tied to the other at the back of the chair.

"Wait! Please! You're making a mistake! I'm not a spy!" he called out.

"I don't care if you are a spy or not, Jacob Ramsay," shouted Hamid, stepping in front of him, slinging Michael's beige canvas bag to the ground beside his chair.

"Please. My name is not Jacob Ramsay. My name is Michael Thompson. I work in a school in London. I was taken by two pupils at the school and from then I don't know what happened. Please believe me! Please!" Michael cried.

"Tonight we will film your first message to your loved ones. You will tell them to help. You will tell your country to help. Then we do another message where you will tell America to help you. You will tell America not to invade our country. You tell them how bad the West is and if any NATO or Allied Coalition Force enter Iran then you will be killed. Then we do another video message where your death is filmed for the world to see. You see how this works? This is how it always works, bro. Message, message, message then death. Always death. You will be killed today, bro," stated Hamid. He cocked his pistol and turned away.

The Black Hawk helicopter raced across the desert sands of Iran. It was like a gigantic, mechanical beast in a mystical fantasyland.

Edward sat inside. He flexed his black-gloved hand as he watched the Special Forces team blacken their faces, readying for an impending assault.

Two balaclava-wearing Iranian men stood either side of Michael.

One gripped an AK47 assault rifle tight. The other held a nasty-looking sabre. Its blade caught the light of the spot-lamp as well as the shine of a laptop computer that was positioned on a table nearby. It was connected to the video camera that was filming Michael.

"Please. My name is Michael Thompson. I am a British citizen. I ask my family to help me in this tense, political time. I ask the Western world to remove their armed forces from the shores and lands of the Islamic world."

Siamak rolled his one open eye around the room as he curled himself in a darkened corner. He could clearly see Michael on the chair and the two men either side of him. He could see another man behind the video camera and one more tending to the laptop. Each one was armed with a pistol and an AK47. He could see a bulk of shadows cast in front of him from behind. He felt that there were definitely more than three men. He turned his eye back to the man filming Michael, who held his hand up as he halted the filming and ejected the tape, fumbling for a new tape within a carrier bag. The only sound was Michael's panicked breathing and the unwrapping of a new DV cassette.

It was then that a new sound was heard, but it was not coming from within the room. It was coming from elsewhere.

Michael tilted his head.

Siamak sneered.

The two Iranian men stood either side of Michael and exchanged a look.

The one with the sword lowered it, but tightened his grip.

The video and laptop men also exchanged a look. They frowned as the sound became more distinct.

The distinctive sound of an electric rhythm guitar delivered a familiar chord sequence. The churning, progressive beat was quickly accompanied by a lead electric guitar, a Rickenbacker Combo 600 single. It provided the melody, which was soon joined by a Hammond organ.

The corners of Michael's mouth began to curl as the combined sounds of those instruments together became more and more familiar to him.

The Black Hawk helicopter swooped across the sands of Kavir-e Lut, blasting out, incredibly loudly, the heavy metal classic 'Born to be Wild' by famed 1960s' band Steppenwolf.

The Iranians were confused and masked their sudden fear by a frantic rage, not knowing what to do as they stepped away from their positions.

Tears welled up in Michael's eyes as the lyrics from the song kicked in and his quivering lips mouthed the words. He started to sing along quietly.

Hamid strode into the room. He was fuming. He gripped his pistol tight and eyed his men.

"Where is this music coming from? Is it the computer? Where is it?" Hamid bellowed. He looked around the room and up at the ceiling.

Hamid locked eyes with Michael and stared down hard at him, trying to figure out if he had anything to do with the music that was becoming louder and louder, closer and closer.

The Black Hawk lowered onto the sands outside the submerged, dune-hidden industrial base. Its team of Special Forces exited, advanced on the structure and positioned themselves, strategically. The light of the moon occasionally picked them out.

An Iranian captor emerged from a door and rapidly fired his AK47 into the darkness. A member of the Special Forces spotted the Iranian clearly with his infrared goggles and took him out with his own semi-automatic weapon. His chest, arms and legs were punctured by the Special Forces hail of bullets, which were suddenly let loose into the night air, forcing him to shake violently and drop to the sands.

Hamid marched toward Michael and pointed his pistol down at him. He pressed the barrel hard against his forehead.

"Did you bring the sound of the devil to this place?"

Michael continued to sing quietly. He was filled with a surge of hope, singing the rock classic, softly, under his breath, as if it was the Lord's prayer.

Hamid signaled his men to leave the room, speaking in Farsi and issuing instructions.

"Hamid! What are you doing Hamid?" cried Siamak.

Hamid turned to Siamak, curled upon the floor several feet away. He pointed his gun at him.

"I saw barrels. Drums and rockets," Michael blurted.

Hamid quickly turned and aimed his gun back on Michael again.

"Barrels? Shit. What kind? Dammit," Siamak called out in his American accent, causing Hamid to frown and scowl.

Hamid was confused. He turned his gun back and forth.

"You! You lying, American pig!" he yelled as machinegun fire sounded out, echoing along one of the corridors below.

The bullets were accompanied by screams that erupted from more than one man.

Hamid gripped his pistol tight and stood to one side in a darkened section of the room as more gunshots rang out, joined by cries of Arabic and a sudden explosion.

Michael jolted, but continued to mutter his lyrics.

The sound of gunfire was like a pneumatic drill pounding a concrete pavement.

He heard the cries of men dying and being shot, accompanied by flash-bombs brightening up the darkened corridors beyond the generator room which housed Michael and Siamak.

A Special Forces member paced along the corridor. His night vision goggles depicted a clear path and every detail ahead, including doorways, stairways, cells and the occasional Iranian rebel, who leapt out suddenly, yet, equally as quick, was shot down.

Two more men hurried along the corridor and branched off into different sections. They reeled off their bullets.

One of the team screamed out in the darkness that he had been hit.

The Master Sergeant advanced on a stairwell. His boots thumped loudly upon each metal step when BANG! BANG! He was shot twice by one of the Iranian captors: once in his thigh and once in his left arm. It brought him to his knees.

The Iranian with the sabre sword stepped out of the doorway at the top of the stairs. He held the blade aloft, ready to strike it down onto the Master Sergeant's neck.

The Sergeant winced with pain and struggled to retrieve his sidearm, as he looked up at the shiny sword with absolute fear as it made its way down from the ceiling towards him. A white light cast by the blade shone down upon him like it was his time to leave the world.

A slew of silent bullets suddenly riddled the sword-clutching Iranian, blasting him several feet away and into the pitch-black corridor beyond. His body clanged against unseen metal.

The Master Sergeant turned his head to look behind him, frowning, but relaxing simultaneously as a figure hurried ahead of him.

Two members of the Special Forces team entered the room containing the plastic barrels and the wooden crate housing the shells.

"CWs detected! Repeat, CWs detected!" called one, into his radio.

"We've got a stockpile here, sir. Chemical weapons. Nerve and blister agents. Look like shell and bomb delivery systems too. Shit. We gotta get outta here."

A magnificent light illuminated the room, picking out the entire array of chemical weapons kept there. Rows of red plastic barrels, with some kind of lettering written in permanent marker, indicated what was contained inside. They lined one wall. Against another was a row of white plastic barrels with a yellow liquid clearly visible inside each of them. The wooden pallets displayed artillery shells of some sort against the back wall.

The men exchanged a look of concern as they turned to exit, when one suddenly received a shot to the neck. It sent him staggering backwards and spurted blood, forcing him to drop to the ground.

The second man blasted the Iranian who had just downed his fellow soldier, tearing his chest apart and screaming as he did so. He looked down at his team member and his wound and then applied pressure to it with his hand.

Michael wriggled his wrists as the sound of gunfire echoed all around him. Hamid looked at the video camera and the laptop and then Michael sitting on the chair in front. Hamid's expression was filled with tremendous anger as he turned his attention to Siamak, looking helpless on the cold, concrete ground, but smirking from the shadows at him. That only made him more furious.

Michael rolled his eyes up to meet Hamid's.

Hamid stepped to Michael and with one hand he grasped his hair, yanked his head back so he faced the camera. With the other hand, he pressed the barrel of the gun against the back of his head. Hamid towered above his hostage with the Islamic wording on the sheet backdrop behind. Hamid stared at the camera.

"The sound of Western thunder can be heard around us, invading our land, taking from us, but we will defeat the devils and send them back to hell."

The viewfinder of the video camera fixed on Michael, with his eyes staring straight at the lens. Michael's eyes quickly rolled up and widened with complete surprise. Tears began to stream down his face. His body just couldn't take anymore, yet through his utter exhaustion, he managed a smile. Then he saw his father.

Edward, in combat gear, stood in the doorway. He gripped and aimed a Sig Sauer P226 handgun. His eyes glazed over as he fixed on his son, in the chair, with Hamid looming behind him. Edward formed a half smile.

Michael managed a blood-stained smile through his fear.

Hamid looked past the camera, and as soon as a muscle began to move in his face to form an expression, a shot was fired.

BANG!

Hamid was shot in the forehead.

BANG!

Hamid was then shot in the chest. It forced him backwards, stumbling into the sheet, fixed by pegs, bringing it downwards as he dropped to the floor. Dead.

Edward took three big steps to reach his son and knelt in front of him. He bit the fingertips of his gloves to remove them and gently cupped Michael's face and looked deep into his eyes with nothing but love.

Michael sobbed with relief. Seeing his father confused him, but brought him so much joy.

Edward released a tear.

Siamak squinted his one good eye across the room at Edward clutching his son and untying his wrists, with Michael wrapping his arms around his father, hugging him tightly. Siamak was bemused by the odd sight. He looked up.

The Special Forces Captain stepped into the room and trained his weapon around. He saw blood on Edward's hands, then noticed a gunshot wound.

Edward winced. Pained. He had been shot.

"We've gotta go," ordered the Captain, who looked down to Siamak.

Siamak looked up and gasped.

"Emmett Smith, sir. Codename Siamak. CIA Middle East."

"I know, sir. OK, gentlemen. We're moving out," said the Captain.

Michael eyed his surroundings one last time.

The cold, dark room where he was first questioned. The terrifying chair he had endured many a beating on. The dead captor, Hamid.

Michael was buckled into the rear of the Black Hawk as the helicopter swiftly rose above the sands and into the night sky.

The morning sun had risen, shining down onto the Turkish US airbase of the Izmir Province. The Black Hawk gently touched down upon the tarmac and the two injured members of the Special Forces team were hurried out and tended to by a medical unit on standby.

Watching with concerned, keen eyes in the doorway of the aircraft hangar were Rebecca and Violet.

Edward clambered out of the Black Hawk. He aided his frail son, Michael, who turned to face a third casualty being helped out by another medic.

Michael extended his hand to grip the other man's. It was the hand of Siamak, also known as Emmett Smith. He helped him upright which enabled him to sit on the edge of the helicopter to face him.

"I tried to tell you who I was many times," Siamak said.

"I did tell you who I was time and time again," Michael replied.

"I'm sorry," said Siamak.

"It didn't start with you," said Michael.

Siamak patted Michael on the back as he was helped into a wheelchair and pushed elsewhere. He looked back to Michael and nodded his head to him, before he was escorted away.

Michael squinted ahead as he cast his eyes on his true love. He trod wearily away from Edward to be met halfway by Rebecca.

She was already in tears and as Michael neared her, she wrapped her arms around him, holding him tight.

Edward looked up and smiled at his wife.

Violet rubbed her crying eyes and saw that Edward's arm was in fact in a sling. She shook her head, giving him a look as he made his way to her on the tarmac.

"Don't give me that look. What was I going to do, leave our boy out there?" Edward said, casually, smirking and kissing his wife. He placed an arm around her, clutching her tight, pulling her close to him.

Despite Mubarak's resignation, mass demonstrations continued in Egypt's capital Cairo, as they had done in many other Middle East countries, including the Yemen, Syria and Libya, where civil war raged.

The Libyan leader, Muammar Gaddafi, was sixty-nine years old and died on 20th October 2011. It was reported that Gaddafi's convoy was attacked by NATO warplanes, after which he was captured alive. The world was informed Gaddafi was beaten and then killed by forces loyal to the National Transitional Council of Libya.

Iran had its share of violent protests. However, there had also been reports since suggesting mass censorship of media coverage of any form of uprising.

A candle flickered on the coffee table as Michael and Rebecca hugged one another tightly in their flat as they sat on the sofa. They reached for a glass of red wine each and toasted one another before kissing.

"I love you," Rebecca said.

"I love you, too." Michael sipped his drink and reclined. It had been a month since he had been back in the UK. He was healthier, clean-shaven, fresh-faced, clean-clothed, relaxed. A D Notice was still firmly in place and he was officially signed off sick, with 'work-related stress', covering up any form of doubt from his workplace. When he did return, however, Helen had decided to resign, taking early retirement. She felt it was either that or stay under the reign of Queen Josephine of the PRU and suffer a heart attack during the process. Michael moved to the main site of the PRU, working with permanently excluded children and an entirely new staff team. As luck would have it, bitter head Josephine also resigned, paving the way for a younger more enthusiastic male head teacher, who wanted a child-centred environment and valued his experienced staff members. Nobody at the workplace knew of Michael's traumatic ordeal; his kidnapping in Greenwich or him being held hostage in Iran. They also didn't suspect him of working for the police. Staff just believed he was off with work-related stress.

Michael exhaled a sigh of happiness. "You never did ask me how my day at work was," Michael quipped, receiving a look from Rebecca, who released a nervous laugh and a sudden flood of tears.

"Stop it! That's not funny," she giggled again, then smiled as she leaned across and kissed him on his lips, nestling herself into his arms, against his chest, closing her eyes, pressing her head to him tightly.

He kissed the side of her head and closed his eyes for a few seconds. He smiled and sipped his wine again. He placed the glass on the coffee table just as his new iPhone vibrated to announce a call from a withheld number.

Rebecca jolted with shock as the phone rumbled on the table.

Michael reached for the phone and took the call. "Hello?"

A male American voice replied to him.

"This is the CIA. Am I speaking with Jacob Ramsay?"

ABOUT THE AUTHOR

Ben Trebilcook is a Screenwriter / Producer from London. He has balanced his work in film by working in the Education Service, with over ten years of experience as a qualified Learning Mentor and Seclusion Manager. His main focus within education was the management of behaviour of permanently excluded Young People within the Royal Borough of Greenwich, in south-east London. He has strong family connections with the police and secret intelligence services.

Ben Trebilcook can be found on various social media platforms, including Twitter under the @BenTrebilcook handle.

Printed in Poland
by Amazon Fulfillment
Poland Sp. z o.o., Wrocław

53801738R00202